THE DISAPPEARED

WITHDRAWN

Also by David B. Silva

The Presence

THE DISAPPEARED

David B. Silva

Copyright © 1995 David B. Silva

The right of David B. Silva to be identified as the Author of the Work has been asserted by him in accordance with the Copyright, Designs and Patents Act 1988.

First published in Great Britain in 1995
by HEADLINE BOOK PUBLISHING

A HEADLINE FEATURE hardback

10 9 8 7 6 5 4 3 2 1

All rights reserved. No part of this publication may be reproduced, stored in a retrieval system, or transmitted, in any form or by any means without the prior written permission of the publisher, nor be otherwise circulated in any form of binding or cover other than that in which it is published and without a similar condition being imposed on the subsequent purchaser.

All characters in this publication are fictitious and any resemblance to real persons, living or dead, is purely coincidental.

British Library Cataloguing in Publication Data

Silva, David B.
Disappeared
I. Title
823.914 [F]
ISBN 0-7472-1300-3

Phototypeset by Intype, London
Printed and bound in Great Britain by
Mackays of Chatham PLC, Chatham, Kent

HEADLINE BOOK PUBLISHING
A division of Hodder Headline PLC
338 Euston Road
London NW1 3BH

For Rich and Alicia, lovers of books
(though they have a terrible habit of dog-earing the pages),
fine coffee, needful dogs, and a competitive game of Shanghai Rummy.

EAST GRID STAMP						
BB		SS		MM	07.95	
BA		SB		MW		
BT		SC		MC		
BR		SD		MD		
BY		SE		MO		
BC		SW		MY		
BG		SL				
BH		SV				
BS						
BN						

Acknowledgements

My sincere gratitude to Bentley Little, a fellow traveler in this strange world of storytelling, and without whom this novel may never have been written.

My continual appreciation and wonder to Alicia Dayton, who is still willing to answer the phone no matter how many times I call her with silly questions.

For Dean Koontz, I wish there was more I could say than simply thank you. For his generosity, his guidance, his friendship, I will forever consider myself fortunate.

For Paul F. Olson, who has never stopped being there when I began to feel a little too isolated from the real world. Thank you, Paul, and please, pick up a pencil and write another story for us!

OPENINGS

In autumn, a leaf drops off a tree and flutters this way and that on the afternoon breeze, a butterfly languidly strolling the currents. It touches down on the clear, calm surface of a pond. A ripple is brought forth. The ripple expands outward in a series of concentric rings. It is these rings that represent closest the true nature of time.

Time is not the linear propriety we have come to believe in. We speak of the past as something that has come and gone and is lost except to our memories. We speak of the future as that which is yet to be. There are many pasts, many futures, each arising from the moment like ripples from a fallen leaf.

Transcending Illusions

1

How had it come to this?
 Hiding in the shadows of her own house.
 Keeping the drapes drawn, day and night, summer, winter.
 Wearing sunglasses in public to keep others from looking in, to keep herself from having to look out.
 Fading mindlessly into the fantasy of television, where hours turned numbingly into days, days into months.
 No drinking, at least.
 No cigarettes.
 Thank God for little favors.
 But still, how had it come to this?
 She didn't want to think about it.
 And *that* was precisely the point, wasn't it?

2

Sometimes when Teri Knight came home after work she would sit in the living room in the dark, trying to quiet the demons that had been singing their dispirited songs to her for longer than she cared to remember. It was never completely dark, though. There was always a slit of light from a neighbor's house, a patch of pale from a nearby street lamp. And it was rare when the songs fell silent. Demons, once they've found their voices, do not easily quiet.
 Tonight Teri was sitting in the dark again, a Diet Coke in one hand, the music of Sting playing depressingly in the background. It was a little after eight. She had been home for a couple of hours now.
 The post office had been miserable today, even though deliveries were light and she had finished her route early. The problem had been a headache that had come on late this morning, just before

her lunch break. She had carried it with her through most of the afternoon, despite four doses, 600 milligrams each, of ibuprofen. There were some things you just couldn't medicate. No matter how hard you tried.

The pain was finally beginning to ease, though. At least she thought it was. Sometimes it was hard to tell if the pain was actually backing off or if she was simply growing accustomed to it. At least this headache hadn't been a migraine. You never grew accustomed to a migraine.

Teri put her feet up, leaned back on the couch and draped her forearm across her eyes to block out the light. Sting's voice softened a bit, then began to mingle with the rain outside. It had been raining on and off for several days now, ever since a low pressure system had settled in just east of the valley. The morning had been overcast and drizzly, but now it sounded as if the clouds had finally opened up. Outside the sliding glass door, she could hear the rain pounding angrily against the patio awning.

In the distance, a crack of thunder exploded.

Just the rain, Teri thought wearily. She let out a slow, deliberate breath.

Her headache ebbed and rose, then ebbed again, noticeably this time.

The sound of the rain drifted aimlessly into the distance, in pursuit of the music.

And gradually Teri found herself slipping into a dream, where she was struggling to escape something that was in pursuit of *her*.

It was on the dark side of twilight, and she was crossing what appeared to be a college campus. On her right: a maze of tall, cathedral-like buildings. On her left: a topiary and a fountain and a statue of a spectacled elderly man, holding a book against his chest. In that way of dreams, she understood perfectly that she was alone here. It was spring break, or some such thing, and the campus was deserted. It was like an old house. The occupants had all moved on, but their spirits, lost and unhappy, still lingered.

The sky was a psychedelic poster, a swirl of back-lit blues and yellows and reds.

Out of the corner of her eye, Teri noticed a small chip of granite break off the base of the statue. A crack spider-webbed every which way up the right leg and across the statue's torso. An arm fell off. The face shifted, granite veins splintering its features.

Terrified, Teri stumbled forward over a rise in the concrete. A twinge of pain shot through her right calf as she caught her balance, then suddenly she couldn't seem to get her legs in gear again.

Her next step barely moved her forward, and it was everything she could do to get her right leg out in front of her.

The colors turned muddy.

Behind her, a gray-black mist rolled up to her heels and hungrily nipped at them. Lightning exploded across the top of the nearest building. A crack of thunder rolled across the earth, and Teri found herself standing at the edge of a huge crevice, teetering forward, only a careless breath away from falling.

There was another crack of thunder.

She felt herself begin to fall. Then a shudder rattled through her body, and Teri came instantly awake. She found herself balancing on the edge of the couch. The Coke in her hand had dropped to the floor and rolled under the coffee table. Its contents had left a dark stain in the carpet.

Teri sat up. With the back of her hand, she wiped the drool away from the corner of her mouth.

Outside, a streak of lightning flashed across the sky, followed several seconds later by a roll of thunder. Behind the thunder came another sound, and it took a moment before she was able to realize what that sound was.

Someone was knocking at the door.

3

That *someone* was a young woman, perhaps twenty-six or twenty-seven years old. Her hair, which was light brown, was pinned at the back. Her face was slender and youthful, marred only by an expression that Teri would have described as anxious.

Those were the things Teri noticed first.

The only thing that mattered, though, was what she noticed next: the boy standing with the woman. He was gaunt and a little on the pale side. It had been some time since he had washed or cut his hair; it was stringy in front and looked both oily and dirty. From beneath his fringe, he looked up at Teri and ...

... and

... and he looked

... *oh, Jesus, he really did*

... he looked

just

like

Gabriel.

Teri felt herself tremble, and crossed her arms beneath her breasts.

It had been nearly ten years since Gabe had turned up missing. The anniversary, in fact, was coming up next month, on the twenty-seventh. Ten long, lost years. Just the thought of it brought up the feeling of dread. Gabe had been her only child.

'Mrs Knight?' the woman asked.

'Uh-huh.' Teri nodded, only distantly aware of the question. She glanced at the woman, then back at the boy. He looked exactly like Gabriel, even down to the clothes he was wearing: Levi's, a black T-shirt, the blue-and-white windbreaker she had bought for him at Penneys only a day or two before he had disappeared. There was part of a white sock showing through a rip in the toe of one shoe, and though Teri didn't remember a rip, she *did* remember those shoes. They were a generic brand that K-Mart had quit selling a number of years ago.

'I think he's missed you, Mrs Knight.'

Behind them, the rain was coming down in sheets. Once, when Gabe had been young, he had come home from school and asked her about God. Someone had told him that whenever God cried, it would rain. But there was something he didn't understand, he said. What was so terrible that it could make God cry? Teri had been at a loss for words. And here she was again at another loss. She looked at the woman and smiled, numbly trying to comprehend what she was failing to grasp.

'He's not a hundred percent, Mrs Knight. He needs to sit down.' The boy did not look well. His eyes were droopy, his color pasty. He had snuggled into the woman's arms, but it wasn't so much that he needed her comfort as he seemed to need her for support. The woman switched what was apparently the boy's walking cane from one hand to the other. 'Please.'

Teri nodded numbly. She stepped back inside the house, inviting them in.

'Come on, Gabriel,' the woman whispered.

Gabriel.

She had called him, *Gabriel.*

Teri felt shaken. She blinked, and in that second, the boy started to sink under his own weight. Together, the two women managed to get him into the living room and onto the couch. Teri went back to retrieve the cane. It had fallen out of the tangle and was lying on the floor near the front door, in plain sight now, like an ugly secret finally out in the open. On her way back, she turned it over in her hands, wondering what was wrong with him.

'His muscles are still a little weak,' the woman said defensively. 'Ten days ago he couldn't have even stood. He's getting stronger.'

Teri hooked the cane over the back of the couch. The boy, his head propped up by a pillow, had closed his eyes and seemed to be resting comfortably. His breathing was deep and rhythmic. The woman gave the back of his hand a pat and smiled weakly.

'Is he going to be all right?' Teri asked in a near whisper.

'I'm just a little tired, Mom,' the boy said, without opening his eyes. 'Just a little tired, that's all.'

'What?' Teri said. She heard exactly what he had said, but she wasn't sure she could trust what she had heard. She leaned against the wall for support. *Mom.* He had called her *mom.* She had nearly forgotten the sweet sound of that word.

'Oh, my God.'

'Mrs Knight . . .'

'It's really him. It's Gabe.'

'Yes.'

'But how? I mean—'

'You've got your son back, Mrs Knight. Does it matter how?'

'But I—'

'Please. I'm sorry. Really, I am. I wish I could explain everything to you, but the less you know, the better off you are.'

'Can't you tell me anything?'

'Nothing that won't lead to trouble.'

'But where's he been all this time? Why hasn't he—'

'Please, Mrs Knight.'

The woman, who had been kneeling next to the couch, brushed the hair back from Gabe's forehead and kissed him on the cheek. She smiled fleetingly, her lips trembling. 'You take good care of your mother now.'

'I will,' Gabe said, his eyes briefly fluttering open.

They stood over him a moment, side by side, Teri and this woman who had brought him home. Gabe curled up. A sad, parting smile crossed the woman's face. She looked as if she might cry, but she didn't.

'I should be going.'

'Please don't,' Teri said.

'He'll probably sleep more than normal the next week or two.' The woman brushed past her, not in any particular hurry, but clearly in evidence that she wouldn't be staying. 'You'll need to push him, to make sure he gets enough exercise and keeps his strength up.'

Teri followed her down the hall. 'You're beginning to scare me.'

'Don't be. He's gonna be all right. He's just a little out of shape, that's all.' She paused in the entry, her fingers wrapped around the edge of the door as she held it open. 'Oh, there's one other thing you need to know. Gabriel doesn't know how much time has passed.'

'What?'

'He doesn't know. He thinks it's only been a couple of weeks.'

'It's been ten years!'

'He thinks there was an accident on his bike.'

'That doesn't make any sense.'

'I'm sorry. I wish I could tell you more.' The woman tried another smile, this one clearly out of place. Sometimes you know a person for years and still not really know her at all. Other times you meet someone on the street and instantly it's as if you were sisters. Teri knew this woman. And without knowing why, she felt frightened for her.

Looking wistful, a little regretful, the woman stared out at the rain. 'It must have been awful losing your son.'

'It was,' Teri said.

'I can't imagine.'

'Are you going to be all right?'

'I don't know. I think so.'

'Thank you for bringing him home.'

'I couldn't have lived with myself otherwise.' Admonishing herself in some internal dialog, she shook her head, then stepped off the porch and started down the walkway.

Teri cupped her elbows in her hands. She watched the car pull away from the curb, a cold uneasiness rising inside her. Secrets dwelled inside the soul of that woman, she thought. Dangerous secrets.

4

By the time Teri returned to the couch, Gabe had fallen asleep. She stared down at him, feeling a combative mix of disbelief and joy. A miracle had happened, if she were to believe such a thing. A miracle had happened and her little boy had been returned to her.

Outside, the sound of the rain had softened to a quiet murmur.

Inside, the voice of Sting had become a distant memory and the ghosts of the past had all fallen silent.

Teri ran her hand across Gabe's forehead, brushing back the damp hair. He was soaking wet. A rivulet of water ran down the side of his face and dripped onto his T-shirt.

He needs a towel, she thought. It wasn't that easy though, because she couldn't seem to get herself to move. Somewhere inside her, a hole had been hollowed out the day she had given up searching for Gabe. It had been filled with guilt ever since. But it was fear that was residing there now. What if she didn't keep an eye on him this time? What if she blinked or looked away even for a moment? And what if her son was gone when she looked back again? Would it have all been a dream? A horrible, horrible dream?

You're making yourself crazy, girl.

I know.

She watched another rivulet of water run down the side of his face, and finally pulled herself free from the nonsense of her thoughts. It took a little work, but she managed to peel off Gabe's jacket without waking him. He rolled toward the back of the couch, then curled up again. Teri dropped the soggy jacket on the coffee table and went down the hall to retrieve a towel from the linen closet.

On her way back, she paused at the door to Gabe's room long enough to take a peek inside. If you could look past the dust that had collected, the room was exactly the way he had left it the day he had gone off to the park. The day he hadn't come home. She had only been in his room three times since then. Once so that the police could take a look around. Another time, when she didn't think she could hold herself together any longer and she had come here looking for the strength to get her through another day. And finally, when she had closed the door for what she had thought would be the last time.

But now the door was open again.

Over Gabe's bed, which he was supposed to have made that afternoon and never did, was a poster of Sly Stallone. It was from the movie *Rambo II*. He was wearing a ragged strip of cloth across his forehead and holding some sort of gun in one hand – an M-something or other, according to Gabe. Teri hadn't allowed Gabe to see the movie; he had just turned nine, and nine was too young as far as she had been concerned. But she *had* allowed him to have the poster. It was a compromise that had managed to keep them both happy.

On the far wall, between the corner and the window, was a poster of Haley's Comet. On top of the dresser was an army of war toys: tanks, rocket launchers, soldiers, jeeps, the same kind of toys Teri's brother had collected as a boy. And above the light switch on her right was a bumper sticker that said: I BRAKE FOR MUTANTS.

Nothing had been touched. Not even the small pile of dirty clothes he had hidden in the corner on the other side of the dresser, where it was supposed to be out of sight. Standing there, in the doorway, it was almost as if Gabe had only been gone a day or two. Maybe off to day camp or off on a school trip of some sort.

Almost.

But then not like that at all.

Back in the living room, she found Gabe with his eyes open again. He was sitting up, looking tired and sad and strangely out of place. Though more than out of place, Teri thought he looked as if he feared he was going to get into trouble. Big trouble. It was a familiar expression, even after all this time: the slightly-slumped shoulders, the downcast eyes, the expressionless face.

'Can't sleep, huh?' Teri said.

He shrugged, a little boy's ambivalence.

Teri unfolded the towel, her hands shaking slightly. They hadn't stopped shaking since she had first opened the front door. 'You're wet as a tadpole, kiddo.'

'Mom, I can do it.'

'No, not this time,' she said softly. 'I get to do it this time.'

5

It was like a dream, at the same time both real and fanciful.

Teri ran the towel through Gabe's hair, took in his sweet, marvelous scent and knew it couldn't be a dream. In her thoughts, he had always remained the same eleven-year-old boy who had gone off to play and had never come home again. That picture of Gabe had never changed for her. And now it was suddenly real again.

'I'm sorry about my bike,' he said.

'Your bike?'

'The accident. I'm sorry my bike got wrecked.'

She mussed his hair affectionately, and sat on the couch next to him, the towel in her lap. A look of guilt had fallen like a dark shadow over his face. It was a precious sight if ever there was one.

'Do you have any idea how much I've missed you?' she said.
'No.'
'More than you'll ever know.'
'This much?' Gabe asked, the guilt vanishing into a grin. He held his hands up, shoulder-length apart.
'More.'
'This much?' Slightly wider.
'More.'
'*This* much?' He held his hands out as far as they would go, a fisherman's gauge of the one that got away.
'You can't stretch them far enough,' Teri said. She thought, if she let herself, it would be easy to break down and start crying now. But she had done enough crying. 'No matter how far you stretch them, you can't stretch them far enough.'
'Is that a mother thing?' he asked.
'Yeah, I think you could call it that.'
Gabe, who had somehow taken over possession of the towel, ran it across the back of his neck a few times, then dropped it on the coffee table. They had both been a little out of synch thus far, like two oarsmen working against each other. But he was staring at her now, and Teri realized with suddenness that he had stepped outside himself for a moment, and had realized that something wasn't quite right.
'You look different,' he said, his forehead furrowed.
Teri felt herself smile uncomfortably. It wasn't just that she was ten years older now. She knew she hadn't taken very good care of herself. What little incentive she might have had after Gabe had disappeared, had walked out the door with his father, some four years ago. It had been a long time since she'd had the courage to face herself in the mirror.
'It's been a long time, Gabe,' she said, brushing the hair back from her face. 'A person changes.'
'Not that long,' he said. He gave her an odd look, as if she were the only person in the next car and he had just caught her talking to herself.
For a moment, Teri didn't catch what was going on, and then she remembered what the woman had said. Gabe didn't know how long it had been. It had only been a matter of days in his mind. He had gone out to play and there had been an accident and he had found himself...
Where had he found himself? she wondered.
And how did he get there?
And why hadn't he aged?

'Mom?'

'You don't have any idea, do you?' she said.

'Any idea?'

'About what's happened. You don't have any idea what's happened.'

He stared at her in silence, a quizzical expression etched into his brow, until a horrible thought came to mind. 'Something's happened to Dad. That's why he's not here, isn't it?'

'Oh, no, sweetheart, your father's fine,' she said. 'I'm sorry. I was just rambling, that's all. I didn't mean anything.'

'Where's Dad?'

Your father hasn't been here in years.

She fought the urge to sweep Gabe up in her arms and smother him in a hug. It hadn't even occurred to her that he had no way of knowing his father had walked out. Gabe had come home expecting to find everything the way he had left it, but unfortunately that wasn't the case. It wasn't the case at all.

Your father hasn't been here, and neither have I.

6

Here was everything Teri had gathered so far: Gabe remembered going to the park on his bicycle to play, which was something he did almost daily after school. He remembered fooling around on the baseball diamond, running the bases a couple of times, tossing some rocks from the pitcher's mound to the backstop, and he remembered getting a drink from the water fountain behind the little league dugout. After that, though, he wasn't sure exactly what had happened. He had looked up at the sky one moment and the sun had been bright and well above the horizon, and then the next thing he realized he was lying in the hospital.

'The hospital?' Teri asked. 'What made you think it was the hospital?'

Gabe shrugged. 'There were these machines and things, like the ones you see on television that make that beeping sound like your heartbeat.'

'An EKG.'

'Yeah. And I had this tube coming out of my arm, and there was this clear stuff dripping, like water. It didn't even hurt or anything.'

He fell asleep again, he said, and when he woke up there was a woman standing over him. The covers were pulled back, exposing his legs, which were very nearly the color of notebook paper. The woman said her name was Miss Churchill. She said he had been in an accident on his bike, and it was going to take awhile for him to get strong again. He wasn't positive, but Gabe thought he had been in the hospital ten or eleven days.

Try ten years, Teri thought numbly.
'Was that Miss Churchill with you tonight?' she asked.
'Uh-huh.'
'And she took care of you?'
'She was my nurse,' Gabe said, as a shudder went through him.
'Cold?'
'A little.'

She made some hot chocolate and brought a blanket out from the linen closet. Even so, he seemed to struggle to get warm again. For awhile, a rash of goose bumps broke out up and down his arms. Teri wrapped him up like a mummy, but he still couldn't seem to get the circulation into his hands. They felt like ice cubes, and she found herself wondering if maybe he'd caught a virus or something. That would help explain some things, wouldn't it?'

No, not really.

Not the things that really mattered.

Gabe took another sip of hot chocolate and replaced the cup on the coffee table, next to the damp towel. His hand quickly retreated back beneath the blanket. Teri took him into the fold of her arms.

He had never seen a doctor in those ten or eleven days, he said. It had always been Miss Churchill who had come to check on him, to bring him food, to get him out of bed and walking around the room. She told him his muscles would be weak for awhile, but that everyday, if he worked hard, they would get a little stronger. And when they were strong enough, she had told him, then he could come home again.

And that was pretty much what had happened.

Teri felt another shiver run through Gabe's body. His eyes had grown heavy, though he seemed to be doing his best to stave off the sandman awhile longer. He stirred, let out a slow breath, then smiled at her.

She wasn't sure how much she wanted to tell him, or if she wanted to tell him anything at all. Some things were better left unsaid. For the time being, she didn't think he needed to know that ten years had passed, or that his father had left so long ago she sometimes had trouble picturing his face. And she didn't think he needed to know that she wasn't the same woman she had once been. He would learn that soon enough. The rest would have its own time.

'So where *is* Dad? Is he working late?'

'No, he's not working late,' Teri said. 'But I don't think he'll be home tonight.'

'Why not?'

It was Teri's turn to stir this time. She sat a little higher, feeling trapped and not knowing what to do about it. Across the room, the television flickered and she wished she hadn't turned the sound off. It would have been nice to have had the distraction. Anything not to have to answer that question.

'Mom...'

'I'm sorry,' she said, having not the vaguest idea of how she was going to handle this. A lump rose in her throat. She swallowed it back as if she were trying to swallow the truth before it could get loose and expose her. 'I...'

And then a lucky thing happened.

At least she thought it was lucky.

Someone knocked at the door.

INTERMEDIATES

You live in a house that serves as your sanctuary. It is your shelter from the water when it rains, from the cold when it snows, from the wind when it turns ugly. You sleep there against weariness, eat there against hunger. It is a reflection of who you are and how you see your place in the world. It is all these things that constitute your perception of yourself, and yet it is not you. It is only your sanctuary.

Your body is the sanctuary of your soul. It is how you perceive the world, how you feel and taste and hear. It is your window to the sunset, to the orange full moon, to the storm in the distance. It is the receptacle of your expectations, of your experiences, of your beliefs about yourself. But it is not you. Be careful which axioms you ask it to follow.

Transcending Illusions

1

When Teri opened the front door, she found two men standing on the porch. The one closest, the one she assumed had knocked, was tall and heavyset. He was wearing a blue suit, with a light-blue shirt and a dark tie, and she had the immediate impression that this was the kind of man who was all business. His expression was grim and no-nonsense. Just above his left eyebrow there was a jagged scar that seemed to confirm his general temperament.

Behind him, the other man, who appeared much smaller, maybe only five-seven or so, seemed somewhat edgy. He rocked back and forth on his heels, like a five-year-old needing to go to the bathroom, though maybe not quite that conspicuous.

'Mrs Knight?'

Though Teri had never formally divorced Gabe's father, she had also never retreated back to the use of her maiden name. Still, it was rare to hear herself referred to as Mrs Knight. She blinked, and wondered distantly who these two men were and how they happened to know her name.

'Yes,' she said.

'Teri Knight?'

'Yes.'

'We'd like you to step back inside the house, please.' The front man, the one with the scar above his left eyebrow, pulled back the lapel of his suit jacket, and there, behind expensive lining, in a holster under his left arm, was a gun. 'If you would, please.'

'Who are you?'

'All in good time, Mrs Knight. Please step back inside the house.'

Don't, a voice sounded inside her.

Teri folded her arms across her chest and wondered if Gabe was aware of what was going on. The living room was slightly offset and you couldn't see the couch from the entryway. But voices echoed down the short hall like thunder along a mountain canyon.

'Please,' she said. There wasn't a muscle in her body that she thought she could depend upon at this moment. The feeling had already drained from her legs.

'Mrs Knight.'

'What is this? You don't have any right—'

'Now, Mrs Knight.'

She looked past the two men to their car, which was parked at the curb out front. Kids had broken out the light on the street corner a couple of days ago, and it was darker than usual out there. Still, it didn't appear that anyone else was waiting. The car, which she had hoped would at least look something like a police cruiser, was a late model Japanese import. Red, no less. These weren't cops. Of course, she had already known that. It had just been a prayer, that last little breath you hold onto even though you know there's not a chance in hell you'll make it back to the surface.

'Last time, Mrs Knight. Step back inside the house.'

Teri stared at the gun one more time, then looked up at the man's face, which was stone cold and uncompromising. It wasn't so much a conscious decision she made then, as it was an automatic reaction to a situation in which she felt she had no other choice. She took a step back as if to invite them in, then in the same motion, depressed the lock button on the knob, swung the door closed and broke for the living room.

There was no way to know how long it would hold them. Maybe only a couple of seconds, because she wasn't entirely certain the door had actually latched. But that was behind her. In front of her, Gabe was sitting up on the couch. His expression was less surprise than curiosity.

'What's going on?'

'We've got to get out of here.'

At her back, Teri heard the thud of a shoulder being thrown against the door. It was followed closely by the sound of glass shattering against the tile floor inside the house. She heard it, clearly, sharply, and did her best to sweep it out of her mind as quickly as possible. But at least one frightening realization lingered: they had broken out the small rectangular window adjacent to the door, and in no more than a second or two they were going to be inside the house.

Gabe remained frozen, a look of puzzlement etched into his face.

'Come on! Let's go!' Teri screamed. She grabbed him by the shirt sleeve and did more harm than good as he fell off the edge of the couch and onto the floor. He landed hard on his side, his shirt still balled up in Teri's fist. She let go of it immediately.

'Mom . . .' Gabe grabbed his cane off the floor next to him and climbed to his feet.

'I'm sorry,' she said, one hand in the small of his back, nudging him toward the family room.

'What's—?'

'I don't know.'

Behind them, the lock on the front door popped. Half-a-beat later, the door slammed into the wall and sent an explosion reverberating down the hall. Whoever they were, they were in the house now.

'Out the back,' Teri said. She pushed him toward the sliding glass door, where the curtains were drawn. The room was bathed in evening shadows. A grayish cast blocked out a rectangular area of the floor. The corners were black charcoal.

Gabe leaned heavily against the wall, breathing hard, already exhausted.

'You okay?'

'Yeah.'

She swept the curtains aside with one hand, and grappled frantically with the lock. When she heard it pop, she pulled on the handle and the door swung back five or six inches before she was able to catch herself.

There was a man standing on the other side.

He was wearing a black, oversized trench coat. He looked like a man who had spent a great deal of his time sitting at the counter of a coffee shop, endlessly downing doughnuts and cigarettes. His face was puffy, and purple veins coursed the rough landscape of his nose. It was an alcoholic's face, Teri thought in that brief moment.

'In the back!' the man hollered to his buddies.

She managed to hold the door in place, him on the outside, her on the inside, neither of them giving an inch. It wasn't easy, though. Not for either of them. She could already see the strain showing in the man's face, which had turned a bright, sun-burnt red.

He shifted his weight in her direction. The opening expanded slightly. Sooner or later he was going to win this battle and there wasn't much Teri thought she could do to stop him.

'Gabe, get upstairs! Hurry!'

She braced her foot against the aluminum frame, locked her knee, and managed to take some of the pressure off her arms. In return, the man somehow managed to curl his fingertips around the edge of the door's sash. He anchored his weight, and she could feel him ease up a bit, preparing for one final push. If it came to that, there was no doubt in Teri's mind that she would lose.

Maybe if she let go, though... all at once... maybe it would catch him off balance... and maybe that would give her enough time to make it to the kitchen... or to the stairs... or

... *oh, sweet Jesus*...

She felt her left knee tremble, then start to weaken.

Gabe moved in behind her to help.

'I told you to get upstairs.'

'I will in a minute,' he said with sweet defiance. He braced one end of his walking cane against the bottom left-hand corner of the frame, and did his best to force the rest of it into the track. But when it was obvious the cane was too long, he glanced up at her, the defiance replaced by a hopeless, defeated exhaustion.

'Try pushing with me,' Teri said, every muscle straining.

Together, they were able to mount a sudden surge. The sliding glass door tore free from Teri's grip and rode the track the full six or seven inches, before slamming full-force into the forward stop. Only it wasn't the stop. The man had gotten his fingers in there and he hadn't been able to get them out in time.

The glass shattered and an ice-storm of splinters came raining down all around them like hail. Teri crouched and covered her head, defending herself against some of the fallout while her bare arms took the brunt of the sharp edges.

The door slowly rolled back in its track and came to a stop.

His eyes white and distended, the man let out a horrible scream. He staggered back, holding his hand in front of his face as if he couldn't quite believe what had happened. Three of the fingers had been badly mangled. One was broken at the second knuckle and appeared as if it were hanging on by a thin thread of flesh. If he didn't get help and get it soon, he was going to risk losing one of those fingers.

Teri found some distant satisfaction in that thought, though it was short-lived.

The other two men couldn't be far behind.

'Now get upstairs!' she said.

Gabe grabbed his cane off the floor, and Teri found herself tugging at him again, trying to keep him moving in front of her as they made their way out of the family room and into the kitchen.

The house had been built in the mid-Sixties. It was one of those tract homes that had seemed to sprout up out of nowhere overnight, sitting just outside the city limits in a little suburban neighborhood where everything was vanilla-flavored and cookie-cutter perfect. At this end of the house, they had the garage in front of them or the stairs that were a straight line to the office that Gabe's father had added over the garage not long after Gabe had been born.

Teri went instinctively for the stairway.

She pushed Gabe ahead of her through the kitchen. On their left was an oak pantry, and somehow Teri managed to cut the corner a little short. She smacked her elbow against the edge, hit her funny bone, and fell back a step or two, surprised.

Gabe disappeared up the stairs ahead of her.

Teri was a step too late, though. Just as she was reaching for the handrail, someone grabbed her from behind. In one swift motion, she found herself turned around, staring into the face of the man with the scar over his eyes. He had gotten a fistful of her blouse, and he wasn't letting go.

'Settle down, Mrs Knight.'

He spun her backwards against the pantry. She hit her head hard and slumped to the floor, her legs rubbery beneath her. The pantry door swung lazily open. A gray-black shadow seeped into the outer edges of her vision and Teri closed her eyes, feeling slightly disoriented.

The man motioned toward the stairway. 'Get the boy,' he said. Teri looked up, thinking he was speaking to her, which didn't make any sense. But then the small, edgy man who had stood in the shadows on the porch, suddenly stepped out of nowhere and started up the stairs.

Teri tried to clear her head.

'It didn't have to be like this, Mrs Knight. I'm sorry.'

'You better not hurt him,' she said, rubbing the back of her neck. Things had gone gray for a moment, even rippling, but they were clearing now. She sat up, catching a breath, and listening to the footsteps of the other man as he climbed the stairs. 'I swear, you better not lay a hand on him or I'll—'

'No threats, Mrs Knight. It doesn't become a lady.' She leaned forward, and he shoved her back against the pantry. 'Stay put.'

'Who are you? What do you want?'

'It doesn't matter.'

'Please, just leave my son alone.'

'You'll do your son and yourself a big favor if you keep your mouth shut, Mrs Knight. You understand?'

'Yes,' she said, hating the bitter taste it left.

'Good girl.'

Upstairs, the echo of footsteps fell silent. It was like a small death for Teri. She held her breath and the thump of her next heartbeat went unnoticed. The man, who had been standing next to her, moved to the base of the stairs, and peered up into the darkness. Apparently, the uneasy silence preyed on both their nerves.

'Hey, Jimmy! Hurry it up, will you?'

Behind them, the man who had been on the other side of the sliding glass door came dragging into the room. His face was ashen. There was a thin sheen of perspiration across his forehead and a sick, twisted grimace cutting into his cheeks. He held his damaged hand out in front of him, making certain to keep it elevated. The pain had to have been something awful.

Too bad for him, Teri thought guiltlessly.

'You gonna be all right?' his partner asked.

He shook his head, a naked fear looking out from behind his eyes. 'I don't know, man. I think they're worse than broke. I just don't know.'

'Christ.'

'I gotta get back.'

'We aren't finished here, yet.'

'I'm gonna lose my fingers, man.'

It lasted only a moment, but Teri caught a clear, unmistakable flash of anger as it passed over the other man's face. He glared at his injured partner, scowling, until he couldn't stand it any longer. Then suddenly he reached out and clamped his hand around the man's wrist. Teri watched the fingers instantly blanch from the loss of circulation.

'Jesus, Mitch!'

'Hurts that bad, huh?'

'Like a fucking hot iron!'

'Wait in the car, all right? We'll get there when we get there.'

'All right. All right.' It was clear that whenever the man dropped his hand below the height of his elbow, the blood did a mad dash for his fingertips. Obviously an excruciating explosion of pain followed shortly thereafter. Still, he did manage to drag himself out of the kitchen and disappear from sight with little more than a whimper or two. Teri had to admire him for that.

'Goddamn idiot,' Mitch said. His face was tight, the scar above his eye stretched taut and wide, looking as if it had been much larger at one time, maybe the thickness of a shoelace. 'How in the hell did you—?'

Teri turned away from him and stared into the upstairs darkness where she had heard something stir. Actually, she had heard more than that. They had both heard more than that. It had sounded a little like a bat against a baseball, only slightly muffled. Following that – in perfect progression, she imagined – came the sound of a weight collapsing against the wall. It made a hollow thud and rattled the china in the cupboards behind her. Then everything fell silent again.

Somewhere in the distance a dog barked.

Mitch, who was still standing at the foot of the stairs, called out anxiously: 'Jimmy? What the hell's going on up there, Jimmy? You got him or not?'

Outside, a car backfired, the shot echoing down the street and back again. Teri shuddered and felt her heart skip a beat. The dog stopped barking. The car turned the corner and disappeared into the eerie blanket of nightfall.

'If you know what's good for you, you'll stay put,' Mitch said, pointing across the room at her. 'You hear me? Because if I come back down here and find you've taken off...'

'I know,' Teri said. 'You'll still have my son.'

'On the money, Mrs Knight. On the money.' He took two or three steps up the stairway, then paused and turned back. Mistrust was suddenly alive and etched into his face, replacing that somber, all-business cast that Teri had nearly come to expect by now. 'On second thought, you better come along with me.'

2

'Jimmy?'

The top of the stairway was cast in gray shadow. It was as if the fog had moved inside and was creeping across the upper floor to greet them. Mitch stopped halfway up and wiped the back of his hand across his face.

'Christ, where's the damn light switch?'

'At the top, on the left,' Teri said. It was the truth, though it wasn't the whole truth. There was another switch near the bottom landing that was easy to miss if you weren't looking closely. Mitch had walked right passed it.

'Keep it slow,' he said, guiding her. Teri stood one step up from him. He had the tail of her blouse wrapped in his fist, making every effort to keep her close at hand. 'One step at a time. Nice and easy. You got it?'

She didn't answer.
Behind them, the last of the kitchen light quietly fell away.
A thick darkness lay ahead.
'Jimmy?'
No response.
'That jackass,' Mitch mumbled grumpily.
They were nearly at the top landing now. Only two more steps and they would be standing at the head of a short hallway, with a door to the left and another door straight ahead. Teri took a step up, her legs weak and unsteady.
A near perfect darkness shadowed the back end of the hallway. Someone had left the door on this end open, though. It was the bathroom door. A faint, grayish cast of light spilled into the hall. Teri thought it was probably coming from the small window over the tub.
'Where's the damn switch?'
'On the left,' she said.
Something moved, and as she leaned toward the light switch, intending to turn it on, she thought she saw a shadow slip furtively across the gray cast.
'Hold it. I'll get it—' Mitch started to say.
But if he got that far, he certainly didn't get any farther than that. Teri thought she might have heard him say the word, *bitch*, but she wasn't sure, because the door on the left swung open at that moment and Gabe stepped through. He brought the cane down full-force across the man's outstretched arm.
Mitch let out a sharp, immediate yelp and pulled his arm back. Somehow, he still managed to hold onto Teri with his other hand, though that didn't last for long. Gabe brought the cane down again. It struck at a ninety degree angle across the man's forearm.
Mitch yelped again.
He stepped back, his face ashen, an expression of shock in his eyes. Teri's blouse slipped out of his hand. That was all he had left to hold onto and suddenly he was grasping at thin air, trying to maintain some semblance of balance. Teri wasn't going to help. She stepped out of his reach and watched the terror cross his face as he tumbled backwards down the stairs. At the bottom, he spilled bonelessly out across the linoleum and lay there without moving.
'Is he dead?' Gabe asked, stepping out of the shadows. He stood beside her, his hands trembling. The cane slipped out of his grip and dropped to the floor. It made a lonely, hollow sound that Teri didn't think she would ever forget.
'I don't think so,' she said. 'Are you all right?'

He nodded, shaken. He had stepped out of the shadows, fearlessly, with the courage and strength of a man. But suddenly he was a little boy again, frightened by what he had done, and by the significance of the man lying so motionless at the bottom of the stairs.

Teri picked up the cane, then swept him up in her arms. She kissed him. 'You did great, honey. I know it must have been scary for you, but believe me, you did great. You did the right thing.'

She didn't know how much time they'd been afforded. Maybe minutes. Maybe only seconds. There was no way to tell how long it would take for Mitch to clear his head and start back up the stairs. For the moment, though, she became aware of the dark outline of the other man, the one called Jimmy. He was lying on the floor off to the right, apparently another victim of Gabe's cane. Teri stepped carefully around him.

'You're one brave little kid, you know that?'

A stream of cold air circulated down the hall. It was coming in through the sliding glass door downstairs and slipping out through the office window just ahead of them. Teri thought she had probably left the window open the last time she had been up this way. The chill slid across her arms like the cold flesh of a snake and she realized she was trembling.

That's your fear, my dear lady.

I know.

Inside the office, Gabe immediately wanted down. She sat him on the corner of the desk, and took an extra second to look him straight in the eye. 'You sure you're okay?'

'I'm fine, Mom.'

'Good boy,' she said, giving him a reassuring pat on the leg.

Now, the phone. It was a combination phone/answering-machine, black, touch-tone. The receiver fell out of the cradle and into her grasp, and it was a good thing, too. She didn't think she would have been able to find it in the shadows if she had let it slip away from her. It was a matter of blindly tapping out 911 next, and only when she raised the receiver to her ear did she realize there was no dial tone.

'Mom?'

'Just a minute,' Teri said. She tapped the cut-off switch half-a-dozen times, as if that might actually make a difference. But, of course, it didn't. There was still no dial tone. The line was dead.

'Mom?'

'What is it, Gabe?'

'Listen.'

3

The sound that Gabe had heard was the sound of someone behind them, climbing the stairs.

Mitch was awake again, though it was unlikely he was one hundred percent, yet. His movement up the stairway was plodding and uneven. Teri could hear the squeal of the handrail as he used it to pull himself up one step at a time, stopping occasionally to catch his breath or to change his grip.

'Mom . . .' Gabe whispered.

'I hear him.'

They couldn't go back. That would only lead them into the man's waiting arms. No, the only way out from here was through the window. Teri had caught Gabe climbing out this same window onto the ledge over the garage once when he was eight or nine. He had been playing Frisbee in the front yard and the disk had ended up on the roof. Gabe had somehow got it into his head that if he could climb out on the ledge, then he might be able to work his way around to the side of the house and up to the roof. Teri had put a quick stop to that idea. But if they could drop from the ledge to the ground . . .

'Out the window,' she whispered.

She took the cane out of his hands and motioned for him to get going before it was too late. Somewhere behind them – near the top landing, she thought – voices had broken out. One clearly belonged to Mitch. The other most likely belonged to Jimmy, who must have finally come up from his blackout.

'Hurry up, Gabe!'

Gabe slipped through the opening feet first, then reached back to help.

'No, you go on,' Teri said, handing him the cane. She waved him on, then watched as he disappeared off into the shadows on the left. It would be an easy drop from the side of the garage into the ivy below, no more than eight feet or so. She might even be able to hear him hit the ground and know he was safe.

Only there wasn't enough time to wait for that.

Teri climbed up onto the desk. She opened the window as wide as it would go, wishing she had taken better care of herself the last couple of years. This wasn't going to be as easy for her as it had been for Gabe. With a hand braced on each side of the window frame, she managed to pull herself nearly all the way through, only dragging one leg.

That one leg, though, was all it took to get her caught.

'Where do you think you're going, Mrs Knight?'

It was Mitch.

'Come on, now.' He gave her leg a playful tug, keeping her ankle firmly in his grasp. 'Come back in here and we'll see if we can start all over again, all right?'

'I'm going to fall,' she said.

'No you aren't, Mrs Knight. I've got you.'

'Please, don't let go.'

'I won't. Just inch your way back in. You'll be fine.'

Awkwardly, with one hand on the frame and the other against the shingles for support, Teri managed to get herself turned around. She crawled back through the window and sat on the front edge of the desk, her heart pounding like a Paul Simon song against the inside of her chest.

Mitch, his thick fingers clamped around her ankle, eased off on the pressure slightly. 'There, that wasn't so bad, now was it?'

God, how she hated this guy. And she wasn't going to let it end like this; she had already decided that. 'Not so bad,' she started to say. In that same moment, she braced herself against the desktop and fired off a kick that struck him squarely across the bridge of his nose.

'Jesus!'

Mitch fell back, stunned. He looked as if he might not be able to hold his balance, teetering there on the edge of an invisible line. Teri's shoe, which he had been holding in his right hand, slipped out of his grasp and fell to the floor.

Mitch grabbed for his face.

After that, her getaway took only a matter of seconds (and later it would be little more than a blur of time in her memory). She found herself outside, standing at the edge of the garage, looking down on the patch of ivy they had planted the first spring after moving into the neighborhood.

She had never been fond of heights, but she got down on her knees and let her legs dangle as far over the edge as possible. It was mostly a matter of trust, and then she closed her eyes, said a little prayer, and pushed off. The landing was harder than she had expected, especially on her left knee, which came up sore. Still, she managed to climb quickly to her feet.

By the time she got there, Gabe was already at the car, waiting.

4

This was the call generated from a phone inside the house shortly after Teri Knight and her son had escaped:
'We've got a spill.'
'How bad?'
'Looks like a Code Red.'
'Christ. What's the damage?'
'Both drums were identified and temporarily contained. We were unable to maintain possession, however. Current location and status are unknown.'
'Any contamination?'
'Jeffcoat sustained trauma to the head. Kellerman mangled his hand.'
'You need a clean-up?'
'Yes. Immediate.'
'Degree of hazard?'
'Some breakage, mostly glass.'
'Are you mobile?'
'Yes.'
'Get out of there.'
'We're on our way.'

5

It was after midnight.

Teri fumbled a dime into the coin slot and followed it with two nickels. The number she wanted to call was circled in red ink on a page torn out of the local phone book. It belonged to Walter L. Travis, a man she hadn't seen in nearly four years.

She finished dialing as two young men walked past the phone booth and filed through the front door of the 7-Eleven. Gabe waved at her from behind the foggy windshield of the car. Teri forced a smile and waved back.

They had been lucky to escape at all, and even luckier to have escaped with the car. If she hadn't been bothered by the headache when she had arrived home, she would have taken the time to park inside the garage. That would have put the car out of reach. And if Michael, her ex, hadn't always insisted on keeping a spare set of keys in a magnetic box in the wheel well, it wouldn't have mattered where she had parked. Teri had kept the habit even after Michael had left and Gabe had been the one who remembered the spare keys.

It had all been an adventure for him. Once they were out of the neighborhood, he had turned to her, his face bright, his smile alive. 'What now?'

'I don't know,' Teri said, still shaking.

'Did you see that guy when he caught his fingers in the back door? I thought his eyes were gonna pop out. Jeeze, that must have hurt.' He climbed up on his knees and stared out the back window as if they had just finished a roller-coaster ride and he wished he could go back and do it all over again. 'Who do you think those guys were, anyway?'

'I don't know that, either, Gabe.'

'What do you think they wanted?'

You, Teri had thought. That much seemed perfectly clear to her. It hadn't been money they were after. Three men with guns could do a lot better at an automatic teller machine. It hadn't been sex, either. If you're going to take it, you don't dress up and bring along your associates. And it hadn't been a case of mere chance. Mitch had referred to her as Mrs Knight a number of times. He had known who she was, where she lived.

No, they had come looking for something they had lost.

And what they had lost was Gabriel.

Teri dropped her smile and listened as the phone on the other end rang a fourth time. The ring was followed by a click and then a message:

Hi, this is Walt Travis. Sometimes I'm here, sometimes I'm not. Looks like this time you're outta luck. Leave a message at the beep.

The tape rolled another second or two, then beeped.

'Walt, it's Teri Knight. I need to talk to you. It's important. Unbelievably important. Uh... it's a little after midnight, if you happen to come in before—'

'Teri, good to hear from you.'

'You're there!'

'Yeah. Bad habit, hiding behind the answering machine. Sorry.'

'No, that's okay. I'm just grateful you're there. I've been driving around in circles, trying to figure out what I should do next, who I might be able to call. I'm scared, Walt. I've never been so scared before in my life.' She gulped down the last word, her mouth dry, her throat raspy. 'I need to see you.'

'Name your time.'

'Tonight.'

'How about Denny's in forty-five minutes?'

'That would be wonderful,' Teri said, taking in a deep breath. She stole a quick glance at the car, where Gabe was hunched over the dashboard, a Big Gulp in one hand, the other hand apparently flipping through the stations on the radio. 'There's something I should prepare you for, though. I've got Gabe with me.'

'Jesus, Teri, you found him?'

'It's more like he found me.'

There was a short pause on the other end, and Teri did her best not to analyze it. If she thought about it at all, she'd probably conclude that Walt was trying to decide if he wanted to believe her or not. A mother's sorrow was like a dream. It could take you places that never really existed. Teri had been trapped in her own sorrow for a long, long time now.

'Gabe's really back?' he finally said.

'Wait 'till you see him.'

6

Walt hung up the phone, took off his glasses and rubbed his eyes. In front of him, on the kitchen counter, the *Chicago Tribune* was open to the Tempo section. It was the top newspaper on a stack of papers from across the country: the *San Francisco Chronicle*, the *LA Times*, the *New York Times*, the *Washington Post*, the *San Jose Mercury News*. Walt folded the *Tribune* into fourths and tossed it aside.

Gabriel Knight had come home.

Walt had been a lieutenant in the Juvenile Investigations Bureau when he had first been drawn into the Knight case. The facts, as he recalled them, had been sketchy at best. Gabe had attended school that day, his behavior nothing out of the ordinary according to teachers and classmates. After school, he took the bus home and got off at his usual stop with three of his friends. He made it to the house. His books and backpack were left on the kitchen table along with a short handwritten note that said: GONE TO THE PARK, GABE.

Mrs O'Brien from down the block saw him ride past her place a little after three o'clock. He cut the corner a little tight and left a tire track across the edge of her lawn. She made a mental note to herself to speak to his parents about it the next time she bumped into them.

Jonathan Chambers, who was in Gabe's fifth-grade class at school, passed him on Sycamore Street a short time later. It was only two blocks from there to Kaplan Park. No one, though, had stepped forward to say that they had seen him at the park.

Gabriel Knight had simply disappeared.

As with most cases of this nature, Walt's focus had first turned to Gabe's parents. Michael and Teri had been married thirteen years. From all outward appearances, it was a good marriage. No financial troubles. No affairs. No history of child abuse. In addition, both parents had been working that afternoon, with a handful of co-workers on each side willing to substantiate that fact.

There was no reason to believe it had been either of the parents.

In fact, a short time later, Teri Knight had taken a leave of absence from her job and had begun spending all her time trying to keep Gabe's disappearance in front of the public eye, doing interviews, sending out press releases, distributing flyers, anything and everything. When public interest began to wane, she even took on the task of tracking whatever leads the department was willing to make available to her.

Michael Knight, on the other hand, had found his own way to deal with the loss of his son. He had buried himself in his work.

And Walt, well, Walt eventually came up against a dead end.

The case had never been solved.

Several years later, Walt found himself embroiled in another disappearance. This one involved a seven-year-old girl, Andrea Kennan. She had been abducted on the way to school by a man, who witnesses described as a white male in his early forties with long brown hair and eyes as black as night.

Walt was one of three investigators on the case. Nearly a hundred interviews, some twenty suspects and five months later they had fished the pond dry and moved onto other waters. Andrea's fate remained a mystery for better than two years after that. Then her abductor suddenly resurfaced. He tried to pick up another little girl outside the Town & Country Mall. This time, though, the girl managed to get away.

A witness jotted down the man's license plate number.

Within a matter of hours, they had the guy in custody.

During the follow-up investigation, it came out that the man had been responsible for kidnapping and murdering at least eleven other little girls over a four-state area. Andrea Kennan, it was believed, had been his first victim.

It was that knowledge that preyed most on Walt's psyche. For months afterward, the world felt like an ever-tightening noose around his neck. Sleeplessness became a nightly visitor. He found himself afraid to close his eyes, afraid of the nightmares that would take him to the cemeteries where the children roamed, lost and abandoned. No rest for the innocent. No sleep for the guilty.

Eventually, Walt resigned from the department.

For a long time afterward, he felt like one of the lost ghosts he dreamt about. No sense of time or place. No belonging anywhere. No sense of the world beyond his apartment walls. Then Teri had called. She said she had heard about his resignation, and she was wondering if he'd be interested in helping her follow up a lead in Gabe's case. There was no way out for him. If there had been, he would have taken it. But he had already let her down once and he wasn't going to do it again. And so he agreed.

As it turned out, the lead was a case of mistaken identity. A Virginia woman thought she might have spotted Gabe at the local swimming pool. The boy had been with a man in his late forties and a heavyset woman with a streak of gray in her hair. Walt called a friend back east, and in a couple of weeks they managed to track the family down. They were from Mexico. It was their first trip to America. Their son, Roberto – who had been named after Roberto Clemente, the Hall of Famer – was nine. Gabe would have been nearly fifteen by then.

Another dead end.

It hadn't been all for naught, though. The idea of actually solving the Knight case rekindled a flame in Walt. For the first time in months, it allowed him to look past the helplessness he had felt as a detective. Maybe he could still make a difference. If he could solve one case, save one life . . .

He had Teri to thank for that little ray of hope. It had steered him back into investigative work, specializing in missing children.

And now Gabe was home again.

The circle was complete.

7

Teri and Gabe sat in the car outside Denny's as Walt pulled into the parking lot. They had been waiting for a good fifteen minutes. In that time, Teri had tried to explain to her son that more than a few days had passed since they had last seen each other. It had gone down like a glass of sour milk.

'Then I should be older,' Gabe argued.

'I know,' Teri said. 'That's the part that doesn't make any sense.'

'And I'd remember, too. Wouldn't I?'

It was a good question. She mulled it over for a moment or two, then asked a question of her own. 'Exactly what *do* you remember, Gabe? You remember the accident?'

'Huh-uh.'

'None of it?'

He shrugged. 'Maybe little things.'

'Like what?'

'Like when I left the note for you on the table. And some junior-high kids getting off the bus at Bascom. One of them threw a banana peel at me; he missed by a mile.' Gabe grinned. It was the most precious sight Teri thought she had ever seen, and it frightened her to think how close she had come to never seeing it again.

'Anything else?'

'I don't know. Just little things, I guess.'

'How about after the accident?' she asked. A car pulled into the lot. Teri looked up, saw that it didn't belong to Walt, then tried to return to her thought. 'What do you remember *after* the accident? Anything?'

'I woke up in bed and it was dark. There wasn't anybody else there.'

'That must have been scary.' She thought to ask him if he remembered anyone besides Miss Churchill, but about that time Walt finally drove up. He climbed out of the car, jiggled the handle to make sure the lock was set, then entered the restaurant.

'Is that him?' Gabe asked.

'Yeah.'

'He doesn't look like a cop.'

'Well, he isn't. Not any more. He works by himself now. He's like *Spencer For Hire* or *The Equalizer*.'

'Who are they?'

Teri grinned, feeling oddly estranged from her own son. There it was again, that ten year gap. Under different circumstances, she might not have even given it a second thought. But it seemed so stark, red ink on white paper. This was how much time they had actually missed together. 'I'll explain later,' she said.

Through the restaurant windows, they watched a waitress show Walt to a booth. He sat with his back to them, and said something to her that Teri assumed had to do with the fact that he was expecting two more people.

'So let's go,' Gabe said.

'Not just yet.' She held him back with one hand, and watched as Walt thumbed indifferently through the menu. She wasn't sure exactly what it was she was waiting for – paranoia wasn't always that telling. But she thought it might be smart to wait a moment longer and make sure no one showed up behind him. She trusted Walt. Right now he was the only man she trusted. Still, it was better to be safe than sorry.

After a few minutes with no one else showing up, Teri and Gabe climbed out of the car. It had been raining on and off all day. Now, though, even as they were trying to walk around the puddles, she could see a patch or two in the clouds overhead where the sky was blacker than black and Lucy was there with her diamonds, as Lennon had once sung. It was a beautiful night.

She took his hand, and he surprised her by not putting up an argument. Some things had definitely changed. He wouldn't have let her get away with that ten years ago.

'You look silly, Mom,' he said as she tiptoed around a puddle. She had lost a shoe back at the house. The other shoe was in the front seat of the car, stuffed into the crack between the seat and the back.

'Oh, I do, do I?'

'Yeah.'

When they entered the restaurant, Walt looked up and smiled. She thought she might have roused him out of his sleep earlier, but that didn't appear to be the case now. His eyes were bright. No bags. No redness around the outer edges. And his hair, which was blond and wavy and a little longish in the back, didn't appear to be watered down as if he had done a quick job of trying to keep it in place.

'Sorry about bothering you so late,' Teri said, slipping into the booth beside Gabe.

'Lost your shoes, I see.'

'You noticed.'

'Hard not to.' Walt glanced at Gabe, giving nothing away. 'So who's this?'

'Who do you think it is?'

'Well, he's too young to be Gabe, that's for sure.'

'Not if he hasn't grown any older,' Teri said, fully aware of how it made her sound. The problem was – there was no other way to put it, was there?

'You trying to tell me that *this* is Gabe?'

'Yes, as crazy as it sounds, that's exactly what I'm trying to tell you.'

'Teri, he'd be in his twenties by now.'

'Twenty-one, to be exact.'

'Right. Twenty-one.' Walt took a closer look at the boy, a mirthful smile playing at his lips. 'He doesn't look twenty-one to me.'

'That's because he isn't.'

'Because he hasn't aged?'

'Yes.'

'Uh-huh,' he said, more doubtfully now. He took a moment to pat down the pockets of his jacket, first the two inside breast pockets, then the right front pocket, until he pulled out a sheet of paper. 'I thought Gabe might be interested in seeing how hard we looked for him, so I brought along one of the old flyers.'

He unfolded the paper, then flattened it out against the table. Across the top it said: MISSING! GABRIEL KNIGHT. Below the headline was a photograph of Gabe in his Little League uniform. They had printed nearly a hundred thousand copies of this flyer. It offered a reward of $10,000 for his safe return, every penny Teri and Michael had been able to come up with.

Walt stared down at the photograph a moment, then up at Gabe. The photo had been taken three months before Gabe's disappearance. He was kneeling on one knee, a bat in his right hand, and a grin across his face that was warm and playful. In the distant background, a bright patch of blue sky cut a mat around the treetops. For a flyer, the photo was unusually clear and sharp.

'Okay, I'll grant you that he looks like him,' Walt said.

'Exactly like him,' Teri agreed.

'But it's been ten years for God's sake, Teri. He's not an eleven-year-old boy anymore. I mean . . . how could you believe this?'

'It's him, Walt.'

'Look, I know you've never stopped hoping,' he said carefully. 'But tell me now, honestly, don't you see a bit of him in every little boy you come across? I mean, doesn't his face show up everywhere? In the grocery store? At the park? And haven't there been times when you would have sworn you saw him up ahead of you in line or in the back seat of a car that just passed by, when it wasn't him at all?'

Yes, she thought.

Of course.

She couldn't count the times she had spotted a boy with Gabe's build, with his coloring, his gait. Or the times she had followed after a boy like one of those crazy women who couldn't have children of their own. Walt was right about that. For years, she had seen Gabe's face nearly everywhere.

'Yes,' she said solemnly. 'But this isn't like that.'

Walt shook his head, his discomfort roaming naked across his face. He stared down at the flyer again, studied it a moment, then slid it across the table toward Gabe. 'Gabe meet Gabe,' he said.

'I know my own son, Walt.'

'I know you think you do, Teri.'

'It's him,' she said.

'How can you be so sure?'

Because a mother knows her child, she thought. More important, though, she realized Walt wasn't asking how *she* could be sure. What he really wanted to know was how *he* could be sure. Convince me, he was saying. Make me believe it as much as you do.

'I'll tell you what, Walt. You ask him whatever you want, whatever you think will help you make up your mind. You ask him, and I'll let him answer, and then when you're done and you're convinced, then I've got something else for you.'

'There's more?'

'Yeah, but it can wait,' she said. 'First things first. Go ahead and ask him whatever you want. I'll let you know if it's on the mark or not. Okay? You trust me, right?'

'Of course, I do.'

'Then go on, ask him.'

Walt grinned again, clearly uneasy. He scratched at an invisible itch near his right ear, then slumped resignedly back into his seat. 'Okay, fine. We'll play twenty questions and we'll see where it takes us. But I'm warning you right now, this isn't going to be an easy sell.'

'That's all right, as long as you keep an open mind.'

'I'll do the best I can,' he said, sounding like a man who would do just that. 'This all okay with you, Gabe?'

Gabe, who had been mesmerized by the flyer in front of him, looked up and nodded numbly. 'Sure,' he said, his voice soft and mouse-like. He was getting tired, Teri thought. He had that rheumy-eyed look of an old dog before it's had a chance to lie down and take its afternoon nap. Without a word, he slid the flyer across the table at Walt, and rested his head against Teri's shoulder. So much the little boy again.

'Okay,' Walt said. 'What were you wearing the day you disappeared?'

'These same clothes.'

Walt glanced at Teri, who nodded and referred him to the description in the flyer. Levi's. A black T-shirt beneath a blue-and-white windbreaker. A generic brand of K-Mart tennis shoes.

White athletic socks. It was all there. Just like the description.

'Okay, what's your middle name?'

The flyer listed him as Gabriel 'Gabe' Knight. No middle name.

'Michael,' Gabe said. 'After my father.'

'And what's your birthday?'

'April 22nd.'

That was information listed on the flyer, as well. The date of his birth. The date of his disappearance. His age. His name. What he had been wearing. A brief description of his physical characteristics. The circumstances of his disappearance (which had been sketchy, since little was known beyond the fact that he had arrived home that afternoon and then left for the park). The amount of the reward being offered. And of course, a phone number to contact. It was all there.

'Okay. At the time of your disappearance, were your grandparents still alive?'

'Only Grandma Knight. She lives in Toledo, so I haven't seen her since I was little. I got to call her, though. On my last birthday, because she sent me twenty dollars.'

Walt looked to Teri for confirmation, and this time, she had to think a little. Edna Knight, Gabe's grandmother, was no longer alive. She had passed away three years ago last Mother's Day, sometime during the night. Natural causes, according to Michael. Teri, who had always got along well with the woman, hadn't been able to make it to the funeral because she had spent that day – as well as the day before – with a terrible migraine headache, something she still felt guilty about. But yes, Gabe's grandmother had been alive then. As for the twenty dollars, Teri just couldn't be sure.

'His Grandpa Knight died in an automobile accident a couple of months after Gabe was born,' Teri said.

'How about on the other side of the family?'

'My side? I grew up in foster care.'

Walt nodded and glanced off into the parking lot, where the lights were shining off the rain puddles like tears in the darkness. Teri thought he probably wanted to say something polite, something like *I'm sorry*, but she hoped he wouldn't find it necessary. That was the way things had been when she was a little girl. Some kids had it better. Some had it worse. She had made the best of it, and spent very little time looking back.

'Okay. What about the birthday present?' he finally asked.

'I'm not sure,' Teri said, appreciating the effortless change of subject. 'It sounds like something she'd do. His grandmother hated shopping for gifts, especially once Gabe started to get a little older. I remember she sent him a check for Easter that year, because she made it out to me and asked that I buy him some new clothes with it. But that Christmas... I can't remember if she sent money or not.'

'She did,' Gabe said.

Walt frowned. 'Maybe we're going about this the wrong way.'

'How so?'

'Well, maybe if there was something just between the two of you. A song you used to sing to him. Or maybe a secret he confided. Something no one else would know about.'

'What do you think? Any secrets between us?'

Gabe shook his head, looking disinterested. Actually, it was more than that. He was getting tired, Teri thought. His face was pale and drawn. Dark circles had appeared under his eyes. He looked like the little boy she used to know who could barely keep his eyes open when he stayed up late on Friday nights to watch *Tales From The Darkside*. God, how she wished she knew what was going on inside his head.

'You all right?'

'Uh-huh.'

Back to the moment, she remembered a song she used to sing to him. This was years ago, when he was still a little tike, maybe four or five. She'd tuck him in bed at night and sing him the *Pajama Song*. Teri had heard the song from her mother, who had heard it from *her* mother, and it had been passed all the way down to Gabe. But it had been a long time since he had been a little tike, and she didn't think there was much chance he'd still remember the words.

'I remember something,' he said quietly. His eyes widened a bit. 'That time I knocked over Dad's model boat. The one he was always working on in the garage. A schooner. Remember?'

God, when had that been? Gabe had been maybe seven or eight years old, and he wasn't supposed to be caught anywhere near his father's workbench. 'Some sort of a sailboat, right?' added Teri.

Gabe nodded. 'I knocked it off the bench and broke it, and you said you wouldn't tell Dad because he'd be madder than hell. You made me promise that I'd never go near his workbench again. And when Dad came home, you told him Marcus had gotten into the garage and knocked over the model and it was your fault because you were busy bringing in the groceries.'

'Marcus?' Walt asked.

'The family dog,' Teri said. 'You remember what happened to Marcus, Gabe?'

'Yeah, we had to put him to sleep.'

'You remember why?'

'Because he started limping and the doctor said he had cancer.'

Walt glanced at Teri for confirmation.

She nodded. 'Bone cancer.'

Gabe nestled back into the fold of her arms. For a moment, they shared the same small space, the same long-ago memories. Marcus had been their only dog. And that sailboat had turned out to be the only boat Michael had ever tried to build. He hadn't been as angry as Teri had expected. Instead, he had said something about not being cut out for modeling anyway, that it took more patience than he thought he might have. That night, he tossed the boat into the garbage, tossed it out and walked away and never looked back. Walking away was something Michael had always been good at.

'Michael never knew any of this?' Walt asked.

'Not about the sailboat.'

'I see.' He sat back in the booth, gazing off through the window into the night, fighting some sort of internal, invisible battle. Then he looked at her, his eyes dull, his face drawn. 'Someone's pulling your strings, Teri.'

'I don't think so.'

'Someone who's close enough to know this kind of stuff.'

'You're wrong, Walt. I'm telling you – it's him.'

'He *can't* be Gabe. It's physically impossible.'

'Maybe if you heard the rest of the story?'

'All right,' Walt said, a touch of impatience finally beginning to show. 'Why don't you try it on me and we'll see where it takes us.'

He's going to think I'm crazy. Teri took in a deep breath, let it out slowly, and proceeded to tell him everything she could remember about what had happened tonight.

8

To her surprise, Walt didn't have any trouble at all believing that three men had broken into her house. And of course, she should have known that would be easier for him. In his line of work, he had heard similar stories before. Maybe not with the exact same twists or the bizarre implications, but stories close enough just the same. They were stories anchored in physical evidence, with at least some degree of scientific verifiability. And in his mind that was all he needed to make something true.

'What do you think they wanted?' he asked.

'Gabe.'

'First he shows up, then they show up. One leads to the other.'

'Exactly.'

'Did you call the police?'

'No,' Teri said, glancing away. Before she had let things overtake her, Teri had made a pest of herself down at the department. Walt had borne the brunt of it, of course, though every once in awhile things had spilled over. Not just to Walt's supervisor, either, but all the way to the Chief of Police. And it hadn't helped – the one time she had tried to prevent a Gabe look-alike from leaving the McDonald's at the Round Tree Plaza. A clerk called the police and once they had established the boy's identity – needless to say, he was *not* Gabe – they gave him a ride home in a police car and Teri got a ride down to the station. After that, she had won herself a reputation with them. And toward the end, when she would call about a lead or a sighting, they had quit listening altogether.

'Why not?' Walt asked.

'Jesus, Walt, you know why. They wouldn't believe me if I had caught the whole thing on videotape.'

Walt smiled, mildly amused by her directness. It was his first smile of the evening, and she probably should have thanked him for it. He had put up with an awful lot from her. And not only the false sightings, either. Twice, when Teri hadn't felt things were happening fast enough, she had gone directly to the press. It had made him look bad, and she hadn't cared, because the only thing that had mattered to her was getting her son back.

Somehow, Walt had understood that.

'No,' Walt said, still grinning. 'I don't suppose they would.'

'And they probably wouldn't believe *you*, either,' Teri added, playfully, though there was a certain thread of truth to it. They had both lost some credibility in certain circles. At times, when she thought about it, she wondered if maybe that hadn't been the basis of their friendship. Two lonely outcasts, clinging to each other.

After the laughter settled again, she turned serious. 'So what do you think we should do?'

'I guess we should start by taking a look at the house.'

9

Something didn't feel right.

Walt was struck by that feeling almost immediately as he rounded the corner and first caught sight of the house. It was a suburban tract home, stucco and wood. A well-kept front yard. The siding would be in need of paint in another year or two. The house sat in the middle of the block. Walt had been here more times than he could remember, though the last time had been a good many years ago now.

The place hadn't changed much.

Teri had taken good care of it.

He parked down the street, near the corner. Teri, who was sitting in front on the passenger side, sank deep into her seat and stared silently up the block at the house. She hadn't said a word on the drive over.

'You okay?' Walt asked.

She nodded.

It was nearly one o'clock in the morning now. Small patches of the night sky had broken through the overcast and it was getting nippy out. Gabe, who was snuggled into a little ball – Walt's coat thrown over him to keep him warm – had fallen asleep in the back. Walt checked to make sure he was all right, then turned to Teri.

'You better stay here.'

'Why?'

'I don't like the way this feels.'

'You don't think they're still there, do you?'

'No, I'd be surprised,' Walt said. 'But you said they knocked out the vertical window next to the front door, didn't you?'

'Yeah.'

There was a street light broken out. A thick, secretive band of shadow had fallen across the front of the house. Still, Walt thought it appeared as if the window were perfectly intact. And though he'd never admit it to anyone, especially Teri – in fact, he was barely able to acknowledge it at all – he wondered briefly if this was another one of those *incidents*, if maybe she had let her excitement about the boy overtake her.

He felt a sharp pang of shame, and brushed the thought away.

'*Did* they break it out?'

'Yes,' she said, a little sharply.

'I mean all the way?'

'What are you getting at?'

'Nothing,' Walt said, a turn of his mouth betraying him. 'I just think it might be better if you wait here with Gabe. I'll do a quick walk through, just to make sure everything's clear, then I'll come back and get you. Okay?'

Teri nodded, and took a quick peek over the seat. Gabe had started to toss a little. 'Sure. I guess.'

'I won't be long. I promise.'

Walt climbed out of the car, slamming the door behind him. He motioned for her to make sure the locks were down, then started across the street without looking back. What struck him almost immediately as odd was that all the lights in the house were off. Teri said she had grabbed Gabe and left on the run. So why were the lights off? Why would these guys, whoever the hell they were, turn off the lights before they left? It didn't make sense.

He stopped at the top of the driveway, next to the corner of the house, long enough to listen to the night sounds. There was a gentle breeze blowing through the shrubs across the front, making harsh whispering noises. What sounded like one or two blocks over, a dog was barking at something in the night. But otherwise, everything seemed quiet, almost eerily quiet.

The front porch was saddled with a blanket of shadows, black and blacker yet. Walt found the knob, tried it, and found the door locked. He pressed his hands against the window and peered in, only distantly realizing that the window had *not* been broken after all. Inside, an eerie, oppressive stillness seemed to huddle in the corners.

He tried the knob again, just in case, and still found it locked.

'Dandy. Just dandy.'

Back at the car, Teri leaned across the seat and unlocked the driver's-side door for him. Walt leaned in, taking a moment first to glance at the surroundings and assure himself that they were alone and in no danger.

'Don't suppose you have a key to the front door, do you?'

'What?'

'The door's locked,' he said.

'You're kidding.'

'Nope. It does sound a little crazy, doesn't it?' He glanced up again at the surroundings, a precaution that had become habit over the years. Night had set a quiet peacefulness over the neighborhood. Overhead, the clouds had opened to the faint glimmer of a scattering of stars. It seemed like a place that had been sleeping for a good long time now, though he knew that was hardly the case. 'You still want to come in?'

'Yes.'

He leaned against the car, his forehead resting against the frame just above the door. You can read a person by listening to her voice or the choice of her words, and you can read a person by the expressions that cross her face. Teri's inner strength had always impressed Walt, especially as Gabe's disappearance had lengthened from days to weeks and then from weeks to months. But he wanted to make sure that strength was still with her and that she was still with him.

'You sure?' he asked.

'I'm sure.'

'Good. It might help if you take me through exactly what happened, step by step.'

'Okay.' She glanced over her shoulder at Gabe, who had settled down again and was sleeping soundly in the back seat. 'What about Gabe? I hate to wake him.'

'He'll be all right here. I'll lock the car up.'

After thinking about it, though, Teri decided she didn't want to chance it. Gabe had been gone too long, she told Walt. And now that he was back, she wanted to make certain she never lost him again.

10

'Try not to touch anything,' Walt said as soon as they were inside.

At the restaurant, he had offered to stop by his place and see if he could scrounge up a pair of slippers or something for her feet. It was a nice offer. But since they'd decided to head back to her place anyway, Teri had told him not to worry about it. She could get something out of her closet.

Standing in the front hall now, she could feel the coolness of the tile beneath her feet. But what was bothering her was the thin, vertical window next to the door. It was completely intact.

She had to remind herself that she hadn't actually seen the window break. She had only heard the sound, the initial impact, the sharp raining down of broken glass. Naturally, her assumption had been that they had smashed the window. But it *had* been an assumption.

'Teri?' Walt said, making sure she was listening.

'Yeah, I heard you. Don't touch anything.'

'You okay?'

'They broke it out, Walt. I could have sworn they broke it out.'

'I heard it, too,' Gabe said, sleepy-eyed.

'Okay,' Walt said. He gave the base of the door a tap with his foot. It creaked up to the jamb, stopping an inch or two short, effectively choking off the outside chill. Teri felt immediately warmer. 'Let me take a look.'

She had no idea what it was he was hoping to find. The window was there, fully intact. The glass – something called bottle glass, tinted green and roughly resembling the bottom of a Coke bottle – had been in style in the late Sixties and early Seventies. It wasn't something you often saw anymore.

'Teri, can you turn on the light for me?'

'Sure.'

'Gabe, how about that flashlight?' Walt had brought three items out of the car with him. One was the flashlight, which he had handed to Gabe and told him to take good care of. The second item was a small, plastic box, which Walt was still holding in one hand. The third item, the one that alarmed Teri when she first saw it, and still alarmed her even now, was a gun. He had tucked it into a shoulder holster, not unlike the one Mitch had shown her, only Walt wasn't wearing a jacket and the gun was always in sight.

Teri turned on the nearest light.

Walt cast the beam of the flashlight across the glass of the window, up one side, down the other, experimenting with various angles. 'No prints. These guys are good.'

'How can you tell?'

'It's a little harder with the green tint, but you can usually pick up a print if you catch it in the right light. It's not likely these guys left any prints, though. I'm sure everything was wiped down. And even if we do come across a print, odds are it won't belong to either of your friends.'

'Who would it belong to?'

'A technician,' Walt said. He turned off the flashlight, handed it back to Gabe, and leaned against the wall. 'Can you smell it?'

'What?'

'Come here.' He motioned her to the window and had her take a whiff. 'Smell that?'

'Yeah.' It wasn't an unpleasant smell, and she knew she had come across it before, but she wasn't sure where or when. It smelled a bit like turpentine or maybe rubbing alcohol or... no, it smelled like linseed oil. That's what it reminded her of – linseed oil. 'What is it?'

'Window putty,' Walt said with a grin.

'They replaced the window?'

'They sure as hell did.' He stuck his thumb into the putty, pulled it out, and there was a beautiful impression of his thumb left behind.

Suddenly Teri understood what he had been getting at: no prints, technicians, these guys are good. After she had escaped, they had brought in some sort of a cover-up team to make it look as if nothing had ever happened here. *I would have sounded like a crazy woman*, Teri thought.

'A few more hours,' Walt said. 'And they just might have gotten away with it.'

11

Walt had been right.

They might have gotten away with it.

They had done an amazing job of putting things back in order. The window had been replaced. The doors were locked. The lights were all off. The sliding glass door in the family room was back on its track, the glass replaced. And the items Teri and Gabe had knocked off the desk upstairs had all been returned (though not in perfect order; the phone was sitting at the front of the desk instead of at the back, where she usually kept it, and the stapler was on the wrong side).

As they toured the house, Teri couldn't help but think how lucky it was she had gone to Walt instead of the police. If they had responded at all, which was by no means a certainty, they wouldn't have spent two minutes here before deciding it was another one of her false alarms. Where was the break-in? Why were the doors locked? Why were the lights off? And even if they had stumbled across the fresh window putty, they would have first suspected her. She had seen that look of suspicion before. Too many times before.

Walt spent some extra time going through the office upstairs, while Teri fixed Gabe some hot chocolate in the kitchen. By the time Walt showed up downstairs again, they were sitting at the counter, Gabe sipping his drink, Teri fascinated by the realization that her little boy was a part of her life again.

'Anything?' she asked as Walt leaned against the corner.

'You've got the cleanest windows in the neighborhood,' he said flatly. 'Probably the cleanest windows in the whole damn state.'

'No prints, huh?'

'Well, I didn't really expect to find any.'

'Want some hot chocolate?'

'No.' He shook his head and seemed to follow his thoughts off into a wonderland of their own. Always thinking, he was. Always trying to catch an angle.

'So what now?' Teri asked.

'I think you better stay with me tonight.'

'You think they'll be back?'

'I wouldn't bet against it.'

Neither would she. Teri ruffled Gabe's hair. 'Some adventure, huh?'

He nodded, and wiped the back of his hand across his chocolate mustache. 'Why are they after us, Mom?'

'I don't know,' Teri said honestly. She ruffled his hair again, then got up to get him a napkin.

'That's something we'll have to talk about,' Walt said, making it perfectly clear that he preferred to talk about it sometime when Gabe wasn't around.

'Sure.'

Teri pulled a paper napkin out of a drawer and set it on the counter in front of Gabe. 'Use it.'

'Use it or lose it,' he said with a giggle. A new mustache had replaced the old one, and he looked a little like a young Clark Gable.

'No,' Teri said lightly. '*You* use it or *I'll* use it for you.'

Gabe giggled again.

'You found yourself some shoes,' Walt said.

'Yeah.' Teri glanced down at her feet. She was wearing a pair of sandals, which tended to go easy on her feet after a long day of standing at the post office. They felt especially good after having gone barefoot for half the night. 'And guess what else I found?'

'What?'

'My other shoe. They stuck it back in the closet.'

'The one he pulled off your foot?'

'That's the one.'

'It was back in your closet?'

'Uh-huh.'

'Why don't you show me.'

Apparently he was hoping that he might find a print on the back of the shoe, where the man had tried to hold on. The shoe was a vinyl pump, the first lucky break. Walt said the vinyl should hold a good print if they hadn't cleaned it off. And that turned out to be the second lucky break.

Teri watched him go through the process of using the flashlight at various angles again. Then, for the first time, he opened the small rectangular box he had been carrying with him. He took out a brush, twisted it in the air until the bristles fluffed up, then dipped it into a small vial of powder. He brushed both sides of the shoe, near the back, and gradually two sets of prints became visible.

'Got 'em,' Teri said optimistically.

'Well, we got something.'

Walt covered the print on the left side with tape, pressed down meticulously, then pulled the tape up in a single, smooth motion. To Teri's eye it looked like a beautiful print. He transferred it to a 3x5 card, then took two other prints on the other side. There were three altogether, though two of the prints appeared to be smudged and run together.

'Well, at least it's something.'

He didn't hold out much hope that anything would come of them, he said, when Teri asked about it. Chances were the prints belonged to a technician and if not a technician, then they might even be her own prints. Just to compare, he took prints from her and from Gabe.

'Guess that's about all we can do here tonight,' he said, closing up the kit. 'You and Gabe might want to grab a few things to bring along since we don't know where this thing is going. For now, at least, you better stay with me.'

For now, Teri thought.

How long did he think this was going to go on?

12

Walt cleared the stack of newspapers off the kitchen table and stacked them in the corner, out of the way. 'Sorry for the mess. A bachelor's life, you know.'

'Actually, I half-expected to be wading through piles of dirty dishes and clothes on the floor. This is nicer than I keep my place.'

'Sundays are my cleaning days. By the end of the week, it'll take a forklift to get around in here.'

It was nearly three o'clock in the morning now. Condensation had formed in the corners of the living-room window, where the cold was fighting to get in. Walt had brought out a sleeping bag and an air mattress for Gabe, who had almost immediately fallen off to sleep in the other room. Teri wasn't sure she'd ever be able to sleep again. Whenever she closed her eyes, she found herself hanging out the office window over the garage. It gave her the creeps.

She sat in the nearest chair.

'Can I get you anything?' Walt asked. He seemed a bit ill at ease, having his place invaded like this, though Teri suspected he wouldn't have had it any other way. 'Coffee? Diet Coke? Water? Anything?'

'No, I'm fine. Really.'

'Okay.' He sat down across the table from her, sighed and asked, 'Quite a day for you, huh?'

'I'm not keeping you up, am I?'

'No, not at all.'

'Because if I am...'

'You aren't. Honest.'

'Okay,' Teri said resignedly. 'It's really nice of you to put up with us this way.'

'I'm glad to do it.' He pulled the fingerprint cards out of his shirt pocket and tossed them on the table. Time to get down to business, Teri supposed. 'So what can you tell me about tonight?'

'Not much, I'm afraid.'

'What time did Gabe show up?'

'A little after eight, I think.'

'And what was the woman's name? The woman you said brought him home?'

'Miss Churchill.'

Walt climbed out of his chair and rummaged around in a drawer in the kitchen until he came up with a pencil and a pad. 'Churchill,' he said, mostly to himself. 'What did she have to say? Anything?'

'Not much.'

'Did she say anything about where Gabe had been the last ten years or why she was bringing him home at this particular time?' He sat down at the table again, immersed in making notes. 'By the way, I want to check Gabe's dental records tomorrow. Just to make sure.'

'You still don't believe it's him, do you?'

Walt glanced up from his notepad, stared at her a moment, then sighed and sat back. 'I want to believe as much as you do, Teri. Let's just make certain, okay?'

'If he's not Gabe, then who is he?'

'I don't know.'

'And why?' Teri asked, knowing these were all the same unanswered questions she had already asked herself. 'I mean... what's the motive? I haven't got any money. I'm not *connected* in any way. What in the world would they want with me?'

'Something's going on behind the scenes, Teri.'

'I know,' she said solemnly.

The mood between them shifted, and they both seemed to realize it at the same time. Teri sat back in her chair. Walt tapped out a handful of beats against his notepad with the end of his pencil, then sighed. It had been a long day, and all of this was new territory.

'We'll get a handle on it,' he said finally. 'One way or another, we'll get a handle on it.'

Teri stared down at her hands, which were nervously picking at the hem of her shirt. She hadn't had a handle on anything in longer than she could remember. Not her family. Not her marriage. Not her job. Everything had seemed to fall apart all at once, right before her eyes. She wasn't going to let that happen again. Not now. Not ever. 'She said he didn't know how long he'd been gone.'

Walt raised his eyebrows.

'Miss Churchill. She said Gabe thought he had been in an accident and that only a couple of weeks had passed.'

'Did you ask him about it?'

Teri nodded. 'He doesn't remember the accident. I think that was probably something that came from her, something to explain about where he was and what had happened.'

'The script being that he had been unconscious since the accident?'

'I think so.'

'So he doesn't have any recollection of the past ten years?'

'Only the last couple of weeks.'

'Which were spent where?'

'Apparently, in some sort of hospital or medical facility.'

'And what did he base that on?'

'I don't know. I didn't have the time to get into it with him.'

Walt nodded, jotted down another note, and took a deep breath. She could see he was burning with raw curiosity now, the investigator poking at the edges of the facts to see if anything protruded from the other side. 'Okay, tell me about these guys who showed up.'

'There were three of them. One man, I think his name was Mitch, was clearly in charge.'

'Were they carrying weapons?'

'Mitch was. He showed it to me at the front door. A little persuader, I guess.'

'And the others?'

'I don't know.' Teri remembered the man with the scar over his eye standing there in the doorway, his suit coat pulled back, exposing the gun. There was something gnawing at her, though. 'It was strange, because that was the only time I saw the gun, when he was at the front door. He never took it out of the shoulder holster.'

'Even when you were close to escaping through the window?'

'Yeah.' She nodded, thinking how odd that seemed now that she looked back on it. 'Why didn't he take a shot at me?'

'Maybe he wasn't supposed to hurt you,' Walt said.

'Why? You think he might have been working for someone else?'

'Oh, they were following orders, all right. This whole thing was orchestrated.'

'How can you know that?'

'The clean-up,' Walt said matter-of-factly. His pencil tapped out another solo on the notepad; the look in his eyes was clear and focused. 'This kid—'

'Gabe.'

'Sorry. *Gabe* probably wasn't supposed to ever leave wherever it was they were keeping him. And that's why they showed up right behind him. Home was the first place to check. And if they found him – which they did – they were supposed to take him back, apparently alive and safe.

'Who are we talking about?'

'I don't know,' Walt said. 'What about Michael?'

Teri shook her head. 'I can't imagine him doing something like that.'

'He loved his son, didn't he?'

'Of course.'

'And the marriage had . . .'

He didn't need to finish. The marriage had fallen apart. But it had been as much her fault as anyone's. After Gabe had disappeared, she had become obsessed with finding him again. She took a leave of absence from her job at the post office and with the help of a small group of volunteers, began an endless campaign of distributing flyers and following up whenever a tip came in. Everything else had been put on the back burner, including her marriage. What had Michael told her? *First I lost my son, then I lost my wife.*

Teri ran a hand through her hair. 'It's got nothing to do with Michael.'

The mood had shifted again.

Walt got up and headed for the kitchen. 'You sure you don't want anything to drink?'

'No thanks.' Teri stared across the table at the notes he had been scribbling. It was impossible to make them out upside down. 'Oh, I almost forgot. The leader – Mitch? He had a scar over his left eye.'

'That helps.' The refrigerator door closed and Walt came around the corner with a Diet Coke in his hand. 'How about the other two?'

'One guy, I think his name was Jimmy, was short and thin. He seemed like the nervous type, always fidgeting, rocking back and forth on his heels, that kind of thing. The other one . . . all I can tell you about him is that his fingers were a mess after Gabe slammed the door on them.'

'So he'd probably need medical attention?'

'If he ever wanted to unzip his pants again.'

'That's good.' Walt made another note, nodding absently as he did so. When he was done, he paused, then said: 'Okay, here's what I think we want to do tomorrow. I've got some friends in the department. I'm going to run these prints by them and see if we come up with anything. We'll also run Mitch and Jimmy through the department's database and, who knows, maybe it'll kick something out.'

'Okay,' Teri said.

'What I want you to do is to take Gabe in to see your family dentist and have x-rays taken. Have the dentist check them against his records and see what he has to say. If he comes back with a match, at least we'll be over that hurdle.'

'*You'll* be over that hurdle,' Teri said. 'I'm already on the other side.'

'Fair enough.'

She wasn't even sure if Gabe's dentist was still in business. She hadn't seen Dr Harding in four or five years and the last time she had been in for a visit, he had been talking about retirement. She'd missed her next check-up, and that easily; her dental care had gone the way of everything else in her life.

'I can't remember if he ever had a filling,' Teri said.

'Well, we'll see what the dentist has to say.'

'Okay.' It wasn't that she was worried, because she wasn't. She knew her own son. But things had gotten so complicated all of a sudden . . .

God, how things had a way of getting out of hand.

13

It wasn't until nearly four o'clock in the morning, with the cold night painting the windows with frost, that they finally headed off to bed. Teri slept in the bedroom, with Gabe on the floor beside the bed in a sleeping bag. Walt slept on the couch in the living room.

Through the window, he could see the tiny puff of a cloud kissing goodbye to the moon, two bodies drifting apart. It had stopped raining. The moon was a huge crystal ball in the sky. If only he could see where this thing was going.

A chill passed through him.

He tried to close his eyes and sleep.

14

Gabe was sitting on the couch, watching an old re-run of *Roseanne*, when Teri came out of the bedroom the next morning. It was a little after ten. The sun was already slanting above the building across the way and there were tendrils of steam rising off the asphalt in the courtyard below.

'About time,' Gabe said, his eyes riveted to the television.

'Where's Walt?'

'Out. He left a note for you on the counter.'

Teri yawned, feeling very nearly as tired this morning as she had last night before she had gone to bed. She didn't get many opportunities to sleep in. Then again, there weren't that many occasions when she found herself up after ten the night before. Strange events made for strange hours, she supposed.

The note, which had been written in precise, draftsman's letters, was short and to the point:

TERI,

THOUGHT I'D CHECK OUT THE PRINTS. CAN YOU GET GABE IN TO SEE HIS DENTIST? HOPE YOU SLEPT WELL. MEET YOU HERE THIS AFTERNOON. AFTER TWO?

WALT.

P.S. MAKE YOURSELF AT HOME.

'Did he say anything?' Teri asked.

'He was already gone when I got up.'

'When was that?'

'About half an hour ago,' Gabe said, without much interest. Teri had to remind herself that while it had been ten years for her, only a few days had passed for Gabe. He was already settling back into the old habit of tuning in the television and tuning out the world.

'Did you get yourself something to eat?'

A mumble.

'Gabe?'

'Uh, I'm sorry.' He glanced up, not exactly annoyed, but not delighted either. 'No, I haven't eaten anything.'

His coloring looked good this morning, and she thought the night's sleep had been good for him. 'Hungry?'

'Uh-huh.'

As long as she had known Walt, she had never been in his apartment before. It was small – one bedroom, one bath – and she imagined he didn't spend a great deal of time here. The refrigerator was sparsely supplied: eggs, butter, lunch meat, cheese, lettuce, condiments, a couple cans of Diet Coke. The stove top, a light beige which matched the tiled, beige back-splash, gave little sign of use.

Teri rummaged around the cabinet beneath the stove and came out with a non-stick frying pan. Since Gabe had disappeared, her skills in the kitchen had gradually deteriorated to microwavable TV dinners. Cooking only for one hardly seemed worth the effort – something she thought she might have in common with Walt. But things were different now, weren't they?

Jesus, weren't they ever.

15

His name was Aaron Thomas Jefferson. He was thirty-five years old, black, and by far the best damn identification technician Walt had ever worked with. His training had come through the FBI, his first on-the-job experience through the Criminal Identification Section of the department. Walt had only a cursory understanding of the deltas and dots and trifucations that defined identification points. Aaron was the expert.

'I've got a full load,' Aaron said without looking up. He was using black ink to trace a photographically-enlarged print onto a sheet of thin tracing paper.

'Something for the FBI?' Walt asked, making reference to the tracing.

'It's from that double homicide on the west side last week.'

'I think I read something about that.'

'Yeah, well, I've had three men working on a non-suspect match and it looks like the guy might not be a local.' Aaron raised the pen off the paper, let out a breath, and sat back. 'So what have you got?'

'I'm not sure.' Walt pulled the 3x5 cards out of his pocket and dropped them on the counter next to the light box. Each card was labeled. One: Teri Knight. Two: Gabriel Knight. Three: Suspect. Instep of right shoe belonging to Mrs Knight. Four: Suspect. Back side of right shoe belonging to Teri Knight.

'I see you haven't lost your training.'

'Like riding a bike.'

Aaron glanced at the cards. 'Isn't she—?'

'Yes,' Walt said quickly.

'Okay. So, what am I looking at?'

'An attempted abduction.'

'Is the department involved?'

'No,' Walt said.

Aaron shook his head. 'Best I can do is probably four or five days. I'll have to handle it myself. After hours.'

'I appreciate it, Aaron.'

'Yeah, sure.' He dropped the cards back on the counter. 'So when you coming over for dinner again? Tina's been asking about you.'

'Soon,' Walt said, feeling a twinge of awkwardness. It had actually been several years since they had last gotten together. At the time, Walt had been going out with a law clerk, who worked for the county. Her name was Rachel Burack. They had met by accident one day, when Walt was searching records for a case he was working on, and Rachel sat down next to him in search of some records of her own. The relationship hadn't lasted, though. She had become impatient with the sometimes unrelenting way he went about his business, the way he let himself become consumed by it. And when he couldn't – or wouldn't – change, she had moved on. It had no longer been Walt and Rachel after that. It had simply been Walt. Walt and his clients. Everything else had fallen away.

'I'm gonna hold you to it,' Aaron said.

Walt grinned.

'I am.'

'All right. All right. I'll give you a call, I promise.'

'Good,' Aaron said, picking up the fingerprint cards again. He tapped them against the counter. 'And I'll see what I can do about these.'

'Thanks.'

'No problem. Now let me get back to work.'

16

Teri had outsmarted herself.

She was standing at the front door of the Evergreen Dental Clinic, a small business space located at the back corner of the West Valley Shopping Center. This was where Dr Harding had maintained his practice for as long as she could remember knowing him. But he wasn't here now.

Taped to the inside of the glass door was a sign that read:
Closed.
May 10th – May 24th
For Emergencies Contact:
Dr Chittenden

Teri's hand fell away from the door handle. She had thought about calling first, but had decided against it, believing the doctor would be more likely to see Gabe at the last minute if they were already in his office. Not the smartest thing she had ever done.

'What now?' Gabe asked.

'Guess I better call Dr Chittenden.'

17

Aaron Jefferson finished the tracing, re-photographed the print and scanned it into the computer. He set the cross hair references on the core and the axis, and the computer began to run through its routine. It was as much of an opportunity to grab a bite as he was going to get today.

He fished his lunch bag out of the bottom drawer of his desk. Tuna fish. Not his favorite. His mother had turned him against tuna when he was a boy. She had always added egg and the combination had never sat right with Aaron. And while there was no egg in this tuna fish, it didn't matter. The taste of egg had long ago become part of his permanent association.

He dropped the sandwich back into the bag, took out a couple of oatmeal cookies, and poured himself a cup of hot coffee. The photographic blowups of the prints Walt had brought in were sitting on the corner of the desk. They had come back nearly half-an-hour ago. Aaron had put them aside until he'd had a chance to look at them.

There wasn't going to be a better chance.

Not today.

He picked up the stack and studied the first print.

Walt had taken the non-suspect latents from the back of a shoe. This set was smudged. They probably shouldn't have even bothered with the blowup. He buried it at the bottom of the stack.

The next photo was also from the shoe. It was a good print, a plain whorl. Probably a thumb print. The big question, though, was did it belong to . . .

Aaron flipped to the next latent.

. . . to this Teri Knight or her boy.

You're gonna owe me for this one, my friend.

He tossed the stack aside, took a bite out of one of the oatmeal cookies, and wondered if he should call Tina and let her know that he was going to be late getting home tonight. It wouldn't be the first time, of course. At least this time, it was for Walt.

18

'No, I don't have an appointment,' Teri said. She rested her head against the glass wall of the phone booth and closed her eyes. 'My name is Teri Knight. My son's name is Gabriel. Dr Harding is our regular dentist, but he's out of town.'

'Is this an emergency?' the receptionist asked. 'Did your son crack a tooth or something of that nature? Dr Chittenden is only seeing Dr Harding's patients in the case of an emergency.'

'All I need is for the doctor to take a look at Gabe's teeth and compare them to his charts.'

'I'm sorry. Dr Chittenden doesn't have access to any patient records. By that, I mean any of Dr Harding's patient records.'

'You've got to be kidding.'

'No. I'm sorry.'

'What if my son did happen to break a tooth?'

'Then Dr Chittenden would be happy to see him.'

'But he doesn't have Gabe's charts?'

'I don't believe the doctor would need them in that situation.'

No, he probably wouldn't now that Teri thought about it. This conversation wasn't going anywhere. There wasn't much sense in stretching it out. She said a polite *thanks*, hung up, and returned to the car, where Gabe was reading a comic book called *The Swamp Thing*.

'Any luck?' Gabe asked.

'Nope. Looks like you've got a reprieve,' Teri said lightly. 'No dentist today.'

'Mr Travis isn't going to like that.'

'No, I don't suppose he will.'

It was mid-afternoon. Yesterday's rain was still evident, though only in traces, mostly by the occasional puddle here and there.

Teri slipped the key into the ignition, and entertained the thought of swinging by the house. If you had asked her why, she wouldn't have been able to provide you with a reason. Maybe it was just curiosity. Maybe it was still a sense of disbelief. Either way, she supposed, it would be something else that Mr Travis wouldn't much care for.

'What now?' Gabe asked.

'I'm not sure,' Teri said. 'You hungry?'

He shook his head. They had eaten lunch almost four hours ago at a drive through called the Pac Out. Gabe had ordered a hamburger, fries, and a chocolate shake. He had left a third of his hamburger and most of the fries. They were still in the bag in the back seat.

'How about the park?' Teri suggested. She gave his cane, which hadn't left his side, a tap. 'I'll race you from the pool to the swings.'

'Mom...'

'Too fast for you?'

'Mr Rogers is too fast for me.'

'Who?'

'You know – that guy on television. *It's a beautiful day in the neighborhood*...'

She laughed, but there was a sting of truth to what he had said and she couldn't just let it go by. 'You'll get stronger, Gabe. It'll take a little time, that's all.'

He nodded.

She started up the car.

On the way to the park, she sang a few lines from *McCarther's Park*: 'I don't think that I can take it, 'cause it took so long to bake it, and I'll never have that recipe again...'

Gabe, who was staring out the window, joined in softly. And

when they were done, they sang it again, laughing hysterically at the nonsensical lyrics.

If Walt could see this, Teri thought, *then there wouldn't be any more doubt. This* was *Gabe.*

19

'So no luck with the dentist, huh?'

Teri took a sip of coffee and shook her head. 'No. He's out of town on vacation. Won't be back for another week.'

'That doesn't help much.' Walt cleared the dinner plates from the table, dumped them into the sink and turned on the water.

On the other side of the wall, coming from the living room, Teri could hear the rise and fall of laughter from a sitcom laugh track. Gabe was in there. He had picked at his meal again, a couple of bites from his garlic bread, maybe half of his spaghetti. She recalled a neighbor's mother once lamenting that 'You can't make a picky kid eat if he isn't hungry.' The trouble was... Gabe had never been a picky eater.

'Sorry,' Teri said, back to the subject of the dentist. 'There's not much we can do about it now.'

'I know. It would have been nice to have put the issue behind us, though.'

The issue.

She had resigned herself to the fact that he wasn't going to give up the issue. At least not until he had some hard evidence. And while that annoyed Teri a bit, it was also something that she greatly admired about him. Walt was a man who sought the truth. Whatever the consequences, good or bad, painful or joyous, the truth was his footing.

He stood at the sink, adding soap to the water, and she thought how lucky she was to know this man. He had been the only person in the world whom she had felt she could lean on during the worst days following Gabe's disappearance. Michael had all but buried himself in his work. And Teri, herself, had become obsessed and distant. Walt, it seemed, had been the only level head around her.

'How about you?' Teri asked. 'Any luck with the fingerprints?'

He turned off the water. 'It'll probably take a couple of days before we hear anything solid. And like I mentioned last night, I'm not holding out any high hopes.'

'So what's next?'

Walt leaned against the sink with both hands, an expression of discomfort on his face. 'I've got to go out of town, Teri.'

'Now?'

'Two days at the most. I'm sorry. I know it's coming at a bad time.'

'No. No. I'm the one who's sorry. You've been great, Walt. Really.'

'It's another case.'

'I understand.'

'I want you and Gabe to stay here while I'm gone.' He paused a moment, as if he were searching for something else to add, and when it didn't come easily, he rinsed off the next plate and placed it in the rack next to the sink. 'You'll be safer here.'

'Thanks,' Teri said, knowing he was right. She wondered how he'd feel about this next question. 'I'd like to take Gabe to see his doctor. You think that would be all right?'

'Worried about his strength?'

'And the fact he's not eating.'

'That shouldn't be a problem. Don't tell anyone where you're staying, though. If the doctor needs to get in touch with you, tell him you'll call him.'

Teri nodded, surprised at how easily she had come to accept this new secrecy into her life. It was frightening how much things had changed in just twenty-four hours. It was also amazing how accepting of the changes she had already become.

Walt rinsed off the last plate and pulled the stopper out of the sink. The sharp, not entirely pleasant aroma of Lux had filled the kitchen, reminding Teri of long-ago nights when she would finish up the dishes while Michael and Gabe played catch in the backyard. Walt dried his hands off on a towel, hung the towel in the crook of the arm of the refrigerator, and swept up the stack of newspapers he had brought home with him. He sat down across from Teri.

'How's he doing?' he asked, in apparent reference to Gabe.

'As well as can be expected, I suppose.'

'Has he asked about Michael?'

'Not really.'

'You still have Michael's number?'

Teri nodded. 'In my purse.'

'When I get back, I'll want to give him a call. See if he has an inkling of what's going on here.'

'He's not behind this, Walt.'

'Maybe not. But I wouldn't be doing my best for you if I took that at face value, now would I?'

Teri smiled.

'How are *you* holding up?'

'Okay.'

'Wish I could tell you exactly what's going on.'

'I wish you could, too.'

'It'll all work out eventually,' Walt said. With the stack of newspapers in front of him, he casually began to glance at the headlines of the local paper. Teri watched him, realizing distantly that what she was witnessing was part of this man's nightly routine.

'You think I should have called the police?' Teri asked softly.

Walt looked up and grinned. 'Caught in a little hindsight?'

Teri laughed to herself.

'What?'

'Nothing.'

'Come on, what's so funny?'

'It's just something Michael used to say.'

'Tell me.'

'It's silly.'

'I don't care.'

Teri shook her head. It was silly, and she preferred not to have to mention it because she knew it was silly. But at the same time, it was still one of those things about Michael that she had always loved, that juvenile sense of humor. 'Hiney-sight. Michael used to call it hiney-sight.'

Walt grinned.

'I told you it was silly.'

'That you did,' he said, somewhat teasingly. 'And you weren't kidding, were you?'

Teri smiled, only slightly embarrassed, then slipped awkwardly into a change of subject. 'Why so many papers?'

'Patterns,' he said. 'The bigger the canvas, the easier it is to spot them.'

'What kind of pattern are you looking for?'

'I don't always know what I'm looking for. Sometimes it's a disappearance or a kidnapping that sounds a little like it might be something similar to what I'm working on. And other times it might be a personal ad or a story about someone who doesn't remember who they are. It all depends.'

Teri nodded. 'Are you looking for anything in particular now?'

'Not really. I've got a case where a father kidnapped his two children. The mother has custody and she hired me to see if

I could track him down. That's what's taking me out of town tomorrow.'

'You think you've found him?'

'I think I might have a lead on him. How hot it is, I won't know until I've checked it out.' Walt slipped the local paper off the stack, set it aside, and began to rifle through the pages of the *San Jose Mercury News*. 'Like all of us, this guy's a creature of habit. First of all, he's a diabetic, so he needs insulin and he needs a prescription to get it. Second, he makes his living as a writer. So he's still maintaining all his old professional contacts. And that's what makes disappearing so hard to do. In order to do it right, you've got to become a completely new person. You can't carry any of the old baggage. You've got to give up everything. Very few of us are prepared to go that far.'

'How'd you track him to the Bay Area?'

'His social security number. I had a female friend call the IRS and talk to one of their female employees. My friend went into this long story about how she and this guy were in love once and how they'd lost contact with each other, and how she was trying to track him down to see if they could maybe start things up again.'

'Isn't that illegal? Giving out that kind of information?'

'You bet. The woman could lose her job if anyone found out.'

Teri grinned appreciatively. 'Clever.'

'Whatever works, as they say.'

They fell silent a moment, Walt lost in thoughts of his own, Teri thinking briefly about how difficult it must be to track someone down once they've made the decision to disappear.

'Did you quit because of me?' she finally asked.

'What?'

'The department. Did you quit the department because of me?'

'No. I quit because I needed a change, Teri. That's all, just a change.'

'Burn out?'

'More like frustration.' He collapsed the newspaper and sat back in his chair. The expression on his face was almost identical to the one he had worn the first time Teri had met him. Not impatience, but a sense of wanting to get on with it. 'Actually, you were an inspiration.'

Teri smiled self-consciously, a bit taken aback.

'You were my ghost of Christmas past, you might say.'

'I don't think I understand.'

'You remember when you called that press conference and made a big stink about how the department wasn't doing anything?'

She remembered. She remembered all too well. That was before she'd really had a chance to get to know Detective Walter Travis. She couldn't have called that same press conference today, and there had been a number of times when she had worried that it might have cost him his career.

'Well, you were right,' Walt said.

'What?'

'You were right. The department was in the middle of a budget crunch and after a couple of weeks, with no evidence that Gabe had been kidnapped, we were told to write it off as a runaway and get on with our other cases. You were right. And that's why I quit. Because I was always going to be under pressure to get on to something else.'

'I always thought...'

'It was your fault I quit?'

She nodded.

'It was,' Walt said brightly. 'And I thank you.'

Teri took that as the compliment it was meant to be, then absently pulled the local paper across the table and glanced at the headlines. There was something about unrest in South Africa, long after the elections, and that seemed to take up the majority of the banner. She flipped the front page and came surprisingly face-to-face with a photograph of Miss Churchill. The slug underneath read: NURSING STUDENT FOUND DEAD. A shudder rose up from somewhere deep inside of her.

'Walt...'

'What?'

'This is her,' Teri said. She spread the front page out across the table and flattened the crease. 'See this picture?'

'Yeah.'

'That's the woman from last night. She's the one who brought Gabe home.'

Walt began to read from the article. 'Amanda Tarkett, aged 26, was found dead this morning near the underpass at Blackmore and Vine after a mugging that apparently went bad. The police have not identified any suspects at this time, though they are following up on several leads, including a possible eyewitness. Miss Tarkett was apparently on her way home from the college when the incident occurred.'

'They killed her,' Teri said, her hands trembling.

'We don't know that.'

'They killed her.'

20

Gabe listened to the voices through the bedroom wall, trying to decide if they were coming from the television or if his mother and Mr Travis had started up another conversation. He decided it was probably the television.

He pulled the sleeping bag up around his neck and watched the shadows go dancing madly across the wall as a car passed by outside. It was always hard to sleep in a strange place. He had stayed over at Ben Sorensen's once and they had stayed up until almost four in the morning, watching videos and playing cards. But this was different. He was alone here.

Gabe closed his eyes.

The voices from the living room fell into a deadening monotone.

And quietly, he drifted off into the warmth of his own little Never-Never Land... behind him, something dark and winged followed into his dreams.

Gabe found himself trying to make his way through a maze of mirrors, some shattered, some whole; some angled to make things small, some angled to make things ugly. It was the ugly thing that frightened him. It was behind him, this thick black shadow that swept down the corridor of the maze like an evening storm over the mountain tops.

Cold.

Graceful.

Dangerous.

Gabe slammed into a mirror image of himself, backed away, stunned, then stumbled through an opening on his right. Somewhere in the beyond, there were candles burning. The light was dim and flickering, disorienting.

He slid around another corner, glancing back over his shoulder at the dark, foggy wave slithering across the floor behind him. A pair of bright, burning eyes stared malignantly out of the nothingness.

Then suddenly he came up against a dead end. He came up to it, going faster than he should have, and rammed the mirror with his forehead before stumbling back. The impact stunned him. He reached for his head and was astonished to find himself looking at three separate, distinct reflections. Each a reflection of himself.

On the left, there was a boy: smallish, maybe five or six years old, with hair that was actually more blond than brown. In the middle was his own true reflection. Then on the right, his eyes were dull, his face weathered, the flesh loose. And while all of this should have made him much older, Gabe knew, without knowing how, that this version of himself, this replica, wasn't nearly as old as it appeared.

'Come into the fold with us,' the old one said.

Gabe screamed.

21

Teri was up early, but apparently not early enough to catch Walt. He had left a note on the counter, weighted down with the salt shaker. It read:

I WANTED TO GET AN EARLY START. I SHOULD BE BACK TOMORROW NIGHT. WEDNESDAY MORNING AT THE LATEST. MAKE YOURSELF AT HOME. KEEP A LOW PROFILE. WALT.

Short and to the point.

Beneath his name, he had added a PS and a phone number where he could be reached. Teri read the note twice, looking for a hint of something but not really knowing what. When she finished up the second time, she folded the note in thirds and slipped it into the back pocket of her jeans.

Gabe was up by then.

She watched him come stiffly down the hall, still half-asleep. His limp was more pronounced this morning, though she chalked that up to the fact that he had just woken up and was moving without his cane. He fell wearily into one of the chairs at the counter.

'You look tired,' Teri said.

'I am.'

'Didn't sleep very well?'

He shook his head. 'What's for breakfast?'

'How about some bacon and eggs? You look like you could use some energy food.'

'Okay.' He toyed around with the salt shaker, and Teri wondered – not for the first time – how well he was handling everything that was going on around him.

She brought the bacon out, managed to tear off a couple of slices, then set them in the frying pan. Last night, Gabe had asked why *The A Team* wasn't on television anymore and she realized that even though she had talked to him about the ten years that had elapsed, he still hadn't worked it out in his mind. And who could blame him? She hadn't worked it out for herself, either. And neither had Walt, for that matter.

'You remember Dr Childs?' Teri asked. She set a plate on the counter in front of Gabe, and watched as he shook a few grains of salt onto it. A little boy playing in the sand.

'Huh-uh.'

'He's your doctor.'

'I thought Chittenden was my doctor.'

'No, he's your dentist. Dr Childs is your regular doctor.'

'You aren't gonna make me go see him, are you?'

'Fraid so, kiddo.'

'Ah, Mom...'

'It won't take long, I promise. He's just going to take a look at you and see if we can figure out why you aren't as strong as should be.'

'I'm strong.'

'I know, honey. But...' But something more than that was wrong. He wasn't as strong as he should be. Not for a ten-year-old. And even though Teri thought he might be gaining strength, something wasn't right. She couldn't seem to put her finger on it. Not directly. It was like one of those heavy, gnawing feelings you sometimes get when something bad has happened and you aren't directly aware of it yet.

Something bad *had* happened.

Maybe that was it.

Maybe *that* was what was bothering her.

'But it's better to be on the safe side,' Teri finished.

22

Teri wasn't willing to play the fool a second time. Yet she wasn't willing to fully commit herself, either. She called the doctor's office this time and spoke with his receptionist, making certain that Dr Childs would be in today. Then, as they say, she showed up on his doorstep unannounced.

Banishment to the waiting room had extended well past lunch and into the mid-afternoon hours before a nurse finally called Gabe's name. She escorted them into a small examination room, took his temperature and his blood pressure, and promised the doctor would be in shortly. By the time the door finally swung open again, Teri was half-way through an article in *Woman's Day* on working out of the home.

'Well, let's see what we have here,' Childs said with barely a glance. He sat on a stool across the room and thumbed through Gabe's records as if he were the only person there.

Teri couldn't remember how long it had been since their last visit. Maybe as long as thirteen or fourteen years. Dr Childs had aged visibly since then. He was wearing glasses now. And his hairline, which was graying around the temples, had begun a noticeable retreat. If pressed, her guess would be that he was somewhere in his early to mid-fifties.

He glanced up, peering over the rim of his glasses, and smiled. 'It's been a while.'

'Yes,' Teri said, hoping that somehow she wouldn't have to explain how Gabe was the same age today as he had been at their last visit.

'So what seems to be the problem?' he asked Gabe.

Gabe shrugged.

'He's been feeling a little tired lately.'

'Tired?'

'Actually, it's not so much that he's tired,' Teri tried to explain. 'He just doesn't seem to have a lot of strength. It's as if his muscles are working against him sometimes.'

'Uh-huh.' Childs nodded, as if he knew exactly what she was trying to describe. 'Has he run a temperature at all?'

'No, I don't think so.'

'Had the flu or any cold symptoms?'

'No,' Teri said, somewhat unconvincingly, she thought. The burden of guilt was beginning to settle in like an unwanted houseguest now. *What kind of a mother am I?* she thought. Maybe he had been running a temperature. Not today, of course. Not yesterday, either. But maybe the day before yesterday. There was no way for her to tell if he had been sick then, was there? 'You haven't, have you, honey?'

'No, Mom.'

'I didn't think so.' She glanced quickly at Childs, and noted with some relief that his expression had remained unchanged. No surprise or disgust there, just a doctor's mask of passivity.

'Uh-hum,' he said absently. He flipped back a page through Gabe's records, then forward again, before placing them on the counter. 'Well, why don't we take a look and see if there's anything going on.'

Gabe, who was sitting on the edge of the examination table, visibly stiffened.

'It's okay,' Childs said. 'I'm just going to check a couple of things. There's nothing to worry about.'

Teri sat nervously watching as he checked Gabe's lymph nodes first, the doctor staring off into nowhere land as his hands tried to determine if there was any swelling. He pulled a penlight out of his breast pocket, and used a tongue-depressor to get a look at Gabe's throat, checked his reflexes, then had Gabe take off his shirt and used the stethoscope to listen to the boy's lungs.

Finally, he asked, 'How long has he been having the problem?'

Who knows?

'I'm not exactly sure,' Teri said. She had hoped that she wouldn't have to elaborate any more than she already had. But in case it had come to this, she had given it some thought and decided it was best that she was as much in the dark as the doctor. Which, of course, she was. She was surrounded by the dark. 'You see, Gabe's been living with his father the past couple of years, and we haven't been on the best of terms.'

Childs nodded. 'Well, I'm not sure what to tell you. At first glance, everything appears just fine. His lungs are clear, his blood pressure normal. His reflexes are a little slow, but beyond that I can't see anything out of the ordinary.'

'Uh-huh.'

'I think I'd like to take a urine sample and maybe a little blood, just to be on the safe side. And after that...' He gathered up Gabe's chart and made a couple of notes at the bottom of the first page.

'What do you think it might be?'

'I'm not sure it's anything at all, Mrs Knight. Maybe a virus of some sort. Nothing that I think we have to concern ourselves with.'

'But I am concerned.'

'I know you are, Mrs Knight, and I don't blame you. But why don't we wait and see what the test results have to say before we start doing any speculating, all right? My guess is whatever it is – a virus or fatigue or whatever – it's already passed and now it's just a matter of building Gabe's strength back up.'

'When will the test results be in?'

'Sometime tomorrow. I promise I'll call you.' Childs glanced down at the chart in his hands. 'We still have your current number?'

'No,' Teri said, a little more defensively than she meant to sound. 'Why don't I call you tomorrow? Things are going to be a little hectic.'

'Sure.'

'Sometime in the afternoon?'

'That should work out fine,' Childs said. He tucked the clipboard under his arm, and reached out to shake hands with Gabe, who seemed suddenly taken aback. Teri thought it appeared to be something more than simple surprise, though. She thought Gabe had seemed almost frightened by the man. He shook hands anyway, politely, and Teri silently explained it away as a combination of the stress and a little boy's discomfort around strangers.

'I'll have the nurse come in to take a little blood and help with the urine sample, and we'll see what turns up tomorrow. Until then, try not to worry about it, Mrs Knight. I really don't think it's anything serious.'

'Thank you, doctor.'

'My pleasure.'

As soon as he was out of the room, Teri turned to Gabe. 'You remember him now?' she asked.

Gabe shook his head. 'I'm not sure.'

23

Walt closed the door to his motel room, tossed his suitcase on the nearest chair, and collapsed on the queen-sized bed next to the window.

The drive down state had taken nearly six hours, largely due to the eight-mile backup in Concord, where a semi had smashed into a small Ford pickup while changing lanes. The semi had flipped onto its side and gone for a long, helpless slide down the middle two lanes of the freeway, leaving a thirty-foot-wide skid mark. By the time Walt had made it to the front of the line, most of the wreckage had been cleaned up. There were a few scattered flares in the road, and off to the right, the semi and the pickup were both in the process of being towed away. The ambulances, if there had been any, were long gone.

Right about now, Walt half wished he had been in one of them.

Not only had the trip been a long one, but he hadn't slept well last night. After Teri had gone off to bed, he had put things away in the kitchen, and re-read the story about the nursing student who had been found dead, the woman who had brought Gabe home. Amanda Tarkett. There was no way that had been an accident. No way it had been part of a mugging, either. Coincidences like that didn't happen nearly as often as we'd like to believe. No, Amanda's death and Gabe's sudden return home were both part of the same weaving.

Walt had thought on that awhile, and then he tried to close his eyes and drift off to sleep. But there was something else bothering him. He hadn't been completely truthful with Teri. The real reason he had left the department was the flip side of the same coin that had initially brought him there. It was the ghost of his past still giving chase.

When Walt had been a boy, he, too, had been one of the disappeared.

Not in the same sense as Gabriel, of course. Walt had never returned home again. And if he had, he would have been older. Much older. And he would have been a dramatically different person.

It had happened not long after his seventh birthday. After a lengthy separation and an even lengthier custody battle, his mother had won full custodial rights. His father was allowed to visit on weekends only, a fate he decided he couldn't live with. Instead, he had picked up Walt after school one day, and they had begun an odyssey through what eventually turned out to be a never-ending succession of new towns and new names, of different haircuts and Salvation Army clothes.

Always on the move.

Always looking over your shoulder, wondering how far behind the Witch was trailing.

The *Witch*.

That had been his father's name for her. 'You've always gotta be on your toes, little guy. 'Cause the minute you relax, she's gonna be there. And when she gets her hands on us, she's gonna throw us both in jail until the day we rot. So you be careful, you hear?'

The *Witch*.

Walt believed most of what his father told him, but even as a seven-year-old he didn't believe everything. He didn't believe he'd have to go to jail. And he didn't believe his mother was a witch. Not the woman who used to tuck him into bed at night and read to him from *The Cat in the Hat* or *Horton Hears A Who*. He never allowed himself to forget that woman.

At the age of sixteen, when he was finally old enough to go looking for her, Walt discovered that she had died some three years earlier from ovarian cancer.

He was too late.

The disappeared had come home too late.

Last night, Walt had played it all over again in his mind. All the way up to three years ago, when he had sat at the side of his father's death-bed and forgiven him for the lost years and the loss of his mother. The trouble was... Walt had never forgiven himself. And that was the reason he first became interested in law enforcement, and that was the same reason he had quit the force and taken up the cause of lost children on his own.

So he hadn't been completely honest with Teri.

And he hadn't been completely honest with himself, either.

Underneath it all, he supposed, he was still trying to make it up to his mother.

Walt stared reminiscently out the window at the Motel Six sign across the street and closed his eyes. Just a little sleep. That's all he needed.

Then the phone rang.

24

Teri unlocked the car door on Gabe's side, then went around and climbed into the driver's side. They were both feeling a little worn down from their visit with the doctor. Especially Gabe, who had been terrified by the thought of some nurse sticking a needle the size of a number two pencil into his arm to draw blood.

'Is it going to hurt?'

'A little,' Teri had told him. 'But if you keep your eyes closed, it won't seem so bad.'

'Really?'

'Scout's honor.'

'Mom...'

'What?'

'You aren't a scout.'

The needle hadn't been as big as he had let himself imagine, but it had been plenty big enough, and Teri had felt that terrible guilt of motherhood when a silent tear had slipped out of the corner of one eye and trailed down Gabe's cheek.

But that was over now.

'What do you say to an ice-cream?' she asked, buckling the seat belt.

Gabe nodded, still a little angry at her.

'Baskin Robbins?'

Another nod, just as unforgiving.

Teri started up the car and backed out of the space. An old Toyota truck had parked right on top of her on the left. She backed out slowly, making a hard turn once it appeared the front bumper was clear. 'I'm sorry it hurt so much,' she said honestly.

'You said it wouldn't hurt that bad.'

'I know, and I'm sorry.' She shifted into first and started out of the parking lot, wanting to be able to look her son in the eye and at the same time afraid of the hurt she might see there. 'It's just that sometimes adults forget how bad things can hurt when you're little.'

'I'm not little, Mom. I'm eleven years old.'

'I know. I'm sorry.'

'So, did you ever have to give blood?'

'Sure.'

'Did it hurt?'

'You bet,' Teri said, checking the rear view mirror. There was a black, late model Ford in the outside lane, maybe half a block behind her. She glanced over her shoulder to make sure she hadn't lost sight of a car in her blind spot, then turned on her signal and moved into the inside lane.

'Sometimes you just have to do things you'd rather not have to do,' she said. 'Like that time when you and your father went to Reno to pick up your grandfather's bedroom set. You remember that? You were seven, I think.'

Gabe nodded noncommittally.

'Remember how you got caught in that snow storm, and how your father had to get out of the truck and put the chains on the tires?' Teri turned left at Bellows Road and moved back into the right lane. Baskin Robbins was another two miles down the road, a small shop that sat just outside the Shasta Valley Mall.

'It really made his hands ache,' Gabe said, clearly recalling the event now.

'But he had to get the chains on, didn't he? Otherwise, you two would have been stuck there.'

He nodded again, mulling it over in his mind. 'I understand. It's like in the summertime when you make me mow the lawn every week.'

Teri laughed. 'Exactly.'

The weather had been moody all morning, a little patch of sunshine here, a little sprinkle of raindrops there. But it was turning serious now. The sky had darkened noticeably, and off to the west, she could see a sheet of rain falling out of the sky and all the way to the ground like a huge drape across the horizon.

'Mom?'

'What?' Teri glanced in the rearview mirror again. There was a white van behind her, keeping a safe distance, and a small foreign car – a Yugo or some such thing – in the other lane, a little further back. Traffic was light for this time of day. She was grateful for that.

'What about Dad?'

'What about him?' she said absently. She had come away from the doctor's office with a feeling of unease at the pit of her stomach. For awhile, she thought it must have been something the doctor had said or done, some little signal that her brain had missed but her intuition had caught. Only now, she was beginning to realize that her intuition had caught something else entirely.

'Where is he?' Gabe asked.

'Who?'

'Dad.'

It didn't have anything at all to do with the doctor. It had to do with the black, late model Ford that she had noticed earlier outside the doctor's office. It was still behind her even now, keeping a safe distance, following behind the white van. Every once in a while, as she would drift toward the inside of the lane, she could catch a glimpse of it. And *that* was the reason for her feeling of unease.

They were being followed.

25

Walt answered the phone in that tone of his that too many people had told him was all business and not terribly friendly. Sometimes that was exactly how he felt. This time, though, it was because he wasn't expecting a call. Not unless it was bad news.

'Yeah?'

'Walt?'

'Who's this?'

'It's Mark.'

A friend of his from the phone company. Walt had met Mark a number of years ago, when Walt was still working with the department and Mark was working the phone company's computer section.

'What's up?' Walt asked.

'I can't talk for long, but I thought I'd let you know that you were right. There was a call made from the Knight house a couple of nights ago.'

'What time?'

'A little before midnight.'

'That's what I wanted to hear, Mark. Hold on a sec and let me get a pencil and paper.' Walt pulled the drawer of the night-stand open and began to rummage around blindly under the Gideon Bible.

'Don't bother.'

'Why? What's the problem?'

'You aren't going to like this,' Mark said, his tone of voice reinforcing the words. 'The number belongs to a phone booth.'

'Jesus.'

'Sorry, Walt.'

'Don't be. I should have guessed that one.' He closed the night-stand drawer, and leaned back against the headboard, suddenly feeling tired again. News had a way of taking its toll when it didn't go the way you had hoped. Something would come along, though. Sooner or later, something would come along.

'It was only a block away.'

'What?'

'The phone booth... it was only a block away. At the 7-Eleven on Kirkwood. I can't be sure of this, of course, but it looks like they linked that number to a number in Chico.'

'Another phone booth, right?'

'You got it,' Mark said. 'And from there, it went down to the Bay Area. After that, it's anybody's guess. Sorry.'

'No need. At least that confirms that we're dealing with a sophisticated operation.'

'If anything else comes up...'

'Thanks, Mark.'

'No problem.'

But of course, there was a problem. Walt hung up the phone and gazed out the window. He watched a puff of gray-white clouds go sauntering past the Motel Six sign and disappear into the distant blue sky like one of David Copperfield's illusions.

And *that* was the problem, wasn't it?

Everything about this case was an illusion.

26

'Gabe?' Teri tried to keep the calm in her voice, as difficult as that was. In the side mirror, she could see the black Ford drifting toward the inside of the lane every so often, making sure to keep her in sight. 'Have you got your seat belt on?'

'Yeah. Why?'

'Because you're supposed to,' she said as evenly as possible.

Lightly, she pressed down on the accelerator, and the car gradually increased its speed. Not enough, she hoped, to be noticeable. But enough to pull away from the white van behind her. Enough to—

The black Ford crossed to the inside lane.

Like a moving picture, the dark, cloudy sky rolled across the car's windshield. Hidden behind it, the driver was faceless, little more than an outline. It appeared, at a glance, that there was a passenger in front, and maybe another in back. But the reflection against the windshield kept changing and the best that Teri could determine was that a side mirror view of the world looked strangely like a Picasso.

'So where is he?' Gabe asked again about his father.

(*Right behind us.*)

'Not now, honey.'

'He's okay, isn't he?'

'Please, Gabe.' She felt the car jump, and realized they had drifted too close to the lane divider. It was a small correction to get back to where she should have been, and then she focused again on the black Ford following along behind and to the left.

'What's going on?'

'Nothing, honey.'

Gabe glanced over his shoulder out the back window. 'It's a cop, isn't it?'

'No.'

The Ford moved up, trailing along slightly less than a car-length behind now. An endless parade of dark-gray clouds went swimming across its windshield, like whitecaps in the ocean. But behind them, in little less than a glimpse, Teri caught sight of her worst fear. The driver of the black Ford was Mitch.

'Oh, my God,' she muttered, feeling something in her chest tighten into a knot.

'What is it?'

'It's him,' she said.

'Who?'

'That man from the other night.'

Up ahead, the next stop light turned to green and Teri prayed a silent prayer that it would hold until she could make it through. Absently, she pressed down on the accelerator and brought the speed up to just under fifty.

'What do they want?'

'I don't know, Gabe.'

They rolled easily through the intersection, thank God, and Teri watched the white van turn off to the right. The Ford immediately increased its speed. It passed on the left – Teri doing everything she could to appear preoccupied and unaware – then switched lanes and slowed down in front of her. Suddenly, it was like *Alice in Wonderland*. Everything was turned upside-down and inside-out, and it was Teri who was doing the following now.

An unwanted thought that spoke the truth a little too plainly skittered across her mind: they were playing a deadly game of cat and mouse. It was a game she didn't think she was going to be able to win. Not as the follower. Not as the prey being led mindlessly into the trap.

The clouds opened, and a light drizzle began to fall. Teri turned on the wipers. They made a maddening, rasping sound as they scraped across the surface of the glass for the first stroke or two, then settled into the steady tempo of a metronome.

'So what are we gonna do?'

'I'm not sure,' she said honestly. She had heard a hint of fear in Gabe's voice. She didn't want to add to that, not even a little, because it was everything she could do to keep a grip on her own fear.

Up ahead, the rear, passenger-side window of the Ford slowly rolled down. She watched a black-gloved hand emerge like a vampire bat flitting out of its cave just after twilight. With the index finger in the air, it motioned toward the curb, and she knew her time was quickly running short.

'You aren't going to stop, are you?'

Teri checked her rearview mirror.

'Mom?'

'Hold on, Gabe.'

The Shasta Valley Mall came into view up ahead on the right. The main entrance was still a block away, hidden between a Carl's Jr that was under construction and a Bank of America that had been there for years. Teri didn't think the black Ford was going to let her get that far, and if that were true, then the moment had finally come when she was going to have to make a decision. When Teri finally did make it, it nearly cost her life.

27

It was happening again.

Walt had hung up the phone, feeling uneasy with the knowledge that whoever was after Teri and Gabe, they were sophisticated and very well organized. He didn't care much for the implications of that thought. There was a chance here, a good chance, that he was getting in over his head. Though sometimes chance was a two-headed coin. It might actually be in his favour that they were sophisticated. At least that narrowed down some of the suspects.

All this whirled around in his head like a wind-storm shifting the sands until the picture was nearly unrecognizable, and finally he fluffed up the pillow and settled back for a short nap.

With the nap, came the dream.

Walt found himself standing at the fore of a hall of doors. The line stretched off into the distant horizon, door after door after door. It felt oddly familiar. He had been here before, he thought, though he couldn't be certain. He *was* certain, however, in that way of dreams when you often know things without knowing how you know, that the doors were waiting to be opened.

They were waiting to be opened by him.

The door on his left was ornately carved, a leaf and petal pattern around the edges, an odd-looking beast-like gargoyle at the center. A thin stream of grayish-blue smoke seeped out of the beast's nostrils like hot, stale breath.

Walt put out his hand and wrapped his fingers around the knob. It felt cool to the touch. He gave it a turn and pushed the door open, listening past its aged creak, hearing nothing beyond. What was on the other side had long been silent.

The door ajar, he found himself staring into a mirror. The reflection was of a young boy, maybe nine or ten years old. His hair was red and grown long, tied in a ponytail in the back. He was wearing baggy jeans with no shirt, shoes with no socks, and he had the vacant look of a boy who has been wandering on his own for a long time now.

Walt slammed the door, fell heavily against it, and tried to catch his breath. His heart did a drum beat against the inside of his chest, but before he had a chance to still it, he found himself standing in front of another door. At the center, a stained-glass design depicted the death of a flower, all white and black and gray.

The door swung open on its own.

Another unfamiliar face.

This of a young boy, perhaps eleven, perhaps younger. His hair was dark, cut short in a military style. He was wearing black slacks and a white shirt with a black tie that looked slightly too large for him. He leaned stiffly against a bookshelf. The fire that had once burned behind his eyes had burned out. So had the fire in this boy's soul.

It's you.

Another door opened.

Another unfamiliar face.

He was eight, here. His hair was black; it had been dyed that color the night before. It was combed back, away from his face, and it gave him the look of a troublemaker. The shirt he was wearing was black and long-sleeved, though the sleeves were rolled up above the elbows. There was a rip across the right knee of his jeans, with white strands of cotton cloth dangling like broken tethers from the hole. His name was Jeff. Jeff Newcomer.

Another door.

Another face.

This one was older, more solemn. The hair was blond, the smile gone. The eyes were dark and tired and had learned to hide the secrets of the boy by now. His name was Raymond Glazier. He was wearing a white T-shirt, gray sweat-pants, black, worn basketball shoes with the laces of the right shoe broken off and retied again. He didn't care anymore.

Another door.

Walt struggled with the knob to keep it closed, but it swung open despite him. This boy was blond and short and thin, and his name was Joseph Browne. He was wearing khaki shorts, no shirt, white socks that came up almost all the way to his knees. He looked as if he might be eight years old. Maybe younger.

'In here,' the boy called, motioning for Walt to enter the room with him. There was a swirl of grayish-white fog around the outer edges of the room. The boy looked lost. But Walt knew better than that. It was not the boy who was lost, it was Walt himself who was lost.

'Your name is Joseph,' the boy said.

'No, you're mistaken. My name is Walter. Walter L. Travis.'

The boy smiled forgivingly, and it was as if he were the wise man amused by the ignorance of his student. 'If you insist.'

'No, really. My name is Walter Travis.'

'Then come in, Walter.'

'But...'

'There's nothing here to fear.'

But that wasn't true.

28

Teri did the only thing she could think to do.

'Mom...'

'Just hold on, Gabe.'

It happened all in one move, though it was anything but smooth. Teri slammed her foot down on the accelerator, and gave the steering wheel a huge tug to the right. The rear tires squealed, kicking up a cloud of blue smoke, before they finally caught and sent the car into a sideways skid.

The front end jumped the curb.

Teri corrected, trying to keep the car from doing a one-eighty. The correction, though, only ended up making things worse. The right front fender clipped a street light, shearing it off near the base. The impact as it came crashing down sounded like a wrecking ball taking its first swipe at an old, tired building.

Teri barely heard it, though.

The car kept going. It squealed across the sidewalk, forcing its way into the space between two parked cars, then suddenly accelerated again. Teri felt the weight of her body forced backwards into the cushion of her seat. It was all she could do to keep her hands on the steering wheel, and...

...and that wasn't going to be enough.

Not this time.

It was going to take more than just holding on.

For a moment, everything seemed to slow down, ticking off the seconds in an irretrievable manner that left no doubt there would be no going back. The car shimmied and rattled, just missed a planter box, then rammed front-grille first into the side of a parked recreational vehicle.

Teri felt her body thrown forward violently, then back into the cushion again.

The engine continued to race, sounding as if it might explode, the noise ear-shattering, almost painful. Then abruptly, it stopped, and everything turned deathly quiet.

Teri unstrapped herself from the seat belt. 'Gabe?'

He smiled at her, struggling with his own belt. 'That was wicked, Mom. Really wicked.'

'I'm glad you liked it,' she said, wishing they had the time to stop and count their blessings. Gabe's side of the car was bulging inward now, in a strange sculpture of metal and plastic that might have been a popular piece if only it had been on display at an art gallery. 'Come on, we're going to have to get out on this side.'

She gave the door handle a tug and realized with dread that something wasn't right. The pull was too easy, no resistance, and nothing happened. She put her shoulder against the door and tried again. Still nothing.

'Break the window out,' Gabe suggested.

In the distance, she could see the black Ford coming back across the intersection into the mall parking lot. She didn't have much time.

'Mom...'

'I heard you!' she snapped. First, she tried to roll the window down, amazed that she had the presence of mind to even think of such a thing. Like the other handle, though, there was no catch here. It dangled from the shaft, useless. Something inside the trim panel had apparently slipped off its track or had become jammed between the inner and outer shells.

'Here,' Gabe said, handing her the small First Aid box that she kept in the glove compartment. 'Use this. It's made of metal.'

She stared at it, toying only a moment with the idea before covering her face and slamming one end of the box into the glass. Instantly, it bounced back at her. Behind, it left little more than a tiny spider-webbed pattern near the heart of the window.

'Hit it harder,' Gabe said.

'I'm trying.'

What scared her more than anything was that she might put her arm through the window and end up cutting herself on the shards of glass. There was that fear, and then there was the fear of being trapped here. The Ford had gotten caught in the backup of rubberneckers across the way. Through the windshield, she watched as all four doors opened almost simultaneously. A small group of men climbed out and started across the parking lot in her direction.

Gabe yelled something at her, something she didn't understand.

'I'm sorry.' Teri took another swing at the window. She hit it hard enough to shatter the glass this time, and it was only a matter of knocking away the shards from around the edges of the opening before they both had a passage to freedom.

Teri climbed through first. Gabe followed close behind, catching his pant leg on the lock, then shaking it loose. He fell to the ground head first, wearing half a grin, half a grimace.

Teri grabbed him by the shoulders. 'The mall!'

The men were only fifty yards behind them now. Mitch was in front, looking like a football player in a suit, only a little heavier and maybe a little slower. Thank God for that. The others had fanned out and were trying to cut them off before they could make it to the entrance.

Teri pushed Gabe ahead of her, between two parked cars, over a small area planted with ivy, across the road, and into the southwest doors of the Penny's. It was warmer inside, and she was struck by the immediate calm on this side of the doors. The chaos outside suddenly seemed a thousand miles away. She glanced back, seeing no sign of the pursuit.

'Where are we going?' Gabe asked.

'I don't know.'

They passed through the cosmetics department, past women's clothing, and followed the tiled walkway out into the mouth of the mall. In the back of her mind, Teri had been thinking – more like *hoping* – that they might be able to blend in with the shoppers and maybe find their way out through another store. But it was late afternoon now, and the foot traffic was light.

Holding on tight to Gabe's hand, she stopped and looked behind her again.

Still no sign of Mitch or his friends.

There was a Gottschalks up ahead on the left, and if they could have thirty seconds, chances were good they could make it there unseen. Teri crossed the floor, keeping Gabe in front of her. He was having trouble keeping up. They had left his cane in the car, and she could tell his legs were already getting tired. Distantly, it crossed her thoughts that there hadn't been a normal, peaceful minute since the moment they had gotten back together.

'Not much further,' she said. 'Hang on.'

'I'm okay.'

But that wasn't true. He wasn't okay, and she had to admire his determination. Especially under these circumstances, when it would have been so easy to let his legs get the better of him.

'In here,' Teri said. They had made it to Gottschalks. Teri was breathing hard, and it suddenly occurred to her how out of shape she had become. Working for the postal service hadn't been as good for her as she had always let herself believe. At least not physically.

They followed the walkway toward the women's section in the back, Teri glancing over her shoulder and trying to convince herself every step of the way that they were okay, that Mitch and his friends hadn't seen them.

A clerk looked up from her register, and smiled.

Teri forced herself to smile back, then pushed Gabe toward the changing rooms. They couldn't go in right away. The clerk kept an eye on them, even if it was a friendly eye, and a heavyset woman was modeling slacks in front of the mirrors. Several minutes passed before the woman went to pay for her merchandise and occupied the attention of the clerk. Teri led Gabe into the changing-room area. They moved to the back stall, closed the curtains, and sat down.

'Mom, this is for girls.'

'Quiet,' she said.

'Sorry.' He sank back against the wall, looking worse for the wear.

The long wait began.

29

Walt woke up in a cold sweat. He sat on the edge of the bed, his heart pounding faster than he ever imagined humanly possible. He slowly rubbed his hands over his face, then stared down at them, studying the wrinkles, the pores, the hair. And gradually, the dream came back to him.

Jeff Newcomer.

Raymond Glazier.

Joseph Browne.

Oh, Jesus.

In an instant, he was up and across the bed, grabbing for his wallet, which was sitting on the night-stand. He fumbled to get it open, then rifled through the photographs and credit cards to his driver's license in the back: WALTER L. TRAVIS. SEX: M. HAIR: BROWN. EYES: BLUE. HT: 6'-0". WT: 175.

Thirty-eight years old.

An adult now.

He closed the wallet, dropped it back on the night-stand, and wiped his hands across his face again. Nothing was quite the way it ever seemed, he thought. He got up, went into the bathroom, washed his face, and spent a long time staring at his reflection in the mirror. There was a part of him that wondered when he had grown up, and how long he had been this man, Walter Travis. Another part of him thought that was the most ridiculous thing that had ever crossed his mind.

He'd always been Walter Travis.

Always.

Except when he had been one of the disappeared.

30

'We lost them,' Mitch said matter-of-factly. They were on their way out of the parking lot, Mitch trying to swing the black Ford into the right-hand lane while still devoting his attention to the voice on the other end of the car phone.

'I'm disappointed.'

'There was an accident.'

'And?'

'Mrs Knight – she jumped a curb and ended up ramming an RV.'

'Any chance she abandoned the car?'

'Yes.'

'Then the police should be looking for her.'

'You're right. I hadn't thought of that.'

'Where'd you lose her?'

'The Shasta Valley Mall.'

'How long ago?'

Mitch glanced at his watch. 'Maybe thirty minutes.'

'How'd the boy look?'

'I didn't get much of a look at him after the accident.'

'He wasn't hurt, though. Is that correct?'

'It's correct to the best of my knowledge.'

'I guess that's something.'

'Yes, sir.'

'Any idea where they've been the past day or two?'

Mitch glanced into his rearview mirror, and saw that the left lane was open. He changed lanes without signaling. 'No. We're still checking out the husband, but it looks like he's living in another state. Could be they've been staying with a friend we don't know about. We'll keep a watch on the clinic in case she turns up again.'

'Keep an eye on her house, too.'

'Of course.'

'Sooner or later, she's gotta turn up somewhere.'

'Yes, sir,' Mitch said, knowing that was true enough. He also knew that he was the one who had allowed the situation to get out of control. It had been a simple assignment to retrieve the boy and if necessary bring his mother back with him. No blood. No unnecessary force. Just a strong suggestion that it would be in their best interests to come along peacefully. Unfortunately, such a sweet scenario would be next to impossible now. And no one knew that better than Mitch himself.

'Sorry about the screw up, DC.'

'You and me, both, Mitch. You and me, both.'

31

He was born Malcolm Winters.

In junior high school, the kids called him Raines, after Claude Raines, because he was the invisible boy. Some days he was there, some days he wasn't. Most of the time you couldn't tell the difference. He was the quiet one who sat in the back and said nothing.

There were no pictures of him in the high school year book.

In college, where he majored in political science, he remained in the background, obscure and unnoticed. He wrote occasional articles for the university paper, most often under the name of Ted R. O'Bannon, though twice he used the name Red P. Covee, an anagram for Deep Cover.

He was approached in his senior year, recruited a short time later.

From that time on, he gave himself to his country.

The Malcolm Winters of old became nonexistent.

In his place came a long procession of new identities: Dexter Clements, a gun runner; Peter J. Thompson, an investment banker; Howard Jenkins, a real-estate investor; Marshal Witmer, an FBI agent; and a host of other characters, some respectable, some shady.

Buried beneath the various covers, a level or two deeper into obscurity, he went by the name of DC. It was from this identity that he kept control of all his operations and kept things in line with the bigger picture of the agency.

There was always a bigger picture.

32

Teri pushed aside the curtains and gave the women's section of Gottschalks a thorough once-over, finding nothing that should alarm her. Better than two hours had passed. It appeared from where she was standing that the traffic in the mall had picked up considerably. And there was a new clerk working now. She was wearing the same smile as the old clerk as she looked up from her register and caught Teri's eye. She smiled like an old lost friend.

'How're you doing back there?' the woman asked. She didn't seem to take notice of the fact that she had never actually seen Teri pass by on her way to the changing room. Or for that matter, that she had never seen Teri before in her life. That didn't seem to matter.

'Just fine,' Teri said.

'Need any help?'

Oh, you wouldn't believe the help I need, Teri thought. But, of course, it wasn't the clerk's help she needed. It wasn't anything as cut and dried as picking out a dress that looked nice and was still in the right price range, or finding out if they carried a blouse in a slightly smaller size. God, if only things could be that mundane again.

'No, I'm fine. Thank you,' Teri said.

It was another ten minutes before the clerk became preoccupied with another customer. Teri and Gabe slipped out of the changing room and out onto the main floor of the mall without anyone apparently knowing or caring. From there, they crossed to the other side, made their way past a Software Etc, and a B. Dalton, past a Payless Shoe Source and a Shear Magic, and into Sears. They exited at the back of the store, out onto Larkspur Avenue, which bordered the mall on the north.

No sign of Mitch.

No sign of any of his friends.

The evening sky, which was just moments away from sunset, was a muddy orange and brown color, streaked with perfect brushstroke clouds that seemed too well defined to be real. Teri took in a deep breath, grateful to be out of that damn dressing room and into some fresh air again.

'What now?' Gabe asked. There was no mistaking the crankiness in his voice. She could hardly blame him, though. It had been a long, difficult day for both of them. Especially for Gabe.

'I don't know. Are you hungry?'

'Starving.'

'Me, too.'

They caught a city bus cross-town to a place called Casa Lupe. Gabe ate a taco-and-burrito plate, with beans and rice, as hearty a meal as he had eaten since his return. At least something good had come from today.

Afterward, Teri used the pay phone on the corner to try to reach Walt in the Bay Area. She had hoped he might be able to tell her what to do next, but there was no answer at his room. That meant she was back to having to trust her own decisions, right or wrong. God, what a difference a few days made. Before Gabe had come back, the biggest decision in her life had been whether she should go to work or call in sick. And now...

... now she was suddenly a mother again.

Teri tossed the quarter from the telephone to Gabe. 'How are you doing?'

'Okay.'

'Well, you're doing better than I am, then.'

'No answer?'

She shook her head. 'No, he must be out somewhere.'

'Why can't we just go back home?'

'Because they might be waiting for us there.'

'What about the apartment?'

That's why she had wanted to talk to Walt, just to make certain that going back to his apartment would be a safe decision. Somehow these guys had picked up her trail and she wished she knew how. Maybe it had been at the doctor's office. Maybe it had been at Walt's. Maybe it had been by chance. The problem was – Teri had no way of knowing.

'I suppose we could go by there,' Teri said hesitantly. She looked down at Gabe, smiled, and pulled him into her for a hug. 'Quite a mess we've gotten ourselves into, isn't it?'

'It'll be all right, Mom.'

'I hope so.'

33

They stood across the street from Walt's apartment for a good ten minutes trying to decide if it was safe or not. The thing that Teri found most troublesome was the light in the kitchen. She didn't remember if she had turned it off or not, but it was on now, and she wasn't sure just what that meant. Maybe Walt had come home early. Or maybe there was someone else waiting for them.

'No one's there, Mom.'

'You willing to bet our lives on it?' she said a little too bluntly. Gabe, who she suddenly had to remind herself was only eleven years old, visibly recoiled. 'I'm sorry. My nerves are a little on edge right now.'

'It's okay. I understand.'

She ruffled his hair, then gazed up at the apartment wistfully. 'Well, I guess if we don't want to stand out in the cold all night, we should check it out. What do you think?'

'Yeah, let's do it.'

They crossed the street, Teri both keeping Gabe in front of her and watching over her shoulder to make sure there was no danger from behind as she had learned to do almost instinctively the past few days.

The apartment building was quiet except for a couple on the bottom floor at the far end, who were yelling obscenities at each other. Teri wondered how often that went on and if Walt, as the ex-cop, usually put a quick stop to it or if he would just grit his teeth and tolerate as much as he could stand. She wasn't sure how he would handle that kind of situation, and suddenly it occurred to her that she didn't really know Walt all that well at all. Oh, she knew she could trust him. And she knew that out of all the policemen she'd had to deal with, he was by far the most honest, the most caring. But she didn't know what made him tick or how he viewed the world around him or even if he had a girlfriend or an ex-wife. Strange how you can know so much about a person and yet so little.

They stayed under the eaves around the outer edges of the courtyard, and took the stairs near the northwest corner of the building where the lighting was better and Teri thought they risked less chance of surprise. At the top of the stairs, she put the clamps on Gabe. 'Let's just wait here a second.'

'What for?'

'Just to be sure.'

The thing that wouldn't let go of her was the light in the kitchen. She couldn't remember having left it on. She might have, but she couldn't remember it. And if she hadn't left it on, then how did it get on?

Gabe toyed with a twig he had picked up off the ground, using it to tease a black beetle that had the unfortunate luck of crossing in front of him at just the wrong moment. Teri watched the apartment. For another four or five minutes nothing else happened, and finally she put her caution aside.

She brought out the key that Walt had given her that first night, tapped Gabe on the shoulder, and led the way down the hall to apartment B-242. The couple who had been arguing had fallen appreciably silent, and it felt almost as if the whole complex had stopped to hold its breath while Teri plugged the key into the lock. She toggled it both directions without success, and before she had a chance to try a third time, the door gradually swung open on its own.

Inside, there was a short entryway. The kitchen was off to the right. The living room was straight ahead, though it sat slightly off center, again to the right.

Teri took a step across the threshold.

Behind her, Gabe grabbed for the elbow of her coat. 'Mom...'

'It's okay,' she said, suspecting that it was a lie she was telling. 'Stay here. I'm just going to have a look. Maybe I left the light on this morning.'

'And forgot to lock the door?' Gabe said unceremoniously.

'Just stay right here and wait for me.'

She moved down the entryway cautiously, then peered around the corner and into the kitchen. It looked as if something terribly violent had gone on in here. Drawers were pulled out, utensils scattered across the floor, the refrigerator door left open. There was a pile of cereal boxes and empty soup cans, jelly jars and empty soda cans in the middle of the room. A five-fingered track of apricot jelly stained the walls from one end to the other.

It was worse than that, but that was as much as Teri needed to see.

'Out, Gabe!' she yelled. 'Get out of here!'

34

It was getting cold out.

Walt blew into his hands to warm them, then settled a little deeper into the front seat of the car. The evening cloud cover had finally dissipated. The sky was a remarkable crisp deep black, sprinkled with a garden of stars.

Four hours had passed since Walt had first arrived here. Across the street, the house had given itself to the quiet of the night. It was a small, two-bedroom Sixties tract home with a flat, gravel roof and an oak tree in the front yard. It belonged to a man by the name of Richard Boyle, though he was currently going by the name of B. L. Richards. He worked at a printing shop off of Fourth Street called the Ace Printing Company. He had been working there for nearly nine months, having moved into the area with his two kids from a small town in upper Oregon. That was the story he had pitched to his employer. It was the same story he had offered up to the secretary at John F. Kennedy Elementary when he registered the kids there. And it was all a lie.

Walt glanced at the clock. 10:20 p.m. He flipped on the radio, met with an instant barrage of static, then grumpily flipped it off again.

'Come on, Richard. Where the hell are you?'

And where the hell were the children? They were the missing puzzle piece here. They were the disappeared in this tragic little episode. So where the hell were they?

He tapped his hand impatiently against the steering wheel. The feeling that he had somehow been made, that somehow Boyle had known Walt was getting close and had pulled up roots, had been eating at Walt all evening.

Where were the children?

A father who steals his children keeps them close. If this was the place and Boyle was B. L. Richards, then the children should be around. Should be ... should ...

No lights, though.

No activity.

The neighborhood kids hadn't seen Christy or Garrett, the Boyle kids, since late last week. The family had crammed into their old Datsun late one night, all three in the front seat, and had apparently driven off to run errands. The kids had waved goodbye on their way down the street. But no one could remember them coming back. And no one could remember seeing any luggage when they had left.

'I thought they were going out to dinner,' one little girl said.

Walt blew into his hands again, and glanced up the street, where a dog was circling a pair of dented garbage cans. The neighborhood had been alive two hours ago, a group of boys playing street hockey, neighbors arriving home after work, a boy going door-to-door collecting for his newspaper route, a woman and her daughter out walking the family dog. Gradually, things had grown quieter, though, and now it was as if the block of tract homes had turned into something of a ghost town.

Walt watched the dog stand on his hind legs and knock over the smallest of the two cans. The lid fell off, rolled over the edge of the curb and wobbled to its death like the last throes of a coin that's been flipped. A loud metallic explosion of noise went echoing down the street. And not a soul stirred. Not a single person in the entire neighborhood.

That was enough for Walt.

He climbed out of the car and started across the street, tired of playing it safe and wasting his time. The Boyles had checked out. It was that simple. Somehow they had gotten word and they had done a quick exit and heaven only knew how far they had traveled by now. Maybe all the way to upper Oregon.

He made a mental note to check that possibility as he opened the side gate and made his way around back. People had a habit of tipping their hands, whether they were aware of it or not. That was by no means only true of poker. A tell was a tell was a tell. Upper Oregon was Boyle's old stomping ground.

To Walt's surprise, the sliding glass door opening to the back patio was slightly ajar. They *had* left in a hurry. He rolled open the screen door, which made an agonizing squeal, then slipped through the opening and into the house.

His eyes made an adjustment.

This appeared to be the family room. Linoleum floor. Sofa. Coffee table. Fireplace. He shuffled through the stack of *TV Guides* on the table, finding nothing of note, then wandered into the adjoining room, which turned out to be the kitchen.

It was darker here. Walt pulled a penlight out of his pocket and did a quick scan of the counter top. A stack of newspapers. A six-pack of Old Milwaukee. An overturned salt-shaker. A toaster. Half a loaf of bread. An open jar of peanut butter. A sink full of dirty dishes.

He hadn't noticed it at first, but he noticed it now ... the strong permeating odor of rotten food. Not only had they left in a hurry, they had left several days ago.

'Dandy,' Walt muttered. 'Two days, three hundred miles, all for naught.'

He turned off the penlight, returned it to his jacket pocket, and took advantage of the nearest light switch. It didn't matter now, did it? *Not unless you're worried about alerting the neighbors.* Which he wasn't. He wasn't planning on being here that long.

In the kids' room, several of the dresser drawers had been pulled out, the clothes dumped in a pile on the bed and apparently sorted. It was much the same in the other bedroom, clothing strewn about on the floor and bed, the closet doors open, a pair of tennis shoes left behind in the corner.

Walt picked up a matchbook from the dresser, tossed it aside, and wondered what had happened. How had Boyle been tipped? He sat down on the edge of the bed, tapped the lampshade with his index finger and watched the dust rise into the air like an angry swarm of bees.

He was going to have to start all over again.

From the beginning.

Social security numbers. Change of address requests. School transcripts.

'Christ.'

Beneath the pile of clothing, the bed sheets were rumpled and dirty. They hadn't been changed in quite some time. Walt slid the night-stand drawer out and rummaged through the contents. A telephone book. Flashlight. A couple of ballpoint pens. A cassette by Counting Crows. An old shoelace. Some paperclips. Another matchbook.

He slammed the drawer, then picked up a scratch pad from next to the lamp on the night-stand. Someone had scribbled a note on the top page, then torn it off. The impression left beneath was faint and mostly unreadable.

Walt pulled the matchbook out of the drawer, struck a match and blew it out. Three matches later, he held the paper up to the lamp. Most of it was unreadable, even after lightly brushing the tips of the matches over the indentations. But the last four letters had come through remarkably clear, and Walt didn't like what he saw.

The letters were: B-242.

35

Mrs Knight, I don't have much time... this is your son, Gabe... I'm fine, Mom... it's not possible... Mrs Knight, if you'll step back into the house, please... run, Gabe!... Teri, he would be almost twenty now... it's him... I'm sorry, I've got to go out of town on business... let me run some tests and get back to you... I think they're following us... are you okay, Gabe?... what now?... we sit and wait... you think someone's in the apartment?... get out!... run, Gabe!... run!... run!...

Teri opened her eyes with a start.

She shuddered, fingered the damp hair away from her face and sat up in the tub.

Run!...

Run!...

Gradually, the nightmare screams drifted away on their own and she was left with the sound of water dripping off her hair into the bath water, that sound and the sound of the television in the next room. She knew where she was now. They had checked into the motel late last night, and though she had slept well, she had apparently drifted off again this morning while relaxing in the tub.

There was a knock at the bathroom door. 'Mom? Are you okay?'

'I'm fine, Gabe.' She realized she must have let out a yelp. 'I'll be out in a bit.'

Just a bit, she thought, letting her eyes close again and settling back into the water.

No one had followed them out of Walt's apartment. Heaven only knew how they had tracked her there, but somehow they had and Walt's interior had paid the price. She had tried to reach him last night, to warn him about the danger of showing up at home. The manager of the motel where Walt was staying took half-a-dozen frantic messages before he finally put his foot down on what he considered her 'damn nuisance calls'. Still, he had promised Walt would get the message when he came in, if she would just quit calling. Teri still hadn't heard anything back, though, and she had a hunch the manager had probably gotten some twisted satisfaction out of tossing all the messages into the round file by the front counter. At least, she hoped that was the reason Walt hadn't called.

'Mom?'

'Yeah, Gabe?'

'Just checking.'

God, who was the child here and who was the parent? Now, *there* was a line that was anything but well-defined. Teri had been nearly hysterical last night. It wasn't just the sight of Walt's apartment, she thought. It was everything together: Gabe coming home, the forced entry, Walt being out of town, the car chase... all of it. Somehow it had all caught up with her last night, and out on the street, trying to decide what to do next, she had simply sank to the ground and started to cry.

Gabe had cried, too.

'It'll be all right, Mom,' he'd said, trying to comfort her.

And maybe it would.

Maybe it would be all right in the end.

Teri opened her eyes again. Television voices were arguing in the next room, sounding similar to the voices that sometimes came from the other side of the wall of post office boxes in the station lobby where she worked. She flipped the drain release with her big toe, stood up, and pulled the white motel towel off the curtain rod.

She had woken with a minor headache that was still with her. It hadn't grown any worse, and as she dressed, she was beginning to feel confident that it wasn't going to spiral into a migraine like so many of them did. It had been three days since Gabe's return, three days of being on the run, and three days without migraine. Try to understand that one.

Gabe, who had been asleep when Teri had gone into the bathroom, was up and dressed and watching *The Phil Donahue Show*. He stared at her as she crossed the room, a look of curiosity on his face.

Just don't ask me what we're going to do now, Teri thought.

'Mom?'

She sat on the edge of the bed, drying her hair with a towel, wishing she had a clean change of clothes, and dreading where this introductory question was going to lead. 'Yeah, kiddo?'

'What about Dad?'

'What about him?'

'You never told me where he was.'

Teri ran the towel through her hair one last time, then dropped her hands into her lap and looked at her son. God, he was having to grow up fast. 'Come here,' she said, patting a soft spot on the bed next to her.

Gabe climbed off what he had happily declared the night before as *his* bed, and moved sullenly to her side.

'Things changed after you didn't come home, Gabe.'

'I know. You told me already.'

'Well, one of those changes was between your father and me. We were both upset and confused, even angry with each other.'

'Why?'

'I don't know. I guess we just missed you so much . . . there was such a huge emptiness in our lives, that we filled it with our anguish and our fears and . . . I don't know, Gabe. It was just hard to look at each other without seeing a little reflection of you, and that seemed to make the hurt all that much worse.'

'So Dad went away?'

Teri nodded, feeling suddenly guilty and regretful. 'Yes.'

'Where?'

She put her arm over Gabe's shoulders, almost as if she were trying to hold the last strand of her family together. He felt so tiny and fragile. 'He lives in Tennessee now. In a little town outside of Nashville.'

'Like Tennessee Avenue in *Monopoly*?'

Teri grinned. 'Yeah, something like that.'

'Will I ever get to see him again?'

'Of course.'

Gabe nodded thoughtfully. He had begun to toy with the wedding band on his mother's finger, and Teri realized for the first time in years that she was still wearing it. Old habits were hard to break. 'You think maybe we could call him?'

'Right now?'

'Yeah.'

'Oh, I don't know, Gabe.'

'Please?'

36

It was a little after eleven when Walt pulled into his parking space right around the corner from his apartment. The morning overcast had burned off; the sun was out; and it was easily ten degrees warmer than it had been yesterday.

He grabbed his suitcase off the passenger seat, climbed out of the car, and locked it up. It had been a good six hours drive up from the Bay Area. Originally, he had considered packing up last night and coming home, but he hadn't been sleeping well lately and he didn't like the idea of possibly falling asleep behind the wheel. So he had called the apartment – ten, maybe fifteen times – trying unsuccessfully to get in touch with Teri. He didn't want her or the boy to be there another night. Not with what he had found at the Boyle place.

B-242.

How had Boyle been tipped?

And how had he tracked down Walt's place? The number was an unlisted number.

It's not hard to find someone who's not hiding, Walt told himself. *You know that.*

The side of the suitcase slammed against the rail near the top of the stairs. He switched it from his left hand to his right, then started down the corridor, tossing around ideas for where he thought Boyle might head next. *Upper Oregon*, he reminded himself, and that was as far as his thoughts took him.

The door to the apartment was open.

Walt dropped the suitcase and hugged the wall. *Maybe not quite as far as upper Oregon after all*, he thought. He reached around the corner and palmed the door. It creaked lightly as it swung open all the way to the stop. Not a sound was coming from inside.

He moved across the doorway and hugged the wall on the other side.

No stirring.

'Teri?'

He took a peek through the kitchen window. Someone had gone out of his way to make one hell of a mess in there. His angle of vision allowed him a look past the kitchen doorway, down the hall to the corner of the living room. There was an eerie stillness over the place, a kind of peacefulness after the body's been lain to rest.

'Teri?'

No answer.

After another peek around the corner, he decided that whatever had gone on here, it had gone on some time ago. The damage was done now. All the participants had skittered back into the woodwork. The apartment was empty.

He listened to the heater kick on, thought distantly that he'd probably been paying to heat the outdoors since last night sometime, then moved down the entry and into the kitchen. A small flurry of white flour blew up from the floor vent. It was only a short stretch from there to the living room, from the living room to the bathroom, and finally into the bedroom.

The apartment had, in fact, been abandoned.

And that abandonment included Teri and Gabe.

That was the single most unsettling thought on Walt's mind as he went to the back of his bedroom closet. After moving into the apartment, he had added a false wall at the far end of the closet. He ran his hand along the top inside edge of the framework, found the release and pressed it. A small side panel clicked open.

The safe had gone unnoticed.

Walt fingered through the combination, having to stop to refresh his memory after the second number. It had been a long time since he had first felt a need to install the safe. He had never before felt a need to open it.

Not until now.

The safe door swung open.

37

'Michael?' Teri switched the phone to her other ear and turned away from Gabe, who was sitting on the other bed and watching her with unbridled anticipation.

'Teri?' There was more than just surprise in his voice. There was something underneath, something that sounded a bit like relief. She had a hard time imagining a situation in which Michael would be relieved to hear from her. After they had separated, he had put a bumper sticker on his car that said, *I still miss my 'ex', but I'm getting closer*. Meaning, of course, that he was still aiming for her. Teri hadn't been completely innocent herself. Her bumper sticker said, *Who cares what Mikee likes?*

'Everything all right out there?' he asked.

'Not exactly.'

'Here, neither,' he said. 'So tell me about it.'

'I'm ... not really sure where to start.'

'The job okay?'

'Yeah,' Teri said. Gabe tugged at her sleeve and when she turned toward him, he mouthed the words: *Is that him?* She nodded and he motioned for her to hand him the phone. 'Uh ... listen ... there's someone here who'd like to talk to you.'

Gabe grabbed the receiver out of her hand. 'Dad?'

There was silence on the other end.

'It's me, Gabe.' A long pause took breath before Michael finally said something back, and Gabe – looking disappointed and more than a little dejected – handed the phone back to her. 'He wants to talk to you.'

She knew what was coming, too. 'Michael?'

'What the hell are you trying to pull?' he said angrily. 'Jesus, Teri. You think I'm that stupid? You think I'm really gonna buy that this kid – what is he? Ten, eleven years old? – is supposed to be Gabe? Not funny, Teri. Not funny at all.'

'Just settle down, Michael.'

'Settle down? Man, nothing's changed, has it? You're still chasing his ghost all over the whole damn country, aren't you? Till the day you die, you're gonna be chasing that kid's damn ghost.'

'It's him, Michael. It's Gabe.'

'It can't be him. Christ, Teri ...' He let out a long, calming breath, the way he always did when he realized he was letting himself become over agitated. And Teri already knew what he was going to say next and how he was going to say it. He was going to tell her, in that almost but not quite patronizing tone of his, that she had to try to keep a perspective on things, that she was losing sight of reality here. Teri had heard it all before. After Gabe's disappearance, it had become her husband's marching song. And who could have really blamed him?'

'Okay,' he said evenly. 'Let's try to think this thing through, Teri.'

'I know what you're going to say.'

'It's impossible. Gabe would be ... what? Twenty? Twenty-one years old?'

'I know. And I know it sounds crazy. But it's him, Michael.'

'What? He just showed up one day?'

'Something like that.'

'Oh, Teri.'

'Michael, he's sitting right here. I'm looking at him. Don't you think I'd know my own son when I saw him?'

'He hasn't changed? Not at all?'

'No.'

'Did you ever think that someone might be trying to con you?'

'Why? It's not like I'm Leona Helmsley.'

'You own the house free and clear.'

'It's him, Michael.' She leaned back against the headboard, feeling tired from having to defend a position that she knew was indefensible. Some things in life, though, you just had to accept them for what they were. Without question. Without explanation. Gabe crawled into her lap and leaned back against her chest, and she knew, as she had known from the very first, that this was one of those things. 'All he wants is to talk to his father.'

'That's why you called?'

'The one and only reason.'

'Did you tell him I'm poor as a dog?'

'No. You tell him.'

'I don't want to talk to him, Teri.'

'Why? What are you afraid of? That maybe it'll really be Gabe?'

'No.'

'Then talk to him.'

'What am I supposed to say?'

'Whatever a father says to his son.'

'But he's not ... Christ, Teri. You aren't going to let go of this, are you?'

'No,' she said flatly. Though if it had been about her and Michael and *only* her and Michael, she might have been persuaded to drop it. And while there was a little piece of her that was saying, *See?*

I told you he'd come home someday. I told you and you didn't believe me and I was right. I was right, Michael, this was mostly about Gabe. Gabe and his father. 'Talk to him, Michael.'

'All right. I'll talk to him.'

38

Walt removed the handgun first.

It was a Ruger P-85 he had bought from one of the detectives down at the station. The frame was a lightweight aluminum alloy, matt-black finish. He held it in his right hand, the trigger finger straight along the frame, the gun tilted to the side. He popped in the magazine. With the heel of his hand, he slammed the magazine home, then retracted the slide to check the chamber. It was empty.

Walt tucked the gun under his belt, against his back where he could feel it.

Next were the credit cards. There were five altogether: two Visa, two MasterCard, and one American Express. Each card had been issued under the name of a different cardholder. Further back was a stack of driver's licenses. Walt removed the rubber band and thumbed through the phony IDs. Good enough to get him through this mess.

He pocketed the cards and IDs, closed the safe and weaved his way through the clutter of clothing and books and sheets on the floor. *You still don't know what the hell went on here, my friend.* No, he didn't. He could take a guess or two, though.

He was halfway down the hall on his way out when something else occurred to him. The files. He backtracked to the living room, where he had set up a small office area in one corner, though it didn't resemble anything close to an office now. The filing cabinet was lying on its side, one end braced against the foot-rest of a stool at the counter. All four drawers were open. One drawer was empty. The empty drawer was where he had always kept his case files.

On the floor, sticking out from beneath the corner of a yellow file folder, the message button on his phone was flashing. Walt, hoping Teri had called, flipped the folder off with the toe of his shoe, and pressed the play button.

'*Things a little messy there, Travis?*'

Richard Boyle.

It had to be.

'Missing a file or two, maybe? Listen, you quit snooping around in my life, you son-of-a-bitch. I know more about you than you do about me, and I'll make things fucking miserable for you if I have to. You understand me, Travis? You better. You damn well better understand.'

Walt leaned back against the wall and swept a hand through his hair. Okay, so at least he knew who was responsible now. And he knew something else. He knew that what had happened hadn't involved Teri and Gabe.

'Yeah, but where the hell are they?' He kicked at a file folder on the floor and started back out of apartment, running the scenario through his mind. They had come back from being out and had found the place ransacked. Teri would have assumed whoever had done it had been after her and Gabe, so they wouldn't have stayed around long, they would have left and . . .

. . . and what?

Teri would have tried to reach him. She would have called the motel and if he wasn't there, she would have left a message for him. That was a place to start, at least. He might be able to talk someone down at the station into tracking any credit card uses as well. And there was always the outside chance that she might have returned home, even though he had warned her against it.

'But she won't be back here,' Walt muttered to himself. He closed the door and locked it. It wasn't likely Boyle would be back, either. Between him and whatever was going on with Teri, things were getting a little too crowded around here. Walt jiggled the doorknob to make sure it was locked, then picked up his suitcase and started toward the stairway.

Richard Boyle could wait.

The big question now was how he was going to reconnect with Teri.

39

Teri wrapped her arms around her son, and Gabe settled back into her fold while he talked to his father. It felt to her like a lost breath had been found. She was whole again. Complete. Every breath he took went into her and out again, every heartbeat struck a chord. Absently, she combed the hair back from Gabe's forehead.

'Mom . . .' He brushed her hand away, a little boy's impetuousness. Then he squirmed a bit, and finally settled comfortably back into her fold again.

'Nothing,' he insisted over the phone to his father. 'She's just being a pain.'

'Don't talk about your mother like that,' Teri said lightly.

'Well you are.'

She mussed his hair again, and, yes, she supposed she *was* being a bit of a pain. But that was a mother's prerogative, wasn't it? Life didn't offer so many opportune moments that you could afford to throw one away. And God, how nice it was to have him with her again. She didn't want to lose another moment with him. Not one. Not ever.

'Mom.' Gabe waved the receiver in the air. 'He wants to talk to you again.'

More than half-an-hour had passed since she had put Gabe on the phone with his father. The maid, a woman who spoke almost no English, had come by and Teri had managed, through a hodge-podge of English, Spanish and arm waving, to convince the woman that it would be better if she came back later. Now it was getting close to their check-out time.

Teri cupped her hand over the receiver. 'How fast can you take a bath?'

'Mom . . .'

'Go on.'

'I just took one,' he said before catching himself. He hadn't taken a bath last night. Nor had he taken one at Walt's the night before. And that left him with a horrible gap, didn't it? When had he taken his last bath? Ten years ago?

'All right.' He climbed off the bed, not thrilled for a moment, and Teri gave him a playful swat on the behind before he disappeared into the bathroom.

She took her hand off the receiver. 'Michael?'

'He really looks like Gabe, huh?'

'What do you think?'

'And you're convinced? I mean really convinced? Not a doubt in your mind?'

'Aren't you?'

There was a period of silence on the other end, then, almost reluctantly, Michael agreed. 'Yeah, I suppose so. But I've got to tell you, it's the damnest thing I ever heard of, and if he isn't Gabe—'

'He is,' Teri said firmly.

'Incredible.' Michael fell thoughtfully silent again. He had always been a man who liked to keep himself under control, a think-before-you-act kind of man. If you hand someone a piece of paper, ninety-nine out of a hundred people will reach out and take it, sight unseen, contents unknown. Michael, though, would catch himself and pause to think about it first. That was his caution, and if she were honest, Teri would have to admit that at times she found herself envious of it.

'What if I came out to see him?' Michael finally asked. 'I mean... that would be all right with you, wouldn't it?'

'Well... things are a little crazy right now,' Teri said honestly.

'No, I understand. They're a little crazy out here, too. I was thinking maybe in a month or two, after things settle down a bit.'

'Let me think about it, Michael.'

'Sure. Teri...'

'Yeah?'

'You always kept the faith, didn't you?'

Not always, Teri thought. The shower in the bathroom went on, and though she didn't recognize the tune, she heard Gabe begin to sing. There was a happiness in his voice that she had once thought she would never hear again.

'I did my best,' she said, trying to work past the layer of guilt underneath.

'Wish I could have been as strong.'

'We both did the best we could under the circumstances.'

'I don't know,' Michael said regretfully. There was an unmistakable hint of his own guilt beginning to show through. No doubt there had been enough for the both of them.

The conversation lay dormant for a moment, then Michael took a breath that was clearly audible, and said, 'You know this isn't possible. I mean, Gabe coming home after all this time and not being any older or anything.'

'That's what's happened, so it must be possible.'

'I don't know. It just seems so bizarre.'

'It *is* bizarre, Michael. What else would you like me to say? That aliens brought him back? Would that make it any less bizarre for you?'

'You always had that sarcastic side, didn't you?'

'It keeps me from going insane at moments like this,' Teri said. She switched the phone from one ear to the other, feeling strangely disconnected and uncertain. There was a part of her that didn't want to end this conversation, a part of her that wondered if since Gabe had come back after ten years, if maybe they could be a whole family again, like the way it used to be. But another part didn't like that idea at all, another part knew that she would never be able to forgive Michael for walking out on her when she had needed him most.

'Teri... what else has been going on out there? Anything?'

'What do you mean?'

'I don't know. I think someone's been watching the house.' His voice fell into something just above a whisper, and Teri remembered that voice. It was the voice of a man who was frightened. It was the voice of a man who wasn't sure what was going on or how to deal with it. It was a voice she had heard often after Gabe had disappeared.

'How long?' she asked.

'Just the last day or two, I think. At least that's when I first noticed it. I woke up late last night, not feeling quite right, and I noticed this car parked across the street. There were two men sitting in it, just sitting there, doing nothing. And then this morning, they were still sitting there, like they were waiting for something to happen.'

'Call the cops, Michael.'

'What am I supposed to tell them?'

'Tell them that out in California, your wife and son have been stalked by persons unknown the last couple of days and now there's someone sitting outside your house. Tell them you're scared and you want someone over there right now.' Teri closed her eyes, feeling tired and burdened and wishing she could be more helpful. 'Christ, that won't do you any good. Not if they try to check us out.'

'What the hell's going on, Teri?'

'I'm not sure, to be honest with you. But whatever it is, I think it's dangerous.' She let out a breath that seemed to take away some of the pressure, at least momentarily. 'Can you sneak out through a back door or a window or something?'

'Yeah, I suppose so.'

'Then do it.'

'Jesus, Teri, is it that bad?'

'Stay in a motel for a few days. Move around. Call in sick at work.'

'What are you saying? What the hell's going on?'

But that was the catch, wasn't it? Because she didn't really have any idea what was going on. 'I'm not sure, Michael. I think it has something to do with Gabe, but right now I'm not sure of anything. Just play it safe for a while, okay? Will you do that?'

'All right,' he said resignedly. There was a touch of unease in his voice now, and she was glad to hear it, because that meant he was going to take this thing seriously. 'Where can I reach you?' At the house?'

'No, I think they're watching the house.'

'Jesus. Are you sure you and Gabe are all right?'

'We're both fine.'

'I can take a flight out and be there tonight.'

'No, that'll only make things worse.' In the background, Gabe's singing fell silent. She heard the shower go off in the bathroom and the curtain drawn back. He'd be toweled off and ready to go in a matter of minutes. 'Look, leave a message with Uncle Henry and let me know where you're staying. I'll do the same, and maybe we can get back together over the phone in another day or two.'

'You sure you don't want me out there?'

'Not right now, Michael.' Absently, Teri had wound the telephone cord three or four times around her index finger, and like Chinese handcuffs, it was a sudden struggle to get herself free again. In some ways, she thought she hadn't been free for many years now. Not from her nightmares. Not from her loneliness. And surprisingly, not even from Michael. 'Uncle Henry's, all right?'

'Sure.'

'Gotta go, Michael. You be careful.'

'You, too.'

40

'Any luck?'

'Don't know yet.'

The man, who was nervously tapping a pencil against the edge of the countertop, sat back in his chair and waited. They had been waiting for nearly three days now, two men crammed into the back of a van, listening, watching, getting nothing until Mrs Knight had finally made the mistake of calling her estranged husband.

'How long does it take, man?'

'Just hold your water. It takes as long as it takes.'

Fifteen seconds ticked by.

'They didn't get it, did they?'

Twenty seconds.

'I don't know.'

Twenty-five seconds.

'Jesus.'

'At least we have a lead to the uncle.'
Thirty seconds.
Finally, the phone rang. Gene, the man with the nervous pencil, sat up in his chair, and grabbed the receiver. 'Did you get it?'

'We got it.'

'Great!' He copied down the phone number, hung up, and immediately dialed the CNA operator. 'I need one on 916-555-3743.'

'Just a moment.' The operator disappeared momentarily, then came back on the line. 'That number is listed to the Royalty Motel.'

'The billing address?'

'Yes... it's 2399 Cypress Avenue.'

'Thanks.'

41

The Royalty Motel.
Room 216.
Time: 1:22 p.m.

The first man took the right side of the doorway. The second man took the left. Mitch, who was ten feet back, braced himself against a six-by-six pillar, and took a solid breath. No mistakes this time. No close encounters. No coming up empty. He drew his gun from its shoulder holster, raised it in a two-handed grip and glanced at the courtyard below just to make sure the situation had remained uncontaminated.

It had.

Though someone had left the door to 216 partially ajar. The curtains were drawn, and there was music playing softly in the background, something that sounded as if it might have been left over from the 'British Invasion' of the Sixties.

Too easy, Mitch thought.

He looked from one man to the other, checked the room number to be certain, then nodded. That quickly there was no turning back. The number one man – James Jacobs, a five-nine muscled man known as JJ – went in low. Alan Moore followed high.

The door flew open, struck the wall and was held there by JJ.

'US Marshal.'

A woman screamed.

Mitch moved up, taking a position to the right of the doorway. He heard Moore shout the command, 'Down on the floor! On the floor! Now!' He followed through the door. J J was on the left, sweeping the bathroom. Apparently the room was empty. Moore stood at the fore of the living quarters, his arms straight, elbows locked, his gun sighted off to the left. He was visibly agitated.

Mitch moved up next to him, halfway through the question, *What's the matter?* when the question answered itself. Face down on the floor, her hands locked behind her head, was a small dark-complexioned woman dressed in a white uniform in need of dry cleaning. The maid.

Christ.

Moore shifted his weight from one foot to the other. In the corner, leaning against the wall, was the boy's cane. At least they had been here. 'What do you want me to do?'

'Shoot me,' Mitch said derisively.

JJ came up from behind. 'What's going on?'

'The maid,' Mitch said. The woman's whole body was shaking and Mitch would later swear that as they stood there, the salt and pepper in her hair had turned decisively more salty. He touched Moore on the forearm – Moore lowered his weapon – then motioned for them to quickly back out of the room.

They would be downstairs, around the corner, and halfway to the vehicle before the woman would have the courage to raise her head. She would see that they had gone and she would cross herself with trembling fingers and whisper a faint prayer to Jesus Christ, the Almighty.

And then she would start to cry.

42

Teri walked the last three blocks from the bus stop with Gabe trailing along in her shadow. They slowed down half a block from the office of Dr Childs, on a side street where they weren't likely to be noticed. She had thought this through last night and had decided that chances were his office was being watched. That's how Mitch and his thugs had caught up with them after their last visit. They were watching her house. And they were watching her husband. And they were watching her doctor.

She stopped and leaned against a fence-post, within sight of the parking lot.

'What are we doing?' Gabe asked.

'Waiting.'

'Waiting for what?'

Teri smiled and ran a hand through his hair, something that had always annoyed him before but didn't seem to bother him now. 'Waiting to make sure that everything's okay and no one's watching the back entrance.'

'You mean like that Mitch guy?'

'Exactly.'

Gabe had been getting around better today. He had forgotten his cane at the motel, though. She hadn't noticed until they were almost to the bus stop, and then she had looked back and watched him struggle down the walkway, using the side of the building for support. It appeared his legs were still fighting him, an agonizing battle, it seemed. She had nearly turned around then and gone back to the room to get his cane – and maybe she should have. But Gabe came to the end of the building, let go, and after a few difficult steps, he easily caught his balance. From there out to the stop, it had been an easy trek for him.

Still, he hadn't looked good.

And Teri knew something terrible was wrong.

She stared down at him now, wondering what it was. The best case scenario, she supposed, would be if Miss Churchill – Amanda Tarkett – had been right. That it would simply take time before he would be up to full strength again. But Teri already knew there was more to it than that. She just didn't know how much more.

'Are you all right?' she asked.

'Yeah.'

'I mean...' His eyes seemed a little red, his coloring pale. And he'd been so quiet since talking with Michael.

'I'm fine, Mom.'

'Good,' she said with a quick smile.

'Does that mean I don't have to see a doctor?'

'No such luck, kiddo.'

She glanced up the quiet street. Both sides were lined with oaks, the gutters filled with leaves and twigs and wind-blown wrappers from the Bartel's Drive-Thru a couple of blocks down. The sound of a distant train rumbled through, and a white station wagon with a woman and two small children crept down the street and turned left at the corner.

Teri wondered if she were growing paranoid. She supposed if anyone had earned the right, she certainly had. Still, it wasn't a trait she liked to see in herself.

'Guess now's as good a time as any,' she said.

Gabe, who had been sitting with his back against the fence, stood up and brushed off the seat of his pants.

43

Teri had not been foolish enough to make an appointment with the good doctor. First, because she hadn't been sure when she was going to have a chance to stop by and see him again. And second, because after the last visit, she thought it might be wiser if no one knew when she was coming.

A little caution never hurt, according to Michael.

She was going to remember that.

They entered the clinic through the back door, which opened to a short hallway, offices on either side. Dr Childs's office was the first one on the left. Apparently, he wasn't that different from the rest of us, Teri thought. Like everyone else, he liked to be the first one out of the door at the end of the day.

'In here,' she said.

Gabe pointed questioningly at the doorway.

She nodded, gave him a nudge into the room, and closed the door behind her. She had never been in the doctor's office before, which surprised her now that she thought about it. Childs had been her doctor since, well, since college. Better than twenty years now.

Built-in bookshelves lined three of the four walls. Open spaces here and there were decorated with diplomas and honorary degrees and awards for community service. The desk was a dark, expensive mahogany. A stack of paperwork looking nearly insurmountable cluttered the desktop. The only window in the room opened to the parking lot in back. Teri could see the corner of the fence across the street where they had waited.

'Now what?' Gabe asked.

'As usual, we wait.'

'Again?'

'You have a hot date this afternoon?'

'Mom . . .' He plopped down in the nearest chair, a swivel chair, and energetically began to pedal himself in circles. It was certain to make him dizzy if he kept it up for long.

Maybe she shouldn't have been concerned about him after all, Teri thought as she roamed aimlessly about the room. She thumbed through a couple of volumes from the doctor's medical library, finding them either over her head or tediously dry. Then she casually shuffled through some of the papers on the desk, hoping she might come across Gabe's file. No such luck, though.

'How long do we have to wait?' Gabe asked again.

'Until the doctor shows up.'

Gabe grumbled under his breath, then gave himself another spin in the chair.

Teri wandered over to the far wall, where a mix of photographs and community service awards had been mounted – quite some time ago, judging by the dust on the frames. *1990: Chairman of the Santa Clara County Health Fair. 1993: Houghton Award for Outstanding Community Service. 1980: Glazier Award for Gerontological Research.* Some photographs taken at a lab somewhere, with everyone dressed in white lab jackets. And then something that caught Teri's attention.

It was a photograph of the steps outside the library at UC Berkeley. She recognized it immediately. Teri had spent two years at Berkeley in the mid-Seventies. That was where she had met Michael, who was studying as an art major at the time. Standing on the steps, at the middle of a semicircle of men, was Dr Childs. He was all smiles then, and Teri shook her head, thinking he must have used them all up that year, because as long as she had known the man, he had rarely worn a smile. Never, ever, a warm smile.

Beneath the photo, the caption read: MAGICAL MYSTERY TOUR. BERKELEY. 1976.

'Wonder what that's supposed to mean,' she said.

And then, behind her, the door to the office swung open.

Dr Childs, holding a folder in the crook of his arm, stepped through, clearly self-absorbed. He closed the door, turned and only then did he realize he wasn't alone. Surprise crossed his face. He instantly covered it. 'Teri? You startled me. What are you doing here?'

'I thought I'd stop by and see what your test results had to say.'

'Oh, yes, of course.'

'You did say you wanted to see us as early as possible, didn't you?'

He looked from Teri to Gabe, his expression an unreadable mask, then back to Teri again. 'I believe I did at that. I just wasn't expecting you to show up in my office without an appointment.'

'Well, since we're already here...' Teri said.

'Yes, well...' Childs removed the folder from the crook of his arm, crossed the room, and sat behind the desk. He seemed caught in some sort of bind, as if he didn't know quite what to say or how to say it. He tossed aside the folder, and looked at Teri with eyes that were a mix of concern and discomfort. He was going to tell her something awful, she thought. Something that would have kept her away if she'd had an inkling of it any earlier.

'I'm not sure where to start,' he said somberly. 'Maybe you should sit down, Teri.'

She sat in the chair next to Gabe, who had ceased his merry-go-round the moment Childs had entered the room. She took her son's hand in her own. 'I don't think I like the way this is starting out.'

'Let me be as straight as I can with you, Teri. Have you ever heard of a disease called Hutchinson-Gilford Syndrome?'

'No, I don't think so.'

'It's a degenerative disease that afflicts children.' He sighed, not for the first time, and Teri realized she had begun to hate the sound it made. It was as if he were trying to lose himself in the air around him. 'We don't really know a lot about it. It's a rare, genetic disease that seems to speed up the aging process.'

'Oh, no,' Teri said softly. She had seen a talk show on it once, now that she knew what they were talking about. *Geraldo* or *Donahue* or one of those other shows. She couldn't remember which. These children, these tiny little children, had displayed all the outward signs of premature aging: loss of hair, loss of weight, frailty. Teri couldn't remember what their life expectancy had been, but she thought it was somewhere around fourteen or fifteen.

My God, she thought. It was all coming around again. Something hideous had come along and swept Gabe up in its jaws as if he were nothing more than a paper doll, and now it was going to fly away with him. Just like it had flown away with him before. Only this time, Gabe wouldn't be coming back.

'I'm sorry,' Childs said.

She shook herself free from the numbness and stared out the window, fighting to hold on to what little control she had left. *This* close. She had come *this* close to having her son again, and now, like a strike of lightning, the dream was suddenly in flames. Gabe didn't deserve this. He didn't deserve any of this. She squeezed his hand.

'So what do we do?'

'First, I want to correct any misunderstanding I might have left with you, Teri. Gabe does *not* have Hutchinson-Gilford Syndrome. What he has are symptoms that closely resemble the disease.'

'What's the difference?'

'I'm not sure. Maybe nothing. Maybe everything. The bottom

line, of course, is that Gabe has begun to age at an accelerated rate, and we're going to have to see what we can do to stop it.'

'How accelerated?'

'That's difficult to say. I'd really hate to speculate at this point.'

'Is...' A lump caught in her throat. She swallowed it back and tried not to imagine that what she had swallowed would soon begin to grow like a cancer inside her. 'Is that the reason he's having trouble building up his strength?'

'That would be consistent with what we're talking about.'

'Uh-huh. Well... then where do we go from here?'

'I think that's largely up to you, Teri. If you'd like, I could make arrangements to have him admitted to a hospital where we could run some additional tests. That would give us the opportunity to get a better feeling for what it is we're up against. That would be my first thought.'

'And if we don't do that?'

'I'm not sure what else I can tell you.' Childs tapped the tip of his ballpoint pen against the desktop, then sat back in his chair, apparently frustrated by his own limited understanding of what was happening to Gabe. 'What seems to be going on here is that something's interfering with Gabe's normal cell regeneration. I don't know what's causing that. I don't know if it's something genetic like Hutchinson-Gilford Syndrome, or something environmental like a virus or an unknown bacteria. It might even be something closer to cancer, where the cells simply start to mutate and multiply at an uncontrollable rate. I can do some research for you, Teri, but beyond that, it seems to me that the best thing for Gabe right now would be a hospital environment where we could keep a closer eye on him and run additional tests.'

'I guess I need to make some decisions, don't I?'

'The sooner, the better.'

44

Walt woke up sitting on the floor, backed into the corner like a caged animal.

It had happened again.

He was somewhere unfamiliar, a small faceless motel room with the curtains open just enough for him to see that it was dark out. A light sheen of perspiration covered his body. He felt a chill rattle through him.

The dream flickered at the back of his mind, trying to hold on a little longer. In it, he had been standing in front of a mirror, transfixed by his reflection. His face was weathered and stubbled, the eyes drawn, nearly lifeless, the mouth straight and cold. He picked at the outer edges with his fingers, and a lappet of skin peeled away from around his ears. The rest followed easily, and underneath . . .

. . . underneath, he found another face. A dark, ragged scar marked one cheek. The eyes were dangerous, the mouth grinning roguishly. And under that . . .

. . . another face. These eyes the eyes of a shark, this smile the twisted grin of a man who has told too many lies, this expression a dare.

And under that, another face.

And then another.

One mask after another torn away until finally a shriek had ripped loose from his throat and he had come fully awake. Only to find himself cowering here in the corner of a place that seemed as strange and unfamiliar as the dream.

Walt struggled to his feet and made his way into the bathroom. He stood before the mirror over the sink, staring at his reflection, wondering if he were to pick at the edge of the mask if he could pull it off as he had in the dream, and if he would find another one underneath. *Jesus.* Would he recognize it if he did? Because he didn't recognize *this* mask.

He splashed some cold water over his face, then studied his reflection again.

A snippet of the dream flashed inside his head.

He closed his eyes, saw a child with a patch-quilt face staring back at him, then shook the image loose and stumbled into the other room. There had to be a clue. Somewhere in here, like a map, there had to be a clue to who he was and what he was doing here.

On the night-stand, next to a Gideon Bible, he found his motel bill. The room had been charged to a Visa card, under the name of Jonathan Chapman. The motel was the River View Inn, and there was an address, so at least he knew where he was, even if he didn't recognize the name.

Beneath the bill, he discovered his wallet. Inside the wallet, he discovered half-a-dozen credit cards issued under half-a-dozen different names. And there were social security cards, and three driver's licenses, and a passport, and a handful of wallet-sized photos of him, one with a beard and mustache, one with long hair, one with glasses and buzz cut.

Jesus, who the hell am I?

He came across a note he had apparently written to himself, taken from a phone conversation last night. It listed a local phone number, someone by the name of Aaron, and then this: *no local match, will try FBI files.*

Walt dialed the number.

'Criminal Identification.'

'Uh, yeah...' He checked the note again. 'Can I speak with Aaron?'

'Sure, hold on.'

A moment later, another voice came on. 'Yeah, this is Aaron.'

'Any luck on the FBI files?'

'Jesus, Walt, give me a break. I told you it'd take at least a couple of days.'

Walt pulled the drawer out of the night-stand, fished around and found a pen. Across the top of the note, he scribbled: *Walt.* 'Guess I'm just a little antsy.'

'I promise I'll get to it as soon as I can.'

'Thanks.'

'Hey, no problem, man.'

Walt hung up the phone and thought a moment. *Walt.* In his wallet, there was an old check stub, folded in thirds. He fished it out, and there, in the upper left hand corner was the name Walter L. Travis. Under that, an address. And under the address, a phone number.

He picked up the phone again, feeling a strange sense of detachment.

The man with no name.

It rang twice on the other end, then an answering machine picked up. '*Hi, this is Walt Travis. Sometimes I'm here, sometimes I'm not. Looks like this time you're outta luck. Leave a message at the beep.*'

He listened to the beep, then hung up and slumped against the headboard. It had been his voice on the other end. Walter L. Travis.

Fly down Death;

Call me;

I have become a lost name.

He had heard those words somewhere long ago, some *time* long ago, living under some name he could no longer remember. And he didn't know whose words they were, but for the moment, they felt as if they belonged to no one else but him.

Walter L. Travis.

45

Mitch parked his car in the lot just outside the tourist center. It was a little after ten. The lot was empty. For the most part, it had been empty ever since the sun had gone down, some four hours ago, though an occasional car would drive by without stopping. It was private here at night.

He closed the door, locked it, and wandered over to the concrete wall that overlooked the lake and the dam. Beneath the dam, the water spilled out in a white, frothy rage and made a mad dash down the Sacramento River. He had been here before, and though he could only hear the white water rage now, the picture was clear in his mind. It was both peaceful and tumultuous, both safe and dangerous.

'You're early,' DC said from behind him.

Mitch turned and saw the outline of a man standing in the shadows. He was on the small side, thin and not more than five-eight or five-nine. It was not the first time he had met DC face-to-face, though such occasions had been rare throughout their association together. 'I didn't want to be late.'

'Appreciated.'

'So what's the problem?'

'The problem is you, Mitch.'

'Bullshit. I've done everything you've asked.'

'Everything except bringing in the kid.'

'That's not my fault and you know it.'

'Exactly who's fault is it, Mitch? Seems to me you were the one responsible for tracking him down after we lost him. And you were the one supposed to apprehend him outside the doctor's office.' DC pulled a cigarette out of his pocket, lit it, and in the brief flare-up of the match, Mitch thought it looked as if the man had been under some pressure lately. His eyes were red and half-lidded. 'Seems clear enough to me.'

'You want to pull me out, go ahead and pull me out. But we both know you aren't going to find anyone any better. You provide the intelligence and I'll bring him home. That's a promise.'

'We don't have much time left. The kid's sick, and he'll continue to get sicker as long as he's out of our control. We need him back as soon as possible. You understand?'

'Yes.'

'This Mrs Knight's no dummy. She'll keep her kid on the move.'

'We've been keeping an eye on his mother's place like you suggested, in case they show up there again. His father lives in

Tennessee. We've got a tap on his phone and a man tailing him. And we're also watching the doc's place, the clinic.'

'What else?'

'We've got an eye on the Royalty in case she decides to spend another night there. And apparently, there's an uncle somewhere. She's been trying to communicate with her husband through him. We don't have a fix yet, though.'

'No more screw ups, Mitch.'

'There won't be.'

'I don't want this whole thing blowing up in our faces. You understand that?'

Mitch understood. He'd been called into this Operation by DC the night the boy had turned up missing. As far as he knew, the bigot list was no more than a handful of agency people. DC was primarily a shadow, someone who preferred to stay in the background of a Black Op like this. He had worked with DC before, though their past Operations together had never carried this degree of security. Once Mitch had received the call, he had contacted a trusted friend to make sure everything was on the up and up, a paranoid habit that came with the territory. This was not a general knowledge Operation, he was told. There was nothing additional his friend could offer him. Just to be careful and to keep himself in a need to know position as much as possible.

So yes, he understood.

But just the same, he didn't like it much.

'You give me some solid intelligence and the job's done,' Mitch said. 'No more mistakes. It'll come down quick and easy and it'll be over before anyone realizes what's happened.'

DC blew out a cloud of smoke that turned the midnight air gray. 'The boy's in danger.'

'From what?'

'He's got a medical condition.'

'You mentioned that.'

'It's potentially fatal.'

Mitch stared off across the dark valley. The sky was clear tonight. The stars were bright and alive. 'Are we helping him or is he helping us?'

'You can serve it up either way,' DC said evenly.

'Yeah, but which way is closer to the truth?'

'Whichever way helps you sleep better at night.' DC took a final drag off his cigarette and flicked the butt at the concrete walkway not far from where Mitch was standing. 'Anything else you'd like to know?'

'You still want him alive, don't you?'

'He's no good to us dead.'

'Same drop-off point?'

'Nothing's changed. Your instructions stand. Just make sure you don't screw it up again, 'cause, like I said, there's a time element involved here. The kid's sick and he doesn't know it and he's gonna get sicker and sicker by the day. That clear enough?'

'It's clear.'

'Good. I'll be in touch.'

Mitch nodded. He leaned back against the concrete wall, feeling the coolness of the night air against his face. DC disappeared into the darkness beyond the shrubbery, and a moment later Mitch heard the car start up and make its way out of the parking lot. Everything fell deathly still again, and in the distance he could hear the sound of the water churning at the bottom of the dam. It sounded like a rumble of thunder.

What kind of a storm's brewing here? he wondered.

46

Teri toweled off her wet hair and found herself staring into the bathroom mirror. Dark circles were beginning to show under her eyes. She looked like a woman who had spent the past several days without any sleep. Which was fairly close to the truth, she supposed.

She felt nearly as sluggish as she looked. Though her period wasn't for another week yet, she thought she had probably started retaining water already. That made for a partial explanation anyway. Closer to the truth, it wasn't her biology that was taking its toll. It was the mental stress of the past few days. Being on the run, always looking over your shoulder, not having the slightest clue of who's after you or why... it didn't take long for these things to start wearing a person down, and the wear on Teri was gradually becoming more visible.

How long was this going to go on?

She finished drying her hair, dressed, and wandered back into the bedroom area of the motel room. They were staying at a Motel Six, just off the highway, a couple miles north of town. There was the constant drone of traffic outside. Instead of being annoying, though, Teri found it somehow comforting, as if it helped to reassure her that she wasn't all alone in this, that there were, in fact, other people just outside her door.

Gabe was sitting up in bed, transfixed by an episode of *Tales From The Crypt*.

'You shouldn't be watching that,' Teri said.

'Why not?'

'You're too young, that's why.'

'But I'm getting older,' Gabe said with an impish grin.

She had tried to explain it to him, the fact that he was aging prematurely, but it was a difficult concept for an eleven-year-old to grasp. Hell, it was a difficult concept for the *mother* of an eleven-year-old to grasp.

'That's not funny,' Teri said, more sharply than she intended.

Gabe's grin disappeared. 'I was just kidding.'

'I know, but it's not something you should be kidding about.'

'Why not? It's not happening to you. It's happening to me.'

'Don't talk to me like that, young man.' Teri sat down on the bed next to him, feeling both angry and dispirited. Gabe was right, of course. *She* wasn't the one it was happening to, and she would probably never know exactly what it was like to be in his position. But she loved him. And she wanted him to know that she was there for him, that she wasn't going to let him slip away from her again. Not now. Not ever again.

'Look,' Teri said, regaining her composure. 'I know the past couple of days haven't been much fun. And I know what the doctor said today had to be a little scary for you.'

'It wasn't scary.'

It should have been, she thought.

'I want to grow up, Mom. I'm eleven already. I'm old enough to watch *Tales From The Crypt*. And I should be able to stay up as late as I want, even on school nights.' He glanced self-consciously down at his hands, which were in his lap. 'You used to let me watch *Tales From The Darkside*. It's the same thing. I'm old enough to take care of myself.'

'I know you are, honey, but that's not what this is about.'

'Well, what *is* it about then?'

'It's about your health, Gabe. Once you start aging, there's no turning back the clock. You'll just keep getting older and older, without ever getting any bigger. Eventually you're going to end up being older than I am.'

'I won't get any bigger?'

'No, you won't.'

'I don't get it then. How can I grow older without getting bigger?'

'That's what I've been trying to tell you.' She put her arm over

Gabe's shoulders and wished she could magically make everything better. It wasn't fair, bringing him back after such a long absence and then giving him something like this. It wasn't fair at all. 'This is different from just growing up, Gabe.'

'How?'

'Well, Dr Childs seems to think that it's something like Hutchinson-Gilford Syndrome. That's a disease that children sometimes get, and it's something that makes their bodies grow old much faster than they're supposed to.'

'Will I get gray hair and have to wear false teeth?'

'I'm not sure about the false teeth,' Teri said, actually finding a breath of humor mixed into the horror. In reality, she really wasn't sure if he'd have to wear false teeth or not. But the question caught her so completely off guard that she found herself smiling without being able to help herself.

'How about wrinkles? Am I gonna get wrinkles?'

'As I understand what the doctor said, the cells in your body will start to lose some of their regenerative abilities. What I mean by that is that they won't replace themselves as often as healthy cells are supposed to. When that happens, your body's going to wear out a little faster than everyone else's.'

'Yeah, but am I gonna get wrinkles?'

'Yes,' Teri said, fighting another grin. 'I think so.'

'Weird.'

'I know. It's very weird.'

'Am I gonna die?'

'We're all going to die, Gabe.'

'Yeah, but am I gonna die when I'm still a kid?'

'I don't know,' she said grimly.

'I don't want to die. Not yet, at least.' He glanced in the direction of the television, looking suddenly as if he were balancing the weight of the entire world on his shoulders.

'Maybe *Tales From The Crypt* wasn't such a big deal after all,' Teri thought solemnly.

'Mom?'

'Uh-huh.'

'What happens after we die?'

47

A small desk lamp cast a circular light over the console and the jumble of folders beneath Gabriel Knight's patient records. Childs stared at the bank of monitors displaying the last cell sample taken from the boy, then sat back in his chair and wondered what was going on.

It was *not* Hutchinson-Gilford Syndrome as he had told Teri Knight. But it was something similar, something potentially even more devastating to the boy's body. As would be expected with progeria, minor signs of aging were already beginning to appear. The boy had visibly lost some of his body fat, especially around his abdomen and his buttocks, and it seemed apparent that his skin had begun to lose some elasticity as well. It wouldn't be long before his internal organs began to suffer. Maybe only a matter of months.

The boy *was* aging.

He was aging at an alarming rate.

Just how fast, though, Childs couldn't say. It was going to take more time before he'd be able to hazard a guess with any accuracy, and he wanted to be sure. He wanted to be sure about how fast it was happening and what was causing it to happen.

It just didn't make any sense.

There had never been any previous symptoms. At least nothing telltale. In fact, nothing even remotely suspect for that matter. So why all of a sudden was this happening? What had triggered the change? And just as important – what was it going to take to reverse it? Was that even possible? And if it wasn't, then what was it going to take to prevent the disease from getting worse?

He wasn't sure if that was possible, either.

It just didn't make any sense at all.

Childs searched out a pencil and pad from the top drawer of his desk, and wrote a quick note to himself: *Is it possible that antisense oligos or oligo subunits might have accidentally integrated themselves into healthy DNA?*

He dropped the pad on the desk, searching for any other possible explanations that might come to mind, and then the phone rang. The call was from Teri Knight. He had given her the number to call in the case of an emergency.

'I didn't really expect to catch you this late,' she said softly. She sounded as if she might have been crying.

'Well, I'm glad you did. What can I do for you?'

'I'm not sure. I guess I was just feeling a little frightened by things.'

'That's certainly understandable under the circumstances.'

'Is Gabe going to be all right, Dr Childs?'

'I wish I could tell you not to worry, Teri, but quite frankly, I'm not sure how this thing is going to play out. As I told you earlier, there are definite signs of premature aging beginning to show themselves. Can we halt it? I just don't know.' He leaned heavily against his elbows which were propped on the console. 'Once again, I want to encourage you to consider having Gabriel moved into a facility for observation. I think that would be the most prudent way of approaching this situation. At least until we have a better picture of what's going on and how we might deal with it.'

There was silence on the other end, except for some background noise that sounded as if it might be a passing truck. Absently, he caught himself thinking: *She's in a phone booth somewhere.*

'Teri?'

'I'll think about it. I promise.'

'Please do.'

'How soon do you need to know?'

'The sooner the better, for Gabe's sake.'

'All right.'

Childs hung up, then thought about it a moment longer. She wasn't going to submit the boy to observation. Sometimes you get a feel for these kinds of things and that was the feeling he was getting now.

'Damn it, anyhow,' he muttered.

Then he took another look at the boy's cells.

48

Teri hung up the phone, feeling as if she had been teetering on the edge of a huge hole that had finally opened wide enough to swallow her altogether. The doctor had sounded more than a little concerned. He had sounded frightened. And that had given Teri a fright of her own, a fright she could have done without.

She stepped out of the phone booth, glanced down the street, and turned in the opposite direction. It was cold out tonight. The sky was clear, the air crisp. The city lights cast a dim wash across the night that made the stars seem farther away than usual. But then, everything seemed farther away tonight.

Gabe was waiting two blocks over, in the magazine section of a 7-Eleven. She went in, fighting back the tears. The right thing, she supposed, would be to let them place him under observation. Anything else, and she wouldn't be fit to be his mother, would she?

No, you wouldn't, Teri thought as she spotted him and went over to stand at his side.

But...

But she just got him back. And...

And she didn't want to lose him again.

Not for a second.

Not to anyone.

Oh, God. It wasn't fair. He didn't deserve this.

49

'Well?'

'We got it, but it's a phone booth.'

'Where at?'

'The corner of Burgundy and Market.'

'Better have someone check it out, just in case.'

'I've already got someone on it.'

'Have them check out the motels in the area, too. You never know, she might have been foolish enough to call from a booth not far from where she's staying.'

'You got it.'

50

'Walt? This is Teri.'

The answering machine was lying on the floor, at an angle, on a stack of file folders not far from the phone. The message light had been flashing furiously when Walt had first arrived back at the apartment. It was a solid red light now, and that meant the first of his messages had begun to play.

'If you're there, pick up, please.'

He grabbed the machine off the floor and made a place for it on the counter between the living room and the kitchen. After a short pause, the message played on uninterrupted.

'I'm not sure how to go about getting back in touch with you. Gabe and I went by the apartment not long after it was trashed. I wanted you to know that we're both all right. I need to get together with you, though, and I don't want to leave anything on the tape that might give away where we're staying. I'll call back, I guess. Maybe that's the best thing to do, to just keep calling back until we connect. Hope everything's all right with you. Sorry about what happened to your apartment, Walt. I never meant for things to get this far out of hand.'

The message ended.

Walt let out a long breath, feeling a sense of urgency and the inability to do anything about it. The pressure had been mounting for a long time now, even long before Teri had shown up again. It had been one little thing after another. And it had all started, he thought, way back when he had first met Teri and became involved in trying to find her missing son.

'Hey, tough guy. Guess who?'

The second message started up. The voice was instantly recognizable.

Richard Boyle.

'You didn't think you could slip away that easily, did you? I've been with you all along, my friend. I know where you stayed last night. I know what you had for dinner. And I know why you're back in your apartment this morning.'

That was interesting. Because Walt wasn't sure exactly why he had come back. Part of it, he supposed, was that he simply resented the idea of letting Richard Boyle force him out of his own home. The more Walt had thought about that the more it had eaten at him. He didn't want Boyle thinking he had won. He didn't want to give the man that pleasure. Not for a minute.

But there was more to it than that. Walt had also come back knowing that there was no other way that he'd be able to reconnect with Teri. He had hoped that she'd either call or stop by and he could put this other matter aside for a while. And, of course, she hadn't let him down, had she?

'You're back because of her, aren't you?' Boyle taunted. 'Just couldn't get along without the little lady and her son. You see? I know more than you ever imagined. Your move, Sherlock.'

The message ended, almost too abruptly for Walt's taste.

He stared down at the answering machine, feeling like a little boy who couldn't lie. *Caught you, young man. Caught you red-handed and dead to rights. No sense trying to deny it. You came back looking for your friend, didn't you? You know you did, so don't you go trying to give me any excuses now.*

Then, mercifully, the next message stepped in to silence the chatter.

'*Me again,*' Teri said, rather evenly. '*Guess you're not there. I'll call back, I promise. It's almost ten-thirty now. I'll try to give you another call in an hour or so. Hope everything is all right there.*'

Not exactly all right, Walt thought. But it could be worse.

He listened to three more messages, all of them from Teri and not another word from Richard Boyle, thank you, thank you, thank you. *Must be my clean living*, Walt thought as he reset the answering machine and wandered back into the kitchen.

There was nothing left to do now, just wait. Her next call would eventually come, not exactly like clockwork but close enough, and when it did he was going to be here, waiting.

It was the least he could do.

He never should have left in the first place.

Not with Teri and Gabe in as much danger as they were.

51

The restaurant, which was a quaint, family-owned place called The Garden, sat on the south side, just off the river. DC was seated on the patio, beneath a canopy of vines and flowers, overlooking a huge bend where the water flowed lazily past.

The sun was out today, casting a warm, amiable blanket over the area. DC looked up from his newspaper (the Warriors had lost again) and glanced up at a white cloud slowly tracking across the sky. The lunch crowd had thinned considerably the past thirty-five or forty minutes, and besides himself, there were only three other customers still left.

His own lunch – he had ordered something called a Garden Burger – had yet to arrive at the table when Webster showed up. The man sat across the table from DC, his chair pulled back, one leg swung over the other.

'And to what do I owe the pleasure?' DC asked, surprised but unruffled.

'Just a friendly visit between two associates,' the man said.

'Your visits are never friendly, Webster.'

The waiter arrived with his lunch, a burger and fries, set in a bed of lettuce, parsley, and two dill-pickle halves. DC rotated the plate a hundred-and-eighty degrees, sat up, and reached for his napkin.

'May I get something for you, sir?' the waiter asked.

Webster waved him off.

'Not hungry?' DC asked.

'I caught a late breakfast,'

'Eating on the run, that's not good for your system, you know.'

'And French fries and a burger are, huh?' The man glanced across the river at the distant horizon, searching for something more than the local sights. DC had only dealt with him twice before, both times he had come out because Washington had grown restless over an Operation. He had closed down one Black Op, something that still stuck in DC's craw. But the other Operation had turned out differently. DC had managed to convince him to leave it alone, and in the end he had been proven right.

'So, I hear things are getting a little sticky.'

'Where'd you hear that from?'

'It doesn't matter. I heard it, that's all that matters.'

'You heard wrong, Webster.'

He shrugged, knowing what they both knew – that he had heard things exactly the way they were, that things *had* become sticky, unpleasantly sticky. 'You've been with this one for a long time, haven't you?'

'Don't bullshit me, Webster, what are you doing here?'

'People are getting nervous. They're worried that things are hanging out a little too far, that you're risking exposure. I've gotta be up-front with you; they aren't all that sure it's worth it, my friend.'

'It's worth it.' DC took a bite out of his hamburger, wiped his mouth with the napkin, then sat back in his chair without taking his eyes off the man across from him. He had been assigned to oversee this particular operation nearly fifteen years ago, after the first man had been lost in a cold-war fiasco in West Germany. The project, which had been code-named Karma, had been initiated in a joint effort between the Department of Defense and the Central Intelligence Agency during the late Sixties, early Seventies. It had been intended primarily as a research project, though things had grown a bit more complicated since then.

'Prove it,' Webster said flatly. 'Because there's not a knowledgeable soul in Washington who thinks this project is worth the paper it was written on.'

'That never stopped Washington before.'

Webster grinned. 'Maybe not, but this one runs the risk of exposing people.'

'Well, we wouldn't want that, would we?'

'You'd be the first one hung out. Is that something *you* want?'

That was telling it straight, wasn't it? DC took a sip from his beer, trying to gauge exactly where Webster was coming from and how much leverage he might have in turning the man around. Not as much as he would have liked. There were some promising things going on here. But that's all they were . . . just promising.

'The boy's begun to age,' DC said.

'What do you mean?'

'He's starting to age prematurely at a rapid rate.'

'How rapid?'

'Maybe ten or twenty times normal.'

Webster glanced past DC, unable to keep eye contact, clearly taken by surprise. 'Not exactly what we had in mind, is it?'

'No.'

'Maybe I better have a drink after all.'

52

Walt had been puttering around the apartment for better than an hour, only half-aware of what he was doing as he straightened things up. He had been pleased to hear that Teri and Gabe were all right, but it bothered him that he had left them unguarded, and it bothered him even more that Teri had sounded more and more anxious with each message she left. Something was going on that he didn't know about, and there was nothing he could do but wait.

He finished in the kitchen, replacing the sugar canister on the counter next to the flour, then wandered back into the bedroom, where it seemed Boyle had enjoyed himself to the extreme. The phone was still on the floor, peeking out from beneath a pillow, and just as Walt was reaching for it, it rang. He snapped it up immediately.

'Yeah?'

'Walt?' It was Teri.

'Thank God. You sure you're all right?'

'Yeah, everything's okay here. We've been moving around from motel to motel, trying not to leave any kind of a trail.' There was a pause on the other end, and he thought he could hear Teri take in a deep breath and let it out slowly. 'I'm so sorry about what happened to your apartment.'

'It wasn't what you thought, Teri. It wasn't whoever's after you.'

'It wasn't?'

'No, it was Richard Boyle, the guy I went down to the Bay Area after. Apparently, he found me before I found him. He's the one who trashed the place.'

'Why?'

'Because he's a mean son-of-a-bitch, that's why.'

'And you're all right?'

'Yeah, I'm fine.'

'Oh, thank God.'

Walt leaned back against the wall and toed distractedly at the edge of a manila folder on the floor. He managed to get the flap open and folded back. It was a case report. He thought they had all been removed but here it was, the one that had been left behind. He glanced down at the title page and immediately focused on the name: Richard Boyle. The man had taken all the case files, except his own. Interesting.

'I went by to see Dr Childs, twice. I told you about the first visit, didn't I? That he had to take some additional tests?'

Why would he have left his own case file behind?

'No.'

'Then I didn't tell you about what happened after the visit, either, did I?'

Why? Walt wondered. With the tip of his shoe, he tried unsuccessfully to flip the title page back, then gradually what Teri had been saying to him came home full force. Walt looked up.

'No. What's going on, Teri?'

'It's been crazy.' She went on to tell him what Childs had said on their first visit, and how they had run into Mitch and his friends outside the doctor's office when they were leaving. She told him about the accident and about hiding out in the mall and about showing up at the apartment and finding the mess there. Then she told him about how they had dropped by to see Dr Childs a second time and how they had gone in the back way. All of that had come out of her matter-of-factly, then suddenly the words seemed to have to fight their way free. 'He says there's something wrong with Gabe.'

'What do you mean?'

'Dr Childs – he seems to think there's something wrong with him.'

'What did he say exactly?'

'He said that Gabe's got something called Hutchinson-Gilford Syndrome. Apparently, it's a disease that only attacks children. And what it does, well, I'm not exactly sure what it does. But what happens in the end is these children, their systems, they start aging much faster than they're supposed to.'

'They grow old? Is that what you're saying?'

'I think it's fairly rare. At least that's the way I understand it, anyway.'

'And Gabe has it?'

'That's what Childs said.'

'He's certain?'

'Yeah. He seemed to be.'

'Oh Jeeze, Teri, I don't know what to say. I mean...' Walt closed his eyes, wishing there was something that might come to mind, something that could take away the sting she had to be feeling. He had never been any good at this kind of thing. And he had never felt any clumsier than he did at this moment. 'Did the doctor say anything else? I mean anything about a cure or maybe a way they could delay the effects?'

'No. I didn't hear anything like that. He wanted to keep Gabe under observation, though. Just to be on the safe side,' Teri said. Her voice was just above a whisper and Walt thought she was close to tears. 'I'm scared, Walt. I don't know what to do. I don't want to lose him. I just got him back.'

'I know.'

'I want to do what's best for him.'

'You will, Teri.'

'I love him so much.'

'I know you do. And believe me, Gabe knows it, too.' Walt sank to the floor, wishing they were face-to-face and not talking over the phone like this. 'We need to get together, Teri.'

'Yeah, I'd like that.'

'Any place you'd like to meet?'

'Somewhere public. I'm feeling a little paranoid these days.'

'You've earned the right. How about the plaza outside of City Hall, the west side, with the statue and the fountain? You know where that is?'

'I think so.'

'In an hour?' Walt asked. He glanced at his watch. It was already a little after three in the afternoon. That would give him enough time to finish straightening up the apartment and maybe stop off to get something for dinner tonight before he had to meet her. The apartment was still the safest place for them to stay until things settled down again.

'Yeah, that sounds fine.'

'Good, I'll see you then.'

'Thanks, Walt. I don't know who else I could have turned to.'

'See you around four.'

Walt dropped the receiver back in its cradle, and dug the rest of the phone out from beneath the pillow. He grabbed the lamp off the table next to the door in the same swoop, and placed them both back on the night-stand, where he had kept them in easy reach since the first day he had moved into the apartment. The bedsheets had been torn off the mattress and scattered around the room as if a tornado had picked them up and toyed with them before dropping them back to earth again. He tossed the blankets off to one side and gathered up the sheets and pillow cases for the laundry.

There were two things gnawing at him as he carried the sheets into the living room and dropped them at the foot of the entryway. First was Dr Childs. There was something about that man, something that didn't want to sit comfortably with Walt. He had never met him, of course. But Walt didn't like the idea of Mitch and his friends showing up right outside the good doctor's office. And he didn't like the sudden diagnosis, either. It just didn't feel right. So try as he may – knowing that Teri trusted in the man – Walt just couldn't seem to bring himself to feel the same way.

The other thing doing some gnawing was the case file Walt had found on the floor in the bedroom. Boyle's file. That hadn't been an accident. Boyle would never have left it behind unless he had wanted it found.

Walt made his way back into the bedroom, pausing in the doorway long enough to wonder how things had suddenly become so complicated. Because if life was anything, it was complicated. Anyone who believed different had been sleepwalking. *Just make do*, he told himself. *Things will settle down again*. He stood the dresser up and maneuvered it back against the wall where it belonged, and wondered once again why Boyle had left his case file behind.

Some things just didn't make sense.

53

Teri hung up the phone and leaned against the side of the booth. She had used the middle booth in a line of five at the Sun Country Bus Depot. Through the glass, she watched a Greyhound bus pull out of the station, turn into the nearest lane of traffic and disappear down the avenue.

Gabe was sitting on a bench across from the telephone booth, where she could keep a watchful eye on him. He hadn't been doing his best today. He was running a slight fever and feeling a little sluggish, and some of that sluggishness had come through loud and clear in his behavior. He was definitely on the grouchy side this afternoon. Of course, having him sit in a bus station, inhaling noxious fumes while his mother made a phone call, didn't help matters any.

Teri forced a smile and waved to him.

Gabe waved back, halfheartedly.

She realized, almost instantly at that moment, something that had been brewing inside her for several days now. She didn't like any of this. She didn't like being on the run, or the loneliness it left her feeling. And she didn't like dragging Gabe around from place to place as if they were homeless and had nowhere else to go. Above and beyond all that, she didn't like what they were doing to Walt.

You aren't doing *anything to him.*

Yes, they were.

They were dropping all their problems in his lap like a sack of hot potatoes. Here, I don't know what to do with this. See what you can do. It felt ... *slimy* was what it felt. Though maybe it only felt that way because she didn't like depending so heavily on anyone, much less someone she cared about. That was something she thought she had overcome after Michael had moved out. But here it was, back again, like a dirty little secret that just won't die.

No, she didn't like any of this.

And yet ... what could she do about it?

54

Webster ordered a beer and downed it in three or four tosses. It was the first time DC had ever seen the man drink and it was not a pretty sight. His hands trembled as he dropped the mug back to the table.

'What do you think the significance is?'

'Of the boy suddenly aging?'

Webster nodded, his gaze slightly more focused.

'It's too early to know.'

'Oh, Jesus, this thing's been going on for better than twenty years now. What do you mean it's too early to know?'

DC leaned forward, wanting to grab the man by the lapels and shake him as long and as hard as it took before his marbles finally fell in line. Didn't he get it? Didn't he grasp any of this? This sudden aging, this was something no one had expected. It was something from out of left field. How in the hell were they supposed to fully understand its significance, especially at this early stage? He wanted to tell him all of that. He wanted to scream it in the man's face. But fortunately that was the same moment DC's pager went off.

He felt the vibration against his side, and sat back again.

'What is it?'

'Nothing. Just a pager.' He switched it off, and glanced at the number. It was from Mitch. 'Look, why don't you let me take this, all right?'

'Yeah, sure, go ahead.'

'It shouldn't be but a minute or two.'

'Fine.'

On his way inside, DC heard Webster call the waiter over and order another beer. Now, two beers for a drinking man doesn't amount to much. But two beers for a nondrinker, now that was something to make you sit up and pay attention. *That* was what a con-man would refer to as a tell. Something was going on here that wasn't completely up front. That concern followed DC all the way out to the phones and back again, and when he sat down he immediately noted that except for some suds at the bottom of the mug, the second beer was already history.

'Anything?' Webster asked.

DC shook his head, and lied. 'No. Just a friend wondering if we could get together for dinner tonight.'

'Any leads on the boy?'

'Not yet, but we'll get him.'

Webster nodded lazily. 'Anything else you want to tell me?'

'Like what?'

'Like why I shouldn't pull the plug on Karma?'

'I told you what's happening to the boy, if that isn't enough to make you hold out a while longer, then screw it, Webster. Go ahead and pull the fucking plug.' DC glanced at a raft full of noisy teenagers drifting down the river. Not a care in the world in that raft, and yet right here, not more than a hundred yards away from them, their futures were being toyed with. 'I mean, Jesus, haven't you ever been so close to a breakthrough that you could smell it? Can't you smell this thing, Webster? Screw the agency and the DOD. We're talking about something with the potential to change the life experience of every single living being on the planet. And you want to pull the plug? What? After twenty years you can't afford to stay with it another month or two? Jesus.'

'Is that how long we're talking about? Another month or two? No longer than that?'

'How the hell should I know? You want something definite? I can't give you anything definite.'

Absently, Webster spun the mug in one hand, stirring the suds at the bottom. He looked like a little boy trying to come up with a good reason for why he had stayed out after dark. 'I don't know.'

'What's to know? If you've got any balls you hold out a little longer.'

'They're not my balls in the ringer, you idiot. They're yours. You're the one making people uneasy with all these wire taps and break-ins. And how in the hell did the kid get loose in the first place? Wasn't someone supposed to be watching him?'

'He got loose, that's all that matters.'

'You're damn right it matters.'

'We'll get him back.'

'When?'

'Soon.'

'How soon for Crissakes?'

'Within a day or two, I promise.'

'And no more mess-ups?'

'What do you want? Scout's honor?'

'I want the boy back under our control.'

'You'll have him.'

55

Teri had never spent much time at the plaza outside City Hall, though she had passed by it on a number of occasions on her way to the police department. She had passed by it, but she had never really paid it much attention.

The plaza was open and airy and a step down from the government buildings that surrounded it on all sides. The light-colored stone forming the outer walls and the walkway made for an uneven surface that was intriguing to the eye. Young junipers lined the east and west sides. In the middle stood a huge fountain with water running over the edges in a clear, perfectly-formed sheet. A statue of one of the city's founding fathers stood at the edge of the fountain. The plaque at the base of the statue read: *Dedicated to Horace Gunthurman. 1917. If a little knowledge is dangerous, where is the man who has so much as to be out of danger?*

Maybe he wasn't a founding father after all, Teri thought as she read the inscription. Maybe he was the town librarian or something of that sort.

She sat down at the edge of the fountain, just outside the afternoon shadow of the statue. Gabe sat down next to her. He was still feeling a bit sluggish, it seemed. She held the back of her hand against his forehead, and thought it felt cooler out here in the cool air and the slight breeze.

'Mom...'

'Just checking.'

Gabe squinted at her, then shaded his eyes from the sun. 'When's Mr Travis supposed to be here?'

'At four,' Teri said.

'What time is it now?'

She checked her watch. It was twenty-five minutes after three. If they had waited for the next bus, they would have arrived a little after four, but Teri had been worried that she might somehow miss Walt. In that case, better late than never might actually have proven to be dangerous. She hadn't wanted to take that chance.

'We're a little early,' she said.

The plaza was deserted, except for two men in business suits who were sitting on a bench across the way. Teri glanced in their direction and made note of the fact that they didn't seem to be doing anything, that they didn't seem to be sitting there for any other reason than to be there.

(*and maybe to be watching*)

She checked behind her, and felt a sway of relief to find that no one else appeared to be guarding the west exit. Still, she wanted to be sure. She stood up and stretched, and started to stroll around the edge of the fountain.

'Mom?'

'Just stretching.'

'How much longer?'

'It'll be awhile yet.'

Across the way, one of the men stood up, then sat down again. They looked like little soldiers, waiting for their orders, waiting for the next move in a deadly game of cat and mouse. Teri didn't like it. She didn't like the feeling that was growing inside her, either.

'Gabe?'

He glanced up from the water, where he had begun to set ripples into motion with his hand, one after the other.

'What do you say we take a little walk? It'll make the time go faster.'

'Sure.' He pulled his hand out of the water, shook it off, and hopped down from the edge of the fountain. It was as lively as he had been all day, and Teri silently prayed that he was finally feeling better. 'Where do you wanna go?'

'I don't know. Where would you like to go?'

'How about...' He did a little spin, one hundred and eighty degrees, his arm stretched out like a compass needle, and when he stopped, he was pointing directly at the men on the bench. Only they weren't sitting on the bench now. They had stood up, like two curious wolves, and were beginning to pace.

'... *there*,' Gabe said.

'How about if we try this way instead?' Teri said. She took him by the arm, none too gently, and pushed him ahead of her around the fountain toward the opposite exit. It seemed as if she had been pushing him in one direction or another from the moment he had shown up on the doorstep, and she hoped he would indulge her awhile longer without too much of a fuss.

'Where are we going?' he asked.

'Let's make it an adventure.'

She glanced over her shoulder. There was no more pretending about who they were or why they were here. The two men were up off the bench and running in a full sprint in Teri's direction. They had already closed nearly half the distance, and she realized with a complete sense of terror, that there was no way she was going to be able to out run them.

'Mrs Knight!'

Frantically, Teri shoved Gabe to keep him in front of her.

'Who's that?' he asked.

'He's not a friend. That's all I know.'

'Please, Mrs Knight!'

They made it to the stone steps at the far end, where they had originally come down. Gabe grabbed onto the railing and pulled himself up, two steps at a time. Right behind him, Teri kept her hand in the small of his back. She thought she could hear herself whimpering, and silently she cussed herself for not being strong when it was most needed. Sometimes it seemed as if she only had so much strength left to draw upon.

'Mom?'

'Just keep moving, Gabe. Please.'

'But, Mom . . .'

She looked up, hearing the disturbing tone in Gabe's voice, and was surprised to discover two more men standing at the top of the stairs, the sun their backdrop. They were dressed in dark suits, white shirts, ties, and sunglasses, and they were standing side by side. The exit was completely blocked.

The man on the left took the first step down and pulled a badge out of his breast pocket. 'FBI, Mrs Knight.'

'What?'

'Your lives are in danger. We'd like you to come with us, if you would.'

56

Walt glanced up from Boyle's file at the clock on the night-stand and was surprised to see it was already a quarter to four. He had picked the file up off the floor with the intent of putting it away, but then he had sat down on the bed and started thumbing through the pages. He had never intended to give them anything more than a quick glance or two. Unfortunately, the quick glance had now consumed nearly forty minutes.

It had surprised him to discover that the initiating date on the file was May 27th of last year. That was the anniversary of his father's death. In all the turmoil, Walt had somehow never made the connection. He supposed that was because he had still been dealing with the death at that time. Even though two years had passed by then, he still often found himself regretful of the things never said, the questions never asked. The third anniversary was coming up shortly. He made a mental note to visit his father's graveside. It was the least a son could do. No matter what the relationship they might have had together.

Sarah Boyle. She was Richard's ex-wife, the one who had made the initial inquiry about hiring Walt to find her children. The police, she had said, had been of little or no help at all. They didn't seem the least bit interested, she said, and Walt understood that better than most. He had been part of it in his own time.

Richard Boyle was a man she never should have married. She was young, she said, and not as wise as maybe she should have been. Perhaps even more telling was the fact that her parents had taken an immediate dislike to Richard. That was all Sarah had needed to love him all the more.

What they say about love being blind, well, that was truer than most such sayings. At the ripe old age of twenty, Richard had already done his fair share of prison time. He had been convicted of auto theft on two separate occasions, and once for manslaughter when a fight broke out at a pool hall and he struck the man over the head with a cue.

Richard Boyle was not the kind of man young girls dreamed about marrying one day. But Sarah had married him anyway. And they had had two children and more fights than Ali and Foreman combined. And gradually, what little love there had been between them – if any at all – had worn away completely, leaving nothing more than a raw and mutual hatred.

From love to hate.

From family to kidnapping.

Jesus.

Walt closed the file and carried it into the living room where the filing cabinet sat in the corner. He had been on the case for nearly a year now and his trip to the Bay Area had been as close as he had come to putting it to rest. He was going to have to start all over now. And Sarah Boyle was going to have to carry on awhile longer without her children.

It was always the innocent, it seemed, who suffered the most.

Walt closed the filing cabinet and grabbed his keys off the counter. A little luck with the traffic lights, and he could still probably make it to the plaza a couple of minutes ahead of Teri. If only he knew what he was going to say to her.

57

'FBI?' Teri inquired, only partially comprehending what was happening.

'Yes, ma'am.'

'Did Walt send you? Walter Travis?'

'Would you come with us, please?'

She glanced back at the two men, who had caught up with them now, wondering if this was everything it appeared to be. Appearances could be deceiving, Michael's mother had liked to say. But it felt right, and maybe more than that, Teri was tired of running, tired of hiding. Maybe this was going to be the end of it.

'Please, Mrs Knight, we don't want you exposed any longer than necessary.' The agent tucked his badge back into his jacket, and smiled. 'We have a car waiting for you. If you'll just follow me.'

Gabe looked at her, his face marked with concern. 'Mom?'

'It's okay,' she said.

They followed the agents up the steps and across the square in front of City Hall. At the far end, on First Street, three cars were parked at the curb. The engines were already running. One of the agents opened the back door and assisted Teri into the middle car. Gabe sat in front, the driver on one side, another agent on the other. All three cars pulled away from the curb in perfect formation.

'Where are we going?' Teri asked.

'Where you'll be safe,' answered the agent to her left.

'Someone'll have to tell Walt.'

'It's been handled.'

'Is he going to meet us there?'

'Yes, ma'am.'

'Oh, that's good to know.'

'I'm sure it is.'

Teri glanced out the window at the scenery passing by. They were heading north, through the downtown section, past the Farmers Market and the Prescott Pavilion and McKinley Park. She watched an old woman dressed in rags, pushing a shopping cart down the street, and a Yellow Cab without a fare pass in the opposite direction.

'Where did you say we were going?'

'Somewhere safe, ma'am.'

'And where did you say that was?'

'I didn't.'

An almost spontaneous discomfort swept over her. This wasn't right. This wasn't right at all. Teri sat forward in her seat and studied the car in front. It was a late model Ford, black, like the others, carrying California plates. There appeared to be two men riding in the vehicle, both in the front seat.

Why don't they have government plates? Teri wondered.

She turned and watched the car bringing up the rear, and suddenly it became all too clear to her. These weren't government cars. And these weren't FBI agents, either. And they sure as hell weren't here to make sure that she and Gabe were kept safe. This all came rushing at her in a wave of realization. And the clincher, if she had needed such a thing, had been this: Mitch was driving the follow-up car.

'Stop!' Teri cried. 'Stop this minute and let us out!'

The agent – correct that, no more sense deceiving herself – the *man* to her left stared out the window, unimpressed, no reaction one way or the other. The man to her right, however, turned and grinned.

'I don't think so, Mrs Knight.'

'This is kidnapping, you know. You're taking us against our will.'

'Did you know there's a warrant out for your arrest? It seems after your little accident at the mall the other day, you forgot to go back and get your car. Now the cops are after you for leaving the scene of an accident. How's that for ironic?'

'You'll never get away with this.'

'Yes, we will. That's the whole point.'

The car turned west on Grove Street and made its way through an old section of town where there were a number of abandoned commercial properties for lease or sale. Teri glanced back to see if Mitch was still following. He was.

'What do you want with us?' she pleaded, trying to suppress the panic that had risen like bile at the back of her throat. 'Why are you doing this?'

'Just settle down and relax, Mrs Knight. No one's going to hurt you.'

'Then let us go, please?'

'Sorry, can't do that.'

She made a foolish and desperate lunge across the man's lap at the door handle. He caught her short and easily shoved her back into the seat between them. He had not been gentle about it, either. For several days to come, her arms were going to be showing dull, discolored bruises as an after-effect.

'Stay put, Mrs Knight.'

'Let us out of here!'

In the front seat, the car phone rang, and the driver picked it up. There was a short pause before he answered, 'She's a little hysterical at the moment.' Then another pause, before the driver called over the seat, 'He wants to know if you think we should sedate her.'

'How much further?'

'Another five miles or so.'

'Nah, she'll be all right.'

It was the idea that there were only five miles left that suddenly sent her panic out of control. Teri lunged for the door again. The man pushed her back forcefully, and she struck out at him with her left hand, dragging her nails across the left side of his face and drawing blood. He let out a groan, then grabbed her wrists.

Teri screamed, and lashed out with her feet.

'Mom?'

The man to her left, the one who had earlier seemed so disinterested, suddenly wrapped his hands around Teri's arms just above the elbow. 'I've got her,' he said, his voice straining from the effort.

The driver glanced distractedly over his shoulder. 'Christ, just sedate her, will you!'

It was at that moment when Gabe made his grab for the steering wheel. He managed to get both hands wrapped around one side, the driver trying to fight him off and keep an eye on the road at the same time. The car swerved sharply to the right, went up onto the curb, barely missed a light pole, and struck a mailbox before swerving back into the street again.

Gabe held on, one hand directly over the other, knuckles white.

Teri had been tossed to the floor. She found herself sprawled across the feet of the man on her right. When she looked up, she could see where he had hit his head against the roof of the car. He was bleeding badly now. His eyes glazed over. A trail of blood chartered new territory down the side of his face. He slumped forward, unconscious.

The car cut across both lanes, sideswiped a pickup truck parked at the far curb, then swung back again.

From somewhere behind, the sound of a horn blared.

Teri fought to keep her breath as the man slumped forward the last few inches and finally collapsed on top of her. And then, like a roller-coaster ride at Great America or Six Flags Magic Mountain, the car did something that felt strangely like a corkscrew. The hood and left front end slammed against the pavement and the car exploded into the air...

... the outside world rolled all the way over, a full hundred and eighty degrees...

... time both expanded and contracted...

... sky blue went flying past the side window...

... the right side of the car touched down and took off again...

... then finally, the Ford came to an exhausted landing, upside-down on its roof.

It swayed from side-to-side a moment, creaking and moaning, sounding as if it were animate and somehow in agony. When it finally came to pause, the only sound left was a soft chorus of weakened voices.

Teri found herself with her knees braced against the man's chest. He remained apparently unconscious. She sat up, feeling a bit woozy, then discovered a trail of blood running down the side of her face, which she quickly wiped away. She raised herself up, struggling to regain her bearings. The Ford shifted slightly, and she could see the sidewalk rise and fall like a wave just outside the window. Shards of glass littered the inside, gathered in puddles here and there where the roof had formed convenient pockets. Someone in the front seat moaned.

'Gabe?'

'Mom?'

'Are you all right?'

'I hurt my arm.'

She found him huddled in a corner near the dashboard on the passenger side. He was curled into a ball, his arm at an odd angle and held gingerly against his body. It was clearly broken.

The driver, who had used his seat-belt, was strapped in and hanging upside-down. The roof had collapsed against the top of his head. He was semiconscious at best, bleeding heavily from several lacerations. The other man hung half in, half out of the passenger side window, his seat-belt in a clump next to the reading light. On a glance, Teri thought he was probably dead.

'Can you move?'

Gabe nodded, tears in his eyes. 'But it hurts.'

'I know, honey. But you've got to try.'

The windshield had blown out completely, which may have explained the scattering of glass shards everywhere. Gabe sat up, keeping his injured arm as immobile as possible. He looked at her, his eyes dark and lost.

'Come on, take my hand,' Teri said.

He reached out in unmistakable pain.

Their fingers touched.

'That's it. Keep your eyes on me, all right?'

She helped him over the mangled legs of the dead man, trying to keep his attention as much as possible. After that, Gabe seemed to take on a strength of his own. Ahead of her, he ducked and went through the gap created by the missing windshield, crawling and still managing to keep the pressure off his bad arm somehow. Teri followed behind, unaware of the gash she opened in her right leg as she dragged it across a piece of glass sticking out of the window frame.

The hood of the car sat little more than a foot or so off the ground, smoke billowing out from both sides. A sliver of daylight crept in through an opening up ahead on the right. Gabe had already crawled out and disappeared. She could hear him calling to her now.

'I'm coming,' Teri said. She slid along on her belly, feeling the heat of the pavement against the palms of her hands, and when she emerged on the other side, it was into the warm face of sunlight. The feeling of freedom, which was as powerful and as exhilarating as anything she had ever felt, lasted only seconds. Mitch was standing over her.

'Put her in my car,' he directed to one of his friends.

'How about the boy?'

'No, keep them separate.'

A man aided Teri out from beneath the vehicle. He pulled her to her feet, wordlessly, then took her by the arm to another car and placed her inside. He set the locks. Teri slumped back into the seat, trapped all over again.

A small crowd had gathered around the outer edges of the accident, curious and uncertain about what was happening. For a few brief moments, Teri held out the hope that maybe she still had a chance here, that maybe someone would realize what was going on and step forward to prevent it. But the one time a middle-aged man did step forward, he was met by one of Mitch's men, who flashed a badge. The man quickly backed off.

Mitch climbed into the driver's seat. Another man opened the door and climbed into the back with Teri. She felt a trickle of blood slide down her forehead and over the bridge of her nose. She closed her eyes. Things were beginning to float now, dipping in and out of clarity.

'What did you do with Gabe?'

'He's going to be fine. We'll make sure his arm gets the proper attention.'

Mitch glanced over the seat, first at Teri, then at the man beside her. 'Everything under control back there?'

'No problems.'

The car pulled slowly around the accident, and Teri could see the smoke still spewing out from beneath the overturned vehicle. A black river of oil and gasoline flowed aimlessly across the street and into the gutter. The pungent odor was nearly smothering.

The forward car remained parked at the curb. As they passed by, Teri saw Gabe in the back seat, between two men. He was crying. He looked up, streaks running down his cheeks. *I love you*, Teri mouthed. Gabe took a swipe at his tears, then the car turned the corner and he disappeared from sight.

Teri sank back into the seat.

Almost absently, she felt the prick of a needle enter her arm. She didn't care anymore. What was the use? The car rounded another corner, then another. Teri began to lose all bearings of where they were. It didn't matter. She had already lost the only person who had ever mattered to her.

Buildings rolled by, monotonously, facelessly.

The motion of the vehicle rocked her gently in its arms.

Somewhere in the distance a siren sang out a sad and lonely song.

Teri closed her eyes.

58

Apparently there had been an accident somewhere on Grove Street. Traffic had been detoured over to Old 44, across to Sweetwater, then back to Market. It had been stop-and-go for nearly three miles before Walt was finally able to slip onto a back street and work his way over to the City Hall parking lot.

He was nearly fifteen minutes late by the time he arrived at the plaza.

Teri and Gabe were nowhere to be found.

The plaza, which was usually teeming with office workers from the surrounding government buildings during the lunch hour, was completely empty now. Walt sat on the edge of the fountain, the soft, whispery sound of the water at his back. He checked his watch, anxiously, then checked it again a minute or two later.

This didn't feel right.

They should have been here ahead of him, waiting.

This didn't feel right at all.

Two women came strolling down the steps, side by side, chatting between themselves. One was in her mid-fifties, Walt guessed. The first hint of gray highlighted the sweep of hair over her right ear, and she was wearing eyeglasses with a strong prescription. The other woman was younger, maybe in her late thirties. She was wearing a dark gray overcoat and had her purse inside, slung over her shoulder.

Walt approached them. 'Excuse me. I was wondering if you might have seen a woman and her son here earlier?'

The younger woman shook her head. 'Sorry. This is the first chance we've had all day to get out of the office.'

The older woman eyed him with suspicion.

Walt nodded and started away. 'Thanks anyway.'

He spent another forty-five minutes at the fountain, pacing on and off, wondering if he had been unclear when he had told Teri what time to meet him. His greatest fear, of course, was that something terrible had happened and that it might not have happened if he had been here on time.

Eventually, he decided the best thing to do was to head back to the apartment and wait for another call.

Maybe they had missed the bus, he told himself.

Or maybe they had gotten caught in traffic like he had.

Or maybe they had simply overslept.

There were a thousand possibilities, a thousand things that might have gone wrong. Most of them were perfectly innocent. But it was the others that Walt didn't want to think about, because it was the others he feared the most.

59

When Teri woke up, she found herself in an alleyway between a Wells Fargo Bank building and an old abandoned bar that had once been called The Brewery. The sun had gone down. Twilight had given way to nightfall. The alley was a patch quilt of shadow and light, of faint outlines and buried figures.

Teri pushed the cardboard boxes off and sat up against the side of the brick building. Her mouth was dry, her throat a little raw, and she could feel the beginnings of a headache coming on. The pain was on the right side of her head, just above her ear. It hadn't started to throb yet, but she was familiar with these things and she knew it wouldn't be long before it did.

The alleyway was littered with garbage, mostly scraps of cardboard and old food wrappers that had somehow escaped the dumpsters at the far end. A swirl of cool night air kicked up. Teri watched a newspaper flap its wings and fly past her. She could hear the rush of air past her ears, and somewhere far away there was the soft drone of traffic, people coming and going, never knowing there was a woman in this alley who had lost her way.

Except she had lost more than that.

She had lost her son.

She tried to stand up, felt woozy, and fell back again. The world wasn't exactly spinning, but it was doing a fairly decent interpretation of both ends of a teeter-totter. Perspiration broke out across her forehead. She wiped it away with the back of her hand, then tried to take a deep breath into her lungs. Whatever they had injected her with, it felt as if it were a miserable winter

cold, scratching and kicking, trying to hold on as long as possible.
She was going to have to be patient, that was all.
Just patient.
The cool night air turned cooler.
Teri closed her eyes and tried to regain both her presence of mind and a little strength. Nausea was stirring inside her belly like a bubbling witch's brew, hot and sour and frightening. The headache began to throb full force, pounding against the inside of her temples.
This one's going to be a migraine, Teri thought.
Her stomach lurched. She bent forward, and the lunch she had eaten hours before came up with a vengeance. When it was done, she slumped back against the brick work and closed her eyes.
The migraine began to recede.

60

DC pulled the Lumina into the parking lot of the Davol Research Foundation and found an empty space not far from the front entrance. The Foundation was set back several hundred feet from the street, secluded behind a wall of dogwood, European white birch, and sumac. DC climbed out, stretched, and wondered if the morning overcast was going to burn off before the afternoon rolled around.

The building was a lone wolf, located on the outskirts of town, not far from the airport. It had been built in the early Eighties and remodeled once in 1994. Three stories high, steel beams, dark-gray reflective glass, it was modern and brooding and a marked contrast to its natural surroundings. The area had once been mostly farm land, but gradually it had begun to give way to commercial zoning as the airport expanded and brought more people into the region. Half a mile down the road, the American Fixture Company had built their headquarters in 1988. They remained to this day the nearest neighbor.

Inside, the lobby was open and breezy, with a marble-tile floor. There were two elevators off to the left, and a grand stairway under a chandelier on the right. DC walked past the receptionist's desk without stopping. She looked up and smiled. 'Good morning, sir.'

'Morning, Jenny.'

He took the stairs two at a time, adding a little pull to the effort by way of the mahogany banister. At the top landing, he turned left and made his way down a short corridor to the conference room at the end. Mitch was already there and waiting.

DC closed the door and leaned against it, his hands behind his back for support. 'Is he back in the fold?'

'As of last night.'

'Good. And his mother?'

'We set her loose.'

'Any problems?'

Mitch, who had been leaning back in his chair, with one leg crossed over the other, suddenly sat forward. 'Nothing we didn't handle.'

'Nothing like *what*?' DC asked, his jaw visibly tightening.

'There was an accident. The boy grabbed hold of the steering wheel. The car flipped. Anderson didn't make it. Zimmerman and Wright were banged up pretty good, but they're gonna be all right.'

'And the boy?'

'He broke his arm.'

'Christ, Mitch. I told you we needed to keep a low profile on this thing.'

'Hey, I had the clean-up crew there in fifteen minutes,' Mitch said anxiously. He climbed out of his chair, and paced back and forth in front of the line of windows on the north side. You could see the faint background of the distant mountains behind him. 'They got in and out in no time. I swear, except for a handful of bystanders, it never happened. No one else knows about it.'

'Was the Knight woman injured?'

'She had some cuts and bruises, mostly around her eyes and scalp.' He paused and made a sour face. 'We had to sedate her. I told you that would be a possibility, remember?'

'Yeah, don't worry about it. As long as there's no chance of her tracing anything back to us.'

'No, we're clean on this one.'

'What about the others?'

'They're already out of the area.'

'And Anderson?'

'Clean-up took care of him.'

DC nodded. He had always been the type of man who liked to walk a fine line, one foot over the edge, just to see if he could keep his balance. It was the adrenaline pumping that he liked. How far could he go before it was too far?

In college, he had developed a particular dislike for a chem. intern. The kid was always hovering around the labs, poking his nose in where it wasn't wanted, taking each and every fucking opportunity to point out your mistakes. He was only a couple of years older than everyone else. And maybe that was what bothered DC the most.

When he'd finally had enough of the kid, he followed him back to his apartment, then waited, and when no one was there, DC broke in and removed a few personal items that he felt would be an easy trace. He used those items to fashion himself a nice little homemade bomb.

It went off the next day, just before lab. The explosion blew a small hole in one wall, shattered some beakers and test-tubes and petri dishes, and tore a couple cabinet doors off their hinges. No one was hurt. He was lucky no one had been in the lab at the time.

A huge investigation followed, and within a month, the bomb was traced back to that fucking little intern. He was expelled the following day. God, how DC wished he could have been a fly on the wall when the regents had met. He heard the kid had cried like a baby.

How far could he go before it was too far?

Too far... was getting caught.

And DC had never been caught at anything in his life.

'I want you to stick around for awhile,' he said. He pulled a white business envelope out of his jacket and tossed it across the table. 'A little something for your troubles.'

Mitch picked it up. He tapped the edge a couple of times, nodding and looking undecided. Then he opened the envelope and fanned through the bills. 'How long?'

'Until things settle down again,' DC said. 'That a problem?'

Mitch held up the envelope. 'Not for me.'

'I want you to keep an eye on the woman.'

'Mrs Knight?'

'Yeah,' DC said, staring absently out of the window. He should have been feeling a sense of relief, but he wasn't. Instead, it was more a sense of having awakened a sleeping beast. Things were going to be tricky for awhile. 'And be careful about it, all right? The only thing more dangerous than getting between a grizzly and its cub is getting between a mother and her child. She's not going to let go of this for awhile, not without a fight. Remember that. You never underestimate your opponent.'

Mitch nodded, noncommittally. 'Anything else?'

'Just keep an eye on her.'

'You got it.'

61

Walt answered the door, and was both surprised and relieved by what he found.

It was around one in the afternoon, and he had spent most of last night and all of this morning puttering around the apartment, trying to keep himself busy while he waited for Teri to call. Waiting wasn't a far cry from dying, he had decided. They could both be agonizing, and they both involved a painful degree of uncertainty. It was the uncertainty that bothered Walt the most.

Sleep had come a little after two last night, while he watched the end of a movie called *Don't Talk to Strangers*. He didn't remember how the movie had ended. In fact, he didn't remember much about it at all. There had been other things occupying his thoughts. More specifically, he had been worried because Teri and Gabe hadn't shown up at the plaza, and it was bothering him that she hadn't bothered to call since.

Something had happened.

Something terrible.

He had awakened several hours after nodding off, the television still flickering its images across the living room walls. An informercial, something having to do with a super absorbent mop, was at the midpoint and an 800 number was on the screen, with a dollar amount in smaller type in the upper right-hand corner. Walt came awake, one eye open, then rolled over and drifted off again. It had been like that all night.

Teri still hadn't called by the time he had finally crawled out of bed, a little after ten this morning. He'd give her until two, he had decided. Then he was going to take to the streets looking for her. Waiting was a death of its own, and he had struggled with it all night. That was long enough. He needed to do something, *anything*, to make the waiting less painful.

Though that was all mute now.

Teri was standing in the doorway.

She wasn't alone, either. She was in the company of two police officers, neither of whom Walt recognized. It wasn't surprising that he didn't recognize them. It had been nearly three years now since he had last worked for the department. Situations changed. No doubt some officers had retired and headed for the countryside. Others had come on as new recruits. Nothing in life was ever static.

'Mr Travis?'

'Yes,' Walt answered, only mildly engaged. 'Teri? Are you all right?'

'They've got him,' she said, her voice caught between something of a whisper and something ever more hollow. A white bandage slanted across her forehead, dotted by a red spot where blood had soaked through. Both cheeks were spattered with a series of cuts and scratches. Thick, dark circles underlined her eyes, giving her what Walt's aunt had once referred to as 'raccoon eyes'.

'They've got Gabe.'

Teri pulled away from the female officer. She fell into Walt's arms. No tears. Just a need to be held by someone she trusted.

'It's all right,' Walt said. 'We'll get him back.'

He helped her into the living room, onto the couch, and brought a pillow out of the bedroom for her. He did this while trying to calm the ugly self-accusations tearing at his insides. If only he hadn't been late yesterday. If only he had left a few minutes earlier, just a few minutes, just to be on the safe side.

Teri closed her eyes.

Walt went back to the officers, who were waiting patiently in the doorway.

'Is she going to be all right?' the woman asked.

'Yeah, I think so.'

'Has this ever happened before, sir?'

'No, of course not.'

'Uh-huh.'

'Why?'

'No reason, sir.' But of course, that was a lie. And they both knew it was a lie. You didn't ask questions like that for no reason. 'It's just that we found her this morning, walking along Brandon Street, looking pretty banged up. We thought she might have been assaulted or something, but she kept insisting that her son had been kidnapped.'

'Yes, last night, I think. I was supposed to meet them at the plaza near City Hall, but I got there late, and they were already gone.'

'And by *them* you mean?'

'Teri and her son.'

'Gabriel Knight?'

'Yes.'

'Have you ever met her son, Mr Travis?'

'Yes, of course.'

The woman glanced down at her notebook again. 'Gabriel Knight? Is that right?'

'Yes,' Walt said, instantly wishing he could catch it and reel it back in. Because suddenly he realized where this was going. Apparently, they had believed Teri when she had told them Gabe had been kidnapped. They had believed her, and they had followed up, and they had come across some interesting background information.

'Are you aware that she reported him missing almost ten years ago?'

Yes, of course, Walt thought, though he had no intentions of saying it out loud. That would only serve up more questions. And then questions on top of questions. And eventually it would all lead back to how he had worked for the department, and how he had worked on the Gabriel Knight case. And how, my dear man, did he intend to explain all that?

'No, I wasn't aware of that,' Walt said.

'I think you might consider getting your friend some counseling, Mr Travis.'

'Yes. I'm sorry. I'll mention it to her.'

'You do that.'

The officer presented him with a business card and suggested he call if he needed anything else. Walt accepted it without comment. He turned it over several times in his hands, glancing only cursorily at the name – Officer Debra J. Pettitt – before thanking her for her trouble and tucking it into his pocket. Neither of them carried any false illusions. The card would be lucky to make it past the first trash can.

By the time he made it back to the living room, Teri had already drifted off to sleep. He brought a blanket out from the linen closet, unfolded it, and covered her. Then he plopped down in the chair across the room and watched her. He watched every breath go in, every breath come out, and he promised himself he would never let another bad thing happen to her.

62

Gabe woke up disoriented and feeling lousy. He had drifted in and out of wakefulness for hours, only dimly aware of his surroundings or the new cast on his arm. What had happened yesterday seemed faraway and dream-like. He *did* remember the accident, however. And he remembered seeing his mother in the back window of the other car. She had mouthed the words, *I love you*, and the expression on her face had been something like that of a woman being burned at the stake. It had been horrible. He didn't think he would ever forget that face.

He sat up and saw that he was alone. Someone had dimmed the lights in here, and a dull hazy cast hovered over the room like a late morning fog. He had been placed in what appeared to be the middle bed in a line of maybe ten or twelve that stretched from one end of the cavernous room to the other. More important, though, he remembered this place. He had been here before. This was where he had found himself after the bike accident, the one that hadn't been an accident at all, according to his mother.

He fell back against the pillow, giving the cast his complete attention for the first time. It was a plaster cast, wrapped around the lower part of his right arm, between the wrist and the elbow. It smelled chalky and a little musty, not unlike the plaster leaf molds he had made at camp one summer. There wasn't a mark on it, not a smudge of dirt, a slight indentation, nothing.

Once, in the second grade, he had bent a finger back while playing wall ball, and everyone had thought it was broken because it swelled up so bad. When the x-rays had come back, the doctor had said it was just a strain and not to worry, the finger would be all right in a couple of days. But this was the first time Gabe had actually broken a bone.

He leaned over the side of the bed and gave the metal railing a whack with the cast to see if it would hurt. It didn't. The arm was going to be all right, too, he supposed. Though it might take longer than a couple of days this time.

He pulled the covers back and climbed out of bed. Someone had taken his clothes while he had been sleeping. He was dressed in his under shorts now, and a hospital gown. Cool air slipped through the long slit in the back and whirled around his legs like cotton candy spinning around the inside of a glass box. He reached back and tried to gather in the flaps, but it was easier thought than done and he finally gave up. What did it matter anyway? He was alone in here, after all.

A pattern of diamonds, black on white, led him across the floor to the only door exiting the room. The door was painted a dull navy gray. It was made of metal, and had a small observation window just above his reach. Even on his tiptoes, it was a little too high to be of any use to him.

Gabe gave the handle a jiggle. It was sloppy loose, with enough play to make him think it might fall right off in his hands. But the door didn't open. Apparently, it was locked from the other side. They had kept it locked the last time he had been here, too. Except when Miss Churchill was in the room.

'Hello?'

No response.

'Anybody out there?'

Another jiggle of the handle, and a lonely echo came back from the other side, like a ghost trying to tap out a message in Morse Code.

'Hello? Anybody?'

He leaned against the door, feeling the frustration building inside him. He pushed away, slamming the heel of his foot into the metal surface. It made a hollow, reverberating sound. He kicked it again, again with the flat of his foot, again with no response from the other side.

After a while longer, he retreated back to his bed. He sat there, brooding, staring endlessly at the door.

Sooner or later it had to open.

63

'Next they're gonna have to put a cast on his toe,' the man said light-heartedly. He was sitting in a small room, with a bank of video monitors across the wall in front of him. The lights were out. The screens cast a dull, gray mood into the room. A shift usually ran four hours max. here, because it was too hard on the eyes if you hung around much longer than that. When the eyes got tired, the mind got tired, and that was when you missed things.

'They oughta cast his whole damn body,' his partner said, placing an eight of hearts on a nine of spades and turning up his next card. It was a king, and there was nowhere to play it, so he buried it in the middle of the deck and turned up the next card. This one was a little better. A seven of spades.

'How do they do that?'

'What?'

'Cast your whole body?' the man said. 'I mean, what do you do if you have to take a leak or something like that?'

'Catheter,' his partner said, without looking up. He had cleared a column and was searching through the deck for a king to drop there.

'Yuck!'

'You said it, man.'

On the monitors, the boy plopped back into the bed, looking restless and unhappy. He was fully awake now, and unless they gave him something to help him sleep again, he was going to be pacing like a caged animal the rest of the day.

'I think we're going to have to order up some nourishment for the little guy.'

'You better clear it first.'

Off to the left, the door leading into the small room swung open and DC poked his head in. He was a man who liked to keep an eye on things, a coach who would much prefer to play the game himself if he were still as sharp as he had been when he was younger. Not to imply that DC was old or anything. He was in his late thirties by appearances. His hair was dark brown, his eyes dark and intolerant, his face a mask that gave away nothing. But he was a much older man beneath the facade. He was intelligent and no-nonsense. There wasn't much you could slip past him without getting caught.

'How's the kid doing?' DC asked.

'He just woke up a couple of minutes ago. He looks a little restless.'

'Have one of the nurses bring down something for him to eat.'

'Okay.'

DC took a quick glance at the monitors, his face expressionless. When he wasn't looking straight at you, you wanted to watch him and try to understand what was going on inside the man's head. But that wasn't an easy task. And it wasn't often, that he didn't look you straight in the eye when you were in his presence.

He nodded, apparently satisfied with whatever he had seen, then started to pop back out of the room again. Before he got the door closed, though, he added this: 'Oh, and put the fucking cards away, will you?'

64

It was nearly two full days before Teri was able to return to the here and now. She had slept most of that time, curled into a fetal position, tossing and turning and fighting with her dreams.

Walt drew the drapes in the bedroom to keep the daylight out, and he did his best to tiptoe around the apartment so he wouldn't disturb her. The one time she emerged from the bedroom, hungry, he sat her down at the counter in the kitchen and made her a plate of bacon and eggs and toast. She wasn't really hungry, though. She picked at the food with her fork, until she started to cry. Then Walt held her in his arms and tried his best to comfort her.

'I let him get away again,' she said, her eyes red and swollen.

Walt still didn't have the whole picture, but he had enough to know that she had done everything that she could have done. 'It wasn't your fault, Teri.'

'I should have known better. Why would the FBI be involved?'

'Hey, we're taught to trust a badge.'

'But I'm not a little girl anymore. I should have questioned them. I should have insisted they wait for you.'

'It's over,' Walt said, doing his best to soothe her. He felt completely incompetent, a man trying to shine a bright light over the mouth of a deep, dark hole. What he didn't understand until much later was that sometimes you have to let the hole completely engulf you before you can find your way out again. 'It's in the past. You can't change that.'

Which had been the wrong thing to say.

It only upset her more.

She went over and over again how she had let Gabe slip out of her grasp and how much she hated herself for allowing that to happen. She would cry, then sniffle awhile, then talk awhile longer, then cry again. And Walt learned to listen without saying anything. That's all she seemed to need. Just someone to listen.

She never did eat more than a forkful or two of her breakfast. It turned cold after awhile, and the eggs turned runny. Gradually, the conversation – what there was of it – died out and it seemed there was nothing left to be said.

Teri stared emptily across the kitchen, her fingers working at the edges of her napkin. 'I think I'll go back to bed.'

'You sure?'

'Yeah.'

'I can put some coffee on?'

She smiled numbly. 'No. But thank you for listening.'

Walt returned her smile, a hesitant, awkward turn of the corner of his mouth, and he watched her climb out of her chair and shuffle back down the hall to the bedroom and close the door behind her.

That had been yesterday morning.

And now she was up again.

She came down the hall, still looking a little on the tired side. Two days of tossing and turning, of nightmares and sweats, had not been good to her. Her hair was a rat's nest, twined and clumped and all out of sorts. Her eyes were still dull from sleep, though beneath them, the dark rings were gone now. She yawned, placing the back of her hand over her mouth, and leaned against the nearest wall.

'How are you feeling?' Walt asked.

'So-so.'

He nodded. 'Hungry?'

'Yeah, a little.'

'What would you like?'

'Anything. It doesn't matter.' She yawned again, and ran a hand through her hair, flattening it against her scalp. 'What time is it?'

Walt had to check his watch. 'A little after two.'

'Another day wasted, huh?'

'I wouldn't call it wasted.' He got up and went into the kitchen. The breakfast dishes from yesterday were still in the sink, where he had simply forgotten about them. He turned the water on and let it run, waiting for it to make the long trip from the heater through the pipes. So many things hadn't gotten done the past couple of days. In a way, he had been sleeping as much as she had.

Teri came up and stood in the kitchen doorway. 'I'm ready now.'

Walt glanced up at her.

'I've done my crying, and I'm done feeling sorry for myself. I want my son back.'

He smiled. 'That's all I wanted to hear.'

65

'Where do we go from here?' Teri asked. She brought a cup of coffee to the table and sat across from Walt.

'After the bad guys, I guess.'

'And how do we do that?'

'First off, we have to figure out who the hell they are.'

Teri nodded. She was beginning to feel better now. After Walt had made lunch and she had showered and cleaned up, she had taken a few extra minutes to sit down and close her eyes, to try to gather up whatever strength she could find inside herself. Walt had been right about what had happened. It *was* in the past, and there wasn't anything she could do about it. The future, however, was still in the making, and that was something she wasn't going to let herself forget.

'You have any guesses?' Walt asked.

'I don't know who they are,' Teri said. She took a sip of coffee, which had been the last of a pot that Walt had made earlier. It was bitter and only lukewarm. 'But they're tied to Gabe somehow. They're the ones who took him the first time; I know they are.'

'You have any theories about why they're interested in him?'

'It doesn't make any sense to me.'

'Okay,' Walt said, looking away. He picked up the pencil he had brought with him to the table and tapped an absent meter against the yellow legal pad underneath. 'What do you know about Dr Childs?'

Teri couldn't keep herself from grinning. 'You're kidding?'

'No, I'm not,' he said seriously. 'There's something about that man...'

She had known the doctor for twenty, maybe twenty-five years, ever since she had first met him at a community health clinic, where he volunteered his time on weekends. That had been long before he'd started up his own private practice, and long before Gabe had even been born. 'I don't know. I know he's a good doctor.'

'Uh-huh.'

'Why him?' Teri asked. 'I mean, why not this Mitch guy? He's the one who seems to be showing up all the time.'

'No, Mitch is just a stooge. There's someone else behind this thing.'

'I've known Childs a long time,' Teri said, feeling uneasy. She took another sip of coffee, trying not to let herself run away with the idea that the doctor might actually have something to do with what had happened. There weren't but a handful of people that you could trust in your life, and you desperately wanted to make sure one of those was your doctor. If you couldn't trust your doctor...

'I don't want to leave any avenues open,' Walt said.

'I know. And I understand that. It's just that...' It was just that *what*? Suddenly it was hitting too close to home? In her mind, Teri had always imagined that the source of their trouble was someone or some*thing* out there, some external, faceless enemy that had picked them at random. *This*, though, wasn't like that at all.

'He may have nothing to do with it,' Walt said. 'But we've gotta make sure.'

Teri nodded, knowing he was right.

'So why don't you tell me what you know about him.'

'Like what?'

'Like how you first met him,' Walt said evenly. He appeared only mildly interested, but that wasn't the case here at all. At least not in Teri's eyes. Walt had done this before. He knew how to keep an even tone in the conversation, how to listen without spooking the person who was doing all the talking. It had all been part of his job at one time.

'It was the first time I ever thought I was pregnant,' Teri said openly. 'Michael and I were going together, and I had missed my period. We were both in college then, and the chance that I might be pregnant... neither one of us was ready for that. We talked about it and talked about it, and it was like running into a mine field. You think you have everything under control and then suddenly there's this huge explosion and all your dreams start disappearing right out from underneath you. It was...'

She stopped and realized how long ago that had been and how fresh it still seemed in her mind. Some things become part of who you are whether you invite them in or not. 'I ended up at a health clinic off campus.'

'And Childs worked there.'

'He volunteered there.'

'Doing abortions?' Walt asked matter-of-factly.

'No, of course not,' Teri said. 'This was before Roe *versus* Wade. Abortion was still illegal back then.'

'That didn't prevent them from happening.'

'It wasn't that kind of clinic.'

'Were you pregnant?'

Teri cast her eyes downward at her coffee cup and shook her head. 'No. We had Gabe four years later, after both of us were out of school and Michael was working for the *Northern Weekly*.'

'You left the Bay Area and moved up here?'

'There was a group of us, a bunch of friends who always hung around together. After college we all decided to stick together if we could. Back then, communal living was a pretty common thing. So we all kind of migrated up here.'

'And you lived together?'

'For a while,' Teri said. She finished the rest of her coffee, and got up to return the cup to the kitchen sink. 'Then some of us got married and moved into our own little places, and others got jobs that took them out of the area, and some just lost interest and drifted away like lonely clouds in the sky.'

'How did you hook up with Childs again?'

'When I got pregnant with Gabe, we started asking around

about a good general practitioner. It was all part of that getting back to nature thing we were trying so hard to do at the time. I was planning on using a midwife for the birth, and after that I wanted to take my baby to a good family doctor, a Marcus Welby type, like they had back in the Fifties, someone who might actually make a house call once in awhile.' Teri finished washing out her coffee cup and placed it in the rack next to the sink. For a moment, she gazed out the kitchen window at the apartment across the way, letting the color of her thoughts melt into the creamy caramel color of the building. 'Someone mentioned to me that Childs had set up his practice in the area. So three weeks after Gabe was born, I took him in to see him.'

'What was Childs doing up this way? Did he ever say?'

'I don't remember exactly. Something about wanting to get away from the city.'

'Like everyone else, huh?'

'Yeah.' Teri broke away from the window and came back and sat down at the table. Her thoughts drifted through the last time she had spoken to Childs and what he had told her about Gabe's aging. Then magically, they drifted to the night when she had put Gabe on the phone to talk to his father. It was the only time she could remember Gabe lighting up with a smile.

'I've gotta call Michael and tell him what's happened,' she said suddenly.

Walt dropped the pencil and stretched. 'Maybe he already knows.'

'No, we talked to him the other night on the phone. He didn't know anything, Walt. I had to convince him it was really Gabe.'

'So you called him?'

'Yeah.'

'Why?'

'Gabe wanted to talk to him.' And then something suddenly occurred to Teri, something she had nearly forgotten. She slumped back in her chair, and felt all the energy drain out of her as if it were one final breath before dying. 'Oh, my God.'

'Are you all right?'

'I just remembered. That thing Childs mentioned, that Hutchinson-Gilford Syndrome. Gabe's aging process – it's speeding up.'

66

For a time after that, nothing more was said. Nothing more needed to be said. The implication was like a dark secret suddenly exposed to the light of day. Out in the open, it was perhaps more manageable, but that didn't make it any less monumental. Time had become of the essence now.

A sense of despondence quietly settled over Teri like a dark thundercloud, and she nearly let herself sink back into the abyss of the last couple of days. That would have been easy for her. So easy. All she would have had to do was close her eyes, and let the sleep come. But instead she got up and stood at the living-room window. She gazed out over the city lights, watching the traffic patterns glow, and thinking how huge the town had grown the past fifteen years.

Gabe was out there somewhere.

And he needed her.

When she came back to the table, Walt took out his pencil and they made a list of things they needed to get done, people they needed to talk to. The list went on for nearly three pages, one item, one line. And they agreed to get started on it the next morning.

It was a little after midnight when Teri finally went off to bed.

Tomorrow was going to be the day she started looking.

And she was going to keep looking until Gabe came home again.

67

Mitch watched the lights go off in the upstairs apartment. He opened his notebook, checked his watch, and made this entry: 12:27 A.M. TRAVIS APARTMENT. LIGHTS OFF.

It was getting cold out. The night sky was clear and according to the weatherman the temperature was supposed to drop below thirty. Mitch closed his notebook, stuffed it back into the inside pocket of his coat, and leaned against the corner of the building. It was best to play it safe for now. A few more minutes in the cold was all it would cost to make certain they had truly retired for the night.

He blew some heat into his cupped hands, then folded his arms across his chest.

It wasn't the cold that bothered him. Nor was it the fact that he still didn't have much of an idea of what this thing was all about. Being out of the know, off the bigot list, he was used to that. It was all part of the deal. In fact, most of the time the less he knew the better off he was. But this time something had stuck in his craw and he couldn't seem to do anything with it. Like a piece of meat that was a little too big, he couldn't seem to get it down, and there was apparently no way it was going to come back up. Not on its own. He was just going to have to learn to live with it.

Only he didn't like that.

He imagined that what was bothering him was the little boy. He had never had to deal with a child before, not in this line of work. It was almost as if he had crossed an imaginary boundary that he had set for himself. It was almost... un-American.

He blew into his hands again, and decided there wasn't much else that was going to happen here tonight, certainly nothing that warranted freezing to death.

The car was parked on the other side of the street, half a block down. As Mitch made his way along the sidewalk, images from the accident the other day came floating back to him like lost, soulless ghosts. Even though he had lost one of his men (something he had experienced only twice before, both times in hostile countries, where the danger was raw and ever-present), it wasn't the accident itself that troubled him. No, what troubled him was the sight of that eleven-year-old kid crawling out from beneath the overturned car. His arm had been broken and hanging at an odd, unnatural angle, his face ashen, the tears already welling in his eyes. And then again, in the back of the car, when the kid had looked out the window and had seen his mother, the way he had started to wail... that troubled Mitch, too.

He arrived at the car, climbed in, and sat there a moment.

The street was deserted. There had been a brief shower earlier in the day, and the sheen of standing water was a mirror to the street lights all the way down the block. A Mercedes passed by, its tires wading noisily through the puddles.

Night... the time of dark secrets and faceless people, Mitch thought remotely.

They had come across Walter Travis by accident, which – if a man were to be honest – was the way most things happened in life. The world was not nearly as organized or purposeful as we'd like to fool ourselves into believing. Chance, Mitch had come to realize, played a bigger role than any of us liked to admit.

Apparently, DC knew someone, who knew someone else, who knew someone in the local police department. And *that* someone was familiar with Mrs Knight and some of her background. He was also apparently familiar with Walter Travis. Mitch didn't have the full story – there it was again, the less you knew the better off you were – but apparently there had been some kind of past relationship between the two of them.

DC had gambled on a tap, and it had paid off.

It was that simple.

Everyone's got an Achilles' heel.

Mitch started up the car, looked over his shoulder, saw there was no traffic, and pulled out into the lane. It was nearly one in the morning now. He'd have to be back here again around seven or so, in case one of them happened to be an early riser.

DC hadn't said anything about how long this was going to go on.

Not too long, Mitch hoped.

He passed a thin man in his late fifties, stubbled beard, gray hair, ragged clothes that were a couple of sizes too large. The man walked as if he had no bones. His arms dangled lazily, his knees seemed to buckle with each and every step. Without looking up, he raised his right arm into the air and flipped Mitch the finger.

Night... the time of dark secrets and faceless people.

68

In what he thought was the mid-morning – there was no clock in the room – Gabe busied himself with a hand-held video game. It was a poker game and it was one of a dozen or so games that had been brought in the day before. They had also brought in a color television set, but it was rigged somehow and all it got was the Cartoon Network. There were only so many hours of cartoons a kid could watch.

The poker game beeped and a new hand was dealt: two fives, a king, a queen, and a seven. No chance for a flush or a straight. Gabe balanced the game on one leg while he pressed the necessary buttons to keep the two fives.

He was gradually growing used to the cast on his arm. There were three things, though, that the cast made difficult. The first was eating, which was fine as long as he didn't have to cut meat or open a milk carton. Last night, Miss Tilley – she was the woman who brought him his meals and had brought him the games – had to come back with another milk after he had spilled the first one all over his bed. It wasn't much fun trying to use the bathroom, either. It was mostly a matter of working out the logistics. But there had been some trial and error involved and a little embarrassment. And finally, the cast was like wearing a lifejacket to bed. It was always in the way, always taking up space, and there were no comfortable positions. He hadn't slept well last night. Not at all.

Another beep from the game and three new cards were dealt: a five, an ace, and a ten. That left him with three fives, a decent enough hand. He pressed a gray-colored button, cleared the screen, and was about to draw a new hand when a knock came at the door.

Gabe looked up.

The door swung open, and Miss Tilley stepped through, balancing a stainless steel meal tray in one hand. 'Lunch time.'

'Already?'

'It's been four hours since you had your breakfast.'

'What time is it?'

'A little after twelve,' she said, placing the tray on a bedside table. She removed the cover from the plate and a cloud of steam rose into the air. Lunch today was meatloaf, mashed potatoes, and corn. There was a wheat roll off to one side, and a carton of milk that she immediately opened for him. 'Hungry?'

'Not really.'

'Well, you need to keep your strength up, Gabriel.'

'Why?'

Miss Tilley was not Miss Churchill. She was an older woman, heavyset, with bright blue eyes that were always averting his gaze. She was as uneasy with him, he believed, as he was with her. Actually, to be honest, he just didn't like her. There was something cold and dishonest about her.

'You sound like you think we're fattening you up for the kill,' she said.

'Are you?'

'Don't be silly.'

Gabe stared down at his lunch a moment, then used his fork to toy with the mashed potatoes. 'When do I get to go home?'

'Not for awhile I'm afraid.'

'Yeah, but when?'

'Look, I'm just here to look after you. It's not up to me when you go home or when you eat your meals or when anything happens. You understand that? I don't make any decisions here.'

'Yeah, but when do I get to go home,' Gabe whispered under his breath. He tried the meatloaf, which wasn't as dry as the chicken had been last night. A little ketchup wouldn't hurt. Neither would salt.

He took another stab at the mashed potatoes and watched Miss Tilley use her keys to unlock the top drawer of the medical cabinet standing just inside the door. She brought out a short rubber hose and a syringe, which she placed on a stainless steel tray. She carried the tray and its contents around the foot of the bed.

'What are you doing?' Gabe asked.

'I need to take some blood.'

'From me?'

'Yes. From you.' She placed the tray on a bedside table, then went about unlocking a nearby drawer and pulling out some cotton swabs and Band-Aids.

'I don't think so,' Gabe said matter-of-factly. He could only recall a couple of occasions when someone had drawn blood from him. His earliest memory was of an incident in the third grade, when he had been drinking too much water according to his mother, and she had grown worried about something she called diabetes. His grandmother had apparently had it and Gabe's mother thought maybe he did, too. It turned out that he didn't, which made it hard for him to understand why he'd had to go through all the trouble of having that huge needle stuck in his arm. More recently, Dr Childs had drawn his blood. Gabe wasn't going to go through that again. And he especially wasn't going to go through it for Tilley.

'Don't be obstinate, Gabriel.'

He pushed his lunch tray aside. 'I don't have diabetes.'

'This isn't about diabetes.'

'Then what's it about?'

She picked up the rubber hose, stretched it, and seemed to take delight at the sound of it snapping back to size again. 'Give me your arm, Gabriel.'

'No.' He pressed his elbow into his side and locked it there tightly.

'Gabriel!'

'*No!*'

'Listen, young man, I don't have the patience for this kind of behavior. Do you understand me? If you want to make this difficult, we'll make it difficult. But either way, we're going to draw blood and we're going to do it now.'

Gabe shook his head.

'Give me your arm!' she screeched. She reached out and grabbed for him.

It was at that moment that all hell broke loose.

Gabe panicked and pulled away. In the process, he backed into the bedside table and his lunch tray overturned and fell to the floor. Corn nibblets scattered in all directions like a thousand frightened insects scurrying for the cover of dark corners. The tray landed with a loud, reverberating clang, and by the time the sound had finally reached its end, the expression on Tilley's face had transformed into a hideous Halloween mask.

'Why you little monster!'

He hadn't meant to knock the tray over. It had just happened. If she would just leave him alone ...

She started around the foot of the bed, her face flushed with anger, one hand gripping the rubber hose as if she were trying to squeeze the very life out of it. Gabe backed into the farthest corner.

'Stay away from me!'

'Not until I get some blood out of you, young man.'

Tilley pushed a chair into the nearest opening, effectively cutting off an avenue of escape. She pushed a cart into another opening, narrowing the room half again as much. Gradually, the space around him was shrinking, one small area at a time.

'You're running out of options, Gabriel.'

He grabbed at a plastic bottle sitting on a nearby counter, caught it, and flung it in her direction. It struck her on the right forearm, bounced off, and fell to the floor with a hollow echoing sound that reminded him of just how lonely and empty this place could be.

What he might have done next, he'd never know. The only door in or out suddenly burst open and two men, dressed in street clothes, came rushing through, their faces a mix of amusement and threat.

'About time,' Tilley said, visibly relieved.

'He's only eleven. We thought you could handle him.' The first man through went directly at Gabe. He swept him up around the waist and tossed him over his shoulder as if he were nothing more than a sack of potatoes. 'Where do you want him?'

'On the bed.'

They pinned him down to draw the blood, and by the time the job was finished, a black, ugly hatred had begun to smolder somewhere deep inside Gabe. He watched Tilley gather up her things, her demeanor subdued, her actions officious again. She was back in charge now, her lips pursed in that prissy little manner of someone who knows she's won.

'Maybe next time you'll make it easier on yourself,' she said on her way out.

The door closed.

Except for the cartoon on television, the room fell quiet again.

Gabe fell back into his pillow, tears welling in his eyes. She had placed a cotton swab and a Band-Aid over the puncture wound to help stop the bleeding. Gabe stared at it a moment, then tore it off and threw it at the overturned tray on the floor.

He had never hated someone so much before in his life.

69

Now that they were both on the same team, they had to see if they could get on the same schedule. Last night had been a troubled night for Teri. She had slept so long the past couple of days that she found it difficult to close her eyes and return to that state of dreams and drifting. Instead, she had tossed and turned most of the night, and this morning she had been up and about by six.

Walt, on the other hand, had had no trouble at all falling asleep. He had snored on and off for several hours last night, the sound often so loud Teri could hear it vibrating through the wall between the living room and the bedroom. And this morning, he hadn't even opened his eyes until a little after ten.

For awhile, they had behaved as if they had been married for a good number of years. Teri busied herself in the kitchen, putting together a breakfast of pancakes, canned fruit, and coffee, all the while trying to suppress her mounting irritation. Walt should have been up hours ago. There were only so many hours in the day, so many days in the week. And how much of it were they going to waste?

When Walt finally emerged from taking a shower and getting dressed, he sat down at the kitchen table and poured himself a cup of coffee. 'How you feeling this morning?'

'Antsy,' Teri said.

'Sorry. Guess the last couple of days finally caught up with me.'

They had caught up with her, too, only a few days earlier. When it had been her turn, Walt had been patient enough to wait. She had to remind herself that he had been patient about a lot of things lately. Certainly more patient that she had any right to expect of him. He didn't have to be helping her at all.

'How about some pancakes?' Teri asked.

'Sounds great.'

It was nearly noon by the time they left the apartment. Walt gave her a ride into town, where she stopped at Enterprise Auto Rental and got herself a '93 Ford Taurus. It was a nice car, dark blue, but the interior had a funny smell that she couldn't quite identify. It wasn't the smell of a cigarette. It was more like the smell of a pipe, though she didn't think that was quite it, either.

Teri finished checking out the Taurus, then walked over to where Walt was waiting for her. 'Everything looks fine.'

'Great,' he said, glancing across the street at a bus that had just pulled up to the curb. It sat there less than ten seconds, then pulled away again, leaving a cloud of black exhaust to linger in the air awhile longer. 'Six o'clock, my place, right?'

'I've been thinking about that,' Teri said.

'Yeah?'

'Maybe we shouldn't meet back at the apartment.'

'Why's that?'

'I don't know. I just think that maybe that's how they knew we would be at the plaza. That maybe the phone's bugged.'

Walt grinned. 'I thought about that, too. It's not bugged, though. At least not anymore. I checked it out a couple of nights ago. Besides, these guys aren't interested in us anymore. It was Gabe they wanted. Now that they've got him, I'd be amazed if they were willing to risk a tap. What would they have to gain?'

'You sure?'

'I'll tell you what, just in case, we'll stay off the phone. How's that?'

'As long as you don't think there's a problem,' Teri said.

'Don't worry about it.'

'Six o'clock, then.'

'Six o'clock.'

She watched him disappear into traffic, then went back and sat in the Taurus a while, letting the old memories stir. This was going to be trip into the past and she wasn't sure if she was going to like it or not. *You can remember fondly*, she had heard somewhere. *But you can't go back*. Of course, this wasn't about nostalgia, was it? It was about Gabe.

The first name on her list was Peggy Landau.

Teri remembered her as the quiet one. She was always hovering around the outer edges of the group, a little fieldmouse who worried about being accepted, but who was too shy to ever feel comfortable enough to become involved. She had been a thin, waif of a girl. Her dresses were all long flowing, flower prints that kept her hidden. When she smiled, it was a child's smile, all innocence and sweet summer smells and soft breezes. Teri had never known her as well as she would have liked, and wasn't that the way life always seemed to be?

Peggy was one of a handful from the old commune who still lived in the area. Her house was out in the country, south of the city limits, where it would be another twenty years before the urban sprawl ever caught up with her. Teri drove right past the house and had to turn around and come back. It was set back from the road, a country charmer with a front porch and white picket fence. Not much different from the kind of place they had all dreamed about when they were still in college.

Teri knocked, then stared out across the field on the other side of the street. Mount Lassen stood majestically in the distance, a white cap of snow against a blue background. At least someone had found her dreams.

The door opened only a crack, and a woman with bright blue eyes stared out.

'Peggy?'

'Yes.'

'I don't know if you remember me or not. It's Teri...' She had started to say, Teri Knight, but that hadn't been her name back then. It had been Teri Cutler in those days, sometimes even Teri Cutler-Knight, though that had come only after Michael had first proposed to her. She finished, 'Cutler. Teri Cutler.'

The crack in the door widened slightly, and a smile of recognition seemed to grow on the face of the woman on the other side. 'You're kidding? Teri? My God, how long has it been?'

'Too long,' Teri said. It had been some twenty-odd years since they had last seen each other. In fact, if she was called on it, she probably couldn't even remember exactly when their last time together had been. After she had married Michael and they had moved into a place of their own, they had seen less and less of the others. Over the years, Teri had come to believe that was the nature of most relationships. They came and they went. Some remembered, some forgotten.

'Well, come on in. Don't stand out there like a stranger.'

The front room was the parlor. Across from the picture window that looked out over the fields to Mount Lassen, stood a wicker sofa with bright, floral-print upholstery. There were huge potted plants on either side, standing nearly six feet high. Teri thought they might be paradise palms, but she wasn't certain. She had never had much of an interest in plants and shrubs.

'Can I get you anything?' Peggy asked.

'Oh, no thank you.'

'It's no trouble.'

'No, that's all right.'

Peggy sat on a wicker chair at the other side of the Shaker-look coffee table, covered with old copies of *Mother Earth News*. Her bare feet, dirty and scarred, stuck out from beneath the hem of her dress. It was a granny dress, similar to what she had worn all those years ago. A patch-quilt pattern, empire style, with the tie just beneath her breasts.

She smiled, appearing genuinely pleased by Teri's presence. 'This is so incredible. I saw Judy a couple of months ago, over at the Farmers Market. First her, and now you. Really incredible.'

'Judy's still in the area?'

Peggy nodded. 'She married a cop. Can you believe that?'

'No,' Teri said uneasily. Going back was a strange and uneasy odyssey, she had decided. As ridiculous as it sounded, because they had all undoubtedly changed over the years, she couldn't stop herself from thinking how much Peggy had changed. Not in her trappings, of course, because those hadn't changed at all. But the wallflower was gone now. Her smile was genuine and easy, and seemed more open than Teri remembered.

'They've got a three-year-old girl,' Peggy said. 'And they just bought a new house in the Henderson subdivision.'

'That's a nice area.'

'Yeah, they must be doing all right.'

'How about you?' Teri asked, trying to be tactful. 'Are you doing all right?'

Peggy smiled. 'Better than ever.'

'You live alone here?'

'Yeah,' she said, nodding. There wasn't the vaguest hint of regret or sorrow in her voice, and it occurred to Teri that her friend had learned something about herself since their last get-together. Peggy was no longer on the outside looking in. She had quit coveting those around her, and she had learned to be happy with herself. It was a lesson Teri wasn't sure that she, herself, had learned.

'It's my own little corner of paradise,' Peggy added.

'It is beautiful here.'

'I like it.'

'Especially the view.'

Peggy nodded. 'So... how about you? You and Michael still together?'

'Separated,' Teri said.

'I'm sorry to hear.'

'No need. It was the right thing at the time.' There was more to it than that, of course. But Teri wasn't in the mood for stirring it all up again. Once the sediment started rising, she was afraid she wouldn't be able to keep her emotions under check and her thoughts clear. So she sidestepped the issue as best she could and left Michael there for some other time, maybe some other occasion that wasn't quite as awkward. In his place, she asked Peggy about the house plants and the furniture and about what had been going on in her life all these years. They reminisced about the old times, about how naïve they had all been, and how the world had turned out to be even scarier than anyone had imagined, and how the good times seemed dimmer and more dreamlike than either of them cared to admit. There was still an aura, as Peggy put it, about those times, even though it had faded over the years. Some of the faces had faded, too, she admitted.

'Have you seen any of the others?' Teri asked.

'Not in years.'

'Me, neither. Funny how easily people drift apart, isn't it?'

'The cycle of life,' Peggy said, philosophically.

'Yeah, I suppose.'

They had come full circle now, and Teri had enjoyed the journey more than she had ever imagined she would. But it was drawing down to the end, and it was time she got to the reason she had come here in the first place. 'Do you remember Dr Childs?'

'From the clinic?'

'Yeah.'

'Sure, I remember him.'

'You ever see anymore of him?'

'Not since college,' Peggy said. She shook her head, a sly smile working its way into her expression. 'Now there was an odd duck if ever there was one.'

'Oh?' Teri said. She had never heard anyone refer to Childs as an 'odd duck' before. In fact, she couldn't recall having ever heard anyone speak ill of him at all. This was going to be interesting. 'How so?'

'Oh, you know, him the good doctor and all.'

'I'm sorry. I think I'm missing something.'

'Genesis?'

The times had been different back then. And they had been young. And what they had put in their bodies hadn't mattered much as long as it swept them away for awhile and eventually brought them back again. Some, like Mark Bascom, didn't even care if it brought them back. He died of a heroin overdose in '71, and Teri had always thought that his death had been the death of the group. Things had never seemed quite as carefree or spontaneous after that.

Genesis, though. Teri had forgotten about that stuff. It was something they were into for about six months during her senior year. Like LSD, it came in a convenient little sugar cube and sent you out into new, uncharted territory every time you took it. She had tried it three, maybe four times altogether, and had quit after that because it always seemed to leave her with a headache that hung on longer than the trip itself.

'Yeah?' Teri said, still not making the connection.

'Where did you think it came from?'

'From you.'

'Where did you think I got it?'

'Childs?' Teri said. It was almost too incredible to believe. They were talking about the man who had been her doctor for most of her adult life, the man who had given vaccinations to her son, who had set Michael's arm after he broke it playing racquetball, who had done the biopsy on the lump under her left breast and had assured her repeatedly that it was benign. Sweet Jesus, what was she hearing?

'I went by the clinic every Friday afternoon,' Peggy said flatly. Her smile was gone now, and her bright blue eyes seemed as if they had faded a bit. She stared past Teri, out the window into the countryside. 'He'd give me enough to pass around for a week or so, no charge. Said he'd rather have us using something he knew was safe than something off the street.'

'You never told anyone?'

'It was the only reason you guys let me hang around,' Peggy said. 'If I would have told you, you would have gone to him yourselves. You wouldn't have needed me then.'

It stung to hear that, though Teri knew it was the truth. They would have gone to Childs directly, and Peggy would have quietly faded into the woodwork, and no one would have missed her one way or the other. She would have become the remnant of a bad trip, a memory better forgotten.

Peggy said something about how lucky they were to have made it through those times alive, but Teri didn't hear the words. She only heard the sound of Peggy's voice. It was a sound that she knew she'd probably never hear again, even as she was leaving and they were both saying how nice it had been to see each other and wouldn't it be nice to stay in touch from now on.

Teri thanked her again, and made her way down the walkway, through the white picket fence and out to her car. When she looked back, the front door had closed. Peggy had disappeared back inside, out of the sun and away from the past. It was a place that Teri thought she wouldn't mind being herself. Sometimes, maybe most times, the past was best left in the past.

70

Aaron was in a hurry. He came out of the building, both hands tucked into his pockets, and took the steps as if he were Gregory Hines in a Broadway musical. It was lunch hour, only he'd gotten himself caught up in a database search and now he had less than twenty-five minutes left.

'Aaron!'

He glanced over his shoulder, hoping it hadn't been his name he had heard. But no such luck. Walt was crossing the commons, hurrying to catch up with him. Aaron tried to wave him off. 'Hey, man, not now. I've only got half a lunch hour as it is.'

'Mind if I walk with you?'

'Are you gonna talk?'

'I was thinking about it.'

'Then try to keep it to a minimum, will you? This is supposed to be my down time. I just want to get a bite to eat and maybe pick up a newspaper.'

'Things that bad down in the dungeon?'

'Hey, to you, its Criminal Identification.'

Walt grinned. They crossed the street at the light, cut around an elderly woman who was walking hand-in-hand with a little girl of maybe five or six, and followed the sidewalk up Reed Street. They were heading to the French Deli, another two blocks up. It was always Aaron's first choice when he was pressed for time.

'So?' Walt said.

'So *what*?'

'So you come up with anything yet?'

'Your guy's name is Mitchell Wolfe. He's a freelancer, mostly for the CIA. I don't know where he came from. I don't know what kind of background he's got. But I'll bet you a pastrami sandwich that he's got himself a horde of phony IDs, including a couple of passports under different names. You're tangling with a pro, Walt. You damn well better be careful.'

'What the hell's he doing out here?'

'That's your job, man. I've done mine.'

They crossed with another light. On the other side of the street, set back into the corner of the Bank of America building, was a small newspaper stand run by an elderly man by the name of Ronnie Tortelli. He had lost a leg in World War II and had only recently managed to finagle a new artificial limb out of the Veterans Administration. He swept a local newspaper off the top of the stack and held it out to Aaron.

'Running late today,' he said.

Aaron took the paper and slipped him a dollar bill. The daily was fifty cents, but Aaron had been paying Ronnie a dollar a paper for as long as he could remember. There weren't too many good, honest people left in this world, but Ronnie was one of them.

'How's the new leg?' Aaron asked.

Ronnie knocked on it twice. 'Still holding me up.'

'Catch you tomorrow.'

'I'll be here. Same time, same station.'

Aaron glanced at the headlines, which seemed to cover everything from the President's decision to reopen migration talks with Cuba to the country's reluctant admission that its 1.2 million dollar computer acquisition of three years ago had been a huge mistake. He folded the newspaper in half and slapped it against his thigh as he was walking. 'I don't know why the hell I read this crap. It's always the same stuff.'

Walt wasn't interested. 'Look, have you got an address on this guy or anything?'

'I told you; he's a freelancer. I'd stay away from him if I were you.'

'How about a city or a state?'

'You're gonna get yourself killed, man.'

'Come on, Aaron. You gotta have something you can give me. We're talking about a little boy who's been kidnapped. How about a photograph?'

'I'll put it in the mail for you.'

'Great. What else?'

'You could try calling up the CIA and asking why they've got one of their men running around out here in the middle of Smalltown, America.'

'Yeah, and we both know what they'd say, don't we?'

'Yeah. They'd tell you that they've never heard of Mitchell Wolfe.'

'So why waste the time?'

'It was just a suggestion.'

The two men weaved their way through a sudden crowd of pedestrians moving in the opposite direction, and when they came out on the other side, they had to backtrack past a jewelry store and a five and dime to get to the deli. This week's special, painted in bright red letters across the front picture windows, read: Italian Meatball Sandwich, Only $2.95.

'Here's where I get off,' Aaron said.

'Why don't we make it my treat?'

'I'm not sure if I feel comfortable taking money from a dead man.'

'Hey, I'm not dead yet.'

'No, not yet,' Aaron said. He held the door open and Walt passed through. 'But you're gonna be if you keep after this Wolfe character.'

71

Her name was Cynthia Breswick, though back in the old days everyone had called her Cindy (and sometimes Flower). Her maiden name was Kutras. She had come to Berkeley from somewhere in Southern California, on family money that had always seemed easily accessible in those days. She was intelligent and happy and easygoing, and she had liked to make bracelets and necklaces and sell them on the streets. In her last year at Berkeley – she had dropped out at the end of her junior year and moved north with the group – she made a perfect 4.0, then burned her grade slips and sent the ashes to her parents. Cindy did not get along with mommie and daddy. They were successful professionals, who lived and breathed their work, and Cindy was an only child, who had spent most of her childhood fending for herself. It had made her a strong woman, but it had also left a hole somewhere inside her. She had always been in search of the perfect family. No one had ever told her that there was no such thing.

What Teri remembered most about Cindy was the stark contrast. Intellectually, she was an independent freethinker, someone who could hold her own with a professor in a debate on situational ethics. Yet emotionally, she was a little girl, always in search of someone to take care of her. For the most part, she had been able to keep the two in balance and properly separated, but every once in awhile, she would let herself get swept away by a professor who seemed to fulfill both of those needs at once. Those had always been the dangerous times, the times when Cindy had been a little girl lost.

Teri knocked on the front door and stood back. The house was a beautiful Italian-style villa, built in the 1920s. The front courtyard was cobblestone, with a small lawn surrounded by a knee-high hedge and several flower gardens. Standing in the doorway, the house seemed enormous, and Teri marveled at how dramatically Cindy's life had changed since their days together at the commune.

The Palladian doors opened, and Cindy stood there, not at all the person Teri had expected to find. She was wearing a peignoir set, with a negligée underneath and a long silk robe hanging freely from her shoulders. Her hair, which had been honey-brown in the old days, was champagne-blond now, cut short and permed. In her free hand, she was holding a wineglass, half-full.

'Yes?' she said.

'Cindy?'

There was a moment when her expression was an empty slate, left completely in the dark. Behind those eyes, though, she must have been searching her memory. It had been a long, long time after all, and Teri had changed, too. More, in fact, than she would ever want to admit. 'Teri? Teri Cutler? Is that really you?'

'Hi, Cindy.'

'Oh, my God.' Cindy stepped through the door and gave her a warm hug. There was the smell of wine on her breath. It mingled in sharp contrast with the scent of a perfume that Teri didn't recognize, and she wondered briefly if the contrast in fragrances was anything like the contrasts that had played havoc in Cindy's past. 'Well, come in, come in.'

She showed Teri past the dining room, which was off to the left, and into the living room. It was huge and airy and full of light. There was a piano in one corner, an incredible marble fireplace in another. Cindy motioned to her to sit in the nearest easy chair, which was done in a warm, white velvet.

'I was just thinking about you the other day,' Cindy said.

'Really?'

'Strange, isn't it?' She sat on the sofa, which was covered in damask, crossed her legs and stared across the open space between them. It was almost as if she were trying to see inside Teri, to see if she was the same person she had been all those years ago. But that wasn't what she was doing, and Teri knew it. She was sizing her up, that's what she was doing.

She took a dramatic swallow of her wine and pinched her face in a smile that required an effort. 'So what brings you around after all these years?'

'It has been a lot of years, hasn't it?'

'Definitely.'

'Almost a lifetime ago,' Teri said flatly. She didn't think she liked this woman sitting across from her. Cindy Kutras, she had liked, even when she had been a fragile little girl following a new professor around like a lost puppy. But Cynthia Breswick, there was no lost little girl in her. The alcohol, Teri suspected, had drowned that little girl a long, long time ago. What was left was...

'I know what you're wondering,' Cindy said.

'Oh?'

'You're wondering what happened to me.'

That thought had, in fact, crossed Teri's mind. She thought she knew a little bit already, and she thought it went something like this: Cindy had found herself a man who liked to treat her more like a daughter than a wife. He liked to think for her and to take care of *things* for her and even spoil her. And in her mind, Cindy liked to think of him, not as her husband, but as her daddy, the one she had always been looking to find. And for a good many years this arrangement had worked well for both of them. But eventually things had changed, and now Cindy wasn't sure who she was or how she had managed to end up like this.

Hence, the booze, Teri thought.

'Well, it's not what you think.'

'No?'

'Well, maybe some of it is.' Cindy grinned and took another dramatic swallow from her glass. It was empty now. She held it up against the daylight shining through the windows and gazed at it as if she couldn't believe there was no wine left. Then she climbed off the sofa and moved across the room to the bar.

'But not all of it,' she added, pouring herself another glass.

'What happened, Cindy?'

She chuckled, and made her way back to the sofa, where she plopped down and immediately returned to her glass. 'Cynthia. It's Cynthia these days. And I don't know what the hell happened. That's what makes life so interesting, isn't it? No matter how smart you think you are, you never really know why anything happens. It's all a game of guessing.'

She fell silent a moment, staring into the marble fireplace as if it might hold some magic answers for her. But apparently there were no answers, and when she looked up again, she raised her glass and took another drink. 'I'm sorry, I should have asked. Would you care for something?'

'No, thank you.'

'You're so quiet. I don't remember you that way.'

'That was a long time ago,' Teri said.

'Oh, yes. People change, don't they? Nothing stays the same for long.' Her gaze went wandering back to the fireplace again, like a moth that couldn't stay away from the flame. This flame was made of old memories and bad dreams, Teri thought. And sometimes it could be dangerous. And sometimes you still couldn't keep yourself from wandering back. It was just too mesmerizing.

'I lost my son,' Cindy said quietly. 'It happened a long time ago, and I suppose I should have learned to live with it by now, but I haven't. I'm not sure I ever will.'

You won't.

Because it won't let you.

'I'm sorry,' Teri said. 'I know how you feel.'

A muted smile rose and fell across her face, and she shook her head. 'No, you don't. You might think you do, but trust me, you don't have the slightest idea.'

'I lost my son, too,' Teri said evenly.

Cindy looked up. For the first time, her eyes seemed to clear a bit. She looked as if she were peeking out from behind a veil of hidden secrets, as if she had suddenly found a reason to come out into the sun and let herself be seen. And she also looked shocked. 'Cody was seven.'

'Gabe was eleven.'

'He went out to play one afternoon, in the front here. We didn't like him playing in the garden or on the lawn, so he used to go across the street and play at his friend's house. He . . .' She swallowed back the rest of the sentence, as if it were bad tasting medicine. The wine glass in her hand looked heavy now. She placed it on the glass end table next to the couch, and tried again to finish the sentence, this time in a near whisper. 'He never came home.'

'When was this?' Teri asked.

'March of '85.'

'Oh, my God.' She put a trembling hand to her mouth. Gabe had disappeared that same month, that same year. Perhaps it meant nothing at all, but if that were true, then this had to be a coincidence and this was one time when Teri could honestly say that she didn't believe in such a thing.

'What?' Cindy asked. 'What is it?'

'That's when Gabe disappeared. March 27, 1985.'

The color, what little there had been, drained out of Cindy's face, and she reached for her glass of wine again. She took a sip this time, only a sip, but her hand was shaky and she was a long time getting the sip down. When she was done, she lowered the glass to her lap and held it in both hands, as if she feared she might spill what remained if she wasn't careful.

'That's not an accident,' she said softly.

'No, it isn't.'

'Why us? Why our children?'

'I don't know,' Teri said.

The mild state of shock hung over her friend a moment or two longer, then her eyes seemed to clear a bit and the color gradually came back to her face. She took a deep breath. 'Is that why you're here?' she asked.

Teri shook her head. 'I'm sorry, Cindy. I didn't know you even had a son.'

'Someone should have noticed,' she said numbly. 'I mean one of the detectives or someone. They should have seen the pattern. They should have checked it out. And someone should have told us.'

She was right, of course. Teri wondered briefly why Walt or someone else in the department hadn't said anything to her. Two disappearances in the same month. Two little boys. Someone should have noticed. *Someone*, Teri thought, *hadn't been doing his job.*

'Did you give up looking?'

Teri nodded, ashamed to admit it.

'Me, too,' Cindy said. 'About three years ago. I woke up one morning and realized I just couldn't go on living like that. It never stopped. I was always checking faces, hoping, praying, that I'd find him riding his bike on the sidewalk or playing catch at the park. He was always the next face, the next phone call. I just couldn't handle it anymore.'

A deep breath filled her lungs, then slowly escaped again, and it was as if she had just emptied herself of a lifetime of shame. She put aside the wine glass, then smiled weakly. 'I'm glad you came by.'

'I'm glad I did, too.'

For a moment, it seemed there was nothing left to talk about. It was strangely out of place to think of bringing up the old days now. They had died a death of their own, Teri supposed, long before either of the boys had disappeared.

'I'm not going to drop it,' Teri said finally.

'You know they're dead, though. After all these years.'

She nodded slightly, hating herself because she didn't believe Gabe was dead and she didn't like playing the charade. At the same time, though, she didn't want to risk getting Cindy's hopes up, either. There was no way of knowing for sure if Cody was alive or not. It had been ten years now. Gabe had come home, Cody hadn't. The thought of anyone having to go through the pain of losing her child twice was more than Teri could stomach. She didn't want to be responsible for that kind of pain. She didn't want to fuel the flames only to have to smother them again later.

'I'd still like to know,' Teri said.

'I guess I would, too.'

72

After awhile, the conversation drifted into private thoughts, and Teri finally made an effort to excuse herself. She was late for a meeting, she said, and even though it had been great seeing Cindy again, she had better get moving.

Cindy walked her to the door. 'Like I said, I'm glad you came by.'

'Maybe we can have lunch sometime?'

'That would be nice. I'd like that.'

There was one more thing Teri needed to ask. The answer was already a given, she assumed, but she wanted to make certain anyway. 'Oh, before I go, I was wondering something.'

'What's that?'

'I was wondering if Dr Childs happened to be your doctor?'

'Yes,' Cindy said. 'Why?'

'Oh, I just found out he had a practice up here, and I was thinking about switching, that's all.' Teri stepped outside, onto the porch and appreciated the warmth of the sun slanting in against her back. 'Was he Cody's doctor, too?'

'Yes. Since birth.'

73

The car windows were rolled down a couple of inches on both the driver's side and the passenger's side. There was a cool, gentle breeze drifting through, and still it felt stuffy, almost muggy inside. Walt rolled his window down further and tried to settle into a new position that wasn't so uncomfortable. He leaned back against the door and stretched his legs out across the front seat. It felt good to move his muscles.

The car was parked on a side street, adjacent to the small parking lot at the back of the good doctor's clinic. Walt had called earlier on the pretext of bringing in his son, who, he said, had fallen out of the tree in the backyard and may have broken his arm. Yes, Dr Childs was in. Yes, they could probably squeeze the boy in for x-rays sometime after three. But if it appeared at all serious, he should consider taking his son to the emergency room at Glenn General.

Nearly three hours had dragged by since then.

It was getting late.

Walt flipped on the radio, listened to fifteen or twenty seconds of the local news, then flipped it off again. The thing that had been bothering him since his meeting with Aaron was this: why? If this Mitchell Wolfe character was freelancing for the CIA, then why was he after Gabe? How on earth could an eleven-year-old kid do anything that would interest the CIA? And if Mitchell wasn't working with the CIA, then who in the hell was he working for?

Across the street, the back door of the clinic opened.

Walt sat up.

Two women stepped out into the bright halogen light over the parking lot. Childs followed close behind. He locked the door, and the three of them chatted casually out to their cars. The women were apparently pooling, because the one dressed in a white nurse's uniform climbed into the driver's side, and her companion climbed in and sat across from her. Childs started up his own car, the engine sounding sticky, and began to back out. As the others drove off, he stuck his arm out the window and waved goodnight to them.

At the street, before finally turning west, he seemed to debate which direction he wanted to take. It was a couple of minutes before six. Twilight had begun to lower its dark blanket over the landscape. Childs moved out of the parking lot apparently in no particular hurry.

'And we're off,' Walt said to himself.

He started up the car, pulled out into the street, and followed along a block or two behind. Not only was Childs in no particular hurry, he seemed to go out of his way to take a number of backstreets. He stayed just above the speed limit most of the time, backing off only once when a patrol car passed going the other direction.

What a wuss, Walt thought.

Childs made only one stop and that was at the Holiday Market. A few minutes after going in, he came out carrying two bags of groceries. By the time Childs finally arrived home, it was seventeen minutes after six.

Walt parked across the street. He took down the license plate number of the doctor's Buick, and made a note of the street address as well. It was getting late now. He had promised to meet Teri at the apartment at six, and that was already a lost cause. But he didn't want to make it any worse than it was. The last time he had been late to meet her ... well, that had turned into something of a disaster, hadn't it?

'Home again, home again,' he said out loud, haplessly.

He hoped Teri had had better luck than him.

74

Forty-five minutes later, after a Swanson Hungry Man dinner of chicken, corn and mashed potatoes, Childs emerged from his house, carrying his briefcase. Twilight had surrendered to the wholeness of night. The stars were out in full force, unmuddied by the usual haze hovering over the cityscape. A sliver of moon shone above the distant mountains like an afterthought to a perfect sky.

He stopped at the corner of the garage and gazed up to the heavens, amazed at how beautiful and infinite the night could be. Sometimes it was frightening to think how small and insignificant we human beings really were. For a moment, he wondered if we had any real control over our lives at all, or if we were simply puppets acting out a scripted tale of life and death.

Not without a fight, he thought.

He threw the briefcase in the back seat of the Buick, backed out of the driveway, and thirty minutes later, only a few miles away, he pulled into the parking lot of the Devol Research Foundation.

75

Lunch hadn't settled terribly well with Mitch. He had pulled into a small Mexican drive-through and ordered himself a couple of tacos and a burrito, and they had gone down quite satisfyingly. But they had begun to kick up a fuss as the day wore on.

He went back to the car and rummaged through the glove compartment. Buried under a map, he came up with an old box of Mylanta II Chewables. The doctor had recommended them after Mitch had had a long bout with stomach acid. He had gone in thinking that he might be having some sort of gallbladder problem, but it had only been gastritis, much to his relief.

He closed the glove compartment, sat back in the seat, and popped two of the tablets into his mouth. They were dry and powdery, and left a funny taste that wasn't much different from the taste this day had left. It had not been a good day.

Around noon, Mr Travis had driven Mrs Knight down to the car rental. They had parted company shortly afterward, and Mitch had stayed with the Knight woman throughout the entire day. She did not seem like the cornered, dangerous mother DC had painted her to be. Today, she had gone visiting, from one friend's house to another's. When Mitch had been growing up, his grandmother used to take him visiting. She'd take him by to see how the Matthews were doing, and maybe take some fresh baked bread over to Molly Jenkins, or drop off some quilting material at Miss Winter's, who had never married. It was one place of visiting after another, morning till night, and as that little boy, Mitch had been just as bored tagging along with his grandmother as he had been bored tagging along with Mrs Knight today.

The two tablets finally disintegrated.

He locked the car up again, and headed toward the laundry room where there was a Coke machine in the corner next to the utility closet. In two days, he had learned his way around this apartment complex far better than he had ever intended. It was quiet here, not much coming and going. Most of the renters were middle-class working stiffs, who put in their eight hours, then came home and plopped down in front of the television.

The Coke machine was out of Cokes, so he got himself a Sprite instead. He guzzled down half of it in a single tug, washing away the chalky film that coated his mouth from the Mylanta tablets. A huge belch came up from the depths, and instantly his stomach began to feel better.

Outside the laundry room, he paused long enough to finish the Sprite and toss the can into a nearby flower-box. The Travis apartment was upstairs, across the commons. Mitch could see it from here, but it wasn't the best of views and tenants did occasionally stop by to do their laundry. It was smarter to watch from the other side, where there wasn't much foot traffic and he could step back into the alcove between the buildings.

He worked his way around the outer edges, hoping against hope that tonight they might retire early so he could get back to his motel room before Letterman. Across the way, a woman yelled at her husband that dinner was on. The husband yelled back that he was in the bathroom and he'd be out when he was done doing his business. Mitch grinned, and when he looked up he saw Walter Travis coming around the corner.

'Evening,' Mitch said.

'Evening.'

The two men passed, Walter Travis barely glancing up from his thoughts. Mitch turned and watched the man climb the stairs. It had never occurred to him before, but suddenly Mitch found himself wondering about the man's relationship to Teri Knight. Was he a brother or something? Maybe a cousin? Or a boyfriend? What exactly was the relationship?

Boyfriend, he decided.

Mitch stopped at the corner, leaned against the wall and stared up at the apartment window. The lights were on in both the kitchen and the living room. Like it or not, he had the feeling that tonight was going to be another long one. He took out his notebook, marked down the time, and noted that W. Travis had just arrived home.

76

By the time Walt arrived back at the apartment it was thirty-five minutes after six and he was feeling guilty about being late a second time. He closed the door behind him, and saw Teri sitting on the couch in the living room. That was enough to alleviate most of the guilt, at least for the time being. She was home, and she was alive and well.

'Sorry I'm late.'

She looked up. Immediately, Walt realized something was wrong. Her eyes were red, her face streaked, and it was obvious that she had been crying.

'Teri? What's the matter? What happened?' Walt sat next to her on the couch, and she melted into his arms, her body an emotional wafer in danger of crumbling. He held her and did his best to comfort her, feeling all the while hopelessly inadequate.

'I'm sorry,' she said eventually, wiping her eyes with a crumpled tissue.

'No need,' Walt replied. 'So what happened?'

A sad smile passed across her lips, then quickly disappeared again. 'He wasn't the only one, Walt. Gabe wasn't the only one.'

'The only one?'

'There was another boy,' Teri said. 'I went to see some of my old friends today, like we talked about.'

'Uh-huh.'

'And one of them, Cindy Breswick, she had a son by the name of Cody, who was a little younger than Gabe. This was the first I'd ever heard about it. I didn't even know Cindy had a little boy. And then today she told me that she had lost him, that he had just disappeared one day.' Teri's eyes began to fill with tears again. 'And... and I asked her about it... and she told me how he'd just gone across the street to play... and... and he never came home again... just like Gabe.'

'When was this?' Walt asked.

'That's the scary part,' Teri said. 'Both of the boys... they both turned up missing in the same month, Walt. March of '85. The same month. Both boys. This thing was no accident.'

'Cody Breswick,' Walt said, remembering.

'You knew, didn't you?'

'I'd almost forgotten,' he said honestly. 'But, yes, we knew.'

'Why didn't you do anything?'

'We did the best we could at the time, Teri. No one took it lightly. There was a huge debate about it. And there were some of the guys who thought we might have a pattern developing. Most of us, though – and I confess I was one of them – just didn't see any link between the cases.'

'Didn't anyone think it was a little unusual? Two boys in the same month?'

'Of course, it was unusual. That's why we had the debate.'

Teri shook her head in disbelief. She had stopped crying now, and Walt could see that she had managed to replace her tears with something a little closer to anger. That wasn't necessarily a bad thing, though he would have found it a little more palatable if the anger wasn't directed at him.

'We might have solved this thing years ago, do you realize that?

I mean, who knows how many other children might have been saved?'

It was a good question, and one that Walt tried not to think too long about. There were some things in life that you simply couldn't change. It didn't matter how much you wished you could, once the card had been turned it was yours. This card had been a particularly painful one. They had missed an important link, and it might very well have cost some children their lives. Walt wasn't sure how he was going to be able to sleep with that knowledge.

'Jesus, Walt, I trusted you!'

'We just didn't know,' he said quietly. His throat had tightened, and when he swallowed it was as if he were swallowing a lump of burning coal. 'There were two others after Gabe and Cody.'

'What?'

'A couple of weeks later. The same thing. They went out to play and never came home again.'

'I can't believe this.'

'The department soft-pedaled it. They were afraid things would get way out of hand, that people would panic and vigilante groups would start popping up everywhere. Some innocent people were going to get killed if that happened. And nobody wanted that. So the department kept the wraps on the second two disappearances.'

'They didn't do any investigating at all?'

'Yes, of course they did. They put together a task force of – I can't remember exactly, but I think there were eleven, maybe twelve detectives. And there was nothing to go on, Teri. These guys worked around the clock for the next six months, and they couldn't come up with anything. Not a license plate number. Not a witness. Nothing.'

'And no connection between the boys?'

'No,' Walt said regretfully. 'I'm sorry.'

She nodded. 'So am I.'

They both fell silent for a time after that. Teri stared vacantly out the window, across the city lights, into the darkness beyond. She had stopped crying, and Walt didn't think she was still angry with him. But she *was* mournful – they were both mournful – and that wasn't going to go away for a good long time.

77

He came crawling up out of the depths like a salamander out from beneath a rock. His eyes fluttered open, caught a faint glimmer of light, then shut again. In that glimpse, he realized he didn't know this place, and he didn't know what he was doing here.

A sound came up from his throat, raw and dry.

He rolled onto his side.

A deep, spiraling soreness dug into the muscles of his legs, feeling – oddly enough – both good and bad at the same time. It made him momentarily aware of its presence, like a knock at the door, and then the soreness gradually evaporated as if it were a visitor who couldn't stay.

Somewhere far away, a rhythm tried to draw him even further out of his sleep. He listened to it, briefly, wondering what it was that made a sound like that. Then bit by bit it slipped away from him and he found himself drifting back into the silence that had already kept him for so long.

It was safer here, more comfortable.

No bright lights.

No loud noises.

Just peaceful.

Peaceful.

Peaceful.

78

The phone rang half-a-dozen times before Teri gave up.

'Not there?' Walt asked.

She shook her head and slumped back against the couch. She had been trying to reach Michael for the past two hours, getting nothing more than that irritating ring at the other end that went on and on, unanswered.

'Worried?'

'Yeah,' Teri said honestly. A lot had happened in the last few days, and she had wanted to catch Michael up on everything. But more than that, if she were going to be honest with herself, she had hoped Michael might volunteer to fly back and help out for awhile.

'Is there someone else you can call? Maybe someone who could check on him and make sure he's all right?'

'No, no one I can think of. We haven't exactly kept in touch the last few years.' There was no denying the odd arrangement between them. Michael had left because he felt like he had not only lost his son, but he had lost his wife as well. And to a large extent, he had been right. Teri never missed a beat. She went right on looking for Gabe, barely noticing that her husband had also quietly turned up missing. And it wasn't because she didn't love him, because she did. Even to this day, she felt she loved Michael. It had simply been a matter of priorities. That's why she had let it happen, and that's why they had never gotten a divorce. In the back of Teri's mind, she had always thought that once Gabe came home again, then Michael would follow him back and things would return to the way they had been before.

'I might be able to get someone from the department to call back there tomorrow,' Walt suggested. 'Maybe have a patrol car stop by and check his place.'

'Really?'

'I don't think it'd be a problem.'

'Okay,' she said softly. 'I think I'd feel better.'

'Consider it done.'

79

'Write your name, Mr Travis.'

Walt looked up from his desk. He was in the first row, second to last seat, farthest from the window that looked out across the school yard. Someone had carved the initials WT into the desktop, and circled it with a black permanent marker. It was not a nice thing to have done.

'Huh?'

The teacher, who was a man of about forty and stood almost as tall as the top of the chalkboard, held out a piece of white chalk in his hand. His eyes were red embers, his brow creased and stern. He was a familiar man, and Walt thought if he resembled anyone it would be his father.

'You heard me, young man. Come up to the chalkboard and write your name.'

The rest of the class all turned in their seats and waited to see what he would do.

'But...'

'Now, young man.'

'I...'

The teacher glared at him a moment, an if-looks-could-kill kind of glare. Then suddenly he slammed the palm of his hand against the board. It made a huge, terrifying noise, sharp and jarring. A cloud of chalk dust swirled madly into the air. Not a single child in the room didn't jump from the sudden explosion, and there wasn't a single heart that didn't skip a beat or two.

'Now!'

Walt climbed out of his seat, his legs rubbery beneath him. He passed through a row of strange faces, girls and boys that he couldn't remember having ever met before. Distrustfully, he took the chalk that was presented him.

'Your name, Mr Travis. On the board. Fifty times, if you will.'

Walt looked from the chalk to the huge, empty board that towered over him like a mountain waiting to be climbed. Slowly he began to write: J-E-F-F N-E-W-C-O-M-E-R.

Giggles erupted from behind him.

'That's not your name, Mr Travis.'

'Yes—'

'That's not your name!' A ruler slammed across his buttocks, nearly standing him as high as the teacher's chin. 'Now do it right!'

R-A-Y-M-O-N-D.

'That's not right!'

Another slap across his back side.

J-O-S-E-P-H.

'No! that's not who you are! Do it again!'

S-A-M-U-E-L.

'No! Again!'

B-E-R-R-Y.

'No!'

R-I-C-H-A-R-D B-O-Y-L-E.

'Richard Boyle. Now remember that,' the teacher said sternly. 'It's Richard Boyle. That's your name now. You understand me? It's yours.'

'It's yours!' the class yelled in unison, a sick delightful sound of harmony.

'It's yours! It's yours!'

'Yours,' Walt mumbled, coming suddenly awake.

A shudder rattled through his body, and he opened his eyes, finding himself sitting up on the living room couch. The room was washed in dark shadows, made all that more ominous by the ill-defined glow of the city lights slipping in through the window.

He fell back against his pillow, and closed his eyes. An afterimage flashed across his vision: the teacher standing over him, eyes blazing, a ruler in one hand, a piece of chalk in the other. This wasn't going to work. Walt wasn't going to be able to fall back to sleep that easily, not without bringing up the dream again.

He pulled the pillow out. It was warm on one side, cool on the side that had been turned down, facing the couch. He buried his face into the cool side, and gradually came to the realization that he wasn't going to be getting back to sleep for a long time yet. Sleep never came easy for the restless, and Walt had been restless for as long as he could remember.

He sat up, and threw off the pillow.

Outside his window, he could hear the soft hum of traffic going by.

He checked his watch. Seventeen minutes past two. This was going to be a long night, the kind of night when he might be lucky to get back to sleep at all. He pulled back the blanket, got up off the couch, his muscles stiff, and turned on the nearest lamp. The shadows that had owned the room quickly scurried back into the corners.

He climbed off the couch, wishing distantly that he would have had the time this evening to stakeout the doctor's house. After Teri had settled down a bit, she had mentioned that Cody Breswick and his mother had both been patients. That was all the verification Walt had needed. Childs was the common denominator. Follow him and eventually he'd lead to Gabe.

If only things were that easy.

Walt wandered down the hall, used the bathroom, and splashed some water on his face. If he was going to be awake, he might as well be fully awake. On his way back, he stopped outside the bedroom door and wondered how Teri was doing on the other side. He had seen her angrier, especially in the early months after Gabe's disappearance, when it appeared that Gabe had simply vanished and no one had a clue as to how or why. But Walt had never *felt* her anger before. Not like tonight. What had hurt most was that she was right. They should have seen the pattern. If they had, they might have been able to save some children.

'I'm sorry, Teri,' he whispered into the door. 'You've got to know I'm sorry.

80

The name of the store was After A Fashion. It was a small boutique in the Town and Country Village shopping center on the west side of town. Teri only occasionally came by here, and most often that was to browse through the bookstore at the other end. She couldn't recall having noticed the boutique before.

It was the kind of place she imagined she would want for herself if she were ever to go into business. Intimate and modest. A small, eclectic selection of styles (were the Sixties coming back?). And the atmosphere not so much that of a store as that of spending an afternoon over at a friend's, rummaging through her closet. It had a nice feel to it.

A bell over the door rang as Teri stepped through. There was no one behind the counter. In fact, there was no one else in the store, at least not up front. She sidled over to the casual wear and pulled out an adorable outfit with a smocked, high-waist skirt made with a two-tier flounce.

'I'll be right out, if you need any help,' a voice called from in back.

'No hurry. I'm just looking,' Teri said. She checked the price. $65.00.

'I'm sorry. Things have just been crazy this morning.' The woman came bouncing out, her eyes bright, her smile wide, and Teri recognized her immediately. Judy had always been a fireball, full of energy and laughter, the kind of woman you enjoyed being around. Time had treated her well. She hadn't aged a day, since Teri had last seen her.

'Teri?'

'Hi, Judy.'

Her smiled grew even wider. She opened her arms and gave Teri a hug that immediately closed the gap of time that had grown up between them since they had last been together. There weren't very many people you met in your life who could do that. It had been twelve, maybe fifteen years since Teri had last seen her, and yet instantly it felt as if it had only been yesterday.

'My Lord. It's so wonderful to see you again,' Judy said.

Teri didn't want to let her out of the hug, but she did, reluctantly. 'You, too.'

'How long has it been?'

'Too long,' Teri said. Yesterday she had visited with Cindy and thought how much the woman had changed, how much – no doubt

– they had all changed. But that wasn't as true today. Because somehow, Judy had managed to hold onto the essence of the old days. She hadn't changed much at all. 'We never should have let it get away from us like that.'

'Life does that, doesn't it? Just keeps us on the run all the time. Always busy, never seeming to get anywhere.'

Teri smiled, thinking that was probably true for most of them, but she wasn't sure it was true in Judy's case. 'I like your boutique.'

'Do you? Eddie – he's my husband – he says there's not much money in it. And he's right. He's always right. But I like this place. I really do like it.'

'I can see that.'

The bell over the door rang, and a young woman with a little girl in tow entered. The woman smiled courteously, then wandered off to the other side to browse through some hand-knitted sweaters.

'Just yell if you need any help,' Judy said.

'Thank you.'

Teri shifted from one foot to the other, suddenly feeling like an imposition. 'Well, I don't want to take too much of your time.'

'Don't be silly.'

'I heard you had a little girl.'

'Yeah, she's three. Her name's Genevieve. You think that sounds stuck-up? Eddie's mother says it sounds like some prissy little European duchess.'

'No, I like it.'

'Yeah, me too.' Judy pulled a black jumper with a pink cotton T-shirt out from the nearest rack and studied it absently. 'At least I didn't name her Moon Shadow, huh?'

'I'm sure she'll appreciate that when she gets older.'

'She better.'

Another customer came in. She looked to be someone who had shopped here before. She was wearing a stretch, twill jumper with mock belt buckle and an acrylic knit T-shirt with padded shoulders. It was a Nineties twist on the Sixties revival that had only recently come into style.

Judy put the outfit she had been studying back on the rack, and smiled at the woman. 'Let me know if you need any help.'

The woman smiled in return, without saying anything.

'It's getting busy.'

'We have our moments.'

'Well, I won't keep you,' Teri said. 'I just wanted to see you, and see how you've been doing. Find out if you've been in touch with any of the old crowd.'

'A few. Most everyone scattered, you know.'

'Did they?'

Judy nodded, browsing through the rack as if she were looking for something for herself or maybe something she could put aside for when Genevieve was older. 'Oh, yeah. Jack moved out to Boston to run a restaurant with his brother. I haven't talked to him in over a year. And Jeremy followed Michelle out to Chicago. They got married and had a little girl who must be twelve or thirteen now.'

'You kept track of everyone?' Teri said.

'Yeah, most everyone.'

'How come I never heard from you?'

'I sent you a card when your son disappeared,' she said, looking up, surprised. It was very nearly a look of accusation, and Teri felt herself immediately fighting off the guilt. 'And I called, maybe half a dozen times. I always got your answering machine, though. You never called back.'

Teri remembered those calls now, though only vaguely. There had been literally hundreds and hundreds of calls for several months after Gabe's disappearance. People offering their condolences. Psychics claiming they'd had a vision. Cranks who seemed to always call in the middle of the night with something sick to say. After a couple of days, she had quit answering the phone, and Michael had taken over the duty of listening to the messages.

'It was a terribly difficult time,' she said, defensively.

'I can't imagine how horrible that was. To lose your son like that.'

'I'm sorry I never called you back.'

'It's all right,' Judy said. 'I understood. I just wanted to let you know that my thoughts were with you.'

'That was nice of you.'

She smiled, modestly. 'You ever miss the old days?'

'Sometimes,' Teri said. It wasn't often, though. The music usually brought it back for her, when she'd hear *I Ain't Marching Anymore* by Phil Ochs or *Here Comes The Sun* by Richie Havens or *Big Yellow Taxi* by Joni Mitchell. The world had been a different place then. Time had moved slower. Life had been bigger and brighter, somehow. If she had it all to do over again, she'd do it exactly the same. But she didn't miss those days, not really, and how odd that seemed.

'I still long for them,' Judy said.

'Do you?'

'I guess what I miss most is the feeling of family we had.'

'Me, too,' Teri said. She thought how crazy the circle of life could be. The little girl she had once been was hardly more than a dream now, another spirit belonging to someone else's past. And it wasn't much different when she thought back to those high school and college years, either. The memories were fond, but they were memories pasted in a photo album, and sometimes when you flipped through them, it was hard to recognize yourself. She remembered the sense of family, though. *That* had never left her.

'What happened to us?' Teri said.

'I don't know. I guess we changed.'

'It feels like a waste, doesn't it?'

'Sometimes.'

The young woman and the little girl walked by, on their way out. They paused briefly at a rack near the front window, then the bell rang again and the woman held the door open for her daughter.

'Thanks for coming,' Judy said.

The woman smiled.

The door closed.

Judy pulled out a two-piece jacket dress, black with turquoise, and padded shoulders. She held it up, pressed against her body. 'What do you think? Too simple?'

'Not at all.'

'Good. I like simple. But I like elegant, too.' She replaced the outfit and nodded to herself, as if she had finally come to a decision of some sort. 'How about if I get you some phone numbers and addresses?'

'The old gang?'

'Yeah.'

'You'll never know how much that would be appreciated.'

'Maybe we could throw a reunion one of these days? What do you think? You think anyone would come?'

'It worked for Woodstock.'

Judy smiled. 'Yeah, I guess it did, didn't it? I'll be right back. Just give me a second. My address book's on the desk.'

'No rush,' Teri said. She wandered across the room and browsed through a rack of sweat suits, finding a pink shirt with kittens on it and a matching plaid design that went great with gray sweat pants. It came in a medium or a large junior. She took out the large and held it up, thinking it looked better than anything she had bought for herself in a long, long time. The price was a very reasonable thirty-five dollars. It would be the least she could do, she thought, after all the help Judy had offered.

The pager went off.

Walt had given it to her this morning on his way out the door. He had picked it up over a year ago, he said, so his clients could get hold of him on the spur of the moment. This was only the second time he had actually used it, though.

Teri glanced down at the strange vibration at her hip. The phone number where Walt was calling from was listed at the top of the black box. It wasn't a familiar number. She turned the pager off, and carried the outfit she had chosen over to the cash register.

Judy came back a moment later with her address book waving in one hand. 'I never realized how many of us came up from the Bay Area. Did you know there were almost thirty of us?'

'No,' Teri said, surprised at the number. It had never felt like that large a group. Now, looking back, she found it rather amazing that they all got along as well as they did. If the years had taught her anything, they had taught her that relationships were infinitely more complicated than you ever thought they were.

'Listen, Judy, I've got a page. I was wondering if you had a phone I could use?'

'Oh, sure. It's in the back, right around the corner, on your right.' Judy handed her the address book. 'Here, why don't you take this with you. There's paper and pencils in the upper right hand drawer of the desk. Go ahead and pull out whatever names and addresses you need.'

'You're a blessing, Judy. And I want that outfit on the counter.'

'You don't have to—'

'I want to. It's a nice outfit, especially the kittens on the shirt.'

In the back, Teri pulled out a chair and sat down at the desk. She dialed the number on the pager, and waited for someone to pick up the other end.

'Walt's Fake and Bake. We fake it, you bake it.'

'You better have something more than that to say.'

'Well, if it isn't little Miss Sunshine.'

'Walt, I thought you were only going to page me if it was something important?'

'This is important. I needed to make sure the pager was working.'

'Well, where are you?'

'In a phone booth across the street from the clinic. Our Dr Childs, being the true conscientious professional that he is, has been conducting business as usual all morning.'

'Nothing new at all then, huh?'

'Nope. Sorry. How 'bout on your end?'

Teri picked up the address book and and turned it over in her hands. 'I'm still at the boutique. Judy's given me a good list of phone numbers, though. I think I'll head back to the apartment and call from there.'

'No more fears about the place being bugged?'

'No, I think you were probably right. They got Gabe. That's who they really wanted.'

'We're going to find him this time, Teri.'

'God, I hope you're right.'

'And it isn't going to take ten years, I promise.'

81

Walt had known it would be wearisome. That was the nature of the beast. Any kind of investigative work requiring a stakeout was going to be wearisome. You had to like cramped spaces and eating on the run and talk radio. You had to live and breathe and sleep on someone else's schedule. Your time was their time. Walt had always found it to be like that. This was proving to be no exception.

Childs had left the house a little after seven-thirty this morning and had arrived at the clinic just before eight. He had taken a different route this time, down Fremont and over to El Camino West. That was an unusual thing for a man to do. Most people preferred to stick to their routines. It might mean nothing at all, of course. Childs might simply be a man who liked to keep the scenery in his life fresh and imaginative. Or it might indicate a little paranoia, which would be an interesting touch. But what concerned Walt the most was that it might indicate that Childs suspected he was being followed. That would be an interesting touch of a different nature.

The car windows were down, and a lazy afternoon breeze filtered through.

Walt glanced up from his newspaper, looked at the back door of the clinic, then went back to reading about US Air Flight 427 that had crashed last night outside of Pittsburgh. It had been a quiet morning at the clinic. Maybe half-a-dozen patients had come through. The last had been a woman who looked to be in her early sixties and in fine health. She had left nearly twenty minutes ago and no one else had come or gone since.

It was one-fifteen now.

Walt dropped the paper again and debated about running

around the corner and grabbing a hamburger at the Bartel's Drive-Thru. If he hurried, it shouldn't take any longer than ten minutes, over and back. But of course, he knew what would happen if he left. As soon as he rounded the corner, Childs would come bounding out and climb into his Buick. He would be off and running then, and Walt would be left with a full stomach and no idea where the good doctor had gone. Wasn't that the way it always went?

'Come on, doc. Take me to your leader.'

That was the hope.

The truth of the matter was that Walt couldn't even be certain there was a leader. He carried no doubts that Childs was involved somehow. Teri had done well in putting that much to bed. But how the rest of it fitted – that was still anybody's guess at this point.

The back door to the clinic slowly swung open.

Walt sat up, feeling an instant surge of adrenaline.

''Bout time.'

Childs emerged, carrying a briefcase in one hand. It was the same briefcase he had brought from home this morning, and Walt wondered if that meant the good doctor's day at the clinic had officially concluded. Childs crossed the lot and climbed into his Buick.

Walt rolled up the windows.

'Come on, make it worth my while, you turkey.'

He had no idea how worth his while it would actually turn out to be.

82

Teri sank back on the couch, feeling tired. Her neck ached. She had slept on it wrong last night and gradually throughout the day it had grown stiffer and stiffer. It didn't help that Gabe had been out there somewhere, on his own, for nearly five days now.

'Uh-huh,' she said, switching the phone from one ear to the other.

She was talking to Peter Brenner, one of the old college gang. She'd had a crush on Peter once, in her sophomore year before she'd met Michael. It had never gone anywhere. Peter had his eyes on Drew. They were married now, with four children, two boys and two girls. Their first daughter, Kala, as Teri had just learned had become one of the disappeared in April '85, less than a month after Gabe's disappearance. Kala had never returned home.

'I'm sorry. I'm trying to get this straight in my mind. Where were you and Drew living when Kala disappeared?'

'That was about a year after we first moved to Houston.'

'And you hadn't been back this way?'

'No,' Peter said. 'Still haven't. Drew's parents are out here and we've kind of settled in like natives. Except for that Southern drawl, which I think we've both come to envy.'

'Sounds wonderful.'

'It has been. Everything except for Kala.'

Teri hadn't told him yet about Gabe, and she wasn't sure she was going to. You never put it completely out of your mind when you lost a child. One way or another, it was always with you. But some days were better than others, and it sounded to Teri as if Peter and Drew had managed to handle their loss as well as any two people could be expected. Teri didn't want to pop that bubble. And she didn't want to add any false hopes to it, either.

'You ever see anyone from the old days?' she asked.

'No, not really. Drew and Judy write back and forth, but that's about it.'

'Who's your family doctor?'

'Oh, well, there's someone I guess we still see. It's Childs. You remember him from college?'

'Yeah, I remember.'

'He's got a clinic out here.'

'Really?'

'It's a small, general practice that he set up shortly after we arrived.'

'Were you a little surprised to see him out here?'

'Amazed. He said he had some relatives here and had decided the old saying was true: there was no place like home.'

Teri's pager went off, sending a tingling vibration into her hip. She glanced down at it, wondering briefly if something was up or if Walt was just testing her again. She shut it off.

'I've got a call I better take,' she said.

'Sorry you missed Drew. I know she would have loved to talk to you.'

'Well, maybe next time.'

'That would be nice.'

'Peter, one more thing before I have to go.'

'Yeah?'

'Do you take all your kids to Dr Childs?'
'Sure do.'

83

The phone rang and Walt grabbed it immediately. 'Teri?'
'Is everything all right?'
'You'll never guess where I am.'
'Where?'
Walt turned and looked out across the gateway. A businessman, dressed in a dark blue suit and carrying a briefcase, passed by. He was followed by a couple of teenage boys who stopped at the newsstand across the way and leafed through the current issue of *Playboy*.'
'The airport,' Walt said.
'What are you doing there?'
'Believe it or not, I'm on my way to Chicago.' He shook his head, then glanced down at the ticket in his hand. It was a 3:30 flight to O'Hare. Absently, he tapped the corner of the document against the metal face plate of the phone. 'Ever been to Chicago?'
'No.'
'Me, neither. Guess there's a first time for everything.'
'What's going on, Walt?'
'I'm not sure exactly.' He glanced across the way at the seating area, while Childs was reading a newspaper and waiting for the boarding call. 'Childs knocked off early this afternoon and now he's on his way to Chicago. I just thought I'd go along for the ride, that's all.'
'He's got another clinic in Houston.'
'You're kidding.'
'No. I just got done talking to an old friend of mine. Apparently, Childs followed them to Houston and set up a clinic there. He's been taking care of their kids, Walt. And their oldest one, a girl – her name is Kala – she's been missing almost as long as Gabe.'
'Christ.'
'I'm beginning to hate this man, Walt. He's been doing something awful to our children. I don't know what it is exactly, but . . .' She sounded as if she might break down and cry. There was a long pause, then a deep breath. 'We've got to stop him.'
'We will.'
'No, I mean now. We've got to stop him *now*.'

'Teri, we don't know enough. Not yet.' Walt stuffed the ticket back into his pocket and checked to see if Childs had moved. He hadn't, though he *had* set the newspaper aside and appeared a little anxious all of a sudden. 'We still don't know where he's keeping Gabe.'

'Well, it's got to be somewhere local.'

'Not necessarily. For all we know, he could be holding him anywhere in the country. In Houston or Chicago. Anywhere. And we still have no way of finding out, not yet at least.'

There was complete silence on the other end.

Walt switched ears. 'Teri?'

'Yeah,' she whispered, clearly unhappy.

'Hey, listen to me. I know this is hard, but you've got to hang in there. We're getting closer to him, Teri. I'm telling you, his time's running out, and sooner or later he's going to lead us right to Gabe. But you've got to be patient.'

'I've *been* patient.'

'I know you have, but you've got to be more patient, you understand? If we spook him now, we're risking our only connection to Gabe, and I know that's not what you want.'

'Of course not.'

'Then hang in with me, okay?'

'I will.'

'Good.' Walt glanced across the boarding area and noticed that Childs was standing in line now. It was still twenty minutes to take-off. 'They're starting to board. I better get going. Are you gonna be all right?'

'Yeah, I'll be fine.'

'Okay.' He pulled the ticket back out of his pocket, searching for something else to say, something that might help her to hang in a little longer. But what was there to say? She had been going through this roller-coaster of a nightmare for ten long years now. She knew the turns, the ups and downs, and far better than him, she knew how to keep herself on track. 'Oh, there is one last thing.'

'What's that?'

'Your friend, the one who gave you the lead to Houston, did she have anyone living in the Chicago area?'

'Let me check.'

The boarding line stretched around the outer edges of the room. It was going to be a full flight. Walt watched Childs move forward in line, one step at a time, like a good little soldier. *That's what you are, isn't it*? he thought. *A little soldier, following orders.*

Teri came back on the line. 'I don't know if it's the Chicago area or not, but Jeremy and Michelle are in St. Charles.'

'Great. You better give me their address and phone number in case I need it.'

84

In the Sixties, endocrinologists began to understand the true nature of chemical messengers in assisting the release of hormones in the body. It wasn't long after that, that we were able to synthesize these chemical messengers and thus trigger specific hormonal reactions. Somatostatin, which inhibits the pituitary growth hormone, is an example of these messengers. Today, we can already see synthetics playing a role in everything from diabetes control to fertility drugs.

More recently, as we've come to discover the role that our genes play in the natural process of aging, we have to wonder how much longer it will be before similar synthetics will be used to artificially trigger the functions of these genes. It is not outside the realm of possibility that by the end of this century we will be able to manipulate the on/off switches responsible for the onset of aging.

We may, in fact, actually be able to cease the human aging process.

Dr Timothy Childs
University of California, Berkeley
1975

85

They landed at O'Hare twenty minutes late due to a strong head wind. Childs didn't leave his seat the entire flight, and seemed in no particular hurry to get off once the plane had touched down. He calmly collected his briefcase from the overhead storage compartment and stood in line like everyone else.

It was after one in the morning by the time they were both out of the airport. Childs rented a new Buick and took I-90 westbound past Rolling Meadows, Schaumburg, Barrington and into Elgin, where he exited at Route 25 and drove south into a place called St. Charles. Walt followed along behind, trying to stay awake, in a Ford Taurus.

They ended up on the east side of town off Route 63 on Kirk

Road. It was primarily an area of corporate and industrial parks, places like the Coca Cola bottling plant and the DuPage Airport and the Norris Cultural Arts Center. At the very outskirts, set well back from the street and hidden behind a wall of trees and shrubbery, was a building called the Devol Research Foundation.

Childs pulled into the lot and parked near the front entrance.

Walt passed by, not wanting to be noticed. He circled the block twice, then came back and stopped near the mouth of the long driveway. A scattering of lights gave shape to the building in the distance. In front, parked under the only light in the lot, Walt spotted the rented Buick. It wasn't likely the good doctor would be going anywhere soon. He was probably going to spend the night here.

'Which means *I* need a place to sleep,' Walt muttered to himself.

86

'How have things been?' Childs asked.

'Fine, sir.'

'Any changes?'

'No, sir. None.'

He stood at the back of the elevator, admiring the woman's near-perfect form. Her name was Pam, or more formally, Pamela Sergeant, and she was thirty-seven years old. She had been running this facility for nearly ten years now, overseeing a full-time, skeletal staff of four. Three of those under her watchful eye maintained the monitoring system, the fourth served as the receptionist and public liaison. Four times a year, for a period of two weeks, a team of lab technicians were brought in to work upstairs. It was Pam's job to supervise them as well, and to make sure the Foundation kept an overall low profile, while they continued to collect and preserve project data.

'Everything set for tomorrow?'

'As always.'

The elevator came to a stop at the basement level. The doors slid open and there was a long dark hallway in front of them, the only source of light coming from two seventy-five-watt bulbs over the doorway at the far end. 'After you, Dr Childs.'

'No, please.'

She nodded, officiously, and led him down the hall to the far door, where she fumbled with the ring of keys dangling from the belt of her skirt. She had used one of the keys to enter the elevator, another to access the basement, and now she used a third key to unlock the door. She stepped aside.

Childs stepped through.

On the other side, three more doors sided the small square room. Pam glanced questioningly at Childs, who pointed to the door on the right. The face-plate on the door said: KARMA SIX. Pam sorted through her key ring, came up with the right key, and unlocked the door.

'Any changes at all?' Childs asked as he stepped through.

'Nothing,' Pam said.

The room was long and narrow, with a line of beds on each side. Not all the beds were occupied. In fact, most of them were stripped of their sheets and buried beneath a blanket of shadows, clearly indicating that they were empty. But of the seven that *were* occupied, all seven had been occupied for a good long time now, and they were all occupied by children.

Childs stopped at the foot of the first bed, glanced through the chart, then hung it over the frame again. The girl in the bed was eight years old. Her name was Rebecca Wright and she had been eight years old for nearly ten years now. She had also been comatose.

He went to her bedside and pulled the covers back, exposing her legs. Even with the daily routine of manipulating and massaging the muscles, the legs had lost some of their mass. Not enough to cause concern, though.

'She's stabilized at fifty-five pounds,' Childs noted.

'Yes, she has.'

'That's remarkable when you think about it.'

'Is it?'

'Oh, yes.' He dropped the bed sheet back in place, and checked the girl's pupils as a matter of routine. There was no reason to believe there would be any change and of course he found none. Still, after what had happened with the Knight boy, he had cautioned the staff at each of the centers to keep a closer eye on any changes in a child's condition. No one wanted to take anything for granted.

'All it would take is a couple of weeks of physical therapy and strengthening and she'd be up and around, almost like new.'

'That *is* remarkable,' Pam said.

'Yes, indeed. You've done a fine job here, Pam.'

'Thank you, sir.'

He moved down the line of occupied beds, one at a time, going through the same routine of first checking their charts, then their pupils. No change. Not a single hint of change anywhere in the room. It had been this way for years now.

The comas had swept through nearly half of the participants of the research study in less than a month. It had taken that long to link the protracted unconsciousness to the administration of an experimental drug called AA103. Use of the drug had been halted immediately.

At first, Childs thought the mishap would prove to be the end of the Karma Project. But he managed to convince DC that they had nothing to lose by monitoring the children another six months. As it turned out, it was a lucky thing they hadn't scrapped the study after all. In those six months, not a single child, not one, demonstrated a single sign of growth or aging. It was the result they had been chasing all along and suddenly they had it. Somehow, they had managed to halt the aging process. The only glitch, and it was still a glitch to this very day, was that they didn't know how they had done it.

At the last bed, Childs nodded and dropped the bed sheet back over the boy's legs. The children had always been well cared for. Their fingernails and toenails were clipped, their hair groomed, their bodies washed. They were fed a high-protein, vitamin-rich solution that helped them maintain their body mass, and there wasn't a child in the study who wasn't within five or six pounds of what was the natural weight for his age and height.

'Ever wonder what would happen if one of them came out of the sleep?' Childs asked casually. He stopped just outside the room and waited as Pam locked the door again behind them.

'I'm not sure I understand what you mean, sir.'

'We have a room full of ageless children, Pam. As far as we can tell, they're ageless because the coma has somehow suspended a process which we've always believed was unalterable. Have you ever wondered what would happen to that process once the coma ended?'

'No, sir. I can't say that I have.'

'I hadn't, either. Not until recently.'

87

'Wake you?'

Teri opened an eye to the clock on the night-stand. She groaned and rolled over on her side, away from the luminous dial. 'No, I'm always wide awake at three-thirty in the morning. I like to get up early so I don't miss anything.'

'Sorry,' Walt said. 'I just thought I'd better check in.'

'Where are you?'

'In a dumpy motel on the outskirts of St Charles.'

'You're kidding.' Both eyes opened and Teri sat up on one elbow. She wiped away what little sleep was left. 'I just talked to Michelle tonight. It's the same thing, Walt. Just like the others. They had a baby girl. Her name was Rebecca. She was eight years old when she disappeared.'

'It keeps getting more interesting, doesn't it?'

'We've got him, Walt. Everywhere this guy goes another kid disappears.'

'We're definitely getting there.'

'Jesus, what more do you want?'

'I'm not sure,' Walt said, his voice suddenly subdued. 'I guess I'm feeling a little confused about what went on with you and our good doctor back in your college days. Was that all he was to your group of friends? Just the guy who ran the off-campus health clinic?'

'No,' Teri said, finally coming fully awake. She had forgotten to tell him about her conversation with Peggy the other morning. 'No, there was more than that. I didn't know this until a couple of days ago, when I was talking to Peggy. There was a drug that was going around then... I mean, well, there were lots of drugs that were going around, but this one was different. It was called Genesis, and it was something of an hallucinogen, not much different than LSD if I remember correctly.'

'You're lucky you still have a brain, you know that?'

Oh, she knew it all right. She knew it better than most. Michael Jacobson hadn't been so lucky. They called him Michael the Second because he joined the group a few months after Michael the First. Teri had married Michael the First. After they had married, they had decided to have children, and once they had made the decision to have children they had quietly moved out of the drug scene, giving up everything from Genesis to LSD to pot.

Having children wasn't their only reason for quitting, though. Several weeks before, Michael the Second had taken the kind of trip that very few people ever came back from. He had never come back from it, either. As far as Teri knew, he was still swimming in a world of nightmares and twisted images. He was staying at Agnew State Hospital the last she heard. That was before it had changed to the Agnew Developmental Center. Now, whenever she was in the City, she would search the faces of the panhandlers and the schizophrenics who were out on the street, looking lost. But as far as she knew, Michael the Second had become a faceless soul by now, one of the disappeared, living in a strange alienated world that belonged only to him.

'Yeah, I know,' Teri said sadly. 'Anyway, what's important is that Peggy told me Childs was the only supplier for the drug.'

'For Genesis?'

'Yeah.'

Walt fell suddenly quiet on the other end of the line. Teri reached for the lamp on the night-stand, behind the clock. The room brightened. It felt like an old sweatshirt, soft and familiar, and Teri realized she had begun to feel comfortable here.

'Walt?'

'You know what this probably means, don't you?'

'What?'

'Teri, this guy wasn't trying to help you enjoy a little recreational mind tripping. He was using you. You and your friends, you guys were all guinea pigs. That's how this whole thing got started. I'd bet the ranch on it.'

'Oh, no,' Teri said softly. She took in a breath that felt cold and foreign, then expelled it as quickly as she could. The next breath came out a little harder. 'And whatever it was he did to us, we passed it down to the children.'

'I'm sorry,' Walt said.,

'How could anyone . . .' The thought fell away naturally, because there was no sensible way to finish it. Some things, some people, simply defied understanding. It wasn't bad enough that this man had kidnapped their children, he had somehow managed to poison them as well.

Except that wasn't entirely the truth, was it? If she were going to be honest with herself, there was a point here where Teri needed to take responsibility for her own misdeeds. The late Sixties and early Seventies had been her playground, a time of naïveté and taking chances. It was Woodstock and *Easy Rider*. Don't trust anyone over thirty. And bumper stickers that said: *Tomorrow is canceled due to a lack of interest.* She had played recklessly and with abandon, as had Michael and most of their friends. But it was Gabe who was paying the price.

So, yes, she hated what Childs had done – what he was *still* doing – but there was little saving grace for what she had done as well.

'What do we do now?' Teri asked.

'Take a look in the bottom drawer of the night-stand and see if there's a phone book in there. I want you to look up the Devol Research Foundation. See if they happen to have a local listing.'

The phone book was buried beneath a stack of old *Time* magazines. Teri dug it out and spent a minute or two thumbing through the yellow pages, wondering in the back of her mind where Walt had stumbled across the name Devol. 'What do you want me to look under?'

'You better try the white pages.'

'Devol? Right? D-e-v-o-l?'

'Yeah.'

When she couldn't find it under Devol, she tried Devole, and then finally Devoule. The results were all the same. The closest she came was Devon's Dry Cleaning, off Hartnell Avenue. 'Sorry, I can't find anything even close. A research foundation, you said, right?'

'Yeah,' Walt said, the disappointment clear in his voice. 'I thought we might be onto something there. Just to make sure, after you hang up will you do me a favor and call the operator and see if maybe she has a listing?'

'Sure,' Teri said. She opened the top drawer of the night-stand and rummaged through the books and old magazines until she came up with a pencil and a piece of paper. On the paper, she wrote DEVOL RESEARCH FOUNDATION in bold, block lettering. 'So what's this place supposed to be?'

'It's where we ended up after our flight. Childs went straight there, like a spaniel to water. There's not much to see from the street. It looks like just another business building from the outside.'

'Maybe it is.'

'Now there's a story for the papers. Idiot private eye tails suspect halfway across the country while the suspect attends a seminar on the proper filing of Medicare forms. God, it better be more than just a business building.'

Teri grinned, and it struck her how lucky she was to have this man on her side. He had, indeed, just flown halfway across the country for her. How many people did she know who would do that for her? Only one that she could think of.

'Go to bed, Walt.'

'Why? Am I starting to sound crabby?'

'Definitely.'

88

Teri did as she had promised.

After she hung up, she called directory assistance and told the operator that she needed a number for the Devol Research Foundation in the 9-1-6 area code. The clickety-clackety patter of computer keys sounded in the background.

'Could you please spell that?'

'D-e-v-o-l,' Teri said.

'I'm sorry. I have no listing for the Devol Research Foundation.'

'Could it be an unlisted number?'

'As I said, I have no such listing.'

'In other words, you can't tell me.'

'That's correct.'

Teri stewed on that after she'd hung up. It wasn't as if she had asked to speak to the President. She didn't even need to know what the number was, just that the damn thing existed. If the number existed, the Foundation existed.

Sleep had gone the way of the Ford Edsel; it was a thing of the past, now.

She threw back the covers, started to get up, then fell back again. It had suddenly occurred to her: what if the converse was true? If the Foundation existed, then the phone number must exist.

Two calls later, she had learned this much: there was no listing for the Foundation in Houston, and there was no listing in St Charles, either. Which meant they were keeping an absurdly low profile for a Research Foundation. And it meant something else, too. Even though there were no listings in Houston or here, locally, that didn't eliminate the possibility that there were offices in both places.

89

Someone had cracked the mirror.

Walt stood in front of it, yawned, and splashed some water on his face. His reflection was a montage of fractured features: an eyebrow here, a sliver of nose there. It was the composite of a man's entire life, and that's what made it so frightening.

He stared at the Picasso-like reflection, transfixed by its alienness, until he couldn't resist reaching out to it. The tip of his finger slid across the cool, smooth surface of the glass until it came to the jagged edge of a crack. The crack instantly sealed. Two of the pieces of the montage fused together. One piece, the shape of a scissors' blade, was made of loose flesh, dimpled and unshaven. The other piece, shaped something more like a domino, was soft and firm.

Another crack sealed itself.

Two pieces of an eye came together. One side bright and alive, with a dilated pupil and a light blue, mesmerizing color. The other side was dull and lifeless, the color of an old cup of black coffee.

Another crack sealed.

Two pieces of a nose melded together, neither one belonging to the other. They were two incompatible pieces, only barely recognizable as part of a nose.

Walt felt his insides tighten.

Then another crack.

Two more pieces of a nose this time. One, shaped like the crescent of a moon, clearly belonged to a young boy, its color pinkish-white and unblemished. The other had spent too many days in the sun, the flesh dark and peeling.

Another crack.

Bits and pieces of a mouth. The middle of an upper lip, softly lined and beaded with sweat. The corner of a bashful smile, curved gently upward, nearly invisible if you weren't looking close enough.

Another.

The face had become a patch quilt of faces, a hundred bits and pieces taken from here and there. This boy at age nine with red hair and freckles. That boy at age eleven with blond hair and blue eyes. This man in his early twenties with furrowed eyebrows and a constant frown. That man in his late teens with cold steel eyes and a straight mouth and a preoccupation that drifted past the curiosity of anyone trying to see inside.

They were all him.

And none of them were him.

Walt screamed and buried his face in his hands. He came awake suddenly, sat up in bed and found himself in a night sweat that had literally soaked through his pillow. With a corner of the sheet, he wiped the perspiration away from his face. A quake went dancing through his upper body, and he held himself.

It would be fifteen or twenty minutes before his heart would settle down again and he would realize where he was and what had happened. Dream or not, though, he would not be able to fall back to sleep again.

Because they were all him.
And he knew it.

90

It appeared very much as if it had been prearranged.

School was out and the park had started to fill with children. Walt parked near the picnic tables not far from where the youngest children were swinging on the swings and building castles out of sand. Across the park, near the baseball diamond, Childs sat in the bleachers, shading his eyes against the afternoon sun. He had a woman in his company this afternoon. She appeared to be in her mid-to-late thirties, her hair cut short in front. She was wearing a modest, gray pants suit that seemed somewhat out of place here at the park on a sunny day.

Walt climbed out of the car and moved over to sit at one of the picnic tables. An old oak tree provided a canopy of branches and leaves, blocking out all but a few tiny patches of sunlight. Behind him, a little girl screamed with delight as she came down the slide and was caught at the bottom by her mother. This was the way it was supposed to be, Walt thought. Children playing with their sand castles, thrilling at their new rides, not a care in the world. Children weren't supposed to have cares. Those were for the adults, the ones who had forgotten what it was like to be children.

He noticed the initials carved into the corner of the picnic table. DE. Nothing else. No postscript above love. No misshapen heart. No giant plus sign connecting the initials to another pair of initials. Not even a hint as to whether a boy or a girl had done the carving, though Walt assumed it had been a boy. It seemed like the kind of thing a boy would do without thinking. Some hot summer afternoon when nothing was going on and no one else seemed to be around, the knife had come out almost unconsciously and an hour had passed.

He looked up and watched Childs nudge the woman next to him and point across the park to the snack bar. The snack bar was closed for the winter. A crudely painted sign the size of a kitchen window made that perfectly clear. But it wasn't the snack bar that had caught the doctor's interest. It was the small group of boys that had congregated next to the snack bar.

They weren't doing much, just hanging around like kids did. A couple of them had shown up on bikes, most of the others had apparently made the journey on foot. A girl with beautiful brown hair, an oversized sweatshirt and a nose-ring, laughed loud enough so that Walt could hear her. The boy next to her laughed, too. He reached into the pocket of his shirt and offered her a cigarette. She nodded and they passed one back and forth while Walt watched.

He couldn't be certain, but he didn't think there was a kid in the group who was over the age of fifteen. It was hard to tell these days. Kids were always in such a hurry to act older than they were. What was it that was so damn appealing about being an adult, anyway? He didn't think he'd ever understand that.

Across the way, the woman asked Childs a question. He nodded and offered her a hand as she climbed to her feet. She made her way down the bleachers one cautious step at a time, again seeming curiously out of place here. This was not a place she came during her off hours.

She strolled across the park and loitered around the grassy area near the restrooms. This was maybe within thirty feet of the group of kids, close enough to be noticed but not so close that she seemed conspicuous or threatening. It was hard to imagine her as threatening anyway. She was a tiny woman. It wouldn't take much to quell any trouble she might kick up.

Two of the kids broke off from the group. They kept talking as they backpedaled off the gravel and onto the grass, then they turned around and started off in Walt's direction. The next kid to wander away looked to be in his early teens, no older than fourteen at most. He raised his hand and pointed apologetically toward the bathrooms, then nodded and started in that direction.

Almost immediately, the woman took notice.

Whatever it is, it's going down, Walt thought.

She moved across the grass, not seeming in any particular hurry. That was because everything had to be timed. A moment or two late and she might miss bumping into him. But a moment or two early and suddenly she risked becoming conspicuous. She would have to stop and wait and then it would be obvious to anyone paying attention that she was waiting for him. No, she took her sweet time, but she took it in such a way that she crossed the boy's path at just the right moment.

Walt stood and stretched, trying to appear casual in his movements.

The two kids, who had been the first to leave the group, passed in front of him. One of them was rattling on zealously about a group called the *Cranes*. It seemed he liked the moods they left him with, though Walt wasn't sure if he had heard that part correctly or not. He went and stood near the barbecue pit, focusing his attention instead on what was going on across the way.

The woman stepped onto the walkway, turned and brushed past her target. Their encounter lasted only a matter of a couple of seconds and then it was over. A snap of the fingers. Just like that. All she had done, as near as Walt could tell, was put her hand on the boy's shoulder and whisper something to him. What she had whispered, Walt had no idea. But it couldn't have been more than a word or two.

The boy gave no noticeable acknowledgement; he simply stayed on course to the bathroom. The woman stayed on a course of her own. She circled around the perimeter of the park and again joined Childs in the bleachers.

What the hell was that all about?

Maybe nothing.

No, it was about something. Walt just didn't understand it yet.

The boy emerged from the bathroom and stood at the entrance a moment, looking lost. He shaded his eyes against the sun, glancing across the grass to where his friends were still huddled together, talking. And then he did a curious thing. He turned and went the other direction.

Suddenly Walt found himself in a quandary. He watched the kid disappear behind the foliage at the far side of the park, then edged around the barbecue pit, out onto the grass. Childs and the woman had not budged from their spot in the bleachers. Whatever or *who*ever they were waiting for, their wait was still on. And that left Walt with a decision to make. Follow the boy or join the wait.

A bird in the hand, he told himself.

But his instincts told him otherwise. Childs had come here for a reason. He had not flown out from California so he could simply sit in the bleachers at the park and watch the children play. No, he had come here to make contact, and the boy was the contactee, so to speak.

Decision made.

Walt cut across the picnic area, around the outer edges of the ball field and slipped out through the wall of oak-leaf hydrangea at the far side. The boy had crossed the street half a block up. His hands were jammed into the front pockets of his jeans, which were at least four inches too large around the waist and held up by nothing more than a length of rope. He did not appear to be a boy with a mission. His head hung low as he shuffled along in no apparent hurry.

Walt kept a safe distance.

At the next corner, the boy turned right and continued on his odyssey through the suburban territories. And maybe this wasn't such a good idea after all. If you followed half-a-dozen regular kids walking down the street, this one would blend in seamlessly, a chameleon with all the right colors, all the right moves. He was invisible if you weren't looking, reticent if you weren't listening. He was a thousand other kids, a single faceless child. All of these and none of these.

So what was going on here?

Why was he tailing the kid?

They moved in make-believe tandem three blocks down, two blocks over until the boy stopped outside a small, cubby-hole-of-a-store set back from the street. It was shouldered on one side by a coffee shop called Mimi's and a Coin-Operated Laundromat on the other. The boy raised his head and read the sign over the store. It read: *The Book Mark. New and Used Books. Buy or Trade.*

This was where he had come.

He sat on a reading bench outside the bookstore, his hands out of his pockets and clasped behind his head now. He crossed his legs in front of him and stretched and stared off into the endless blue dreams of the afternoon sky.

Walt went on by and got himself a window table at Mimi's, where he could keep an eye on things without looking as if he were keeping an eye on them. He ordered a slice of lemon-meringue pie and a Diet Coke, then sat back and watched.

A few minutes later, a girl, who looked to be a couple of years older than the boy – maybe sixteen or seventeen, it was hard to tell these days – came down the same street, in the same direction. She was dressed in jeans with holes in the knees and an oversized sweat shirt with the sleeves rolled up above the elbows. Sunlight glistened off a string of four earrings dangling from her left ear.

She stopped and looked up at the sign over the bookstore, the one that said: *The Book Mark*. Like the boy, she was apparently satisfied that she had found her way to the right place. She sat on the bench opposite him, curled protectively into the little space afforded her.

As far as Walt could tell, they didn't exchange a glance or a word or any other form of communication that might indicate they knew each other. They sat like two strangers sharing a park bench out of necessity, neither liking nor disliking the need. And perhaps that was what they were. Two strangers. Walt had no way of knowing for sure.

It was another fifteen minutes before the third one came along.

Walt hadn't recognized the girl from the park, and he didn't recognize this second boy, either. The kid sat between the other two, his arms folded defiantly across his chest, his gaze faraway and out of touch.

Walt finished his pie. He wiped his mouth and downed the last of the Diet Coke. This was beginning to get interesting now. Three kids, all in their teens, parked on a bench outside a bookstore, waiting. Waiting for what? was the question.

Childs, of course. They're waiting for the good Dr Childs to come and pick them up and take them back to the Devol Research Foundation. That's what they're waiting for. Only they don't know it, do they? That's what the laying-on of hands and the whispering was all about. It was the Pied Piper piping. And now the children are all in a line, waiting to follow the music wherever it takes them.

Walt crumpled up his napkin and sat back in the booth. He didn't have to wait long before Childs and the woman showed up, only a couple of minutes. The doctor was punctual if nothing else. He pulled up to the curb and without a word, the three kids climbed off the bench and into the back seat of the car. Nothing to it. It was that easy, that quick, that inconspicuous.

Slick was the word that came to Walt's mind as he watched the car pull out into the street again.

The man was slick.

91

The empty elevator car, which had been parked on the top floor where all the lab work was being done, started its slow descent toward the basement. It would take several more days before all the test results would be completed. By then, Childs would be back in California. In fact, he had a ticket on the redeye heading out tonight. Pam would be faxing him the prelims when they were available, and if there were any surprises – which he had no reason to expect – then she'd express the samples to him. That had only been necessary once before, when they had first tried AA103. Nothing even remotely as intrusive had been introduced into the study since.

The lab was fully equipped, though it hadn't always been. Most of the money had poured into the project in the mid-Eighties, after the incident with the AA103. The abrupt comatose states brought about by the experimental drug had initially been thought disastrous. People in the CIA and the DOD were in a panic, fearing that if the project were exposed the entire government might fall. But then an interesting thing happened. The subjects, still comatose, stopped aging. It was the result Childs had been after all along. Only he had stumbled across it accidentally and didn't clearly understand why or how the natural process had been interrupted. Hence the money came pouring in. Find the answers and everything else would work itself out.

Childs was still looking for the answers.

The upstairs lab was primarily a biochemistry lab, though there was also a seldom-used bacteriology component. The blood and urine samples were already in testing. Some of the blood had been inserted into a special glass tube, then placed in a centrifuge and spun at a rate of several thousand revolutions per minute, separating the blood cells from the blood serum, which remained at the top of the tube. The serum went into little plastic cups next, then into an automatic analyzer that measured the color by shining lights through the sample plus a reagent solution. Other blood samples were given a flame photometer test for certain elements such as sodium and potassium. The examination of the liver cell samples under an electron microscope would come later.

As the elevator neared the halfway point of its descent, everything was moving along smoothly, all on schedule. The routine examinations on all three subjects had been completed in a little more than forty-five minutes. In addition, Childs had already debriefed and reprogrammed the subjects, which was and always had been the trickiest element of the entire operation. The past five years, they had developed a system of hypnotic and subliminal commands in conjunction with a virtual reality simulator that actually reconstructed a powerful false memory in the minds of the subjects. They had spent the afternoon, the entire afternoon, at the park. That would be their only memory of their afternoon activity. Everything else would be masked. It was a remarkably effective system.

Before virtual reality had been an option, the use of drugs and hypnosis in combination had served in a similar role. While the doctor had not been able to substitute a false memory, he had been able to erase any memories the subjects might have had of being at the lab. It was a process that left them not quite knowing what had happened. They simply closed their eyes at the park and when they opened them again, two hours had passed. In the place of those two hours sat a blank spot. No explanation. Like many of the cases of UFO encounters, while the blank spot was odd, it was generally accepted and left unchallenged.

The elevator arrived at the basement. The counterweight set, the car settled onto the buffer, and the doors opened. Childs escorted the three teenagers into the car. They were the walking dead, fixed gazes, expressionless, going through all the motions and only distantly aware of their surroundings. He pressed the button for the first floor. The elevator doors closed.

Pam was waiting in the lobby for them. She checked her watch as the doors opened and the four passengers stepped out. 'Right on schedule.'

'Couldn't have gone any smoother,' Childs said.

'The lab's got everything?'

'They're already doing the work-up.'

They went out through the back entrance, where the Buick was waiting. The kids climbed into the back seat. They would be back at the park, innocent and safe for another three months, in less than the usual two hours. Childs closed the door behind the girl.

'I think I'll go straight from the park to the airport,' he said. 'No sense in hanging around here twiddling my thumbs for the next three hours. Maybe they'll be able to get me on an earlier flight out.'

'I'll fax you the prelims tomorrow.'

Childs paused a moment, the driver's side door open. He looked across the top of the car, a wistful longing in his eyes. 'You know, we've been doing this for I don't know how many years now. I sure as hell wish we could get over that last little hurdle.'

'We're getting closer.'

92

For many years we believed that aging was a process beyond our control. There was only so much punishment the body could take, we believed, before it lost its ability to renew itself. Death, we believed, was inevitable.

I'm here to tell you tonight that we may very well have been wrong.

Please, let me explain.

The most interesting development to come along in recent years has been our increased understanding of the nature of a genetic disease called progeria. More specifically Hutchinson-Gilford

Syndrome. This is a degenerative disease which afflicts children. By the age of ten or twelve they begin to demonstrate many of the signs of old age. These signs may include gray hair, baldness, loss of body fat, and atherosclerosis, which refers to the fatty deposits lining the arterial walls. While the cause of progeria is still unknown we have discovered that its victims demonstrate a dramatic reduction in the number of times their cells are able to regenerate themselves.

We know that progeria is a genetic disease and therefore we can now conclude that the aging process is a genetically controlled process. If we're able to learn to identify and manipulate the gene or genes that trigger this process there's no reason to believe we won't be able to delay and perhaps even permanently suspend the aging process.

This is not idle speculation, ladies and gentlemen.

This is, in fact, quite achievable. Perhaps even as early as the end of this century.

Dr Timothy Childs
Commission on Death and Dying
1982

Beep... beep... beep... beep...

Cody Breswick heard the beat of his heart on the ECG machine before he heard anything else. It made a sound like the old Pong video game his father had shown him at the San Francisco Exploratorium when they were last there. *Beep. Beep. Beep.* A steady, almost monotonous sound that called him up from the black, murky waters where he had been floating aimlessly for longer than he could imagine.

The ring finger of his left hand twitched, then fell motionless again.

Air escaped from his lungs in a short, sharp burst.

He tried to swallow, but his mouth was dry and what little saliva he could gather together wasn't enough to coat the inside of his mouth much less the inside of his throat. It felt raw and burning when he tried to swallow.

He moaned.

Beep. Beep. Beep.

At the edge of the darkness, he could see the first bluish-purple glow of a sunrise. There was light out there somewhere beyond the darkness, beyond the black, formless landscape. He sensed it more than saw it, but it was there all right, gradually drawing in the surrounding darkness the way a Black Hole draws in the light.

The black sky turned dark blue... turned light blue... turned white-orange... turned

... turned bright and illuminating, a burning, sparkling sun.

His eyelids fluttered open against the light, and he was startled by the intensity. He blinked back the glare several times, felt his eyes water, then raised his hand to shade his eyes against the brightness. Overhead, a small fluorescent lamp cast its gaze over his pillow and halfway down the bed.

Beep. Beep. Beep.

The machine making that rhythmic sound stood against the wall, next to the bed. Across a screen near the top, a graph line moved from right to left, spiking in unison with each new beep. Cody didn't know exactly what it did or how it did it, but he thought the beeping had something to do with his heart. Small round bandages on his chest and wrists and ankles were connected to long wire leads that seemed somehow to join him to the machine.

At least it didn't hurt.

He couldn't say that about everything. When he tried to move his legs, they felt as if they were cased in concrete. A dull throbbing pain went all the way up his calves and through his thighs. His right arm was sore, too. It lay in some sort of a contoured half-cast, strapped across the biceps and forearm. A needle protruded from beneath several layers of medical tape across the inside of his elbow joint. The needle ran into a tube, the tube ran into a machine that sounded as if it were gnawing on something, and above that a couple of bags with clear liquid hung from a metal stand.

'Mom...'

Cody glanced to his right, beyond all the machinery, and realized he wasn't the only person in the room. A line of beds stretched from one end to the other, each with a little light overhead, each with its own staff of monitors and whatever, each with its own patient.

There was a girl in the next bed. She looked like she might be a year or two older than him, her hair blond-brown, her fingernails unpolished and long. She took in a shallow breath and her chest expanded briefly then fell back again. Cody wondered distantly if she was dying.

'Mom...'

It was scary here.

'Mom...'

Before the door finally opened, Cody had to call out another half-a-dozen times. When it did open, a woman he had never seen before walked through. She seemed as surprised to see him as he was to see her. And though later he would wonder about his mother and why she wasn't there, initially he didn't care that the woman wasn't his mother. Initially, all that mattered was that an adult had arrived.

An adult who wasn't hooked up to a machine.

94

There had been no early flights out of O'Hare and Childs ended up hanging out at the airport for nearly three hours before his eight o'clock flight was ready to board. The plane landed a little after ten, Pacific Daylight Time. It took him another thirty minutes to retrieve his luggage and make it to his car, which was parked in the overnight lot half a mile from the terminal.

By the time he made it home, he had begun to feel the effects of the trip. He dropped his suitcase in the entryway and headed for the wet bar in the living room, where he poured himself a Vodka Collins. There was a slight chill in the house, though he preferred it a little on the cool side and didn't have the energy to bother with the thermostat, which was mounted on the wall at the other end of the hall.

Instead, he collapsed on the couch.

It had been a long haul. Not just the trip and the flight home, but everything that had happened over the past twenty years: the first administration of Genesis, the disappointment when it didn't appear to have any effect, the follow-up with the children just in case, then the mishap with the AA103. A long journey, and he still wasn't sure how far he had come.

DC had instructed him to dispose of the AA103 and all his research notes shortly after the comas had started to crop up. If the public ever found out, he said, all hell would break loose. The entire government would be in danger. Of course, that had been before they discovered the other side effect: that the children had stopped aging. By then, DC had already supervised the burning of the notes and the disposal of all ten vials of the drug.

Childs had been devastated. He had naïvely allowed himself to believe that he had been part of something important, so important that the CIA and the DOD wanted him on their team. That was the only way he had been able to justify to himself what he had done. It had been for the good of the country. He had been called and he had answered and how could anyone expect any less of him?

Not all the AA103 had gone down the drain, though. Childs couldn't bring himself to dispose of all of it. Shortly after the first child had fallen ill, he had set aside a single vial, replacing it with distilled water. He was perhaps naïve, but he was not stupid. He had no doubts that once word got out about what had happened things in Washington would heat up and eventually he'd feel the pressure. So he had covered himself.

Childs took another swipe at his drink.

AA103.

How close could a man come to uncovering the key to aging and still not quite figure it out? All he had to do was take a look at any of the two dozen sleepers scattered around the country. In ten years, not a single child in the group had grown older. Not a single child. Not a day older. They had all beaten Old Man Time's ticking clock, and they had done it because of Childs. And now the only thing that remained between him and history was understanding the connection to the AA103. How close could a man come? So close that he might wake up one morning with no idea of where he was or how he had gotten there. So close he might have a line of drool driveling out of the corner of his mouth like his last rational thought slipping away into the night. So close it could make a damn fool of him.

He gulped down the last of the Vodka Collins and nearly missed setting the glass on the coffee table. There was a quote he had picked up in college, though he couldn't remember who had said it. It was this: *I was never afraid of failure; for I would sooner fail than not be among the greatest.*

'Not so me,' Childs said, knowing that the fear of failure had been a harbinger perched upon his shoulder for as long as he could remember. It was always there, always whispering calamities in his ear, rarely letting him sleep the dreamless night, rest the wakeful morning.

'Not so me.'

The phone rang. It startled him, and he nearly kicked the coffee table over as he sat up. He barked the shin of his right leg against the edge. It hurt something awful as he limped into the kitchen and grabbed the receiver off its cradle. 'Yeah?'

'You're back?' Elizabeth said, surprised. Her last name was Tilley. She was in her late-fifties, and she had an extensive background in nursing, which was how Childs had first met her back in the days of his off-campus clinic near Berkeley. They had been together, professionally, ever since. If there was anyone in the world he trusted, it was Elizabeth. She was his adviser, his confidant, the only person who had truly shared his vision all these years.

'Just got in,' he said.

'I left a message on your answering machine.'

'Yeah?'

'Another sleeper woke up today.'

'Jesus.' Childs pulled out the nearest chair and sat down. Earlier, he had been willing to succumb to the numbing effects of his drink, but he came fighting back now, suddenly wide awake and clear-headed. It hadn't been a fluke after all. When the Knight boy had come out of his coma, no one had been sure what to make of it. 'Which one?'

'Cody Breswick.'

'How old was he?'

'According to our records, almost eight.'

'And when did he go under?'

'Two days before the Knight boy.'

'Incredible.'

'You think they might all start coming up?'

'I don't know. Your guess is as good as mine. I wish I understood what the hell was going on.' Childs ran a hand across his face. He hadn't had a chance to shave this morning. He wasn't one of those guys who had to shave twice a day or otherwise risk walking around with a ragged five o'clock shadow, but the stubble was beginning to irritate him a bit. He needed to clean up. More than that, he needed a good night's sleep.

'You monitoring all his vitals?'

'Of course.'

'Anything out of the ordinary?'

'As far as I can tell, he's as healthy as the day he went under. We've already started him on physical therapy and we did a complete blood work-up. No surprises so far. The kid's eating like he's trying to fill a hollow leg.'

'I can't believe this,' Childs muttered. He let out a breath that felt cool against the inside of his throat, and wondered if he might be coming down with a cold. Things had been stressful lately. That wasn't something he liked to admit to himself. He preferred to think that over the years he had learned to roll with the punches when things got to be a little overwhelming. Sometimes, though, you fooled yourself without realizing it. 'Okay, I'll be in first thing in the morning. Is he sleeping now?'

'Like a baby.'

'Good, then first thing in the morning.'

'He's your patient.'

95

Teri was asleep by the time Walt arrived home. She had learned, without intending to, how to sleep lightly these past few days. As soon as the front door opened, she was sitting up in bed, the covers already thrown back. He came down the hall, whispering her name, and it was a good thing, too, because if she hadn't recognized who it was she might very well have jumped him, and someone might have gotten hurt.

'Walt?'

He pushed the bedroom door open. 'I didn't wake you, did I?'

Teri stepped out from behind the door, the *Webster's New World Dictionary* in her hand. 'Jesus, Walt, you nearly scared me to death.'

'Sorry.'

'You would have been sorry if I hadn't recognized your voice.'

She returned the book to the top of the bureau, next to the manila envelope that had come in the mail for her this afternoon. It was addressed to Teri Knight, written in a bold, almost childlike scrawl that slanted downward, left to right. The address under her name, written in that same crayon-like scrawl, had not been her home address, though. The address was Walt's. Somehow, someone knew where she was hiding out. She had opened it apprehensively, curling back the corner of the flap and peering in as if she were afraid something might leap out at her if she wasn't careful. But it had only been a letter and some personnel files. The letter had been written by Richard Boyle.

For a moment, Teri debated showing him the contents, then decided against it. It was late now. They were both tired. There would be another time to share with him what Boyle had sent along. She moved the dictionary on top of the envelope and went over to sit on the edge of the bed. A yawn came crawling up her throat. She held her hand over her mouth.

'What time is it?'

'A little after midnight.'

'You just get in?'

'Yeah.'

'How did it go?'

'He's still doing it,' Walt said. He sat next to her, his eyes bright, his voice bubbly, a little boy who just discovered that tomorrow's Christmas Day. 'Whatever he did to Gabe, he's still doing it, Teri. I saw him pick up a group of teenagers, drive them back to the

Foundation for a couple of hours, then return them to the park again. And these kids, they were like the walking dead. Eyes glazed over. No reaction to their surroundings. He's got 'em programmed somehow. That's how he gets them to the Foundation and back again without anyone taking notice. The damn kids don't even know what's going on.'

And neither do the parents, I bet, Teri thought. That had been her biggest fear as a parent—that somehow she wouldn't be able to protect Gabe from the horrors in the world. She wondered how long Childs had been picking him up and dropping him off again before whatever it was that had gone wrong had forced the doctor to keep Gabe permanently. And beneath that, she wondered what kind of a parent could have been so blind to such a thing?

'And you think that's what happened to Gabe?'

'Of course, it is.'

'It might have been going on for years,' she said, her body feeling as if it had taken a sudden beating. 'Maybe all of Gabe's life. And I never did anything to stop it.'

'You had no way of knowing, Teri.'

'I should have known, though. I should have seen a sign or something. He's my son. Maybe if I'd kept a closer eye on him, if I hadn't been working, or maybe if . . .'

'Shhh,' Walt said. He took her into the fold of his arms and she stared vacantly across the room at the hall light seeping in through the open door. 'That's enough of that. None of this was your fault, you hear me? You can't let him off the hook that easily, Teri. He's the one who has to take responsibility for what happened to Gabe. Not you. It wasn't your fault.'

Maybe so, but that didn't make it hurt any less.

'We still don't know where he is, do we?' Teri said softly.

'Maybe not the exact location, but at least we've got some leads.'

'The Devol Research Foundation?'

Walt nodded.

'It's not a registered foundation,' Teri said.

'What?'

'The Devol Research Foundation. I checked. It's not registered.'

'I guess I would have been surprised if it was.'

'So how are we supposed to find him?'

'The same way we found the building in St Charles,' Walt said evenly. 'We'll sit at the good doctor's curbside tomorrow and follow him around all day, and the next day and the day after that, and we'll keep following him around until he takes us where we want to go.'

'That easy?'
'That easy.'
'God, I hope you're right.'

96

We're getting close, my friends.

HGH. Human Growth Hormone. We've been using this hormone for some time now, most notably to assist the growth potential of children whose physical development is lagging behind the norm. It has proven to be quite effective within this given context. However, we're coming to believe that HGH may actually have a much larger role to play within the arena of human aging.

For example, we've recently learned that most people, when they enter what we've come to think of as our twilight years – the sixties, seventies and eighties – these people stop producing HGH. More important, when we give these same people regular injections of the Human Growth Hormone some interesting things begin to happen. They begin to increase bone density. They increase muscle tone. They lose an average of twelve percent of their body fat. And they find they have recharged energy levels.

In essence, ladies and gentlemen, we're able to chart an array of specific, measurable changes in these population groups that indicate something remarkable is going on. It appears that HGH, administered to the elderly, might actually bring about a process of age reversal.

These people get younger.

Dr Timothy Childs
Bay Area BioTech Conference
June 1989

97

Walt was already awake when the alarm clock brought Teri out of her sleep at a couple minutes of six the next morning. She found him in the kitchen, sipping a cup of coffee, waiting for the toaster to finish its business with a slice of bread.

'Morning.'

'How long have you been up?' Teri asked, plopping down at

the table, wishing she'd had another three or four hours. It didn't come easy anymore, a good night's sleep. And she almost always felt a little worse for the wear in the morning.

'I don't know. Not long,' Walt said quietly. The tone of his voice immediately caught Teri's attention. He sounded as if he might be a bit under the weather. Or worse, he sounded as if he might actually be upset about something.

'Are you all right?'

'You'd think after three years...' He looked at her, something frighteningly unfamiliar behind his eyes, then looked away.

'What is it, Walt? What's the matter?'

'Did I ever tell you about my father?'

'I don't think so.'

'He was one hell of a son-of-a-bitch, that man. He died alone in a hospital in Nevada, at the age of seventy-three, after a bout with pneumonia. We didn't get along very well, and I guess somehow, over time, I came to think of myself as not having a father. I hadn't seen him in eight or nine years.'

'I'm sorry,' Teri said.

'Today's the third anniversary of his death. I guess I'm a little surprised it still comes after me.' The knob on the toaster popped and Walt took possession of the bread almost the second it appeared out of the furnace. He dropped it on a plate, slapped on some butter and strawberry jam, and carried it over to the table. 'Here, a little something to get you going. You look like you need it.'

'Thanks.'

'You want some coffee?'

'Black?'

'Coming up.'

Teri took a bite of her toast and dropped it back to the plate. She really wasn't that hungry. 'Want to talk about it?'

'Not really,' Walt said flatly.

For the second time, she considered showing him the envelope that had arrived in the mail yesterday. It seemed ever more pertinent in light of the anniversary of the death of his father. All things had their time, though, and she didn't think now was the time to bring out the skeletons. Maybe there would never be such a time for all she knew. Maybe it would be best if the closet door was nailed shut permanently. For the time being, she decided to let it pass.

'What do you think Childs does with them?' Teri asked abruptly.

'I don't know,' Walt said. He placed the coffee cup in front of her and sat down in the adjacent chair. 'It's gotta be part of some sort of research project. Something to do with aging, I imagine.'

'I keep thinking about what he told me.'

'What was that?'

'About Gabe getting older.'

'Yeah, well, you've got to remember who we're dealing with, Teri. This guy's been using children as guinea pigs for the past twenty years. I'm not sure you should be listening to anything he has to say, much less anything about Gabe.'

'But if he was telling the truth...'

She let the thought trail away, and it wasn't because the thought had come to her incomplete and wanting. It was something fully developed, something she had previously considered any number of times already.

'What?' Walt asked.

'If he *was* telling the truth, then that means... it means Gabe's dying.' It was out there now, plain to see. Ignore it or fear it or try to make do.

Walt didn't say a word.

'And there's something else,' Teri said.

'What?'

'Dr Childs might be the only person in the world who could save him.'

98

Childs came out of the house, checking his watch. He dug into his right front pocket, pulled out his keys, locked the front door, and started down the walkway. He had parked overnight at the front curb instead of in the garage where he usually kept the car.

It was ten past eight.

Walt and Teri had been parked across the street, half a block up, for over an hour. She had found herself an oldies station on the radio and a song called *Breakdown* by Tom Petty & the Heartbreakers had just come on as Childs emerged from the house.

Walt tapped Teri on the forearm and pointed up the street. 'We're on.'

Teri turned off the radio and buckled her seat belt. Between the coffee and the cold morning air, she had finally come fully awake and alert. Added to that now was a sudden rush of adrenaline. 'About time. I was beginning to wonder if he was taking the day off.'

'Me, too,' Walt said, starting the engine.

They pulled out, went down the block a couple of houses, then pulled into a driveway and turned around. Childs was making a right-hand turn, two blocks up, by the time they were headed in the right direction.

'Don't lose him,' Teri said.

Walt grinned. 'I won't.'

He had warned her that she was going to have to be patient, that Childs might not lead them anywhere except to the office and back. And not just today, but tomorrow and maybe the day after and maybe the day after that as well. It could turn out to be long and arduous, he had said.

But Teri already had the feeling that this was different. Over the next hour, Childs had taken them on a sight-seeing tour through a maze of neighborhoods and twice around the business district. He wouldn't be doing that if he were going to the office or downtown to the mall to do some browsing or over to the Holiday Market to pick up some groceries. Even a careful man didn't waste his time worrying about being followed when he made a trip to the market.

'What's he doing?'

'Making sure no one's following him.'

'He's not going to the clinic, is he?'

'Nope,' Walt said.

'You think we hit a jackpot first coin in the slot?'

'That I do.'

It was almost nine by the time Childs finally pulled into the entrance of the Devol Research Foundation. Walt slowed down out front and watched the Buick make the long straight line down the driveway to the parking lot. Someone had turned the sprinklers on during the night. The landscaping glistened and there were a number of small puddles in the road that seemed to explode under the weight of the car's tires.

'You were right,' Teri said, feeling a strange sense of dread settle over her. It was almost as if she had come to a fork in the road and deep in her heart she knew that neither of her options would take her to where she wanted to go.

'Lucky guess.'

'You think Gabe's inside somewhere?'

'He's in there, all right.'

'Can we get him?'

Walt pulled back into the street and accelerated. 'Not yet. We have a little researching to do first.'

99

Mitch, who had pulled over to the side of the road in front of a trash bin, watched the Pontiac Sunbird slow down outside the entrance to the Foundation. This was not a good thing. Not a good thing at all.

Odd as it was, he had grown to admire Mrs Knight. She was one tough woman, stubborn as could be. He still had the bruises to prove it. But what she didn't seem to realize was that she was putting herself into the kind of jeopardy that could get her killed. She wasn't supposed to know about this place, and now that she did, something was going to have to be done about her.

The Sunbird pulled back into traffic and started down the street, gradually accelerating until it disappeared into the horizon. Mitch watched it go with a feeling of unease, the kind of thing that sometimes settled over him when he knew things had gotten out of hand. No sense following them any further. Not now. All bets were off now that they had found their way this far.

He waited for an opening, then drove down the street, talking to himself before pulling into the Foundation entrance. DC was not going to be pleased with this new development; Mitch knew that without having to give it much thought. And what a shame, because the man was like a mountain lion. As long as you steered clear of him, gave him a little breathing room, he wasn't dangerous. But the moment you backed him into a corner, he'd turn on you, vicious and snarling and ready to pounce.

No, DC wasn't going to like this at all.

And that was too bad for Mrs Knight.

100

When the door opened, Gabe was watching *Huckleberry Hound* and absently scratching at the upper edge of the cast on his arm. He looked up, fully expecting to see Miss Tilley step through, a slick smile on her face and a man or two behind her, just in case things got a little out of hand. That seemed to be the way things had shaped up around here. There were only two reasons that door ever opened. First, if she was bringing in a meal – and it wasn't meal time, he knew that much, because he had just finished eating a tuna-fish sandwich and a bag of potato chips for lunch.

Or second, if she was bringing him grief.

The worst of that grief had come yesterday. Gabe had learned not to put up much of a fight when she was after another sample of his blood. It didn't seem to hurt as much if he just closed his eyes and let her take what she wanted to take. But it hadn't been his blood that she had wanted yesterday.

'We're going to take another sample,' she had said, matter-of-factly. 'And this one's going to be a little different from the others. I don't want to have any trouble out of you, do you understand? You can make it easy on yourself by just relaxing and keeping your eyes closed like you do when I'm drawing blood. And if you do that, you'll hardly even notice what's going on.'

It hadn't been that simple, nor had it been as horrific as he imagined it would be after that little speech of hers. Gabe did his best to keep his eyes closed, but when he felt the first pin prick over his right lower ribs, he stole a quick peek. Miss Tilley had given him some sort of a shot. She wasn't taking things out, she was putting them in.

'You rest for a few minutes and I'll be right back,' she said. When she returned, she pinched that same spot, complaining to herself that he was all skin and bones and they were going to have to do something about that. 'How does that feel?'

'Numb,' he said, only mildly aware of the pressure.

'Good.'

She had him close his eyes again. Seeing the needle, she said, would only make the pain seem worse that it actually was. It hurt, just the same, even without seeing the needle. Maybe that was because what he *did* see was enough to scare him half to death. Miss Tilley had taken a knife and cut a slit into his side, just above his lower ribs. She was twisting and turning a needle in there, hunting around for just the right prize the way you hunted for the biggest stuffed bear at one of those crane-like vending machines you see at carnivals.

Gabe snapped his eyes shut.

'There,' she said, a moment later. 'That wasn't so bad, now was it?'

He looked down and saw a Band-Aid covering the damage. It was one of those children's Band-Aids, the ones with the bright colors and shapes, as if that could somehow make what had happened less horrifying for him. It didn't. It made it worse, in fact. Because suddenly he had a longing to be home again, with his mother, where there were no needles, no antiseptic smells, no witch posing as a nurse.

God, how he was beginning to hate this place.

There had been very little pain initially. Late last night, though, when he rolled over in his sleep, the soreness brought him suddenly awake. He peeled back the Band-Aid and saw a small black-and-blue circle where Miss Tilley had pinched him. The slit underneath, where the needle had gone in, was nearly invisible.

Gabe fell back against his pillow, closed his eyes and cried.

So the worse of Miss Tilley's grief had come yesterday, and now, as she was stepping through the door, he wondered what kind of grief she was bringing for him today.

101

'I need to make a stop,' Walt said flatly. They were on their way back to the apartment after visiting the Building Department at the County Offices, where they had picked up the blueprints to the Devol Research Foundation. Walt had seemed draggy the last thirty or forty minutes, not tired so much as maybe a bit self-absorbed. He had been distant and uncommunicative, and Teri wondered if maybe he knew something that she didn't, if maybe it had something to do with Aaron Jefferson.

They had bumped into Aaron on the steps outside the County Offices. It was the first time Teri had ever met the gentleman. He was tall and thin and had a smile that came easily. It left you feeling as if you had been friends most of your life. For the most part, they had all exchanged small talk, Aaron mentioning something about a proposed change in the structure of the department, Walt remarking on how easy it had been to get the set of blueprints. The exchange had been short and affable. It was only after they had parted and they were well on their way to the parking lot when Walt mentioned that Aaron was the man who had run the fingerprint checks on her shoe.

'Did he find anything?' Teri asked, not remembering if they had discussed the results or not. So much had happened the past week or so, it was hard to keep track of everything.

'Nothing important,' Walt had said, and then he had fallen uncharacteristically silent. He climbed into the car, turned on the radio and lost himself somewhere in the lyrics or the music of Neil Young's *The Needle and the Damage Done*. And for a man who purported to abhor the Sixties, wasn't that a little red flag going up? Teri let it flap in the wind, without making an effort to extract any kind of explanation. If he had something on his mind that he wanted to talk about, then sooner or later it would come out on its own. As long as he understood that she would be there to listen...

The stop Walt wanted to make was at the Hillcrest Cemetery, off of Remington Drive just north of the city, overlooking a small agricultural valley nestled in the foothills. They parked out front, next to the Hillcrest Chapel.

'My father's buried here,' he said, unbuckling his seat belt. He sank back, his hands still wrapped around the steering wheel, and stared out across the graveyard, a man who had seen his share of ghosts in his life.

'You want me to wait?' Teri asked.

'No, you can come.'

They got out. Walt locked up the car and waited for Teri to join him. A gentle afternoon breeze kicked up, whistling through the trees, stirring the souls of all the ghosts that still made their residence here.

'My father's greatest fear was dying,' Walt said solemnly as they walked through the huge ironwork gate. 'I never understood that.'

'A lot of people fear death,' Teri said.

'I don't.'

As strange and as stark as that might have sounded, Teri didn't doubt it in the least. In fact, she thought she might even understand it. She had felt much the same way after Gabe had disappeared, especially after she had reached the point of giving up her search for him. After that, whether she lived or died hadn't mattered much to her. Death, she had decided, was something you feared when you had a reason to live, and her reason had gone the way of the wind.

'My father died a thousand little deaths in his life,' Walt said. 'Every time he changed a name or quit a job or moved to a new town. Each and every one of them, they were all little deaths and he never even realized he was dying.'

They came upon the grave site, which was at the far end of the third row, just out of the shade of an old oak. It was marked by a marbled headstone set flush into the ground, the grass long and unkempt around the edges. There was a small bouquet of yellow daffodils above the name on the marker.

WILLIAM JACOB TRAVIS

1919–1992

The Last Enemy That Shall Be Destroyed Is Death

Walt knelt and crossed himself, then brushed away the debris that had collected around the chiseled-out letters. Underneath a matting of oak leaves and pine needles, he stirred up a red-ribbon bow, faded and pinkish and curled at the edges, that had found its way to the grave site all on its own. He stuffed it into a pocket.

'I hated him as much as I loved him, you know. He was that kind of man.'

Teri stood back, silent, not knowing what to say. She wished now that she had opted to wait in the car. She felt out of place here, a voyeur catching a glimpse of a moment best left private.

'We moved around a lot when I was a kid; I ever tell you that?'

Teri shook her head.

'That was because we were running most of the time.' He sat back on his haunches, then raised his eyes to the sky, which was still overcast, though you could catch a patch or two of blue trying to battle its way through in the distance. 'Oh, Christ, what we do with our lives.'

Teri placed a hand over his shoulder. He covered it with his own.

'Ever wish you could go back and start all over?'

'Sometimes,' she said.

'Me, too. I'd live in a small town, in an old Victorian. Maybe go to the same school all my life. Come home to Mom baking cookies, the smell in the house warm and delicious. I'd play catch with Dad when he got home, talk about the Giants, oil up my mitt, make plans to go down to the creek and do a little fishing. So many things would have been different.'

'I'm sorry.'

'Guess I'm making an idiot of myself, huh?'

'We all wish things could be different, Walt.'

He nodded and made a face. It was something he already knew, and something she imagined he had already tried to deal with on numerous other occasions. The way a childhood could follow you around the rest of your life, though, like a stalker always there, always looking for that opening, that chance to remind you that you aren't alone... it was such an odd phenomenon when you thought about it. There was no escaping the little boy, was there? He was your conscience, your memory, your teacher, your student.

Walt climbed back to his feet. He brushed off the knees of his slacks where they were grimed with gravel and loose blades of grass. He looked at her, almost apologetically, then leaned over and picked up the bouquet of daffodils. A bright yellow ribbon formed a bow around the middle. Beneath the bow was a card. He opened the card and read it twice before handing it to her.

She accepted it reflexively and might have even opened it and read herself if Walt had given her the chance. His hand was shaking as he passed it to her. His eyes widened a bit. Teri felt a momentary urge to draw back. *He's going to snap*, she thought, hating that she had found that thought inside her own head.

'Walt? Jesus, Walt, are you...?'

The color drained from his face. He fell to his knees.

'Walt?'

'Oh, God.' He buried his face in his hands, and began to sob.

Teri fell silent.

If she hadn't felt the voyeur before, she felt the voyeur now.

102

It wasn't a gift of grief this time after all.

Miss Tilley stepped through the door and asked Gabe how he was doing today. All right, he told her, having learned never to offer anymore than he absolutely had to. You never knew what the crazy woman was going to do. She could be your grandmother when she wanted. Or she could be Nurse Ratched, depending on what kind of mood she was in or if you happened to say the wrong thing.

She did not come all the way into the room as was her usual routine. Instead, she stood by the door, her hands clasped behind her back. 'Got a surprise for you,' she said.

Gabe didn't say a word.

'How'd you like to have a room-mate?'

'Depends.'

'On what?'

'On who it is.'

'Well, to tell you the truth,' Miss Tilley said, slipping instantly into her Nurse Ratched persona, 'It really isn't up for debate. Like it or not, you've got yourself a little playmate now.'

She wheeled in a boy who looked like he might be nine or ten years old. He was pale and on the thin side, had blond hair and a spattering of light freckles across the bridge of his nose. He looked frightened and confused. Tilley wheeled him over to the first bed on Gabe's left and helped him out of the chair and into bed.

'He's still a little weak,' she said. 'But he'll get stronger.'

His name was Cody, and he wasn't nine or ten; he was eight.

After Tilley left, they talked for awhile and he told Gabe that he didn't remember how he had gotten here, only that he had gone to the park to play. He tried not to cry, but eventually he lost the battle and tears filled his eyes. He missed his mother, he said. And he didn't like it here. And he wanted to go home again.

Gabe missed his own mother.

And he wanted to go home, too.

103

'It's the same scenario,' Childs said, doodling absently on the calendar pad on his desk. There were two other participants in this meeting. One was a muscleman by the name of Mitch. The other man, Childs knew as DC, though he suspected this man – who had been his primary contact almost since the very beginning – was a man of many names. They were names you didn't want to know, because when you started to know too much about these guys, you made yourself dangerous to them, and dangerous men lived short lives.

'What about the others?' DC asked.

'What about them?'

'You tell me. Are they *all* going to start coming up?'

'There's no way I can answer that.'

Mitch was standing in the corner, his arms crossed, leaning against the wall. It was the same position he had taken up every time he had been in this room. He coughed into his hand and crossed his arms again, not saying a word. He had said more than enough already, Childs supposed.

DC had perched himself on the folding table, next to the copy machine. His hands were curled around the edge, elbows locked, knuckles white, and he was swinging his legs through the air as if he were trying to pick up speed. He was not terribly pleased about anything he had heard here this afternoon.

'You *can't* answer that or you *won't*?' he asked.

'I never imagined any of them would wake up again,' Childs said.

'Well, they did. And now we're going to have to figure out what the hell we're going to do with them, aren't we?'

'Time,' Childs said. 'All we need is a little time.'

'How much time are you talking about?'

'Six months, eight months, maybe a year. Both boys are already showing signs of aging. They'll die naturally if we just wait it out.'

'I'm sure Mrs Knight won't mind waiting,' Mitch said.

'She's gonna be a problem, doc. No matter what we do.'

'I know,' Childs said, leaning back in his chair. He studied the ceiling, which had a dark gouge over the conference table where two years ago the janitor had crushed a spider under the handle of his mop. 'We could transfer the kids to another facility until things settle down. Maybe Houston or St Charles.'

'The two boys?'

'Yeah.'

'What about the sleepers?'

'We could move them all, I suppose.'

'How soon?'

'It wouldn't be easy, not with the sleepers,' Childs said. 'They'll need special care. I'd have to make some arrangements.'

'How *soon*?'

'Maybe two weeks.'

Mitch grunted. 'Like I said, I'm sure Mrs Knight won't mind waiting.'

'Then for Christ's sake just get rid of her!' Childs erupted. He surprised everyone in the room, including himself. For a moment, his entire body shook. He looked away. 'I'm sorry. I didn't mean that. It's just that . . .'

'You can't go around killing off everyone,' Mitch said.

That was exactly what things had turned into lately, or at least it seemed that way. There had only been one death, of course, but it had turned Childs into something of a basket case and barring the sudden outburst, he really didn't want to see anyone else getting hurt. He looked up at Mitch, quietly disdainful. 'Tell that to Amanda Tarkett, why don't you?'

'That was an accident, and you know it, you son-of-a-bitch.'

'Gentlemen, please,' DC said. 'Let's try to stay on subject, all right? We've got enough on our plate without tossing around insults and accusations.'

The pencil Childs had been holding, suddenly snapped in half. He stared at the two uneven pieces, the cylinder of graphite exposed beneath the jagged yellow edges, then tossed them at the wastepaper basket next to his desk. One piece bounced off the rim and fell silently to the carpet. The other hit home, making a hollow, clanging sound.

'Done?' DC asked.

'I hate this.'

'I know you do.'

'It's a fucking nightmare.'

'So let's see if we can find a way out of it then, all right?'

Childs nodded, wearing the lost and lonely face of a man who wasn't sure of anything anymore.

104

Teri went into Walt's bedroom after the manila envelope that had arrived in the mail yesterday. It was sitting where she had left it on the bureau, under the dictionary. She pulled it out, studied the name in the upper left-hand corner – Richard Boyle, and wished she had mentioned it to Walt last night or maybe this morning. Maybe it would have saved them both the incident at the cemetery.

Following that incident, which had left Teri nearly as shaken as Walt, something had changed between them. Teri wasn't sure exactly what it had been, but she thought maybe they had both lost a little of the trust they had had for each other. The trip back to the apartment was a silent, reflective drive for both of them, a straight line from the cemetery. Walt went immediately to bed (in his own room for a change), saying he felt as if he might be coming down with something. He slept through the rest of the afternoon and most of the evening.

Teri found it a little more difficult to hide. Maybe that was because she wasn't sure what they were hiding from. She made a casserole for dinner – the recipe was on the back of the elbow macaroni package – and didn't give the note a thought until several hours later. She might not have given it a thought at all if she hadn't found the note in her purse while looking for some aspirin to go after a mild headache before it developed into something worse.

This is what the note said:

    The face in the mirror is an old friend.

    So sorry to hear about your father's taking leave.

It was signed: Richard Boyle.

The man was a busy little bee, wasn't he?

Now, at the bureau, Teri wondered how it was that Richard Boyle seemed to know more about Walt than Walt knew about him. The contents of the envelope were remarkable, both in their substance and in the fact that Boyle would have had access to them. The first item was an anonymous letter, addressed: *To Whom It May Concern*. The letter went into a detailed account of Walt's childhood. His parents' divorce when Walt was only six. How his father kidnapped him a short time later. The years they spent on the move, changing names, towns, schools, altering their appearances, adopting new backgrounds.

What a nightmare, Teri had thought her first time through. By her second time through she had already decided that it must have been something closer to a personal hell. How could a child grow up with any sense of identity under such horrible circumstances?

The second item, in some ways, carried an even bigger shock. It was a copy of Walt's personnel file when he was with the department. More specifically, it included an internal memo from the department's psychologist recommending that Walt's employment be terminated with disability pay. Most of the gobbledygook went over Teri's head, but she understood enough of it to garner two things. Walt's problems began to surface shortly after the death of his father, as if the childhood nightmare had finally caught up with him once the man most responsible was no longer a threat. And the problems were not superficial. Words like *delusional*, *paranoid*, *schizophrenic* jumped off the page like embossed lettering.

And then there had been the incident at the cemetery this afternoon.

105

'No,' Walt said, standing at the living-room window, looking out across the valley. A thin band of twilight colors edged the distant mountain tops. A few more minutes and nightfall would own the sky. 'I didn't quit. I'm sorry I didn't tell you, but it's not the kind of thing that a person likes to slip into the conversation.'

Teri listened, hating herself for having put him in this position.

'And yes, I had some psychological problems. And yes, they got me herded out of the department.'

'I'm sorry.'

'For *which*,' he added, without leaving the window, 'I received counselling.'

'I'm sorry,' Teri said again, a little louder this time.

'And that thing at the cemetery – well, my apologies. I was tired. I didn't get much sleep last night. And it was my father's grave, my own *father's* grave. The thought that Boyle had been there...'

'It's all right,' Teri said. 'I was just worried about you.'
'No need.'
'I should have known that.'

He turned away from the last sliver of sunset. His face was drawn, though he managed to find a place on it for a grin. And not the tragic grin Teri half-expected to see there, either. It was a break in the ice that had formed between them on the way home this afternoon. A look of forgiveness.

'Yes, you should have,' he said.

Teri managed a grin of her own. 'Friends again?'

'Friends again.'

106

'What we need to do is get Gabriel Knight and that other little kid moved out of here as soon as possible. If the Knight woman starts nosing around – and I think we all know she's going to do just that – then we damn well better not have her kid in the basement, yelling for his mommy.'

'We can move them into a motel in the morning,' Mitch said.

'And then move them out to Houston from there,' Childs suggested.

DC studied the doc, looking for anything that might indicate what was really going on inside the man's head. He had watched Childs swing from one mood to another like a chimpanzee trying to find a vine that might support him. It appeared the man had finally gotten himself under control, but as far as DC was concerned he was running out of vines.

'How long will it take?'

'To get them to Houston?'

'Yes,' DC said sharply. 'To get them to ... *Houston.*'

'The same day, if there's a flight going out.'

'Tomorrow?'

Childs nodded.

'Then why don't we do that.'

'What about the others?' Mitch asked.

'Well, since we can't move them all—'

'We could try a little sleight of hand,' Childs said. 'What I mean is – we could leave them right where they are. No one's likely to stumble across them in the basement, anyway. But just to be on the safe side, we could set up the first floor to at least give the appearance of a research project in progress. Maybe move down some of the equipment from upstairs, bring in some monkeys and rats, maybe pay a few indigents to let us draw blood, that kind of thing. Make it look good for whenever she decides to come around.'

'Not bad,' DC said, pinching his face. Between the troubles with the Knight woman and the awakening of the second boy, he had already come to the conclusion that things had gotten too far out of hand. The question was – what should he do about it?

Somewhere down the road – not far down the road, either – they were going to have shut this thing down. All of it. The operations in Houston and St Charles and Reston. The operation here. It was his guess that the only person in this room who didn't understand that was Childs. And DC had no intention of warning him.

'It would probably take two, maybe three days at the most to get it set up,' Childs said. 'And it would buy us enough time to work out a more permanent solution.'

'All right, then why don't we give it a try.'

107

Outside the grounds of the Devol Foundation, Walt pulled the Sunbird off the road, into the shadows. He looked across the seat at Teri and raised his eyebrows questioningly. 'You sure you want to do this tonight?'

'I want my son.'

'I know you do. That's not what I asked you.'

'Yes, tonight. I want him tonight. No more waiting. They've had him long enough, and I'm not planning on letting them have him another moment.'

'Another day or two and we'd have a much better idea—'

'Tonight,' Teri said firmly.

'All right.' Walt leaned back and brought the blueprints out from behind the passenger seat. He slid the rubber bands off each end, unrolled the plans, and used his flashlight as a weight to pin the top against the dashboard. 'Let's take a look at these. How about a little light?'

Teri took the flashlight out of her backpack, turned it on and held it over the plans.

The building was three stories high, plus a basement. There was an open receptionist's area when you first went through the front door, and two elevators off to the left. Only one of the elevators went down to the basement level. Upstairs appeared to be mostly office space, including a myriad of small cubicles, a couple of conference rooms, and a huge open area that was labeled *The Lab*. The intended use of the basement appeared less certain. Labeled as *Storage*, it appeared to be well wired, with an unusual array of electrical outlets. At the back of the building, sat a loading dock, and next to that, a set of glass double doors. The only other way in or out besides an upstairs window would be what looked to be an emergency exit, next to the only staircase in the building.

'What do you think?' Teri asked.

'My best guess would be – if they have him, they have him in the basement.'

'How do we get down there?'

Walt pointed to the back of the building, at the emergency exit. 'See the stairway? That's the only way down unless you want to walk through the front door and try the elevator.'

'And what if he isn't in the basement?'

'Then I guess we'll take a walk upstairs.'

108

Childs had found his way back to the lab, glad to be out of the presence of his quote – *associates* – unquote. It wasn't that he didn't like them, he had *never* actually liked them. And he had never actually doubted that their feeling for him was mutual. But sometimes when people were forced together in a common goal – or what might appear to be a common goal – it was necessary for the personalities involved to overlook some of the petty quirks of the other group members. And yes, it sounded like a group therapy session, but that was the dynamics of interpersonal relationships. You learned to tolerate your differences.

He pulled out the most recent sample of liver cells taken from the two boys. The first sample belonged to Gabriel Knight. He placed it into the specimen chamber of the electron microscope, positioned it, then turned to the control panel. When he finally brought up the visual, he compared it to a visual display of the cells taken when the Knight boy had still been comatose. There was a marked difference. The mitochondria, which had been round and smooth and resembled the basic form of a grape while the boy was comatose, now looked something more like a raisin. It was shriveled and misshapen. And instead of dividing every five to six days, it teased you, threatening to divide but never quite getting around to it.

There was no denying the evidence. Somehow, through an interaction that Childs still did not fully comprehend, the AA103 had served to keep the Knight boy both comatose and ageless for a good number of years. But suddenly, without an obvious trigger, that causatum had mysteriously shut down. More than that, it appeared the process had actually reversed itself. The body was making up for lost time, so to speak. It was aging at such an alarming rate that before long the boy's physical maturation might very well overtake his chronological maturation.

And after that ... death, Childs thought glumly.

He pulled out the liver-cell sample of the Breswick boy, and exchanged it in the specimen chamber. It was mostly a matter of confirming what he already knew at this point. Then a most interesting, errant thought went rambling through his head like a forbidden tease. Maybe the DOD would be interested in what he had here? Premature aging. Maybe, if they were able to sit down and do a little brainstorming, maybe they'd be able to come up with some sort of military application? That would keep things going, wouldn't it?

Probably not, he had to admit. It didn't take a genius to realize that things were rapidly drawing to a close around here. DC wasn't going to tell him that, of course. He wasn't even going to hint at it, if he could help it. But Childs could read the writing on the wall without much effort. DC was getting worried that too many risks of exposure were beginning to pop up like little leaks in the dike, and he wasn't interested in playing the little Dutch boy. It was easier – and probably smarter in the long run – to drain the water under his own terms. If he did that, he was going to leave Childs out to dry.

He positioned the specimen, then turned his attention to the control panel. It was frightening how quickly things had sprung out of control the past couple of weeks. Suddenly a lifetime of work was on the verge of being scrapped. Just like that. No second thoughts. No regrets. Scrap it and move on before someone finds out.

What an ungodly waste, Childs thought.

109

They had made their way around the perimeter of the Foundation property, staying close to the fence where the shadows were darkest. There was a sliver of moon out tonight, just enough to cast a grayish tint over the landscape. It was that grayish tint that served as their eyes.

At the back of the building, they kept low and moved along the line of shrubbery until the last twenty or thirty feet, where they were forced to scamper across an opening. Walt held Teri's hand all the way. They reached the emergency exit door, Teri breathing hard on one side, Walt scanning their surroundings on the other.

'So far so good,' Teri said.

'That was the easy part.' He grinned at her, thoroughly enjoying himself.

'Great, now you tell me.'

It was a matter of picking the lock next, and it took Walt less than thirty seconds to do it. Teri watched him, amazed at how simple he made it look. The lock popped. He turned the knob slowly, then opened the door a crack and waited.

'What—?'

'Shhh.' He waited for another five counts, then motioned her on through, and entered right behind her. Inside, a short hallway faced them. At the far end, the darkness was spotted by a couple of overnight lights in the receptionist's area. Off to the right, just as the blueprints had shown, was the stairway that was supposed to take them down to the basement. What the blueprints hadn't shown was the locked door that blocked access to the stairway.

'Christ!' Walt muttered. He ran the palm of his hand over the surface and Teri could see that the door was made of metal. It was painted an ugly navy gray that contrasted sharply with the large black lettering. The lettering said, simply enough: STAIRWAY.

'Can't you pick it?'

'Yeah, but it's a mortise lock. It'll take a little longer to play around with the cylinder.'

'I'll cancel our dinner reservations,' Teri said without a smile.

'You do that.'

It didn't take as long as he had led her to believe. Maybe a minute and a half. Two minutes at the most. He worked with it intensely, then suddenly whispered, 'Got it!' and fought a moment longer before Teri heard the dead bolt slide back from the strike plate. The door swung out.

'I'll see if I can get our reservations back.'

Walt pulled the flashlight out of his backpack, and they started down the stairway.

110

'That guy really is an asshole,' Mitch said.

'I know. Even worse, he's a skittish asshole.' DC had his feet propped upon the desktop, the heels of his shoes resting on the top page of a computer printout. The cubicle where they were talking sat in the middle of a maze of cubicles on the third floor. The only light on in the room was the Luxo fluorescent lamp above the desk. 'He's going to panic and do something stupid one of these days.'

'How'd you ever hook up with him anyway?'

'It was a long time ago,' DC said with a touch of sarcasm. 'I'd like to think I've grown a little wiser over the years.'

Mitch let out a huff. He was standing at the corner of the cubicle, leaning against a divider, his arms crossed, all business. You never had to guess with Mitch, and you rarely had to watch over him the way DC had always had to watch over Childs. Some men you could trust, some you couldn't.

'Things are getting tight,' DC said.

'I know.'

'We're going to have to do something about this mess before it gets so far out of hand we can't bring it back under control again.'

'You have something in mind?'

'I don't know. I guess if I thought I could get away with it, I'd be tempted to try taking our asshole little doctor out of the picture entirely and see where that leaves us.'

'Scrap the project?'

'The project's already dead in the water. The guy's been working on this thing for twenty years and he still doesn't have a fucking clue to what's going on.' DC, who had been toying with a rubber band, tossed it aside and sat up. He felt tired, a little bit from stress and a little bit from the fact that he still hadn't had dinner. 'And with this Knight woman and her friend poking around – Christ, this thing's a bomb waiting to go off, and we're sitting right on top of the damn thing.'

'So?' Mitch prompted.

'So, I wish I knew what the hell to do about it.'

'I'll take him for a ride, if you'd like.'

'Thanks, but we'd still have a room full of sleepers to worry about,' DC said. He paused, anticipating that Mitch might make an offer to take care of the kids as well. That would be the kind of tell that would worry him, DC thought. Because it was one thing to be all business, and quite another thing to be a fucking loon. If Mitch had mumbled a single syllable about handling the kids, DC might very well have stood up and shot him right on the spot. *Bang, you're dead.* One less psycho in the world to worry about. Thankfully, Mitch made no such offer.

'Are your hands dirty?' Mitch asked.

'No, of course not.'

'And the agency?'

'Everything's clean. Why?'

'I don't know, it just seems like maybe the easiest thing to do would be to get up and walk away. Leave the whole thing sitting in the doc's lap.'

'He'd squeal.'

'Anything to back him up?'

'No, nothing I'm aware of.'

'Well, then.' Mitch shrugged, enjoying the scenario. 'Mrs Knight stumbles onto the scene, she finds the doc here with her kid and a whole other room of other kids just like him, and who's she gonna point her finger at? Hell, the only way they found this place is by tailing Childs.'

'And everything's in the name of the Foundation. And he's registered as the President of the Board of Directors on all the paperwork. It might work. It just might work.' DC steepled his fingers and rocked back in the chair, running it through his mind in case there was something he might be missing. You had to be careful with something like this. Overlook one small detail and you could find the whole thing blowing up in your face. 'It does have a sweet sense of irony about it, doesn't it?'

111

The room was completely dark except for the gray cast of the four video monitors mounted at the back of the console. Just at the periphery of the man's vision, the nearest monitor reflected the slow, sweeping movement of the camera over the receptionist's area on the main floor. The screen flickered and the picture changed. This camera was mounted near the ceiling above the basement landing, just outside the elevator. It did a slow, deliberate sweep across the open space.

Jake, who was working alone tonight, briefly glanced up from his checkbook then returned to the task of trying to find the one hundred and forty-seven dollars and thirty-six cents that was missing from his account, according to his current bank statement. He'd had this problem with the bank before, though it had always been a couple of dollars here, a couple of dollars there. That kind of difference wasn't worth the time or effort to track down. But a hundred-and-something dollars, that was *real* money. You could make a down payment on a fine stereo system with that kind of money. He wasn't going to let it slide this time. The bank was going to have some explaining to do.

The nearest monitor flickered and changed pictures to the room with the two boys. The youngest boy was asleep. The other kid, the Knight kid, he had settled back into the pillow and was trying to read a Christopher Pike book with his arm cast across the top of the page to keep it from turning.

The far monitor flickered and the camera swept across the lab where Dr Childs was hunched over a console, his glasses sitting on top of his head. He sat back, ran his hands down his face, then sat forward again, apparently refreshed enough to continue.

The right middle monitor flickered and the picture from the loading dock changed to the room in the basement where the *sleepers* were housed. Jake glanced up again, then started back to his checkbook when he thought he caught a movement at the corner of the screen. He sat forward, pressed a button, and froze his monitor at that location.

'What's going on here?' he muttered.

At the lower right-hand corner, two adults emerged from out of camera range. They moved only a step or two into the room, then stopped, side-by-side, their backs turned away from him. He wasn't sure who they were, but he thought it might be Dr Childs and Miss Tilley. They tended to make their rounds at odd hours, whenever it seemed to convenience them.

'Come on, turn around now. Let me see your faces.'

The woman, who was standing on the left, suddenly sank into the man's arms. That was something Jake had never seen between the doctor and his assistant. Not that he would know if anything were going on. He only came in for a couple of hours a night. It wasn't as if he were privy to anything.

Finally, the man turned toward the camera, where Jake could

clearly see his face. It was not Dr Childs. And it was not one of the other two who were always hanging around, either. This guy – he was a man Jake had never seen before.

'Oh, Christ,' Jake said, reaching for the phone. 'Oh, Jesus Christ Almighty, we got one.'

112

'My God,' Teri whispered. She could barely believe her eyes. They were standing just inside the door of a room that was maybe thirty by sixty, looking out across two rows of hospital beds. Half of those beds were occupied, and all of the occupants were children. 'What has he done?'

She sank into Walt's arms, overwhelmed. 'How could he—?'

'Shhh,' he said, giving her a hug. 'I know it's horrible, but we've got to keep moving, Teri. We don't have all night here.'

'I know. I'm sorry.' She did her best to buck herself up. It was just that—

'You take that row, I'll take this one.'

Teri nodded. There were four occupied beds on her side. The first two were empty and cast in a thick, neglected shadow. There was a small fluorescent lamp above the third bed. Its light fell over the soft face of a little girl who looked to be ten or eleven years old. Teri stopped and held the girl's hand, amazed at how tiny and delicate her fingers were. How old was she really? And how long had she been here? And who were her parents? Had they searched for their daughter the way Teri had searched for Gabe? Of course, they had.

'Teri!' A sharp whisper of admonition from Walt.

'I'm sorry.'

She went down the row, one bed at a time, and Gabe was not one of the occupants, thank God. This was what he had been, though. She had no doubt of that. He had slept here in this cold room, maybe in one of these darkened beds, a tube going into his arm to feed him, another coming out to drain him. No love. No mother. No father.

Oh, Gabe, I'm sorry. I'm so very sorry.

'He's not here,' Walt said.

'What are we going to do?'

'Keep looking.'

'No, I mean about these children. We can't just leave them here.'

'Teri, we can't take them with us, either.'

She knew that, of course, though it was not something that she readily wanted to admit to herself. She had already let Gabe down, how could she do the same to all these other children?

'We'll make a report,' Walt said. 'Tonight. As soon as we get back, all right?'

Teri nodded.

'All right?'

'Yes,' she said.

And then the door behind them opened.

113

'Cody!'

Gabe sat up in bed, leaning on his casted arm. He thought he had heard something that had sounded like voices. Cody, who had been asleep for a good long while now, stirred uneasily.

'Cody!'

'What?' he moaned, opening one eye reluctantly.

'Listen.'

114

'Excuse me, you folks lost?'

Teri Knight looked like she might clutch her heart and fall over dead right there. Her mouth opened, her eyes widened, her coloring went instantly white. Walter Travis, on the other hand, hardly seemed surprised. He pulled the woman to his side, and shone his flashlight in Mitch's face.

'Get rid of the light,' DC said.

Obediently, Walter Travis turned it off and dropped it to his side.

'No, I think I better take it, thank you,' Mitch said.

The man passed it handle first, no resistance. Folks tended to be cooperative when they had guns pointed at them. DC had learned that years ago, and it was just as true today as it had been the very first time he had tried it. Mitch frisked both of them, finding a nice little Ruger P-85 strapped under Mr Travis's left arm. He took possession of it, along with both of their backpacks, and stepped back again.

'So, now that we've checked in your luggage, to what do we

owe the pleasure of your company?' DC asked.

'Where's my son?'

'And you are?'

'Teri Knight.'

'Well, Teri Knight, if he's not here, then it's my guess you're probably looking in the wrong place. Maybe a day care centre would be a better place to check. Wouldn't you agree?'

'I want my son,' she said firmly.

'We don't always get what we want, Mrs Knight.' That was as true for him as it was for her, of course. DC had not wanted to find himself in this position. It wasn't going to make Webster happy, him with his blunt warnings. Nor was it going to make walking away from the Foundation any easier. 'Though, I suppose it never hurts to ask. Why don't we take a little walk.'

He took them upstairs to a small office on the second floor, using the elevator this time. There was only one door. Plenty of windows. No way out unless they were tempted to try a swan dive into the rock walkway below. Not as secure a room as DC would have liked, but secure enough to hold them until he could decide what to do next.

Ah, things are getting exciting now!

115

'Did you hear it?' Gabe asked.

'Sounded like some people talking,' Cody said, still trying to wipe the sleep out of his eyes. He sat up in bed, looking a little younger, a little more fragile than he had when he had first been wheeled in by Miss Tilley.

'Exactly.'

'So what?'

'So did you ever hear any of those voices around here before?'

'I haven't heard any voices period, except yours. Oh, yeah, yours and the *Witch's*.' The *Witch* was as nice a word as they could agree upon for Miss Tilley. Gabe had been partial to something a little meatier, but he tried to remain mindful of the fact that Cody was only eight.

'Besides me and her.'

'No.'

'You know who it sounded like?' Gabe asked, almost afraid to say it out loud for fear that it might jinx the possibility of it being true. 'It sounded like my Mom and Mr Travis.'

'Who's Mr Travis?'

'He's a friend of my Mom's. He's one of those private detective guys.' Gabe threw off his covers and climbed down from the hospital bed, the tail of his gown hooking on the side railing until he pulled it free. The floor felt cold against the bottom of his feet. He went after his slippers. 'My Mom said he used to work for the police department.'

'Really?'

'No lie.'

'Maybe he came looking for us?'

'Bet he did,' Gabe said. His slippers had somehow made their way underneath the bed, all the way to the other side. He found the right one first, underneath the box top to the Monopoly game the *Witch* had brought in when he'd first arrived. He leaned against the edge of the bed, balancing on one foot, and managed to get the slipper over his toes and hooked across the back of his heel. Then he went about finding the other one.

'What are you doing?'

'Trying to get their attention.' The left slipper was stuffed into the corner between the bed frame and the wall. Gabe dug it out, got it over his foot, and went to the door. He pressed his ear against it.

'Hear anything?'

'Huh-uh,' he said, shaking his head. It was completely silent on the other side, not even the restless sound of the ocean, like you heard when you held a sea shell to your ear.

'Maybe they left already.'

That's what Gabe thought, too. They had come downstairs to check on something and they hadn't seen the door, of if they had, they hadn't imagined anyone would be on the other side, and they had left without checking to make sure.

He slammed the palm of his hand against the cool, smooth metal surface, and heard it echo on the other side. Somebody had to have heard that. It sounded as if a cannon had gone off. Somebody had to have heard it.

Another slam, harder this time.

'What are you doing?'

'Help!' he screamed, feeling it sting the inside of his throat. 'Help! We're in *here*! Please! Help!'

116

'It seems like every time I turn around, I'm asking this question again,' Teri said, sitting on the edge of the desk. The fear that had screamed its lungs out at her downstairs was quiet now, subdued by the knowledge that at least for the moment they were out of danger. It didn't prevent the queasiness from churning in her stomach, though. That might not settle for several more days, assuming the two of them were afforded several more days.

'But here it goes again,' Teri finished. 'What do we do now?'

'Try to find a way out,' Walt said evenly. 'Any suggestions?'

'Don't look at me. It was everything I could do just to get us in here.'

He grinned, and Teri had to admit that she didn't know where the humor had come from. It was something she wouldn't have had two weeks ago, before Gabe had come back. She might have cried then, or she might have grown tired and lain down and fallen asleep. But she wouldn't be able to laugh. Not in the best of circumstances.

'Can you pick the lock?'

'They took my backpack with my tools.'

Teri hopped down from the desk and pulled out the middle drawer. A tray had been built into the front span and filled with pens and pencils, rubber bands and paperclips, old pennies and a couple of letter-openers. She plucked out a paperclip.

'How about this?'

Walt looked up from the lock. 'You've been watching too many movies.'

'Okay.' She dug around a moment longer and brought out one of the letter-openers. It wasn't anything fancy. Not one of those engraved ivory-handled things or even an antique sterling pewter opener. Just an everyday straight-and-narrow stainless steel letter-opener. That was all. 'What about this?'

'No,' he started to say. Then he caught himself. 'Well, let me take a look at it.'

Teri passed it to him.

He turned it over in his hands a couple of times, as if he were trying to get a feel for what it might be able to do. 'Even with the tapered end, it's too big to pick the lock,' he said thoughtfully. 'But then, picking a lock isn't the only way through a door, is it?'

'It isn't?'

'You better hope not.'

117

Jake had put aside his checkbook. There was too much going on tonight, and DC had told him no more screwing around. He hated the idea of losing more than a hundred dollars to the bank, but he hated the idea of losing his job even more. He could always pull out his checkbook and have another go at it tomorrow.

The nearest monitor flickered from the room with the *sleepers* to the room with the two boys. One of the boys was sitting up in bed, his face pale, a pillow pulled into his lap. The other boy was barely visible out of the corner of the camera. Jake sat forward. It appeared that the kid had gotten out of bed and moved to the door. He was pounding against it with his good hand, his arm coming down again and again and again, with the passion of a caged animal.

Jake flipped an audio switch.

'Help! We're in *here*! Please! Help!'

He flipped it off again.

Christ, what next?

He sat back again, and moistened his lips, which had begun to chap a couple of days before. The question he had to wrestle was this: would this be something DC would need to know about. Jake didn't think so, though with DC you had to be careful. Jake hadn't told him when Amanda Tarkett had taken the kid out of the room for the first time, and everyone knew how that had turned out. Sometimes the little things that you didn't think mattered much, mattered a whole lot more than you'd ever imagine.

Still, he didn't think this was one of those times. At the very worst, the kid might scream himself raw. He certainly wasn't a threat to break out. Not with that door. It was as solid as they came. Even screaming the way he was, it was debatable that anyone might actually hear him from the other side.

The monitor flickered and changed to a view of the lab, where Dr Childs was hunched over the console of his electron microscope. Jake let the image change without trying to freeze it. He'd keep an eye on the basement whenever it came around, but he wasn't going to bother DC. Not without good reason. DC was the kind of man you did your best to avoid unless it was an emergency. And some kid throwing a tantrum and pounding on the door was hardly an emergency.

The monitor flickered again, from the lab to the conference room on the second floor this time. All was quiet.

118

The door opened on the other side of the room, and Childs looked up from his work, disappointed to find that he hadn't escaped DC after all. The man came through the door with Mitch at his side, where he seemed to have been permanently attached.

'Got a problem,' DC said, pulling out a nearby chair and plopping down. 'That Knight woman and her boyfriend showed up. We've got 'em downstairs, locked in an office.'

'And what do you intend to do with them?'

DC glanced at Mitch and they were like two hungry vultures contemplating their next meal. *Jesus, they want to kill them*, Childs thought. He looked from DC to Mitch, trying to find something in there that might assure him he was wrong. But these eyes – they had lied before, many times before, and effortlessly. They had learned to keep their secrets.

'You aren't thinking about—'

'Lighten up, doc. We aren't going to hurt anyone.'

'Not unless we have to,' Mitch added.

'And I bet you'd like that, huh, Mitch?'

'All right, kids, break it up.' DC slid his chair against the side of the console. He braced an elbow on the beige corner and leaned against his arm. 'Listen, I don't know how to say this except straight out: it's over, doc. It's been one hell of a roller-coaster ride, but it's time to get off now.'

Childs slumped back in his chair. He had known this was coming, he had prepared for it, but all the same, after twenty years, after coming so close . . . 'All I wanted was to find a way to keep people from aging.'

'Hey, we gave it a good shot.'

Childs looked up from his muse, hating the faces that met his gaze. These guys – they were idiots. They didn't understand any of this. Not a single, solitary word of it. Mitch with his folded arms and that crooked little scar over his eye. DC with that cocky little grin and his who-gives-a-fuck attitude. It was just a game to them, a chance to play cops and robbers. They didn't appreciate any of it.

'Hurts, huh, doc?' Mitch said, thoroughly enjoying himself.

Childs glared at him.

'Listen,' DC said. 'We've got to clear out tonight.'

119

It certainly helped to be on the right side of the door. In this case, the door swung into the room, which meant the hinges were on the inside and accessible. Where there were hinges, Walt had learned years ago, there was a way out.

He muscled the last pin out of the hinge, using the tapered end of the letter-opener. The pin popped out with sudden surprise. It glanced off the door, fell to the carpet and rolled under a nearby chair. The door shifted instantly and slanted off center to the left. Walt caught it and wrestled it aside.

'Bring along the Scotch tape and a handful of business cards, will you?'

'Already got 'em.' They had found the business cards in the top right-hand drawer of one of the desks. A single card placed over the lens of a camera and secured with a little Scotch tape was as good as a can of spray paint.

'Where now?' Teri asked, sticking close to him as they moved down the hall.

'Back to the basement,' he said. 'That's where they've got Gabe.'

'How do you know that?'

'Because they moved us out of there as fast as they could.'

Teri could have sworn the stairway was on the other side of the building, behind them. But apparently she had turned herself around. Up ahead, she saw a grey metal door blocking the end of the hall. Like the door downstairs, it was marked with a sign that said: STAIRS. Above the sign was the number: 2.

Walt held her up. 'How 'bout we take the elevator this time?'

'Only one of them goes to the basement.'

'You remember which one?'

'No,' Teri said, amused by the thought.

'A lot of good the blueprints did.' Walt pressed the down button and within fifteen seconds the doors to both elevator cars opened simultaneously. 'Your choice.'

'Eenie–Meenie–Minie–Mo.' Teri pointed to the car on the right. 'I'll check this one.'

The other car turned out to be the one that could take them where they wanted to go. Walt called Teri over, the car doors closed, and he used a clip he had broken off the cap of a ball-point pen to pick the basement lock.

'You're getting pretty good at that.'

'I'm getting lots of practice.'

120

'So we're really clearing out tonight?' Mitch asked as they came out of the lab on the third floor and started down the hallway to the elevators.

'Unless you've got a better idea,' DC said.

'What about our company downstairs?'

'The Knight woman and her buddy?'

'Yeah.'

'Let's just leave them,' DC said. He checked his watch, wondering how long it would take to clear everything out and still make it to the airport tonight. He could always have the agency arrange for a private plane. Only that would alert Webster, and he didn't want that bastard to know what was going on. Not until after the fact, when the dust had settled and it was too late for him to stick his nose into it. 'We've got other things to worry about.'

'Like our good Dr Childs?'

'Why? Does he worry you?'

'You know someone's going to eventually track him down.'

'So.'

'So the first thing he's going to do is start pointing fingers.'

'Yeah.'

'And the first finger he points, he's going to point at you.'

'And what do you suggest I do about that, Mitch?'

'I'll take care of him for you, if that's what you want.'

DC stopped outside the first elevator car and stared at Mitch a moment, both amused and a bit intrigued. 'You really got it in for the guy, don't you?'

'Just trying to cover your ass.'

'Jesus, Mitch.' He reached out to press the down button, his mind toying with the idea of giving Mitch the go-ahead to handle the doc in whatever fashion he deemed necessary. It might be easier on everyone that way. Just walk away and never have to worry about looking over his shoulder to make sure the Karma Project wasn't coming back at him. He toyed with that a moment, and then his mind went to the DOWN light illuminated over the elevators and made a jarring new connection. Someone was in the elevator, going down.

'Where's Tilley?'

'She went into town to pick up supplies.'

'Christ! Someone's in the elevator!'

As part of the building's security system, emergency in-house call boxes had been situated on every floor, directly across from the elevator shaft. DC dug his keys out of his pocket, unlocked the door, and grabbed the receiver off the hook. It was the first time he'd ever had to use the system. There was dead silence on the line.

'Come on!'

And then finally someone picked up.

'Jake.'

'Override the basement elevator. Now! Do it now!'

121

Jake reached across the console to the elevator control panel and depressed the red, emergency STOP button, which activated the terminal stopping switch. He had already begun to suspect that something was wrong. The monitor on the far end had flickered from the receptionist's area to a black screen and Jake had been fiddling with the contrast when the phone had rung.

'Got it,' he said.

'Great. Send the car back up to the third floor.'

'Will do.'

122

Somewhere between the first floor and the basement, the elevator car made a strange winding-down noise, like an engine after it's shifted into a lower gear. It shuddered violently, then came to an abrupt stop. The overhead fluorescent lights flickered and went out momentarily, then slowly climbed back to full strength again.

'What's happening?' Teri asked.

'My fault. We should have taken the stairway.'

'You mean they've shut us down?'

'Looks that way.'

'Can't you override it?'

'Not likely. Not from in here.'

Walt took a look at the control panel anyway. There wasn't much to play with: the emergency override button, the basement key lock, the buttons for the lobby and the two floors upstairs. He toyed with the panel faceplate and almost had it off when the car suddenly shuddered and began to rise.

'Now what?'
'I think they're inviting us back.'
'Great.'

123

Gabe had flailed with his good arm against the door until he was silly with exhaustion. He sank against the wall, catching a breath and glancing across the room at Cody, who was sitting up in bed, looking horrified.

'We've got to... get out of here,' Gabe said, panting.

'How?'

'I don't know.'

When Miss Tilley had brought Cody in on the wheelchair, she had folded the chair and left it leaning against the next bed. Cody worked himself a little higher on the mattress, pulled the covers off and swung his legs around.

'What are you doing?'

'I wanna help.'

124

There had been a sound, a little like the cargo hatch of a 747 snapping shut, and then the DOWN light over the elevator had suddenly gone off. DC waited anxiously until the UP light finally illuminated several seconds later.

'Got 'em!' he cried.

'Nice job.'

'When they show up, take 'em back to the lab and keep them there along with Childs. I'll catch up with you as soon as I can.'

'Where are you going?'

'It's time to start shutting things down.' The doors to the second elevator opened. DC entered. He pressed the button for the lobby and stood at the back of the car, his hands curled around the rail. 'Don't do anything until I get back. Got it?'

Mitch nodded.

The elevator doors closed.

DC sank back into the corner, feeling hopped up, his adrenaline keeping every muscle taut and on edge. It was all going to come crashing down soon, anybody's guess who'd be left standing and who wouldn't.

Hold on, Karma, 'cause the ride's just beginning.

125

Enough was enough.

Childs had turned away from the console and watched DC and Mitch leave the lab, knowing that it might very well be the last time he ever saw either of them again. It had all come to a head now. There was no sense in trying to save what he had already accomplished. It was lost. Forever. A life's work. Just like that.

The door closed and he scrambled to his feet. He went to the cabinet at the far end of the lab, unlocked it, and removed the only vial of AA103 that remained. He set the vial aside, then removed the tray of test-tubes at the back of the cabinet, and slid open the false back wall. Behind it, set into the wall of the building, was a combination safe he had installed several years earlier. He opened the safe and removed its contents, which included: fifty thousand dollars in cash; a Visa, MasterCard and American Express, all made out in the name of William Devol; some obsolete research notes, which he tossed aside; a California driver's license in the same name as the credit cards; a medical board certification and license to practice; two diplomas; and a set of car keys.

'Okay, what else?'

He took his wallet out of his back pocket, and emptied it of everything except the sixty-seven dollars in cash. No sense throwing away good money. He was going to need every penny he had if he wanted to start over again. Into the wallet went the credit cards and driver's license. The wallet went back into his pocket.

At the door to the lab, Childs stopped and checked the hall both ways. Mitch was standing outside the elevators near the other end. He was leaning over, apparently tying a shoelace. Childs stepped out of the room, guided the latch bolt silently into the strike plate, and hurried to the stairwell. His keys got him through the door, down the stairs, and through the exit door on the first floor then out into the great open spaces behind the Foundation.

It was cold out. The night sky was clear, the air crisp. A sprinkling of stars could be seen just beyond the haze of the city lights that hung over the entire valley. Childs filled his lungs with the fresh air.

A good night to start a new life, he thought.
Then he started on his way.

126

'Is there anything we can do?'

'Nope,' Walt said nonchalantly. 'I think we're along for the ride on this one.'

A bell rang, and the light over the elevator doors moved from left to right one number, signifying that they were at the second floor now, still rising. Walt moved away from the control panel to the back of the car, next to Teri. She reached out and took his hand.

'Scared?' he asked.

'A little.'

The bell rang again before he could tell her not to be, that everything would work out all right. The elevator car lugged, then settled back into place. For a moment, nothing else happened and it was as if all the anticipation had been for naught. Then gradually the doors opened up to the third floor.

Mitch was standing on the other side of the hall, leaning against the wall. In his hand, he held a gun. On his face, he wore the kind of smile that let you know how much he was enjoying himself.

'Well, well, well. Who do we have here?'

'Nice to see you again,' Walt said.

'I bet. I know how tickled I am.' He waved the gun at them, an invitation to exit the elevator. 'Please, why don't you two join me.'

They did.

127

Gabe helped Cody into the wheelchair, then went back to the door to see if there was a way they might be able to pick the lock or break it down. *Something. Anything.* It wasn't that easy, though. Back home, he could pick the door between the garage and the kitchen with nothing more than a paperclip. All he had to do was jiggle it around in the lock a few seconds and before he knew it – *click!* – the door was open. This lock, this door, they were a different story.

'How about this?' Cody said, coming up behind him. In his hand, he held up a tongue depressor, maybe four times the size of a Popsicle stick.

'Where'd you get that?'

'Out of that drawer over there.'

Gabe shook his head. 'Too big.'

'Then what about *this*?' Cody said, bringing out a q-tip. Only this one wasn't like the q-tips Gabe's mom kept in the bathroom cabinet at home. It was like the tongue depressor, industrial strength, maybe twice the size of a household q-tip and nearly as thick as a water-swollen strand of spaghetti.

'Maybe,' Gabe said, taking it in hand. He flexed it between his fingers to see how brittle it felt. You go sticking things into a lock, you don't want them breaking off in there. Once that happened, you might as well forget it. He had found that out the first time he'd tried using a toothpick. 'Let me try it and see.'

The cottonless end of the q-tip slipped easily into the keyway. Gabe gave it a jiggle, first to one side, then to the other, adding just a bit of pressure with his forefinger. It felt like a good fit, he thought. He jiggled it again, added a little more pressure, and cursed himself when it suddenly snapped off. Half-an-inch of the q-tip was now lost just inside the cylinder case. It was exactly what he didn't want to do.

'Damn it!'

'What's the matter?'

'It broke off.'

'Oh.' Cody looked down, disappointed. 'So, what are we supposed to do now?'

'I don't know.'

'Maybe we could get someone to open it from the other side?'

'I don't think they can hear us from the other side.'

Gabe cast a glance around the room, looking for something, an idea, anything that might draw attention, even Miss Tilley's attention. If they could just get someone to open the door, then ...

'A fire,' Gabe said suddenly. 'If we can start a fire, a small fire, then they'll have to open the door.'

There was no shortage of combustible material in the room. Cody stripped the covers off the nearest bed, while Gabe went through the cabinets and pulled out the Kleenex and tongue depressors and sterile gauze pads, anything and everything he thought might burn. They piled all of it high in the middle of the room, then pulled a fluorescent lamp off the wall and ran it over to the pile.

'Think it's hot enough?' Cody wondered.

'I think so.'

Gabe got down on his knees, stuffed the Kleenex tissues into the tight space around the bulb, then added some bedding on top of that. He stood up and backed away.

'How long you think it'll take?'

'Not long.' After a few minutes, though, when nothing had happened, he realized that the bulb probably wasn't hot enough after all.

'It's not burning,' Cody said.

'We need something to get it started, lighter fluid or gasoline, something like that.'

Gabe went searching again, and this time, in the corner of a cabinet, he came across a bottle labeled: *Isopropyl*. A yellow warning notice cautioned that the contents were highly flammable. He removed the cap, and gave it a sniff. Instantly, his eyes watered. It was alcohol. *Isopropyl* was alcohol. Perfect.

He sprinkled a couple of Kleenex tissues with the liquid, tossed them onto the fluorescent bulb, then stood back and waited. After awhile, when nothing happened, he tried pouring the alcohol directly onto the lamp itself. The bulb might not have been hot enough to ignite the sheets, but it exploded furiously at the moment of contact with the alcohol.

Gabe covered his face and turned away. When he turned back, he saw a brown-black circle gradually appear in the middle of one of the bedsheets. It had a raven iris that opened like a fissure in the earth. Cotton-thread edges disappeared into the black rift.

First it was one circle, then it was another, then another, then a whiff of smoke began to rise into the air and it was no longer a question of *if* they could get someone's attention, it was a question of how long it would take.

128

The nearest monitor flickered and Jake felt something tighten in his throat.

The two kids had started a fire inside the room. He watched as the smoke thickened into a dark, angry cloud and began to run the line of the ceiling in all directions. Within seconds the hungry gray mass seemed to consume nearly every square inch of the room.

'Come on,' Jake said, anxiously waiting for the overhead sprinklers to kick on. He didn't think the fire itself was going to pose much of a problem. But the smoke was a different matter. It had already dropped a thick grey curtain over the picture on his monitor. Behind that curtain, in faint outline, he could see the two boys huddled on the floor, next to the supply cabinet.

He watched until the sprinklers finally kicked on, then he crossed to the far end of the room, and pulled down the handle to the fire alarm mounted on the wall. Instantly, the quiet halls, the vacant rooms, the entire building erupted into the deafening rattle of a bell.

'All right, that takes care of that.'

He went back to the console, sat down, and rolled his chair to the left, where a bank of override switches had been built into the panel. He started at the top and threw the switches for all the exits, the elevators, the stairway doors, the offices, the labs, every room, every lock in the building that he had the power to control. When he finished, he checked the monitors and was stunned to discover that the kids were still trapped. The door to their room had not opened.

'What the hell—?' He tried the switch again, once up, once down, and when that didn't work, again, once up, once down, and finally another half-a-dozen times before giving up in frustration. There was only one way that door was going to open. He'd have to go down there himself and open it manually.

He was on his way out, keys in hand, when DC showed up.

'You the one who set off the alarm?'

Jake nodded, and motioned toward the far monitor, which was little more than a dark-gray hue now. 'It's the room with the two boys. The override's jammed. I can't get the door open. I'm going down to see if I can do anything.'

DC sat at the console, and quickly scanned all four monitors. 'Jake?'

'Yeah?'

'Just keep going after you've got it open, understand? I'll watch things here until the fire department shows.'

Jake nodded and went out the door without a word. What he didn't tell DC and had no plans to tell him in the future, was that he wasn't planning on returning anyway. Not tonight. Not tomorrow night. Not ever. Things had finally crossed that line and he wasn't comfortable here anymore. At $6.50 an hour, he could just as easily be playing night watchman at one of the industrial complexes in the area, just cruising around in a car, flashing his spotlight into the shadows and listening to music on the radio. This was not a job he needed.

He crossed the floor to the elevators, entered the basement car, then waited for the doors to close. It was the first time he had ever stopped to wonder if someone was going to watch *his* movements the way he had always watched everyone else's.

129

Teri was the first one into the lab. She stepped just inside the door to the left and turned to wait for Walt, who had kept himself like a shield between her and Mitch from the elevator all the way down the hall.

'How you doing?' Walt asked as he entered.

'Fine,' she whispered.

'Never a dull moment, huh?'

Mitch moved them to the far side of the room, against the windows, and had them face outward. He sat on the corner of the nearest desk, picked up the phone, dialed a number and hung up again after he couldn't get an answer.

'Christ.' He mumbled something else, something about the *doc* not being there.

'Trouble in paradise?' Walt asked.

In the reflection in the window, Teri watched Mitch stand up and start to pace back and forth in front of the desk. He looked like a worried man, and that worried her, because she had always thought of him as having everything under control. She didn't like the idea that something might be going wrong. When things went wrong, people got hurt.

Walt was watching him, too. Only he was watching him for a different reason. Teri didn't immediately realize that, but when the fire alarm suddenly went off, Walt went off with it. He turned and closed the distance between the two of them in less than a second. Mitch never had a chance to use his gun.

Teri turned and screamed. 'Walt! Don't!'

But by then, they were already grappling.

Walt smashed his fist into the man's jaw and Mitch went flying over the desk backwards, Walt on top of him. The gun jarred loose and bounced around on the carpet only a brief moment before they were on it again, each man trying to take sole possession.

Teri moved away from the windows, a hand to her mouth to hold back the scream that was trying to force its way out of her throat. She had stepped forward momentarily when the gun had bounced free, but she had been too slow and now she was backed against the electron microscope with nowhere else to go.

'Please!'

Mitch landed an elbow to Walt's face. His head snapped back, and Mitch met him with another shot to the face, this one so loud that Teri cringed. Walt rolled over, momentarily dazed, blood flowing out of his nose and a cut over his right eye.

The gun was within Mitch's grasp now. He climbed slowly to his knees, breathing heavily, then to his feet, blood dripping out of the corner of his mouth. He bent over to pick up the gun, wrapped his fingers around the handle, and...

... and Walt rammed him from the side, full-body, full-force.

They tumbled over a chair, and it was Mitch who was the first one standing. He slammed a foot into Walt's side that rolled him over twice. Walt grabbed for his ribs and curled into a ball, in obvious pain.

'Don't!' Teri screamed. 'Please, don't!'

Mitch, who was bent over, his hands braced on his knees, trying to catch a breath, looked up at her. His eyes were pure black, cold, empty. This was a duel to the death, she realized bleakly. He was not going to stop, not until Walt was dead. And if he couldn't kill Walt, then he'd die trying. It was all... *right... there.*

'Please?'

He shook his head and bent over to pick up the gun, and this time Walt rammed him going the wrong direction. Walt hit him low, around the waist and it looked like a perfect Sunday-afternoon tackle. He nearly picked him up off the ground and the force of the hit drove Mitch backwards across the room, Walt's legs pumping, Mitch trying to get his feet planted, both men moving straight at the window.

Mitch went through first. The back of his head slammed into the window, shattering the glass and opening a hole big enough to drive a car through. Walt went through right behind him, his hands still wrapped around the man's waist.

It happened that fast.

And then it was over.

Teri heard a faraway scream that only later she would realize belonged to her. She went to the window, and looked down at the two dead men. Walt's neck had been broken, his head twisted back in a hideous angle, a bone protruding out the front.

She closed her eyes and turned away.

130

DC had finally shut down the fire alarm, and had gone out to the lobby to check to see if any trucks had shown up. It was getting down to the final few seconds now, he imagined. Once the trucks started arriving and the fire crews started going through the building floor by floor, then all hell was going to break loose, because sooner or later they were going to stumble across the room in the basement with the sleepers.

The parking lot was empty, except for a pair of tail lights in the distance, on their way out the long drive. DC watched them momentarily, wondering whose car they belonged to, then he went back to the control room to check the monitors one last time.

Downstairs, in the basement, Jake had finally gotten the door open. A wall of smoke came pouring out and immediately filled the basement landing. The monitor flickered, this time inside the room with the two boys. They were huddled together, behind a gray screen of smoke, appearing for all he could tell, lifeless.

Another flicker, and DC found himself watching the last few seconds of the fight between Mitch and Walter Travis. The two men, wrapped together like twine, went sailing out the third story window, a couple of idiot martyrs bent on giving themselves to the afterlife. Foolish men did foolish things.

DC hovered over the monitors, his arms braced against the console, and realized the end had finally arrived. He stood, searching the surroundings, trying to recall if there was anything he needed to take with him, but there was nothing left but trouble here.

He turned the light off on his way out of the room, a habit that was strangely metaphorical. Behind him, the middle monitor flickered, and Jake showed up on the screen, carrying Cody Breswick in his arms. He carried the boy out of the room, over to the stairwell and set him down. Cody took in a spastic breath, then another, and his eyes opened slowly.

Jake went back to look for Gabriel Knight.

131

Teri was on her way down the stairwell between the first floor and the basement, when she encountered Cody Breswick. The boy had made it to the mid-landing and he was lying on the floor, too weak to go any further. His face was covered with soot, his blue eyes shining out like diamonds in the coal.

'Cody?'

He nodded.

'Oh, my God,' she said. She knelt and gave him a hug meant for all the children just like him. Those who had made it. Those who had not. 'I can't believe this. I can't believe you're still alive. Are you all right?'

He nodded again, his eyes clearing.

'Where's Gabe? Do you know where Gabe is?'

'Downstairs,' Cody said.

'You stay right here. And when I get back, I'll help you, all right?'

'All right.'

She discovered Gabe sitting on the last step, just before the basement landing. His eyes were closed, his breathing shallow. She shook him gently and when he opened his eyes to look at her, Teri felt an overwhelming rush of relief.

'Hey, kiddo!'

'Hey, Mom!'

'Think you're ready to come home now?'

'I don't know,' Gabe said with a grin. 'It's only been ten years.'

CLOSINGS

Sleep comes in cycles. It weaves in and out of your experience like a ribbon in the wind. Weariness, exhaustion, boredom, routine, all these call it forth and send it back again, hunkering in the corners of your dreams. Sleep is the way you rejuvenate your body, refresh your mind, change your perspective. It is a necessity, no less important than the food you eat, the air you breathe.

Death is the sleep of the soul. It is a necessity for your renewal, for your expansion. Do not cower in the shadows when death comes knocking. Greet it eye-to-eye with a hardy handshake and know that it comes like sleep in cycles.

Transcending Illusions

1

Teri never saw DC again.

Several months later, after she had learned more about the Karma Project and its history, Teri called CIA headquarters in Washington. She asked to speak to an agent, any agent, and when one came on the line, she gave the man a brief background on the project, how it had unfolded, the people who had died, and how there were now some twenty-seven children scattered around the country, their lives permanently scarred by what the CIA had done.

It wasn't until she brought up DC that the agent began to protest. Before that, he had listened without comment, neither confirming nor denying anything she had said. But the moment DC was mentioned, the man turned defensive. He adamantly denied all knowledge and any records of any DC having ever worked for the CIA in any capacity whatsoever.

Teri interrupted him. 'I really don't have time for your denials. I want you to understand this and I want you to make no mistake about it. If I don't receive notice within one month that this man is no longer involved in the CIA or any CIA sponsored activities, I will immediately go to the press. I will sit down with them and I will share everything I know about the Karma Project and every piece of documentation I have in my possession. Do you understand?'

'Yes,' the agent answered quietly.

'Get notification to me within a month that DC is out in the cold and the issue becomes mute. All my documents will be destroyed, and you'll no longer have to worry about Karma embarrassing the agency or the country. Do you understand?'

'Yes.'

She gave the agent a post office box in Reno, Nevada, where he could notify her, and then she hung up. It was the most frightening thing she had ever done in her life. And it was the biggest bluff she had ever played. Once the phone was back on its cradle and she was out of the phone booth and walking down the street again, Teri felt as if she were walking on water. Maybe next time the children would be left to their innocence.

Four weeks later, a newspaper article arrived at the Reno post office. It was forwarded to another box at another office, and from there another box, under yet a different name. By the time Teri held it in her hands, the news had been old: Malcomn Winters, a man in his late thirties who had always stayed to himself, according to his neighbors, had hanged himself from a chandelier two weeks before. There was no record of any relatives, no knowledge of any friends. He had been despondent lately about money problems.

Across the top of the article, written in red ink, were the initials: DC.

A red line had been drawn through the initials, diagonally, top to bottom.

2

Michael showed up the day after Gabe came home. He apologized for showing up out of nowhere, but he had given it a lot of thought and wanted to see Gabe and had been afraid that Teri would object if he brought it up to her again. Teri didn't object at all. She was glad to have him there.

Gabe was glad to have him there, too. He beamed all day, a little boy delighting in the attentions of his father. They went miniature golfing and to the movies, then drove by the house and picked up Teri for dinner. It was as perfect a day as it could have been under the circumstances.

After Gabe went off to bed, Teri sat at the kitchen table, nursing a cup of coffee and trying to find the words that would explain everything that had gone on the past week or so. It had been a beautiful spring day outside, but inside Teri found the house hot and stuffy. The words came slowly, painfully. She appreciated the fact that Michael didn't rush her. He listened and asked good questions and held her hand when she came close to tears. She had forgotten how good he could be in these kinds of situations.

The hardest part was the very last part. Teri took a sip of coffee and got up to pour herself another cup. It was strange being back home again, even stranger to have Gabe and Michael here. 'More coffee?'

'No, I better not. I'll be up all night.'

She stared down at her empty cup, debating. Last night had been a light sleep, lots of tossing and turning; breezy, unremembered dreams; the sounds of the house bringing her up; her exhaustion taking her down again. It would be nice if her dreams could keep her in their fold tonight. Teri left the coffee cup on the counter and returned to the table.

'So what are we dancing around?' Michael asked.

'You don't miss much, do you?'

'Try not to.'

'It's not over,' she said plainly, her voice soft. 'I think Gabe's got Hutchinson-Gilford Syndrome.'

Michael took the news like a trooper, barely a visible reaction. He suggested they have him tested, since they were relying primarily on the word of Dr Childs and neither of them had reason to trust anything that had come out of the man's mouth. Teri agreed. She called Cindy to let her know what they were going to do, in case Cindy wanted to have Cody tested as well.

At first, Cindy had balked at the idea. She was still whirling from the shock of finding Cody alive, and Teri suspected she hadn't even had a chance yet to deal with the fact that Cody was the same age today as he had been when he had disappeared. When you looked at him, there wasn't a hint of what was going on inside his body. He appeared as healthy and as precious as the day he had been born.

But looks could be deceiving.

'He's the same age, Cindy. How do you think he got that way?'

'What do you mean?'

'Well, it wasn't by the love of God.'

'Maybe not, but it was a blessing, not a curse.'

'The curse just hasn't started yet.'

Teri tried to convince her that she had nothing to lose, but that wasn't the truth. Not the whole truth. There *was* something to lose. It was called peace of mind, and it would be impossible to hold onto it if the doctors came back with bad news.

Cindy said she needed to talk it over with her husband, that they both needed to think about it. It was not something to be taken lightly. The next morning, she called back and agreed to have Cody tested, too.

3

After a barrage of doctors and batteries of tests, Teri finally admitted two things to herself. First, that Dr Childs hadn't lied to her after all. The physicians and specialists all agreed that Gabe's cells were not regenerating the way normal, healthy cells regenerate. It was a classic indication of Hutchinson-Gilford Syndrome, they said. After which, they went into long explanations that all boiled down to the same thing: Gabe was aging prematurely, and as in most cases of progeria, he probably wouldn't survive his teens. The news in Cody's case was equally as grim.

Teri was devastated. The next few days, she fell into a funk that kept her sleeping long hours and fighting against a constant stream of headaches. And that brought about the second thing she had finally come to admit to herself. Like Gabe, she was fortunate to have Michael there. He was as helpful as he knew how to be – making the meals, doing the dishes, mowing the lawn, and more important, spending time with his son.

Several days later, Teri bounced back again. She went to Michael one night after Gabe had gone off to bed and told him that she didn't know *what* they were going to do, but they were going to do something.

'What are the options?'

'I'm not sure,' Teri said. 'Keep searching for a specialist, I guess.'

'Um-hum.'

'If you have any suggestions, I'm open.'

He shook his head, and glanced away.

'Hey, this is Gabe we're talking about. If you've got an idea, I want to hear it.'

'It'll be the hardest thing you've ever done.'

'Just say it, Michael.'

'What about Dr Childs?'

'Oh, Jesus,' she said, climbing up from the couch. 'Oh, Jesus, Michael. How could you even think of such a thing? I mean – this guy is the reason Gabe might die. How could you even—?'

'He's the only one who knows what's going on inside our son. He may be the only one who can put a stop to it. I don't think he could make it any worse.'

'I wouldn't be so sure of that.'

She hated the idea. For awhile, she even hated Michael for suggesting it. But eventually she cooled off enough to realize that Michael was only trying to help. At times like these she sometimes forgot that he was Gabe's father, that he loved Gabe as much as she did and only wanted the best for him.

Regardless of how difficult it might be for her.

And of course, he was right.

4

There were four branches of the Devol Research Foundation nationwide: Houston, Texas; St Charles, Illinois; Reston, Virginia, and the local branch. In those four facilities, a total of twenty-seven children, not including Gabe and Cody, had been discovered. All of them had been comatose.

Twenty of the children were returned to their parents, who had to assume the responsibility of care for a child they had thought had been dead for better than ten years. Seven of the children were placed in state care facilities, some because efforts to locate their parents had failed, others because the parents had no longer proved to be capable of providing care.

Over the next few months, seven other children would come out of their comas.

5

Six Months Later
The Last Day

They left the house around ten-thirty. Gabe was dressed in the same dark blue suit she had bought him for Walt's funeral shortly after that last night at the Foundation. Michael did the driving on the way over. Teri didn't know if it had been the right thing or not, but she had made the funeral arrangements for Walt and she had purchased a plot for him at the Hillcrest Cemetery, next to his father. Maybe in death they could find the peace that had eluded them in life.

Gabe sat in the front seat between them on the ride over.

All three of them were quiet.

It was a beautiful fall day, the sky blue, the temperature in the mid-seventies, a few degrees higher than normal for this time of year. They walked hand-in-hand-in-hand down the row of tombstones, past a family mausoleum, past a cinerarium to the end of the third row where the oak tree was now barren of its leaves.

Teri, who had brought a bouquet of roses with her, stood in silent prayer.

There had been no Richard Boyle.

Teri had suspected that after she had received the manila envelope with Walt's personnel files. The handwriting wasn't a perfect match by any means – there was a slight back slant, and the capital letters were overblown – but it was close enough for her to wonder if Walt himself hadn't sent the package.

She called Aaron a week after the funeral and asked him about it. He was the gentleman that Walt had described as a friend after their brief visit that day on the steps of the County Offices. At first, he went through a painstaking process of sidestepping her questions, not wanting to say anything that might soil the dead man's name. Gradually, though, Teri convinced him that she had no intention of hurting Walt, that she was only trying to understand.

'Richard Boyle was an alias,' Aaron told her. 'His father used it when Walt was a kid and they were on the run.'

And so there it was, out in the open where Teri could no longer deny what she had already suspected. There had never been a Richard Boyle. Walt had left the note and the flowers on his father's grave. Walt had sent the personnel files. Walt had been the one who trashed his own apartment. He had been fighting invisible demons, and because Teri didn't understand, he'd had to fight them alone. She would always feel that she had let him down because of that.

Gabe looked up at her now, his eyes trying to see what was going on inside. A little piece of her was dying, she thought. *That was what was going on.*

'I'll do it,' he said.

She let him take the roses from her hands and place them at the base of the gravestone. Michael, who was standing behind her, placed his hand over her shoulder for comfort.

Gabe looked up. 'You think we should say something?'

Everything she had to say was in her heart. *Thank you, Walt. Thank you for helping me bring Gabe home again. Thank you for beating back your own demons long enough to be there for me. And my apologies, because I should have known. I should have tried to help.* It was all right there.

'He knows,' Teri said quietly. 'He knows.'

6

There were only two things that had needed to be done today. The first was their visit to Walt's grave. As much as it had taken out of Teri, it was nothing compared to what was yet to come.

Michael drove on the way back from the cemetery. Gabe sat in the back this time, quiet as a mouse. What Teri wouldn't have paid for the chance to know what was going on inside his head. The aging had become less theoretical and more physical the past few months. He had lost nearly fifteen pounds, much of it from his face and arms. Streaks of grey had worked their way into his hair, especially over his ears. He had broken his right arm twice since getting the cast off following the automobile accident. Once it had been a re-break. The other time the break had been several inches higher. Both had happened while throwing a baseball with Michael. They didn't play catch anymore.

When it became apparent that Gabe's aging was accelerating at an alarming rate, Teri pulled Michael aside again and together they agreed that it was time to see if they could find Childs. Though luck did play its part, finding him wasn't as difficult as Teri had thought it would be. The key was something that had been bothering her for months. She couldn't understand the name: the Devol Research Foundation. Where had that come from? Why hadn't it been called the Childs Research Foundation? It was something that bothered her endlessly over the span of several months, and then she woke up one night with the answer. Dr Timothy Childs was an alias. The man's true last name was Devol. It made perfect sense.

She checked the California AMA membership list and discovered there was only one Devol practicing in the state. His full name was William Devol and he lived and practiced in a little town east of Sacramento called Placerville. Teri had been through there several times in her life, always on the way to Reno to play the slots or catch a show. Placerville was a five – maybe six – hour trip down the state, almost all freeway.

She was surprised to find that he had set up a nice little family practice for himself. Out front, a sign hung from a four-by-four redwood post, his name routed into the wood: William Devol, MD. And under that: General Practitioner. He practiced out of an old house that had been converted, bedrooms to examination rooms, living room to waiting room, dining room to office.

When Teri entered, she was greeted by the comforting smile of a receptionist. 'I was wondering if I could see the doctor today?'

'Certainly. Have you been in before?'

'No.'

The woman, who was in her late forties and had one eye slightly off-center, handed her a clipboard with a pencil and several forms. 'If you'll have a seat and fill these out. The doctor is busy with another patient now, but he should be available shortly.'

Teri filled out the form, which included a brief medical history and some insurance information, using the name Jennifer Cunningham. The receptionist, who was apparently a nurse as well, took her temperature, her blood pressure, weight, and asked about the purpose of her visit – 'Headaches,' Teri told her – then had Teri wait in the second examination room.

'Dr Devol will be in shortly.'

'Thanks.'

He came through the door several minutes later, reading her chart and introducing himself without even looking up. 'Miss Cunningham, I'm Dr Devol—' The color went out of his face, though he managed to maintain his composure far better than she ever would have imagined possible. He snapped her Cunningham file closed, put it aside on the counter, and sat down.

'You never cease to amaze, Mrs Knight.'

'The feeling's mutual, believe me.'

'So what can I do for you?'

'Not for me, for Gabe.'

'It's gotten worse, has it?'

'Yes,' Teri said, holding on. She wasn't sure exactly when she had started to lose her grip. Maybe when Walt had died. Or maybe when she first realized Gabe's health was getting worse. But being here in this room with the man who was largely responsible for everything that had happened...

'What do you want from me?' Childs asked.

'I want my little boy back.'

He wasn't sure he could do anything, he said. But he was willing to take a look at Gabe and at least talk about the options. The key word: *options*. It slipped past Teri when she first heard it, but later that night when she was in bed, reading an Ed Gorman mystery, that word came to mind again. *Options*. That was a word meant to deceive, she thought. It was his subtle little way of saying that there were some things they might try but nothing that he thought would actually work.

And they did try some things. Childs placed Gabe on a vegetarian diet, limiting his calorie intake and increasing his vitamins.

In addition, he set up a regiment of growth hormone shots, using a derivative he had recently developed himself. And finally, he tried a synthetic version of the original Genesis drug, without the hallucinogen. It was this synthetic version that showed the most promise, somewhat inhibiting Gabe's aging process though falling short of halting it altogether.

Childs felt there was a good chance it might eventually provide the answer.

But time was running out.

Gabe was growing weaker.

7

Michale pulled the car into the driveway and parked. They sat there in silence, Teri not wanting to move because getting out would take them one step closer to what lay ahead and just the thought of it left her feeling empty. It was what Childs had referred to as their 'last great hope'.

Teri glanced into the back at Gabe. 'How're you doing?'

'Okay,' he answered.

Michael took her hand, again for comfort. 'How about you?'

She smiled emptily and started out of the car.

Childs was waiting for them inside the house. He had spent the morning setting up the medical equipment in Gabe's room. Everything was ready, he said as Teri entered the house. She nodded, asked him to give her a few minutes, then directed Gabe into the living room. They sat on the couch together, the afternoon sun slanting through the sliding glass door. It was a warm day. Gabe peeled off his jacket and sat back.

'Come here,' Teri said. He moved next to her and she wrapped her arms around him, thinking distantly how tiny he felt, wondering how much weight he had lost. 'Scared?'

'Huh-uh.'

'Good.'

'Are you?'

'Not scared,' she said. 'Just a little sad. I'm going to miss you.'

'It won't be forever.'

'I know,' she said. She kissed him on top of his head, and they stared silently out the window until Michael came into the room. He asked Gabe how he was doing, and like a trooper, Gabe said fine. Michael picked him up and they spent a few minutes talking,

Gabe looking even more fragile in his father's arms.

And then the time had come.

Gabe's room had been re-furnished, accommodating a new hospital bed, an ECG machine, and in the corner, playing sergeant at arms, a thin, metal IV-stand. Childs stood off to one side, out of the way.

Michael carried Gabe into the room and dropped him playfully on the bed. Gabe bounced and let out a giggle. 'You like that, huh?'

'Yeah.'

'I love you, kiddo.'

'Love you, too.'

It was Teri's turn next. She gave him a long, hard hug, not wanting to let go, even though she knew what they were about to do was the right choice, the only choice. It was going to save his life.

'Mom, you're choking me.'

'Sorry,' she said, pulling away. She smiled and tried to keep the smile from turning to tears. 'I guess it's time, isn't it?'

'I guess,' he said.

Teri pulled a chair next to the bed, took Gabe's hand in her own, and nodded to Childs. A few short minutes later, Gabe closed his eyes and fell into a restful sleep. Minutes after that, he received a dose of AA103 and slipped effortlessly through his dreams and into a coma.

The last thing he said was, 'See you in a blink.'

Teri held his hand and cried and refused to leave his side until late the next morning.

8

How had it come to this?

Hovering over his bed every morning.

Spending nights at the University Library, scouring through medical texts, looking for the last piece of the puzzle.

Trading shifts with Michael, pleased that some of Gabe's weight had returned, wondering how much longer until they would get to wake him up.

Turning him, moving him, stretching his muscles, reading him stories.

Not much longer.

Still, how had it come to this?

She didn't want to think about it. There wasn't time to think about it.

And *that* was precisely the point, wasn't it?